ABOUT THE AUTHOR

Peter Gray has been writing in various guises since he was twelve years old and he has never been able to stop. From plays to magazine articles Peter has produced a plethora of work.

His first 'Sam Series' book "A Certain Summer" has had excellent reviews, one from TV presenter and ex England soccer coach Bob Wilson who grew up in the same area and could easily identify with the character in the book.

With many short stories, articles and celebrated Mummers Plays plus many touring productions under his belt. Peter is always busy writing something or other. He has also acted in and directed some of those productions and one such production played at Warwick Castle for six full seasons. He has also written several scripts for advertisements, mostly with a humorous theme as well as several live shows for the stage. He has now embarked on a new series of Adventure Novels of which more details can be found on his website.

He currently lives in the Highlands of Scotland.

www.petergrayauthor.co.uk

Auld Clootie

by
Peter Gray

Tricky Imp Publishing

Auld Clootie

First edition first published April 2017
Reprinted April 2018

Tricky Imp Publishers
Highlands, Scotland.
Email: books@trickyimppublishing.co.uk

A CIP catalogue record for this title is available from
The British Library.

ISBN: 978-0-9572668-4-1

Cover artwork by the author.

More Information at:
www.petergrayauthor.co.uk
www.trickyimppublishing.co.uk

Printed and bound in the UK by 4 Edge.

Preface

The Avalon Series is a contemporary work set in actual locations in the 'real world', so the usual problems in telling a story in this manner are many and varied.

What makes these stories real for me, (and hopefully the reader) is that you can go and stand on the very spot where the characters in the book stood.

The major problem as a writer is that in *our* reality, crime rarely happens in a convenient place or at a convenient time, indeed by its very nature, crime isn't convenient. So in an attempt to recreate that 'feel' I hardly ever make it convenient for me as an author.

As with the previous book, the most compromised part of the story is making sure that none of the characters are based on anyone in particular and therefore not all procedures and departments are the same as they are in the real world.

If you find the need to visit the places in the book please remember that some locations could be private land, monuments or sensitive heritage sites. To this end, please be respectful of the sites and locations and follow any guidelines or rules you may find there.

I hope you enjoy the second Avalon book in the series.

P Gray February 2017

Chapter One

"How the hell did you come to that conclusion?" asked Ross with a mix of frown and smile on his face.

"Just look at the facts, it's as plain as day," replied Avalon as he opened yet another drawer in the filing cabinet.

"Well it's as plain as day that you need to find another profession because your detective skills are sadly missing," insisted Ross allowing the frown to chase away the smile. Avalon stopped searching the files and looked over to Ross and said,

"I have no idea what you mean but I agree I would use the same criteria to come to a conclusion as I would with detective work."

"Now what are you rambling on about?" questioned Ross.

"Well, for instance, look at this room. What do you see?"

"Don't try and change the subject," demanded Ross.

"I'm trying to make a point," explained Avalon, "just tell me what you see here."

"A straight forward robbery, no ambiguity or doubt," replied Ross.

9

"But that's your problem, you surmise a conclusion, in your mind you've already solved the crime and so you're not so receptive to alternatives," explained Avalon with a slight smile. Ross began to shake his head.

"Problem? Anyway, this has nothing to do with the question."

"It has everything to do with the question," insisted Avalon looking over to Ross for a second, "I use the same logic in my civilian life as I do on a case."

"Well," laughed Ross, "your life must be a real shambles because your logic is going to fail on this one."

"No it isn't, like every good detective I have an open mind at all times," replied Avalon returning to his search of the filing cabinet. Ross walked over to him and said,

"Okay, here we go, I'll humour you," and he turned to face the door, "two persons, unknown, break in through the office window and make their way straight to this door," he pointed to the door showing damage around the lock, "where they proceed to kick it down. Frightened manager picks up this baseball bat and tries to defend himself but is overpowered by assailant or assailants," Ross stopped for breath and took a quick look around the room. "Then, they beat him to the ground as shown by the blood stain on the floor, ransack the office and leave by the same way they came in," Ross shrugged heavily and turned to Avalon. "There is nothing more to be seen here, forensics may add a little here and there but I fail to see how the human eye could see any more at this crime scene," he added. Avalon nodded.

"I wasn't talking about eyes, human or otherwise. You just admitted that we don't know how many were involved in the attack, right?" Ross looked doubtful at this, "yet you tell me *two* people broke in which means you are already convinced that we are looking for two offenders," concluded Avalon. For a moment, Ross stood staring at Avalon. He wondered how such chaotic thinking could ever be harnessed to catch criminals.

"But, we *know* there were two assailants because they were seen leaving the premises," began Ross, "and I'm sure when the victim is well enough to be interviewed he will confirm it. The only thing we don't know yet, is if one or both of them beat the crap out of him."

"What if another assailant left by another exit?" Avalon asked quietly, "but that isn't the point," he added placing a sheet of paper into an evidence bag, "I was trying to explain why you don't see my way of thinking. Even now I'm open to other options here, for instance, why does the victim have a baseball bat in this office? From his description," Avalon looked up at the ceiling as if remembering what he had been told, "and correct me if I'm in error, 'a rotund, short man with a pronounced limp', it's doubtful that he has ever played baseball with it," he said as he sealed the evidence bag.

"But as stated earlier, this is getting off the subject at hand." continued Ross, "my question still stands, we're not talking about a crime scene, so I'll ask again, how the hell did you come to that conclusion?" Avalon sighed and headed towards the door, he stopped and looked back at Ross.

"It's pretty obvious," he shrugged, "the barmaid was looking at me and not you and I came to that conclusion by using the same deductive powers as I would here at this crime scene."

"Go on," smiled Ross folding his arms.

11

"Was she looking at the slightly chubby, gel haired, middle class, lawn mower pusher, or the tall, slim, rugged man that looks as if he's in charge?"

"Slightly chubby?" called Ross with amazement, "and I'm the same height as you," But Avalon had turned and was walking from the building. Outside it was almost dark but the streetlights illuminated the area well enough. He nodded to the police officer guarding the door and made his way towards Ross's car, "and what do you mean by 'lawn mower pusher'?" called Ross as he caught up.

"It was something I heard Frazer say about you, I have no idea what she meant," shrugged Avalon as Ross unlocked the vehicle. They both got in and Ross turned back to Avalon.

"When did she say that?" asked Ross.

"I can't remember, I think when we were at Wilson's birthday party." Avalon looked at Ross, he was sitting, staring out of the window with his mouth just slightly open. "Shall we go or do you want to *mail* this evidence back to the station?" Ross came out of his thoughts and started the engine and the BMW gave a slight growl as Ross 'blipped' the throttle before setting off. Avalon realised Ross was stewing in his own thoughts which was why he was driving a little harder than he would have normally done. "I wouldn't get too upset about it," began Avalon deciding to have a little more fun, "some women like the older man, the experience wins out over boyish naivety." Ross just said,

"Let's change the subject, it's like talking to a character from Star Trek."

"I've no idea what you mean?" replied Avalon.

"Don't even think about telling me you have never watched Star Trek." Avalon was quiet, he was quiet all the way back to the station.

The two of them entered an empty office, the rest of C Section long gone to their homes, homes where they would try to continue with a normal life, maybe to a family or, for some, to an empty house. Avalon hated police stations at night, they developed a sinister feel as the darkness fell, becoming dead and clinical. In the daylight, there was usually bustle and noise with telephones ringing, but at night, a single phone ringing unanswered in the distance had an ethereal sound to it. Ross didn't seemed phased by it and had already slumped down into his chair, though he had omitted to switch the lights on and allowed a single desk lamp to light the room.

"Almost cosy," he smiled pointing to it.

"Cosy? It's not my idea of cosy," replied Avalon sitting opposite in a chair borrowed from another desk, "I think the reports can wait until the morning," he added as he stretched his arms above his head with a yawn. Ross said nothing, he leaned back in his chair and, after a moment, looked at his watch. Avalon thought he was checking if it was too late to go for a quick drink.

"Before you ask, I'm off home," smiled Avalon.

"Yeah, I don't think I can be bothered either," nodded Ross, "what do you think this new DCI will be like then?" Avalon thought for a moment and then offered,

"I'm not sure, but one thing is for certain, there will be changes, there always are."

"I suppose so, he'll want to put his own systems in place and no doubt there'll be upheaval," agreed Ross and he looked at Avalon, "talking of upheaval, how long have you been here now?" Avalon had to mentally count the weeks and convert them to months.

"Nearly four months," he eventually said.

"And you are still living with the Italian beauty?" grinned Ross.

"Well yes but the way you say it, it sounds something that it isn't. I share the house, nothing more." Avalon wasn't lying, the arrangement with Angioletta Carbonna was still in operation, he rented a room and they hardly ever saw each other due to her working long work shifts at night. The arrangement had originally been for just ten weeks but Avalon had been invited to take a more permanent position at Inverness and he had jumped at the chance. Detective Inspector Davies had gone on long-term sick leave and most people doubted he would return. Avalon's arrangement with 'Angie' had benefited them both so Avalon had continued to rent the room from her. DI Lasiter had taken over B Section and Avalon had been promoted to Detective Inspector and put in temporary charge of C Section by Chief Anderson who, since then, had also left for pastures new. This left the post of DCI open so a new Chief had been employed but had not yet arrived. DS Douglas had moved too, he had relocated to Edinburgh after the security van case and DS McGill had taken early retirement, leaving B Section seriously short handed. There were other changes too but in the forefront of most people's minds was the arrival of the new DCI.

"Where's he from?" asked Avalon.

"O-K says she heard he was previously with the Northumberland Division and she usually has good information." O-K, otherwise known as PC Kirk did have many contacts, it was true, and rarely was her information wrong. Avalon stood and said,

"Well, I better get this logged and down to the

storeroom," holding up an evidence bag that held the sheet of paper he had collected earlier.

"What is that by the way?" asked Ross.

"Just a sheet with contacts on it, I thought we may need it to check through to see who the victim knew," replied Avalon, "see you in the morning," and he left. As he returned from the evidence archive he passed through the foyer and saw Sergeant Gregory on the desk.

"Burnin' the midnight oil again Sarg..." began Gregory but then he remembered Avalon's promotion, "sorry, *Detective Inspector*."

"Oh, evening Bob, yeah, I still haven't got used to the title yet either," smiled Avalon.

"Well deserved if y' ask me," Gregory returned the smile, "an' worth all the hassles y' got after the case."

"Thanks Bob, I have to prove that I can do the job now though," he sighed and then said, "right I'm off home, I need to get an early start in the morning to get all the paperwork ready for the new DCI."

"He's already en," whispered the Desk Sergeant nodding to the rear of the building.

"Really?" frowned Avalon.

"Yeah, he arrived about two hours ago an' locked himself away upstairs."

"That's odd," insisted Avalon, "creeping in under the cover of darkness." The sergeant nodded and continued,

"One o' the traffic team reckon they know 'em from old and said they bet he starts tomorrow."

"On a Saturday? It's a pretty odd day to start a new job isn't it?" asked Avalon.

"Aye, a good way tae keep everyone on their toes though," nodded Gregory. Avalon sighed again and then said goodnight. As he drove home he considered this new Detective Chief Inspector, he could only assume that he was in his office doing his homework before surprising everyone with a Saturday morning start, it probably meant he was tight with discipline and difficult to work for. Avalon wondered how it would effect the station as he pulled into the drive of the bungalow. His housemate would have left for work a good five hours previous and so he would have the house to himself as usual and he wouldn't see her in the morning, as she would be tucked up in her bed by the time he awoke. The bungalow was functional yet comfortable and Avalon had set his own room out with a decent bed and a laptop in the corner as a small office area. He had put his house in Wolverhampton up for sale and had arranged for a removals company to bring some of his better possessions and his treasured Triumph Thunderbird motorcycle to Scotland, he had already bought and erected a shed on the back garden to store it. His life in Scotland wasn't complete by any stretch of the imagination but it was improving all the time. The only itch he needed to scratch now and then was the fact that his ex-wife, who he was still very fond of, was now seeing another man on a fairly regular basis. It bothered him, it shouldn't, but it did and no matter how much Avalon told himself he was being a fool he still had thoughts of her before he went to sleep each night. As he made himself a snack and seated himself in front of the television, he suddenly saw a parallel in his life, though here he was in Scotland, hundreds of miles from his former life in England, he was still doing the same things and in private, still living the same life.

He finished the snack and turned off the television and went into his room to pour a single malt whisky. He added a little water to it and walked outside into the

16

reasonably warm air of an Inverness evening. He looked up at the sky and realised why the Scots were so disparaging about their weather, maybe it was just a bad year but most days saw some rain and he couldn't remember the last clear sky he'd seen. He dealt with the weather but if there was anything that would drive him back south of the border it was the midges. The damn things were everywhere and into everything, he wasn't sure if he would get used to them, but then again having to share his life with them for a few months each year seemed preferable to going back to his old job, and for that matter his old life, even if wasn't all that different. He shivered slightly, he wasn't sure if it was the cooling air, or the thoughts of the toxic atmosphere in a particular Wolverhampton police station. He went back indoors, had a hot shower and then went to bed.

Avalon was getting used to Scottish mornings, the weather was always a bit of a lottery but the air was clean and clear. As he drove into work he began to consider what his Saturday might bring, though he knew the new DCI may be ready to force his personality on them all. Even so, he entered the building fairly upbeat and, to offset any foreboding he may have, he thought about his precious motorbike that was to be delivered on Sunday. It had been awkward to arrange and he had been very uncomfortable speaking to his ex-wife about it, but she needed to be there to allow the driver of the van to fetch his things from the house and load up the bike. She had asked why he wasn't coming for it himself and he had told her he was too busy. There was some truth to it, but not that much. He *was* busy but he simply couldn't bear the pain of seeing her and knowing someone else was making her happy. It hurt and he didn't know how to

17

deal with it.

"Mornin'," said a voice, it was PC Kirk passing through the building saying hello quite randomly, without knowing who it was she had spoken to, her eyes fixed on the pile of mail in her hand being delivered to various departments.

"Morning," replied Avalon, inside he was thanking her for bringing him out of his dark thoughts. He climbed the stairs and entered the office he had worked from for some considerable weeks and was surprised to see Ross already there.

"Hells bells, is your bed on fire?" he asked as he sat.

"An attempt at humour I admit but still short of the mark," replied Ross leaning back in his chair, "and anyway, you should thank me for getting the coffee machine ready for your arrival."

"Well done, the first time since I met you," said Avalon and without giving him time to add anything, "I could smell it down the corridor, I wondered if I had left it on all night." He then looked over to Ross and asked, "so why are you here..." he took a quick glance at his watch, "I was going to say early, but I'll amend it to 'on time'." Ross smiled slightly and said,

"I'm turning over a new leaf."

"You? The north wind hasn't turned as many new leaves as you," frowned Avalon as he switched on his computer.

"This time it's for real."

"So why the change in attitude?" asked Avalon, giving him the benefit of the doubt.

"This," replied Ross waving a sheet of paper in the air. There was a slight smile on his face and Avalon gradually followed suit as he realised what it might be.

"You got it confirmed?" grinned Avalon. Ross nodded with a broad smile.

"Yep, DI Lasiter left it on the desk yesterday, I picked it up just after you left last night," and he read from the paper, "*Detective Sergeant* Ian Ross."

"Bloody hell, it sounds exotic, are you actually going to do something now, seeing as they're giving you extra money to attend?"

"I think it calls for a double celebration, we didn't have a drink on the baby's head when your promotion came through," quipped Ross. Avalon allowed the smile to leave his face as he said,

"Not too fast, we might all have the sack when this new DCI hits the fan."

"We still have time before that."

"Not so Watson," added Avalon pretending to smoke a pipe, "Elvis is in the building."

"What are you talking about now?" asked Ross still smiling.

"Our new boss was here last night, there are those that say he'll start today, which means..." he gave a slight pause, "he is here right now." Ross now dropped the smile and stood, he walked to the window.

"On a Saturday? What sort of car has he got?"

"A Bentley... how the hell do I know what car he has?" replied Avalon shaking his head, "anyway, we better get started on the report for last night."

"Sod that, I want to know what sort of weird alien starts his new job on a Saturday."

"What happened to the 'new leaf'?" asked Avalon as he typed at his computer. Ross turned and sat down. Quietly, he set about his report but it wasn't long before he asked,

"I heard the sections are being cut back again."

"It's likely, but with a couple of people moving and a retirement it may not be that dramatic," suggested Avalon.

"It's madness to even consider it when we're so short handed," frowned Ross.

"They have to find money for your pay rise somehow," replied Avalon without any obvious emotion, just as the door opened.

"Er guys," it was Frazer with a doubtful look on her face, "et seems the new DCI es on site."

"We know," replied the two men in unison.

"Et's not normal startin' a new job on a Saturday," she insisted.

"We know," they said again. Frazer folded her arms and said,

"You two need tae find some new friends, you're starting tae sound like each other."

"That's easy for me but how the hell is he going to find any friends," replied Ross nodding towards Avalon, "oh and by the way, I've got mail."

"Jees," sighed Frazer as she read the paper Ross was holding up, "I resign."

"You have to start before you can resign," said Ross with a slight shrug. Frazer held up the middle finger of her right hand and then left.

"You will have to stop baiting Frazer," said Avalon looking up.

"And lose my only hobby," replied Ross shaking his head.

"You could end up working closely with her now," nodded Avalon to the paper Ross was reading through yet again, "or I may make her your regular partner."

"I may not be in your section," insisted Ross,

"you may not even get a section."

"You better hope I do and you are in it, because if you end up under DI Lasiter with Frazer..." he let Ross take in the implications. Frazer seemed to be a favourite of Lasiter, it wasn't clear why but the look on Ross's face showed he realised what Avalon was getting at. Avalon looked for some moments at Ross, the last few months had been difficult for him and Avalon wondered if he was fully recovered. The problem had begun when he and Ross were still working on the Abriachan murder near Drumnadrochit, Ross had returned home on several nights to see a car parked at the front of his house which moved off soon after he arrived. He had checked on the registration number but it didn't belong to anyone he knew and he came to the conclusion that his wife was having an affair. It had been unthinkable to Ross and he struggled with the idea that it was true but he eventually decided to return home early one night and park several hundred yards from his house. He had then watched as the car pulled up with a single male occupant inside. It had waited for thirty minutes and then the male got out and approached the door of his house. Ross later confronted his wife and she admitted to seeing someone. Though she had said it was just a friendship and nothing had happened Ross fell apart, unfortunately, during the case. Avalon was tired of the curse, though neither he or his ex-wife had been involved in an affair, their marriage had come unwound due to the pressures of the job in one way or another and indeed DI Davies was now on long term sick, for much the same reason. Davies had collapsed due to stress and exhaustion, he had suffered a nervous breakdown soon after and many doubted he would return. Davies's marriage seemed to have survived however but for Ross it didn't seem that it would end in a happy way.

"Have you seen Lucy recently?" he asked, Ross looked over to him and shrugged.

"No, I don't think there's much point in keeping any hopes up, we just argue now." Ross had told Avalon everything that had happened and Avalon had listened when Ross poured it all out, but it took a toll on *him* too, it reminded him of his own failure. Avalon stood and poured a coffee for them both.

"There's always a point," he said as he returned to his desk.

"I don't think so, she is living with her sister and I am exploring the exquisite delights of instant soup in a cup and ready meals," replied Ross taking a sip of his coffee.

"Well, I've told you before that I regretted not talking more to my wife, don't make the same mistakes."

"Thanks for the advice," nodded Ross, "but I don't think it will work anymore. She needs something I can't provide, not while I do this job," explained Ross. Avalon knew it to be true, although many police seemed to have blissfully happy marriages, even if he didn't know how they managed it. "Anyway," continued Ross with a distant look on his face, "I feel like I don't have to pretend anymore, it feels sort of-"

The door opened and Detective Sergeant Wilson walked in and looked over to Avalon as Ross went instantly silent.

"Mornin' all, have we heard anythen about the Cave, like when are we gettin' et back?" he asked. Avalon shrugged. It seemed Ross's outpouring would have to wait.

"I don't know, when I spoke to DI Lasiter he said as far as he was concerned we could move the rest of the crap out of there and move back in."

"Can we get et sorted then, this es hopeless bein' in three different offices," asked Wilson.

The 'Cave' was the original office used by C Section, it was just about large enough for them all to work in, but after being used as an incident room during a surge in criminal activity earlier in the year, it had since been used for storage. Recently though, most of the room had been cleared and there had been hopes that they would be able to return to it. Avalon had become used to working from several offices but he did agree the job would be easier with everyone able to offer theories and support lines of inquiries.

"Can do," agreed Avalon, "but the new DCI may have his own ideas." Wilson nodded and turned to leave.

"I'll get Mack to gae me a hand," he said.

"I'm in no hurry to be back in the same room as the others but he's right, it's almost impossible to run the section split up," insisted Ross.

"I agree the Cave would make things much easier," nodded Avalon.

As soon as he and Ross had finished their reports, they went to the Cave and lent a hand in the clear up. The room was much lighter having three large windows, in truth, just about the whole wall was glass. The end nearest the door had a small, sectioned area that had been used as the Detective Inspector's office but Avalon wasn't keen on separating himself off from the team. After a couple of hours work, the room was cleared and two desks were brought in to fill some of the extra space. Avalon's phone rang.

"Avalon," there was a long pause, "yes sir, straight away," and he put his phone away and raised his eyebrows. "The new Chief wants to see me. Finish off in here and I'll see you later," he continued and he left for the new Detective Chief Inspector's office. He knocked loudly on the door but waited for a reply.

"Come in," called a voice from within. Avalon walked in and saw a very different system than Chief Anderson had employed, gone were the piles of paperwork and the box files. All that sat upon the desk was a computer screen and a phone.

"D-I Avalon," he said as Avalon stood in front of the desk, there was no suggestion that he should sit, so he remained standing. The D-I was punctuated by a pause between the letters as if he was questioning Avalon's right to bear the title.

"Yes sir," replied Avalon. The man sitting at the desk was wearing his dress uniform and had his gaze fixed to the computer screen, obviously reading Avalon's record. With the immaculate uniform, his head looked completely out of place, his hair unkempt and his face wrinkled as if he were much older than his years. Not that Avalon knew his age, he knew nothing about him whatsoever except for the name he had given when he asked to see Avalon. Detective Chief Inspector Croker. The man eventually looked up and asked,

"Is there any reason you didn't want to go back to Wolverhampton?" There was a slight Scottish accent in the deep voice, his eyes were dark behind wire-rimmed spectacles and his lower lip seemed to jut out from his frowning visage and flapped as he spoke.

"There was no reason sir, a post was available here and I applied for it," replied Avalon trying to be as noncommittal as he could.

"Seems mightily odd that you found yourself promoted as soon as you were in post," growled the man.

"Odd sir?" asked Avalon looking slightly

surprised, "I have been qualified for DI for some time, I just haven't been offered a suitable post until now," replied Avalon.

"So there was a reason after all, you stayed on due to the promise of a promotion."

"That's incorrect," replied Avalon with a frown, the man may be his new boss but he wasn't going to stand there and be called a liar, "I took the post because I was told that with DI Davies on long term sick, I stood a good chance of being accepted, because I was still working relevant cases, not because of any promise. You are free to consult with DI Lasiter if you wish." Avalon allowed the final clause of the statement to show a slight amount of displeasure in his assumption.

"I have already interviewed DI Lasiter and he told me the same," replied the Chief, "but then he would, wouldn't he?" and he looked back to the screen. Avalon kept quiet.

"Sit down Detective Inspector," the man eventually said. Avalon was about to say that he would rather stand but he wondered if he was being goaded, and so he sat. "You seem to have been instrumental in making a profound breakthrough in the security van robbery back in April."

"It was a team effort sir," replied Avalon. There was no immediate reply, the man just seemed to continue reading from the screen. Avalon was feeling uneasy about the interview, he realised that a new DCI would want to make his impression on the station but he seemed positively antagonistic. Croker seemed to finish reading, he removed his spectacles, and looked at Avalon.

"I realise that you have a reasonable record DI Avalon but I wish to impress upon you that 'reasonable' isn't good enough for me," began Croker, "and I will tell you exactly what I have told the other Detective Inspectors, I want a more exacting approach to police work at all levels and I will not tolerate any slack procedures or misdemeanours. I run my departments by the book and I expect all my officers to do the same, is that clear?"

"I think you'll find that is the case here sir," replied Avalon.

"Not from what I can see, Detective Avalon, for instance there is still an ongoing investigation to find the remaining suspects for the security van case I see." demanded Croker and Avalon wondered if he was surreptitiously referring to Chief Anderson's official warning to Avalon after the arrests were made during that case. Avalon had not stuck to usual procedure and though his quick thinking brought significant results, both DI Lasiter and Chief Anderson had berated Avalon for his actions. Croker seemed to sigh slightly as he continued as if the job he had to do next was beneath him. "As you are the senior detective after DI Lasiter and DI Wick I am placing you in overall command of C Section. I know you have been in temporary control of the section and so it seems prudent to keep you in post," he paused as he replaced the spectacles and returned to reading the computer screen, "but as you probably already know, this station is being trimmed down. I have, however, managed to lessen the cull on the CID." At this point his voice became less harsh and Avalon detected a slightly more 'human' side to the man. "DI Lasiter will remain in command of B Section, you will run C Section, your team will be DS Ross and DS Wilson with constables Frazer, MacDonald and Mackinnon. DS Murrey is transferring to B Section as a replacement."

"Very good sir," replied Avalon trying to recollect the name Mackinnon.

"I wish you to know DI Avalon, I do not take kindly to my officers, *any* officers, whatever their rank, straying from procedure, I will not tolerate any behaviour that causes officers to become a liability," Avalon now knew *he* was being warned, "is that clear?"

"Yes sir," replied Avalon.

"I also see that you have been in the news on occasions in your past life, this is something else I do not wish to see." Avalon was unresponsive to the statement, how could he be responsible if the newspapers got hold of a story? "I want the press kept at arm's length under all circumstances," insisted Croker. Avalon gave a slight nod though he didn't hold out much hope on that score. Croker looked back at the screen for a moment and then said, "I see you have current cases, I expect to see speedy results, any questions?"

As Avalon walked back to his office he had mixed reactions to DCI Croker. He was abrasive but that may soften once he found his feet yet he seemed organised and efficient, so much so that there was no option for discussion whatsoever. Avalon was also slightly apprehensive about the task at hand. Yes, he had his own section, something he could never have imagined at the beginning of the year, but he also felt the pressure of such a post drop heavily on his shoulders like nothing he had ever experienced. Most of that pressure came from the low staffing levels, both B and C sections were shadows of their former selves with an estimated shortfall of twelve detectives. But, it was all down to him now, he was the officer in charge, in charge of *his* team and *his* life and woe betide anyone that tried to take that away from him. He opened the door to the office and stepped inside and was surprised to see how quickly Ross had turned the office around.

"What do you think?" asked Ross. There were four desks set at about equal distance from each other and another within the partition, which formed a kind of booth at the end of the room. "We've put it back more or less how it used to be, DI Lasiter's desk is yours now of course," Ross pointed to the desk in the booth. Avalon had considered that *his* desk would be with the others but he realised the booth was the only place for him, he was the DI, the 'top dog' and that was his kennel. Avalon nodded slowly and walked into the booth and sat. The Cave had plenty of glass to the outside so a good amount of daylight streamed in which made it feel much larger than it actually was. The booth itself was no more than a glass partition across the room with a wide entrance its the right hand side, it did however afford Avalon a little privacy.

"Seems fine," he nodded, "but you need to find another desk."

"I thought the section was to be cut down even more?" asked Ross.

"It seems DCI Croker has other ideas, we've lost Tom but gained someone called Mackinnon." Ross, Wilson and MacDonald looked at each other and shrugged.

"Must be new," suggested Wilson, "never heard o' him."

"Mack, you'll have to take PC Dowd's role for a while, we're losing his assistance I'm sorry to say," said Avalon.

"Aye, I suppose the youngest gets the crappy

job," sighed MacDonald.

"Any other changes?" asked Ross.

"No," replied Avalon shaking his head, "but by Monday I want this office ready to rock and roll."

~~~~~~

Avalon sat at the table looking out from the kitchen window, eating a slice of toast with his first coffee of the day. His bike had been delivered the day previous, along with his helmet, books, bike clothing and a few other items including his old guitar that he hadn't played for years. He was planning when he might take the bike out for a celebratory ride, as it was Monday, it was likely to be the following Sunday but as Avalon considered this he noticed movement. Across the road the strange little woman who he knew only as 'Mrs Pink' due to the fact that every item of her wardrobe was either pink or had pink in it, went off to work. Ironically her equally little car was blue, not pink. Avalon could set his watch by her and indeed almost did, for as she drove away from the street he would finish his coffee and then wash his plate and cup. He would then put on his jacket and leave the house for work. If she was late, there was a good chance Avalon would be late, and so, this Monday morning, he had decided to take no chances and kept a close watch of the time, that was how he knew Mrs Pink was early. It was most unusual for her, Avalon had never seen this before and he wondered if it was a bad omen for the day. It bothered him so much he began to wonder if his watch, the clock on the cooker and the kitchen clock were all wrong. Just to be on the safe side he decided to make a move and he headed off to the station. He arrived early of course but it would give him chance to have a look at the Cave in detail. It was a much better office than the one they had left and, though it looked out from the side of the building, the view was mostly over fields. He thought back to the temporary office he had occupied, just one of the interview rooms with a desk and filing cabinet, now here he was with three large windows and his own space at one end. He looked at the place that Ross had claimed, as usual by the window. He was still concerned about Ross, with the new DCI breathing down their necks he didn't want Ross falling by the wayside. He walked into his booth and sat in the chair he would now run C Section from, it was daunting yet exhilarating and he was looking forward to it, as long as Croker let them get on with the job. The door opened and DS Wilson entered.

"Mornin' Boss," and he walked to the other desk by the windows, it seemed the windows were for the sergeants and not for the constables. DC MacDonald was next in, he smiled and nodded to Avalon.

"Get the coffee on Mack," said Wilson, "the boss had the goodness tae provide for us so we ought to use et."

"So I'm the tea lady as well as the secretary am I?" complained Mack as he walked to the coffee machine.

"We'll get you the uniform later," smiled Wilson. Avalon didn't know these people as well as he ought to, so as he watched them fill the room, he brought up their profiles on the computer. The ginger haired Wilson was thirty-two years old but his deep accented voice made him sound much older. He was confident and competent. Avalon had not worked with Mack all that much but he seemed capable and wiser than his twenty-six years showed. He too had a broader accent that gave Avalon a clue he probably wasn't originally from Inverness. The next through the door were Frazer and Ross, almost together and once again, Ross was on time. Avalon had grown to like Frazer, he could see why Lasiter had thought highly of her. He wondered if some of her bluster and aggressiveness was just her humour, deep down she seemed caring and capable, if a little quiet. If Avalon could have his way Frazer would be a detective sergeant, she had the skills if not the attitude.

And then there was Ross, well Ross was never going to change, even with his life falling apart around him he still managed to keep his sense of humour even if it was somewhat muted. It was probably the best indication of his mood.

With everyone seated and chatting, the office came alive, there were a few smiles too now that they were back in the Cave. The only thing missing was Mackinnon, who the hell *was* Mackinnon? Avalon rose from his seat and walked from the enclosed area into the main room and leaned with his back on the glass wall of the booth.

"Right C Section, a new Monday and a new start for us," began Avalon as the talking subsided and they looked to see what he had to say. Avalon had considered this moment, it wasn't scripted exactly but he did know what he wanted to say, "therefore, I thought I may as well get what I have to say out the way so that we can get on with our jobs." He looked over all their faces, they would be expecting changes so he wasn't too perturbed about altering routines. "Firstly, I have to tell you that yours truly, Detective Inspector Avalon is now officially in charge of C Section," there were a few nods and the odd smile but little other response so he moved quickly on, "I also want to say that as a section I have no doubts of your skills or your integrity and I'm happy that we really have no 'weak link' in the team. I do, however, expect nothing but the best. DI Lasiter always had a tight grip on the reins and that grip will certainly not be relaxed on my watch." He stopped and watched their reactions, there was still little of any sort, but they seemed to be taking in his words. "We are running with a severe shortage to the section, looking at the records from previous years I realise we are at least five officers down but, I know with your help, we can continue to improve and that means catching more bad guys even quicker. To that end we will work in teams as usual. These teams are not set in stone and we will have to swap roles depending on the cases we are given, so that is something you need to get used to," he explained and took a breath before continuing, "on that note, we don't know who Mackinnon is and I have no information on him so we will have to wait and see." New faces, particularly ones from other areas needed time to settle into the routines and Avalon didn't really have the time for such distractions.

"Sounds like he's from another nick, nobody seems to have heard o' him," offered Mack with a smile. He was obviously thinking that he might not be at the bottom of the 'pecking order' if it were true.

"Yes," nodded Avalon, "it looks like it, well DS Wilson, you will be in charge of Mackinnon," Wilson frowned and said with a sigh,

"Yeah, okay Boss," he was clearly unenthused by the thought.

"Mack, unfortunately you draw the short straw and will be in here most of the time when not helping DS Wilson," Avalon looked over to Frazer. "DC Frazer, you will be floating between teams for now until we can assess the new boy," and he looked to Ross. "I know no one will want to partner Ross so I'm keeping him for *special duties*," and he smiled to confirm that humour still had its place in C Section and he quickly moved on. "But that isn't the end of it. When we know more about Mackinnon we will sort something more permanent. Any questions?"

"Yeah," nodded Wilson, "who es workin' on what?" Avalon smiled,

"Well I suppose that's what we're here for," and he moved forward and leaned on Ross's desk, "we were running two main cases, it makes sense to leave them with the people already working on them especially as Ross and me went out late on Friday to a robbery and attack."

"Where wes that?" asked Wilson.

"As far as we can tell it's not tied to your investigation Gordon," Avalon stood straight, "if it turns out to be linked, we'll hand it over. So you, Mack and the new boy will stay on your warehouse break-ins and Frazer and Ross will continue with the two attempted abductions, and I want that one closing down quickly now we have some DNA. I'll have a good look at the attack on Friday but I think that will be sorted fairly quickly due to witnesses. I know there are several other less serious cases such as the missing person but we will deal with those as and when." The door to Avalon's right opened and DI Lasiter walked in.

"Oh sorry DI Avalon, I didnae realise..." apologised Lasiter seeing they were having a meeting.

"We've just finished," said Avalon and he turned back to his team, "okay guys, carry on." He walked over to Lasiter and into the booth. Lasiter was smiling as he spoke,

"Et's good tae see the Cave up an' runnin' again."

"It's certainly better than the interview room," replied Avalon glancing back and he offered Lasiter a seat. "What can I do for you?"

"Have y' been tae see the Chief?"

"Yes," replied Avalon raising his eyebrows.

"So what dae y' think?"

"A bit odd but it's early to say, ask me again in six months."

"Aye you're right about odd, I mean, who ever heard of a CI coming tae work in es dress uniform? He does seem tae be on the ball though, I'll give him that," agreed Lasiter, "he knew everythen' about our cases so maybe he will turn out fine once he gets tae grips with his dress sense," Lasiter slapped his legs and said, "okay, I better get back to et," and he stood.

"I gather you want to ask me something?" smiled Avalon.

"Aye laddie, nothen gets past you, y' ought to be a detective," smiled back Lasiter.

"Well spit it out then," said Avalon.

"Et's just that I asked for Frazer in B Section, the Chief denied the request but I didnae want y' tae find out and then... well, best that y' know."

"Well I've got a question for you," said Avalon.

"Go on," replied Lasiter.

"Why the big interest in Frazer, I mean she's a good detective and all that but you seem to have some greater interest in her career?" Lasiter shrugged and shook his head.

"Nothen in particular, I just didnae want tae see her on the scrap heap just because she doesn't always toe the line."

"I doubt that would happen, she fit in really well during the security van case."

"Aye, I know that fine," nodded Lasier and he stood to leave.

"Well, I better get back to et, lots tae do hey?" he gave a brief smile and left. As Avalon sat, he couldn't shake the idea that there was some link between Lasiter and Frazer but for the life of him he couldn't see what it could possibly be. He looked up for a moment and through the glass he saw his team hard at work on phones, looking at the wall maps and working at computers. It looked good and Avalon should be happy, but he wasn't, and he didn't know why, it was if there was something unresolved. He was about to think through the situation when there was a single knock at the door and PC Kirk entered, she was followed by another person, Avalon guessed it was Mackinnon.

"Mornin' DI Avalon," she said. Kirk was highly professional but Avalon could see the slight smile on her face as she said the 'DI' part of the greeting. She immediately returned to business and continued with, "Thes es DC Rory Mackinnon, I believe he is joining your section," then she turned and left.

"DC Mackinnon, please take a seat," announced Avalon pointing to the other chair in the booth, "your personal file isn't on our computer system yet so you'll have to tell me about yourself."

"Of course sir," replied the young man. He actually looked unfeasibly young to Avalon's jaundiced eye but he had an intelligent face and eager eyes. There was little accent of any sort but he detected a slight Scottish background to it, "what would you like to know?"

"Let's start with your experience shall we?"

"There isn't much to tell in that respect sir, twenty-four months as a student PC, ten months as

Police Constable waiting for my application to join the CID. I passed my exams and then waited another three months for a post."

"Pretty quick even in these days of shortage," said Avalon with a false smile but Mackinnon didn't seem to understand what he meant. "Did you specifically ask for Inverness?"

"No sir, I was eager to start so I didn't try to specify."

"Eagerness can be a bad thing in this line of work Mackinnon," frowned Avalon.

"I suppose so sir, but it's something I always aimed for and I know I can be a real asset," insisted the young man.

"How old are you?" asked Avalon.

"Twenty-five last month," he replied. Avalon began to wonder if a twenty-five year old had seen enough of the real world to understand what he was letting himself into. It was young to be accepted into the CID but then again, MacDonald was young too, but he had probably been brought up in a rough area, he knew what was at stake to be on the wrong side. He had made a choice to be a detective because of the injustice and cruelty he had witnessed at first hand. Mackinnon didn't seem to have that 'edge'.

"I can't promise you're going to be in the front line here and I dare say you're going to find it different to what you expected..." Avalon trailed off with a slight shrug, he knew this new recruit was going to be difficult to assign and if he had known how inexperienced he was he may have made some objections.

"With respect sir, I'm new but I have no delusions about the job or the work involved, I know all about the paperwork, the hours, the lack of clothing allowance and all the other complaints that other officers have but I accept that," insisted Mackinnon. Avalon stared at him for a moment then said,

"Maybe you do but there are parts of this work that no research, no advice and no training can get you ready for."

"I realise that, but that can only come from experience," insisted the young man.

"But it's how you deal with the experience," began Avalon with a little frustration in his voice, "for instance, the first time you spend two years sweating a case, getting everything right, sinking in parts of your soul to bring some heartless villain to justice, to have the CPS or the Procurator Fiscal throw the case out because they don't think it will tick any boxes. Will you just sigh and say 'oh well better luck next time'?" Mackinnon could see Avalon was becoming slightly agitated.

"Sorry sir, I'm being too eager again."

"It's not that Mackinnon, it's just that I'm going to struggle to integrate you into this section so you'll have to accept whatever crumbs you can get," Avalon spoke slightly softer, "is that clear?"

"Of course sir," nodded the young man.

"For now you are going to have to deal with something much more pressing and to a certain degree as distasteful as police work can get, meeting C Section," and he stood and lead Mackinnon in the main part of the office.

"People, this is the elusive Mackinnon." The first to speak was Wilson, who spoke with a southern American accent.

"You've got a pretty mouth boy," and he hesitated before reverting to his usual broad Scottish, "but don't be affraid, I never kiss on the first date." Ross simply nodded, as did Frazer but Mack called over,

"Well I'm glad tae see you ef the others aren't." Avalon pointed the team out and introduced them by name and rank and then Mackinnon looked back to Wilson.

"A quote from 'Deliverance' DS Wilson?" Wilson looked slightly bemused and then said,

"I dunno the name of the film, why?"

"It's a bit of a hobby, well the old B Movies really," replied Mackinnon.

"Great," announced Ross, "the DI quoting poetry and Mackinnon telling us which film it's from." Avalon listened to several other jibes and jokes from the team, it gave him time to reassess how to try and integrate Mackinnon into the scheme of things.

"What are we gonna call hem?" asked Wilson to the whole room, "we cannae have another Mack?"

"Where are you from?" asked Ross.

"I've been stationed at Dunbarton and Oban but I'm originally from Mull," replied Mackinnon.

"Hmm, nothing funny there then," shrugged Ross and he went back to work.

"Aye, we'll have tae *mull* et over," grinned MacDonnald.

"What about the Gaelic word 'eilean', et means 'of the islands' doesn't et?" submitted Frazer.

"Let's not do the Gaelic theng," offered Wilson, "after the cock up on Bute especially."

"What was that?" asked Frazer.

"I heard about that, it was a bit of confusion with the Gaelic language," began Mackinnon, "the council put up a sign saying 'Welcome to the gateway of the beauty of Bute Island' with what they thought was a translation in Gaelic. The problem was, the word for Bute in Gaelic has an accent over the letter 'o'. Without the accent the word means something utterly different and they left it off."

"So what did it say?" asked Frazer.

"Welcome to the doorway to the beauty of 'Penis Island'," smiled Mackinnon. There were laughs around the room.

"Well, that's councils for you," sighed Frazer.

"Aye and et was only there for ten years or so," laughed Wilson. Avalon decide it was time to get to work and he said,

"Mackinnon, you will be with DS Wilson for now and Mack will show you the ropes, an let's hope you can fit in as quick as possible, we are seriously short of manpower," he smiled and returned to his booth but now and then he looked up to see how the new face was settling in.

~~~~~~~

Avalon always struggled with what to do with what was left of the evening when he returned home and this Monday evening was no different, so in an effort to resolve that, he went to the shed at the back of the house. There was no power laid on, so he couldn't stroke or caress his bike, he picked up the box that had been delivered with it and went back to the house. As he opened the flap he saw on the top was his trusty helmet, it was scratched a little bit but it fit like a glove and then he pulled out his jacket and waterproofs. Within the clothing was something white, it dropped and fell on the floor. He couldn't remember putting anything in there so he picked it up and stood looking at what seemed to be an envelope. It wasn't sealed but on the back it said simply, 'James'. He knew the hand writing, it was from Carol his ex-wife and his heart missed several beats, what the hell did she want to tell him that she couldn't say over the phone? He decided to sit, he pulled out a flimsy sheet of paper and he began to read. It contained all the usual introductions, hoping he was well, hoping he was looking after himself and asking how the job was going. It was then he realised he hadn't told her it was permenant or even that he was now a Detective Inspector. He was still struggling with the idea of a thorough conversation with her, he was too afraid what she would tell him.

"This letter may be to resolve that," he thought. He continued to read. The second part was the telling piece.

"I'm not sure if I'm reading this properly but I do think you are avoiding me. I have rung you and left several messages and when I do manage to get through, you tell me that you're busy and you'll ring back. You never do."

Avalon sighed, obviously it was true but no matter how much he tried to think his way through it and no matter how she felt, he just couldn't fully let go of her. He continued reading.

"I assume it's because I said I was seeing someone, but honestly, I can't stay alone forever, you must understand that..." At this point he placed the note on the table and walked into the bathroom, he didn't think that reading anymore would be advantageous, he knew what it was going to say. He threw cold water over his face and reached for the towel, as he looked up to his reflection, he considered what he had to do. He had to write and tell her, 'just get on with your life, I'm fine with it,' no matter what it was going to cost him. Inside

he knew what he felt, he felt just the same as he had when he first met her, outside was a different matter. The reflection he saw looking back was someone he didn't know anymore. There was a confidence, dark eyes looking back from a face that seemed to have an inexhaustable lifeforce. He had been taking his health more seriously, that was true but could such a simple change alter someone that much? He stood back slightly, "Maybe it's the lighting in here," he thought looking up at the lightbulb but as his gaze fell back on the image in the mirror, there was something different, it almost made him shiver. Was he going mad? Had he taken too much on and was he now reaping the whirlwind? He returned to the kitchen, there was the note, he picked it up and sliped it back into the envelope and carried it into the bedroom along with the box with his bike clothing. He ate a light meal, showered and had a single glass of single malt, with water, and then climbed into bed. He didn't sleep, he lived his life over like a dying man, thinking his way back to the present and finally flinging back the sheets and getting up once more. He made himself a coffee, if he was to be awake he needed to think properly, but before he sat to drink, he returned to the bathroom. He looked once more at the face there, but there was no change, it looked back at him as if issuing a challenge. "I hope you know what you're doing," he said and he turned out the light.

Chapter Two

"So what do y' thenk?" asked Lasiter sipping at the coffee Avalon had just poured him.

"It doesn't matter what we think, the DCI seems to be on a crusade to change the whole system here," shrugged Avalon.

"Personally, I thenk et has potential for disaster, the idea of demarcation es good en theory but without enough personnel et's never gonna work," insisted Lasiter.

"I'm not sure what he's thinking but we're already overworked and understaffed and without the ability to help each other out, all the sections are going to feel more pressure." Avalon looked through the glass window into the Cave, there was only Mackinnon and McDonald left in there but he wanted to be sure their conversation went no further and so he lowered his voice. "I think the new lad will get there eventually but, essentially, I'm a man down, well, several men down," and he looked over to Lasiter with a serious look, "we both are." Lasiter nodded,

"Aye, I know what y' mean an' that's more or less what I told him, ef we had another four or five staff en each team we could probably make et work."

"And it didn't make any difference?" asked Avalon.

"No," replied Lasiter shaking his head, "he just said that he had seen a great deal of success with the system en other forces and we would have to make et work."

"I expect the 'other forces' he spoke of have more staff," frowned Avalon.

"I thenk he wants tae create competition between the departments."

"Well if that's true it seems pretty naive," replied Avalon. Lasiter nodded and sighed.

"Blinkered I would call et."

"Well," sighed Avalon, "he's been here three days and already he's causing us more work." His phone rang. "Avalon," there was a pause as Avalon raised his eyebrows to Lasiter, "yes sir, on my way."

"That's him I'm guessing," said Lasiter as Avalon put down the phone.

"Yes, he wants to see me as soon as is practicable," replied Avalon standing.

"I'll see you later as long as you can keep your calm," smiled Lasiter.

With Avalon and Lasiter out of the office, Mackinnon turned to Mack and asked,

"How long have you been here Mack?"

"Oh, I dunno, about eighteen months or so," he replied.

"DI Avalon is new isn't he?"

"Yeah, pretty new, he came from Birmingham on secondment but liked the weather so much he decided tae stay," smiled Mack.

"What's he like?" asked Mackinnon. Mack

shrugged.

"He's okay, I hav'nae worked for him for very long but tae be honest, we have had some decent DI's since I've been here."

"So nothing I need to know about then?" asked Mackinnon with an almost pleading look on his face. It made Mack smile and he said,

"Y' mean how do you get on his good side?"

"More like how do I stay off his bad side," grinned Mackinnon.

"Just do your job, keep all the arsing about to the Cave and never outside, dress tidily, don't bad mouth any other police officers and don't look shocked if he starts rambling out some poetry," explained Mack and then he continued, "apart from that, ef he has that 'dark' look in his eyes, just stay clear."

"Dark look?" asked the young DC.

"Yeah, sometimes he seems tae be..." Mack trailed off and shrugged, "well you'll know when it happens."

"Okay, that sounds easy enough, any odd habits I should know about?"

"Except for reciting poetry you mean?" asked Mack with a grin. Mackinnon gave a look of 'I'm just asking' and so Mack continued, "not odd as such but he hates criminals, and I mean *hates*. There es something different about him when he has to confront them. We've all noticed et, he's like a lion with a gazelle, he seems tae circle them looking for a weak spot, leave him to et when you see that."

"I guess we're supposed to dislike the enemy if we're to catch them," shrugged Mackinnon, Mack smiled and shrugged at the same time.

"Probably," he replied, "he looks after his team

though. Wilson says et's because we're the nearest thing he has to a family, I wouldn't know about that though." Mack seemed to remember something and then continued with, "Oh and he doesn't like swearing."

"No swearing?" asked Mackinnon with surprise.

"It's okay tae use the less severe stuff but not the strong language," explained Mack.

"Does he know this is Scotland?" asked the young DC, still surprised about the rule.

"Aye, we explained et was a national sport but he says that's the reason, 'ef we are tae stand out and above the criminal classes we have tae be different and have higher morals'." Mack recited it as if it was a quote from the DI and so Mackinnon gave a slight shrug and nodded.

"Difficult but if it's a rule..."

"Consider et more of a guideline," smiled Mack. Mackinnon had one more question.

"What's with the nick-names in the office?"

"Et's sort of a tradition en the section, et's dying out more recently but I expect you'll get yours eventually," he paused, "and though I can tell you *what* they are, I'm not saying *why*." He smiled and looked around the room before he continued. "You know mine, Ross was 'Frothy' but that's sort of died out, Frazer es called 'Razor' but only behind her back and DS Wilson es 'Bendy'." Mackinnon smiled and nodded.

"So has the DI got one?" he asked. Mack looked out of the window for a moment at the passing grey clouds, then turned and nodded to Mackinnon.

"Somebody came up with one but I ain't telling you what et es 'cos the DI don't know about et," he frowned a little, "and I hope he never does."

~~~~~~~

"Sit down DI Avalon," said Croker without looking up. Avalon sat and waited for the speech, he hadn't decided exactly how he was going to react but he tried to remain as calm as he could. "I assume you have heard by now that I am planning to change the way that the sections handle cases?"

"I have heard that there are to be changes," replied Avalon, "but no details as such."

"The changes that are most pertinent to you are the roles of both B and C sections. My intent is that B Section shall deal with cases within the city and its environs and C Section will operate in the rural areas outside the main city."

"With respect sir, I don't think that will work."

"And why not DI Avalon?"

"Well sir, I have no idea what size of area you are thinking of, but B Section simply isn't large enough to deal with the amount of crime around Inverness and C Section can't hope to cover the hundreds of square miles in the rural areas and I think with Police Scotland making us 'One Police Force', it seems counterproductive to say the least." insisted Avalon.

"DI Lasiter made a similar point but as I have told him, based on the figures from the database and hours expended on cases, as long as you all work more efficiently we just about have the staff to cope," Avalon didn't answer, he was still trying to figure out what figures and databases had to do with fighting crime. "I admit it would make things easier with more staff but a similar situation exists with C Section, there is less serious crime in the rural environment and, with a more efficient approach, your team should deal with it easily."

Avalon decided that it was time to make a stand.

"You must certainly know that police work isn't like that, you can't just bundle it up into convenient parcels and expect 'more efficiency' to work. I have several cases from the security van case coming to court and some of my officers will have to attend, plus court appearances for other minor cases, meetings with the Procurator Fiscal's office, plus follow up calls on-"

"I know exactly what detective work involves," interupted Croker raising his voice, "and I don't need a lesson from you. My decision stands, from this point you and your team will be dealing with cases outside the juristiction of B Section. Continue with current cases of course," he calmed his voice, but removed his spectacles, to continue with, "is that clear?"

"It's clear but I wish my opposition to this plan to be recorded."

"Noted!" spat Croker, Avalon didn't say anything further, he just left the office. He returned to his seat in the Cave and contemplated how seriously misinformed the DCI was and wondered how it would end. Either way, he and his team still had a job to do and do it they would. Avalon decided not to mention it until everyone was back at base, but their reaction was predictable.

"I wondered what kind of catastrophe he would bring down on our heads, an' thes es et," announced Wilson. Ross wasn't far behind him.

"He must think all we do is find lost dogs and missing bus passes."

"If things get busy we could be in some trouble," insisted Avalon, "but we'll have to adapt and do the best we can."

"Yes boss," began Mack, "but I have a bad feeling about this."

"I agree with Mack," added Frazer, "something es really wrong with his attitude, ef you look at past records, the serious rural cases are few and far between, what are we gonna do when B Section are pulled out an' we are sat on our arses?"

"That's not our issue, we just have to keep to what we have to do, when the system goes wrong, we have to ensure that C Section did what they could to make it work," insisted Avalon.

"Y' mean, don't rock the boat?" said Wilson.

"No I don't mean that," insisted Avalon with a glare.

"He means make sure we just do what we are supposed to do, nothing more, nothing less," sighed Ross folding his arms.

"A work tae rule?" asked Frazer with surprise in her voice.

"Nothing so ridiculous," insisted Avalon, "it's clear the system won't work but we are not to be seen to make it fail." There was silence and some blank stares, it wasn't going to be good for morale if these type of issues were to be commonplace.

"So what about the robbery and attack we went to last Friday?" asked Ross.

"I'm handing that one over to Lasiter, it should be straight forward for them."

"So what about the current cases?" asked Wilson.

"Continue as previous on any cases unsolved, your case particularly Gordon. It's still your case even though it's in B Section's area," announced Avalon. There was a slight knock at the door and PC Dowd came in.

"Ah, Dowd what can we do for you?" asked Ross with a slight grin.

"Er, I just brought this upstairs, who wants et?" he was holding up a piece of paper that obviously held a newly logged crime.

"Where was it?" asked Avalon. Dowd read from the paper.

"Erm, Dalneigh," he eventually replied. Avalon looked to Ross who shook his head.

"B Section," replied Avalon looking straight at Dowd. The PC looked puzzled.

"B Section?" he frowned, but seeing no one in the room showed any signs of taking up the case, he shrugged and left.

"I wonder what it was?" asked Ross to no one as he looked down to his computer screen. Avalon gave an audible sigh and went into his booth sitting down heavily. Ross soon joined him.

"I wonder how long we can keep this up?" he asked as he leaned on the wall and folded his arms. Avalon leaned back and shook his head at Ross.

"You know, it used to be like this at the old office in the midlands, someone would walk in with a sheet of paper and say 'who wants this?' and everyone would look down at their desks," he sighed again before continuing. "Not because of any other reason than they had too much to do," he stood and thrust his hands into his pockets in frustration, "and we are turning them away because they aren't in the DCI's idea of 'our area'."

"What about going above Croker?" Avalon stared at Ross and sat again.

"I may as well hand my notice in now, I've seen too many careers end through moves like that."

"Then we'll have to put up with it then," frowned Ross. Avalon picked up a pencil and tapped it lightly on his leg as if beating out a tune only he could hear.

"For now, yes, so how are the team doing?" he asked trying to change the subject.

"Fine," nodded Ross unfolding his arms looking toward the team through the glass, "Mackinnon is going to be awkward to integrate but we'll find something even if it's making the coffee," Avalon smiled slightly then Ross added, "do you fancy a drink later?" Avalon nodded,

"Yeah, can do."

"I'll drive you home after," replied Ross and he walked back to his desk leaving Avalon with his thoughts. Avalon threw down the pencil and felt himself sigh once more and then he continued reviewing notes on a missing person case that was several days old.

~~~~~~

Avalon took a sip of the drink that Ross had bought at his request.

"Thanks, I'm not really a fan of beer but I'm damn sure I'm not drinking that cheap blended whisky," he complained nodding towards the bar, "why have we come here anyway?" he continued.

"I just can't be arsed to bump into anyone I know," explained Ross as he sat, "it's a bit quieter anyway, he added after taking a sip of his larger.

"Have you admitted defeat about the barmaid in the other pub?" questioned Avalon. Ross just shook his head as he placed his drink on the table and then looked around. "Why does it need to be quiet anyway?" asked Avalon after giving Ross time to settle into his seat.

"Don't worry, I'm not going to spill my guts to you again, I just wanted to ask a question or two..." Ross trailed off as if he was slightly embarrassed.

"Fire away," replied Avalon leaning back into the seat thinking it could be about the Croker's ideas but he saw more doubt the mans face. Ross looked down to the drink and Avalon began to guess what was on his mind, had he considered going back to his wife he wondered? For one moment, Avalon even considered that Ross was about to tell him he was leaving the force. "Well, are you going to ask or shall I see if they have any Tarot cards behind the bar?" Ross looked up to Avalon for a second and then cupped his pint glass with both hands and seemed to be examining its contents.

"Well, it's sort of hard to ask, it seems pretty childish really," stuttered Ross letting go of the glass and making a deep sigh. He then looked to Avalon and said, "I was thinking, you have been divorced for some time now haven't you?"

"Too long," replied Avalon.

"And by that answer you would probably change the situation if you could?"

"Yes, of course," nodded Avalon, "I told you before, I regret not trying harder to keep it all together," Avalon began thinking about the letter Carol had sent him.

"So," continued Ross with more hesitation, "you don't like living on your own then?" Avalon looked to the ceiling, he was beginning to see Ross's tack. He wasn't looking for a way out of his predicament, it seemed he was considering what the future held as a single man.

"No, quite frankly, I don't," replied Avalon looking directly at him, "but sometimes I think it's preferable to ruining another person's life. I can do what I like when I like and I don't have to make excuses when I get home and try to explain why the job is to blame."

He stopped for breath then continued, "but, then again, most of the time I have no real reason to *go* home," he took a sip of his drink, "so you're feeling lonely already?"

"It's nothing to do with that," frowned Ross, "I just find myself laying awake at night, wondering what I should be doing, it feels like I'm in some sort of limbo."

"Well, you probably won't want to hear this but that's how I felt, I still do to a certain degree," insisted Avalon, "because I can tell you, *that* won't go away very quickly. You can learn to live with it but it doesn't really go away," Avalon gave a slight smile, "unless you meet someone else and make *them* put up with your antisocial lifestyle of course."

"I wish I hadn't asked, it's like talking to one of the four horsemen of the apocalypse."

"Well you did ask," shrugged Avalon.

"I wouldn't want to see you and Lasiter out together, there would be suicides in the pub," insisted Ross as he took a large gulp of his drink.

"I can make inane, upbeat chit-chat when the need arises," replied Avalon.

"Oh, and on the subject of 'need arising'?" asked Ross with a pause, "who is the target of your recent health fix?" Avalon genuinely didn't understand what Ross was getting at, he didn't say anything, he just gave a deep, questioning look. "Don't give me that puppy dog expression, you know what I'm getting at," added Ross.

"I haven't the foggiest idea what you-"

"I didn't see it at first because I was going through the crap with my own life," interrupted Ross, "but then I began to wonder about the interest in heath foods and the extra exercise and, worst of all, cutting down your drinking," Avalon began to understand.

"I was just trying to make my lifestyle a little less destructive," he replied.

"Oh yeah?" glared Ross, "it recently occurred to me, there must be a woman involved, care to elaborate?" he concluded. Avalon sat open mouthed for a moment and then shook his head.

"You see," began Avalon, looking at Ross with a more confident expression, "there you go again, making two and two make seven, no woman, no ulterior motive just a consideration for my health."

"More bullshit," grinned Ross.

"No it isn't," replied Avalon with a deadpan face. He now realised Ross was referring to him asking about getting fitter and eating healthier during the security van case earlier in the year. Avalon had found out that Sarah Underwood, of the forensics department, was vegan and that alone was the most likely the reason she had never accepted any kind of date from any of the police officers. He didn't quite see the logic in his thinking now but he had quite forgotten about it. He had found Miss Underwood very attractive and he wasn't the only one, Ross had admitted that he and many of the other officers at the station had tried their 'luck' with Sarah. For a short time Avalon had thought of going vegan himself, maybe just to impress her, but he decided that it was naive and eventually thought better of it. The thing was, he had never told Ross about his findings and wondered if he should now, but looking at the inquisitive face staring back at him, he decided he would hold the information back for some later date. "I have a perfectly good reason, and that is *my* business," he concluded.

"You must think that we Scotsmen are wet behind the ears, you can't fool me, it's either Angie your housemate, or Sarah Underwood," grinned Ross.

"Wrong on both counts," replied Avalon, "if you like, I could give you a few pointers about detection." Ross shook his head slowly.

"You are so full of crap, I can't believe you won't tell me."

"Okay, I'll tell you, it isn't a secret," agreed Avalon opening his eyes wider, "when I first arrived," he continued, "I took one look at you and thought, 'I don't want to end up like that and so I decided to do something about it." Ross simply sighed and shook his head slowly once more as he reached for his glass. Avalon also took another sip of the tasteless beer and smiled a little to himself. The internal smile subsided as the thought of the letter from Carol arose once more and he attempted to shake free of it by asking Ross a question.

"So what do you think of Mackinnon?" it seemed to draw Ross from a thought too, and he blinked several times before an answer was forthcoming.

"He seems a nice enough lad but that might be the problem."

"Well he doesn't have the CID cloud above his head but that'll come soon enough," nodded Avalon.

"I just don't think anyone will want to team up with him until he has more experience." Avalon frowned a little,

"We have to give him a chance, I mean Mack isn't that much older but everyone gets on with him."

"Mack is easy going, he takes the stick and gives it back," replied Ross, "but then again I never want to be on surveillance with him again."

"Why's that?" asked Avalon with genuine interest.

"He can be as boring as shite, all he talks about are computers and American trucks," frowned Ross.

"I knew he was a bit of a boffin with computers but where's the American truck thing come in?" Ross looked a little surprised at Avalon and asked,

"You didn't know?" he waited a moment as Avalon shrugged and then continued, "that's how he got his name, it's Mack with a C-K not just with a C, it's Mack as in American truck Mack. Nothing to do with MacDonald." Ross drained his glass and replaced it on the table. "He used to have a plastic model of a Mack truck on his desk but he got fed up of the jokes about playing with toys."

"But the point is, he *did* fit in and that could be true of Mackinnon?" explained Avalon. Ross just shrugged and nodded at the same time.

~~~~~~

"Mackinnon, can I have a word?" called Avalon and he returned to his booth. The young DC stood and made his way to follow Avalon, straightening his tie as he walked.

"Sir?"

"Sit down," said Avalon not looking up from his computer screen. He hit a couple of keys and then looked towards Mackinnon, "Rory isn't it?" he asked knowing full well it was the lad's name.

"Yes sir, spelled the English way not the Scottish."

"Oh, I see," replied Avalon not having any idea what he meant, "I've got something I want you to work on," he continued looking back to the screen and sensing the young man move slightly in his seat. Avalon could just about remember the first job he was given as a DC, it was sorting out old case files for archiving, boring but he had completed it to the best of his ability. "I want you to go over the files on a missing person case, there's been a snippet of extra information come in and I want to go over the notes again."

"Of course sir," replied Mackinnon, visibly keen. Avalon glanced back to him and said,

"I want you to check through the statements from the family," he returned his gaze to the screen, "and see if there is any mention of a link with the area around Stirling." The DC nodded. "It's nothing profound, his credit card has been found there, we need to know if there is a link with that area." Mackinnon nodded again then asked,

"How long has he been reported missing sir?"

"Just over a week but until something crops up to say otherwise we are ignoring it, I just thought we ought to do a little bit of digging now the credit card has turned up, he probably has a girlfriend or something down there."

"Who's the person?" asked the DC, Avalon looked back to the screen.

"William Thomas Ewart, runs a business hiring out wedding cars and the like. Fifty-two years old, married with two grown up children, lives the other end of the bridge. No record, and as far as we can tell, no reason to go off without telling anyone. He just never came home from an airport job but the car was found abandoned near Nairn." Mackinnon nodded again and then said,

"Okay sir, I'll get to work on it," and he stood.

"If you need anything, ask Mack, he'll show you where everything is." The young DC left the booth and Avalon watched him return to his desk where he seemed to throw himself into the work. Frazer and Wilson were both out of the office and Mack was typing feverishly at his keyboard. Only Ross was seemingly unemployed, he was staring out of the window with a far away look in his eyes. Avalon was beginning to wonder if Ross was not telling him the truth about his recovery and, in an effort to bring Ross out of his dream, he carefully opened and then quickly closed his drawer with a bang, looking down as he did. He looked up, everyone was looking towards him, so, he rolled his eyes in an effort to make it look like the drawer was stuck. It had done the trick, Ross was back at his keyboard.

The door to the Cave opened, it only opened a little way and then the face of PC Kirk appeared and looked carefully round the edge. She looked into the room and then to Avalon giving a slight, but apologetic smile. Avalon raised his eyebrows and she decided to enter but almost crept over towards him in an uncharacteristic way.

"What are you on with PC Kirk?" demanded Avalon.

"Sorry sir but I wanted a quick word," she said with a tentative smile and then, "et's a private nature." Avalon blinked and said,

"Oh?" He glanced into the room, and then back to Kirk saying, "well you better come a little further in my office." She came into the booth and Avalon pointed to the chair,

"Oh et will only tak a moment," she smiled, "I just wanted to tell you that mysel' an' a few others have arranged a surprise birthday party for Angie." Avalon had no idea that his housemate had an imminent birthday, but how could he, they rarely met?

"Oh?" he said again.

"Et's at her house, er your house, on Sunday, an' I

know you live there but I thought I better tell y' about et," the smile had now gone and she looked a little apprehensive.

"Well thanks for telling me, at least I can get her something," he replied.

"I tried tae get them tae make et somewhere else but et wes difficult tae change et."

"It's fine, but I'm glad you let me know," and he gave her a quick smile for reassurance.

"I mean, well, you are invited, er, well, y' know what I mean." Avalon gave her another smile and said,

"It's fine really, is her birthday actually on Sunday?"

"Oh aye, et is, so I'll..." she stepped backwards towards the door, "maybe see you Sunday?" Avalon nodded and replied,

"I'll do my best," and she quickly turned to leave, just as Wilson and Frazer came in. Wilson nodded to Avalon and the two of them entered the booth.

"Any luck?" Avalon asked.

"Not really, one of the suspects admitted tae bein' en the warehouse but said he did'nae start the fire."

"So he broke into a burning building to steal computer parts?" asked Avalon shaking his head.

"Aye that's what we asked, he then said he was looking for his mate and wondered in there, but the other one is keeping quiet," replied Wilson.

"They're both as thick as pig-shit boss, we'll have tae find more on them," added Frazer.

"So the quiet one is probably in charge," suggested Avalon.

"Aye, we thought so anyway, so he's the one we'll work on," grinned Wilson.

"Okay, keep at it people, it sounds like you are

getting there," added Avalon. Wilson nodded and the two of them went to their desks. Wilson had been running a continuous case on warehouse thefts where the perpetrators started fires after they left, and he was close to making some more arrests but he had put a great deal of time into it and he was looking more tired than usual. Frazer still looked the same, she didn't tire, and she didn't seem to get too fazed by the work. As she sat at her desk, he noticed that, unlike Wilson, she didn't acknowledge any of the others. Wilson had joked with Ross and made a comment to Mack, but Frazer, she was straight back to business. Avalon, once again, considered the interest that DI Lasiter had in her career and though he knew he shouldn't, he couldn't help checking on his computer to see if Frazer and Lasiter had any possible connection in a previous life. As he read, he found that Lasiter was born in Glasgow in 1968 and joined the police in 1990 while still in Glasgow. Frazer, on the other hand, was born in Beauly in 1985 and though she *was* just young enough to be Lasiter's daughter, it didn't seem possible, he considered that they were nothing alike in any way. She had joined the police in 2006 and moved to Aberdeen, soon after, she had a period of six weeks leave, three months prior to the move to Inverness. Avalon considered this, had she been pregnant? If she had, she must have lost the baby, because she wasn't known to have a child, then again it could have been an injury acquired in the line of duty. Lasiter on the other hand, had never been posted to Aberdeen, and except for a short stint at Falkirk, he had been at Inverness since 2002. He could find nothing in their records to connect them in any way, there was no evidence and he began to wonder if Lasiter had some sort of 'fatherly' crush on her. She seemed an odd girl to love however, she had a stern look and her slightly drawn face and scraped back hair made her look severe to say the least. She was bright and quick-witted though and knew the regulations, even if she didn't always follow them. Avalon looked up from his screen and peered out through the glass at Frazer as she busied herself with her work, he would just have to accept that some mysteries just couldn't be solved. His internal phone rang.

"Avalon."

"*Oh DI Avalon, et's the front desk, there's someone here wants tae see you,*" said the voice on the other end of the phone.

"Is there no one there who can deal with it?"

"*He's pretty insistent, he wants tae speak to you.*"

"Okay, I'll be a couple of minutes," he replaced the phone and stood. Avalon descended the stairs and made his way to the foyer where all he could see was the duty officer and a seated youth with his head buried in the screen of a mobile phone. Avalon walked to the desk and raised his eyebrows at the duty officer who casually and silently nodded to the lad with the phone. He was about fourteen or fifteen years of age and wore, what Avalon considered was, the 'uniform' of the housing estate brat.

"Can I help you?" he asked looking down to the youth.

"Are you Detective Avalon?" he asked looking up from the phone, he had a thicker accent than most local people. Avalon nodded, "how dae a' know that? You got no ID or nothin'?" Avalon was already tired of the youth and he sighed and turned to leave. "I wis told tae gae thes to Detective Avalon en person, nobody else." Avalon turned and looked, the youth was standing and was holding a small white envelope. The youth looked into Avalon's eyes for the first time and saw something there he didn't particularly like, so he looked at the note and thrust it towards the detective. The fact that it was similar to the one Carol had sent made him feel very wary about it.

"So who's it from?" he asked.

"I dunno, I wes promised a tenner ef I got et tae y', that's all I know," replied the youth, still holding the envelope, the other hand gripping the mobile phone. Avalon pulled out his warrant card, showed it to him with a stern look and replaced it taking the envelope from the youth who immediately turned and began to leave in that strange, bouncing gait that all young people seem to have.

"What's your name?" asked Avalon. The youth didn't turn, he just made a stifled chuckle and continued looking down at his phone as he exited the building. Avalon looked towards the duty officer and said,

"Why is it you never have a baseball bat when you need one?" The officer grinned and nodded as Avalon made his way back to the office, pushing the note into his jacket pocket.

Back in the booth, he pulled out the note and read it. The writing was in blue biro by a hand that looked like it didn't put pen to paper very often.

"*To Mr Avalon, as a sort of thank you for your help in sorting out my problem I thought I would give you a wee snippet of info. If a big truck goes missing you probably need to have a wee look at this address.*" There was a tiny map of a road and two buildings, below the map was part of an address. The note also informed him not to check there before as, "*any snooping may mean the hidey hole changes.*" It was signed A.S. For a moment Avalon remembered seeing a rerun of a 1960s television cartoon serial, 'Journey to the Centre of the Earth', where a team followed in the tracks of a lost explorer and the letters AS written here and there would be their signpost and their guide. He doubted it was actually Arnie Saknusson who had left the message, it was more likely a small time crook who had been offered protection for evidence in the security van robbery, Antony Scobie. The problem was, Avalon didn't trust Scobie and considered that it could equally be a way of ensuring no one would go near the address while he pulled off some petty theft. He decided to sort out some insurance, he called Frazer into the booth and showed her the note.

"Scorguie?" she said as she read the address, "tae be honest boss, there isn't much out there, mainly residential," admitted Frazer looking at the sketch and reading through the rest of the note.

"Can you take a look without being seen?" he asked. She shrugged still looking at the address and the map.

"Et's not the sort of place you can hide a big truck, I doubt ef y' could even get a truck down some o' those roads ef y' get my meanin'?" she looked up at Avalon, "I thenk Scobie es pulling your leg sir."

"Probably," replied Avalon, he certainly didn't trust the man but, being new to the area, Avalon didn't have the usual handful of informers and he had considered 'grooming' Scobie. "But we still have to be on our guard, just in case he has something," he continued. Frazer nodded and handed back the note.

"Do you want me tae go now?"

"Yeah, let Wilson know though."

"I'll get on it, et shouldn't take long."

"Don't take your own car though, just in case you're recognised, get Mack to take you," insisted Avalon. She nodded again and went to speak to Mack. Avalon heard her call out to him.

"Mack, you're weth me. Gordon, the boss needs me tae run an errand, I'll be an hour or so." Wilson shrugged. Avalon was starting to believe that the decisive nature of Frazer was a real asset to the team, she could make quick decisions, and she could lead if the situation required it.

"Where you going, anywhere nice?" Wilson asked.

"Windy Ridge," she replied pulling on her jacket.

"Scorguie?" questioned Wilson as he looked back and saw Avalon coming forward, "you lookin' for a house sir?" he continued.

"Not if the place is called Windy Ridge," smiled Avalon. Frazer and MacDonald left and Avalon walked over to Ross who looked up.

"I had a note from Scobie giving us a tip off of sorts," Avalon explained.

"Don't trust the little toad would be my advice," frowned Ross.

"I don't, but equally, we have to react just in case."

"Is that where Frazer is going?" asked Ross, Avalon raised his brow, "I wouldn't have thought it was the ideal area for the criminal element to hang out," Ross added.

"Like I say, we have to react, if something did happen and we were seen to do nothing the DCI would jump on me straight away," explained Avalon. He turned to look out of the window, it was almost sunny but there were clouds over the sea and the constant promise of

63

rain seemed to be closing in.

"Have you bought a car yet?" asked Ross from nowhere.

"No," replied Avalon turning back to Ross, "I never seem to get the chance or the time."

"How long is it now since your Mondeo gave up the ghost, three weeks?"

"Probably," agreed Avalon, "but like I say, it's finding time."

"Well someone I know is selling a decent car, it's a six year old BMW three series, good condition and he only wants six for it."

"It can't be up to much if he only wants six hundred for it," shrugged Avalon.

"Very amusing," frowned Ross, "you can't get them much cheaper than seven grand even on ebay," continued Ross.

"He wants *six - thousand - pounds* for a car?" spluttered Avalon with the realisation that he was completely out of touch with how much people paid for their vehicles.

"That's nothing for that model, it's low mileage and has loads of paperwork," added Ross.

"Six grand?" Avalon said as he made his way back to his office, but he paused and turned, "six thousand pounds for a car to get from A to B?" he asked again with an amount of doubt in his voice. Ross shook his head and laughed.

"And they say Scotsmen are tight, you need to get out of the 1970s, gone are the days you can buy an Austin Seven for fifteen shillings and still buy three pints of 'Old Almanac', a loaf of bread and take all seven children to the moving picture house to see Charlie Chaplin's latest silent with the small change. We've moved on, well some of us have," and he raised his eyebrows with a sympathetic glare and continued with his work.

"What were you wanting tae pay?" asked Wilson. Avalon paused for a moment then turned and thought about it.

"The old Mondeo cost me eight hundred quid from Slippery Singh in Wolverhampton but I'd not mind paying..." there was a pause as he considered and Wilson looked over to Ross with a startled expression, "say, fifteen hundred." Wilson once more glanced over to Ross and swallowed,

"Well," he began, "I don't know if he's still got it but my nephew did have some wheels for sale, I can ask."

"Yeah, okay," nodded Avalon.

"Have you ever ridden a BMX before?" concluded Wilson before they all burst into laughter, even Mackinnon had joined in, but he was careful to judge Avalon's reaction. As the joke dissipated and left the room with just a whiff of inevitability, Avalon finally admitted he was out of touch, not quite as much as he lead his team to believe however.

"I don't want anything fancy, just transport, is that too much to ask?" he sighed.

"We don't have Slippery Singh, though there are still plenty of back street dealers," smiled Wilson, "but tae be honest, you won't get anythin' reliable for that kind of money."

"Why don't you have a look in town, it's not busy in here at the mo, go and have a look around," smiled Ross. Avalon blew out his lips and made a kind of horse sound, then sat on the desk near his booth. He nodded slightly and then said,

"I probably should, I need something that won't let me down I suppose," he then looked at his watch and continued, "but not today, I still have some business to attend to," and it was true but Avalon also knew that he constantly put off things in his personal life. As he walked back to his desk he wondered if he could find time at the weekend.

"Nothin' there boss," insisted Frazer when she returned from her drive with MacDonald.

"Just what you would expect from suburbia," agreed Mack.

"What about the actual houses on the map?" asked Avalon looking up at the two of them.

"Both just wee bungalows with rose beds and some crappy statues," explained Frazer folding her arms, "equally wee cars on the drive just like all the other wee houses," Frazer probably wasn't the best judge of such things as even Avalon had realised she had a vehement distaste for all things 'normal' when it came to living quarters.

"Aye, nowhere to hide a truck either," added Mack causing Avalon to remember the DC's odd little hobby.

"Okay, we'll put this one down to experience but I want to know if anything comes in about truck thefts or robberies from such a vehicle." The two of them nodded and returned to their places in the Cave and Avalon thought about why Scobie might give him the nod if there was really nothing to be found. Maybe he *was* telling the truth, maybe nothing had happened and when it did, this address may become important. He reached for the post-it notes and made a visual reminder and stuck it on the glass of the booth. He then decided to get a coffee from their machine by the door. He noticed Mackinnon looking sheepishly at him as he turned with his cup.

"Problems?" he asked.

"No, no sir," replied the young man, "I may have found something, but it may be nothing," he almost stuttered the reply.

"Bring whatever you have," insisted Avalon as he returned to the booth. Mackinnon was unsure if the DI wanted him to follow but he took the chance and entered the booth.

"Sit down, so what have you got?" asked Avalon. Mackinnon was holding a notepad like he had just discovered the original bible and he had found himself surrounded by atheists.

"Well sir," apologised the DC, "I don't want to get your hopes up."

"You mean all crime hasn't been eradicated and we have to keep at it?" asked Avalon with a serious face.

"What I mean is," Mackinnon glanced quickly down at his notes, "it's not a breakthrough, it's just..." Mackinnon was clearly hoping that he had kept his theories to himself and kept his mouth shut.

"This isn't an interview for the Chief Constable's job, just tell me what you've found," insisted Avalon, sipping the coffee.

"I have been through the files on the missing man, William Ewart. There was no reference to Stirling and I didn't want to ring his family because, well..." he hesitated, "I didn't know the policy." Avalon nodded,

"You did right, you need to come to me for that."

"Yes, I thought that would be the case."

"Carry on then," nodded Avalon taking another drink.

"Yes, right, well, I did phone the Stirling Central Police station and spoke to the reporting officer," he glanced up to see Avalon's reaction but there wasn't one, "and he told me that the credit card was handed in by a well meaning passer-by thinking it had been dropped."

"So what?" said Avalon without much interest.

"It seems it was found in the grounds of the police station," at this point, he looked down at the notepad, "Ralphfields the place is called."

"So what are you getting at?" asked Avalon placing his cup down.

"I'm not sure but it just seemed odd that the card would be found on the grounds of the police station," the lad swallowed as he began to deal with the realisation that his idea was weak and his governor was thinking that too.

"I don't think it's that odd myself, I think it's more odd that his card isn't with him, but keep it tucked away for a cold night," said Avalon making it clear that he wasn't interested. Mackinnon felt embarrassed, he stood and headed back to the desk thinking that he had approached it wrongly. Ross or Wilson would have just called over and said, "funny place that the credit card was found," but *he* had to make it sound like he had found enough evidence to seal the case. It was true, he had much to learn, he was out of his depth and his boss had ignored the information as if missing men's credit cards were found in police station grounds a hundred miles away everyday of the week. He slumped back into his chair glancing quickly up to the glass of the booth to see Avalon sipping his coffee whilst reading from a small piece of paper. What he didn't know was that Avalon had seen how heavily the young DC had made contact with that seat.

~~~~~~~

Avalon had spent the early morning at the Procurator Fiscals Office just off Leachkin Road dealing with mounds of tedious paperwork that seemed to be his constant companion since becoming DI. He seemed to move from meetings to paperwork and back to meetings with some extra paperwork thrown in. He was beginning to wonder if the jump to DI had been worth it. But then again, it wasn't raining so rather than head back to the office, he decided that it would be a great opportunity to slip into the town and try to find something as a birthday gift for his housemate, Angie. He had no idea if he would be free for the surprise party on Sunday, but he would certainly supply a suitable gift. He had regularly seen a delicate chain and pendant she left on the kitchen table, a tiny heart on a silver rope chain, so he considered he knew the type of thing she liked. He went through the whole stock of three jewellers before he found something just right, ironically in a shop he had been in previously. He had questioned the owner of the business regarding a protection scam earlier in the year and she had been helpful. She recognised him and offered the item he was studying at a good price. It was a silver pendant in the shape of a Scottish thistle and had green and blue stones in it. The leaves were crafted in a sort of emerald stone and above the silver ball of the thistle amethyst set off the top with a purple-blue twinkle.

"It's really pretty isn't it?" she smiled. Avalon nodded and wondered if it was too small. "Is it for a wife? A partner?" she asked.

"No," smiled Avalon glancing back, "just a

friend." He looked at it again. "Is it too small do you think?"

"It depends," replied the woman, "this isn't too showy and it would compliment just about any occasion."

"I'll take it, I'm sure she'll love it," he announced, seeing the clock at the rear of the shop. He had a great deal to do yet and the time was evaporating as it always did, well almost always. He sometimes thought that time would run away from him during the working day, trying to escape and hide. He always found it though, huddled away at the side of his bed at night and there it would uncurl itself.

He was happy he had found a gift for Angie but his plan to do a little shopping for himself would have to be left for another day. He walked towards the car park where he had left the pool car, checking he had the tiny jewellery box in his jacket, and drove away but because of the way he had come into town, he drove down Shore Street and onto Harbour Road. He hadn't noticed before, but the whole of the road seemed to be covered in businesses that sold, repaired, or hired vans and cars, the only differing services on offer were petrol stations. He decided to pull in and examine some of the vehicles on offer. It was clear that business was brisk as he was left alone to browse while both the staff were talking to prospective customers. He didn't really know what he was looking for, he looked for something like his old Ford but that model went out of date with the Lancaster Bomber. So to him, many of the cars on the lot looked like large training shoes with wheels. Everything was made of plastic and it seemed that there were only three shades of colour produced in car paint. Nothing there piqued his interest and so he moved to the next pitch. To his surprise, they were the same cars, in the same colours being sold by the same two men.

"Did everyone want the exact same car as their neighbour," he thought. One of the men quickly scurried over to him.

"Looking at the Cactus sir?" asked the man.

"Eh?" remarked Avalon, "No I was looking at the cars."

"Very funny sir, the Fiat Cactus I was referring to," smiled the man but he may as well have stuck his tongue out from what Avalon could see of his expression.

"It's really called a Cactus?" asked Avalon shaking his head, "it looks like they didn't get time to finish it," he smiled pointing at large black plastic panels on the side.

"What about the DS-3?" said the man pointing to another car. Avalon considered that it may have been more appropriate to him if it had been called a DI-3. The eleven grand price on the windscreen forced him on to the next item.

"What's this?" he asked.

"Peugeot 207, three years old, full service, one lady owner and purrs like a freshly massaged kitten."

"Not at seven grand," quipped Avalon as he moved on, "I like that though," he pointed. The man looked to where he was pointing.

"Certainly sir, Porsche Cayman, forty-two and a half thousand pounds will secure it.

"Wrong colour," coughed Avalon fighting back several swear words.

"I thought it might be," nodded the man, "what colour are you looking for if I might ask."

"Well a sort of dull shade of fairly reliable but

won't make my wallet bleed."

"I see," mused the man holding his chin, "we do have a Citroen Aygo at the back."

"You just made that name up right?" frowned Avalon. The man just glared unblinking. Avalon dropped the smile just as the man seemed to remember something.

"Ah, there is this," he said and he squeezed past two vehicles to the rear of the plot. He was pointing at a small car painted in a dark, gunmetal grey. It was smaller than Avalon had expected, the sort of thing a large dog could accidentally swallow, but it had a Ford badge, something Avalon could recognise. "2003 Ford Focus one point six Ghia, clean inside and at nine-nine-five a snip," grinned the man, "does that *colour* suit?" he concluded. Avalon was interested, true it looked like the sort of thing Mrs Pink would drive but yes he did like the 'colour'. "I could take the shade of the colour down a tad, say..." there was a moment of pause, "eight-fifty for cash." Avalon was about to say he was interested when his phone rang. It rang in that way that said 'if you don't answer you are in trouble' and so he excused himself and answered it.

"Avalon."

"*Where are you?*" it was Ross.

"In town, why?"

"*Do you still fancy that trip up to Beauly Priory?*" Avalon thought for a moment, he did remember telling Ross he wanted to visit it one day but now, at... Avalon glanced at his watch. It was one thirty, not as late as he expected but he realised there must be something important.

"What is it?" he asked with a grim tone, the salesman was considering that the suited man in front of him was probably a copper and began to look for another customer.

"*Body, found inside the Priory.*"

"Any info?"

"*Looks like foul play.*"

"Right, I'm on my way, I'll meet you at the station," Avalon gave a cursory wave to the salesman as he exited the car lot. He had forgotten about the Ford Focus, his focus was elsewhere.

Chapter Three

"So, what do we know?" asked Avalon as he slid into the passenger seat of Ross's car.

"Not all that much, male body found inside the priory by a workman an hour or so ago," replied Ross as he sped off.

"This place is a ruin right?" asked Avalon trying to get a picture of the scene.

"Oh aye, it's a ruin. There is a small portion covered by a roof as I remember but the main part is just a few walls."

"I assume the uniforms are attending," said Avalon.

"Yeah, they have already cordoned it off, I spoke to the Sergeant at the scene while I was waiting," he seemed to hesitate.

"And?" asked Avalon looking over to Ross.

"He wouldn't say too much on the radio, he just said, 'you better see for yourself' so I assume there is a problem," explained Ross.

"So what time does the place open for business?"

"In the summer?" replied Ross concentrating on the road, "nine o'clock until five."

"So if the place is a ruin, it seems odd that the

body wasn't discovered for several hours, doesn't it?"

"I thought about that..." Ross paused as he forced his way past a short line of traffic, "so I rang up the people who run it while I was waiting for you, I asked if it was closed for repairs, they said it wasn't and confirmed it opened at nine."

"So that's the first puzzle to solve then," replied Avalon looking back at the road. Beauly was just over twelve miles from Inverness but even with Ross's 'inventive' driving it took almost twenty minutes before they arrived. To Avalon's eye the town looked very smart even under the cloudy sky, flowers decorated many parts of the centre with baskets hanging from almost every lamp post, showering blooms from their lofty positions. There were displays of flowers around what looked like a large font in the main square and there was space and a feeling of a steadier pace of life. He considered that something this distasteful would be quite a shock to this sort of community, not that he knew anything about it. He also thought of DC Frazer. As they pulled into the square the place was already busy, the uniform officer pointed them to a parking area close to the gate where a flat-back Transit truck with fencing panels loaded on the back was parked. There were several police officers in the grounds and what looked like local press and quite a few of the general public. They got out of the car and moved towards the gate where a young constable looked towards them. Avalon had his warrant card ready and they squeezed past the parked Transit to where the constable gave a fake smile and lifted the police cordon tape so they could enter the grounds.

"It's a nice spot," commented Avalon as he walked past a rather ancient tree.

"For a murder you mean?" quipped Ross.

"There you go again making assumptions," answered Avalon with a slight smile. He hated situations with dead bodies, not technically squeamish, he was just uncomfortable in the company of the dead, he felt embarrassed for them. So, having a bit of light-hearted banter was good for him, it eased him into the horrible task at hand. He stopped suddenly and it took Ross by surprise.

"Problems?" asked Ross turning to him with a slight frown.

"Where was Frazer when we left?" asked Avalon.

"In the office, why?"

"Give her a call and get her up here."

"Any particular reason?" asked Ross as he pulled out his phone.

"She grew up here didn't she? It wouldn't hurt having someone with local knowledge," replied Avalon raising his brow a little. Ross dialled as Avalon continued down the short path to the Priory. The grass was thick and green, growing strongly between massive gravestones, the sort of gravestones you only seem to see in Scotland. Some were in a poor state and Harris-type fencing surrounded the worst of them. To his right, another path came from the square where the gates had been closed and a panel of the fencing had been moved to seal it off with police tape all over it. A PC patrolled the area. Straight ahead, yet another panel of fencing had been positioned in front of the entrance to the Priory and had a blanket draped over it to keep out prying eyes and long camera lenses. Another PC guarded the area, stiff backed with his hands tucked behind him. Avalon gave a slight nod and moved behind the fence to the doorway of the ruined building. Inside he noticed that Scenes of Crime were already there, securing the site and he could

76

also see Sarah Underwood off to the right talking to one of her team. Her photographer was already busy around the site. As Ross had said, there was no roof, the building *was* a ruin, but the place looked well maintained as a tourist site with display boards here and there. It was a long, narrow chamber running down to where the large windows would have been, but now a severe hole presided over the scene. Avalon remembered that the far end was correctly called the 'apse', and the 'nave' was the part where most of the activity was. He knew his architecture study would come in one day. Avalon had his own approach to this type of scene. He rarely looked at the body on arrival, he first appraised himself of the area, and looked for anything surrounding the scene that looked out of place. It was odd to see gravestones actually inside the Priory, obviously added at a later date and on one he caught sight of what looked like a man's bound arms. That was obviously *the* body, but he ignored it for now. He walked steadily in, looking around and taking in all the details he thought may be required later when he put thought into the scene. He noticed he was about to be disturbed as a white suited shape came towards him.

"Detective," there was a pause, "Inspector Avalon I believe is the correct title now," smiled the smiling face of Sarah Underwood.

"Miss Underwood, you made good time, *we* have only just arrived."

"I was in the area as it happened," she said as the smile gradually returned to the businesslike expression she usually provided.

"Have you found anything yet?" he asked looking towards the activity.

"Just a preliminary look until the area has been

processed, but I can tell you it *is* foul play and looks almost ritualistic at first glance." Avalon considered she was another one making assumptions but then again, bound hands certainly put anyone off the idea of an accident or suicide.

"I see," was all he said.

"Detective Avalon?" came a voice from behind, he turned to see a uniformed officer with stripes on his sleeve. "Sergeant Morris," he offered, "er, d' you want tae talk with the lad that found the body?" asked the Sergeant.

"Yes," he paused and turned back to Sarah Underwood, "I'll see you in a moment if that's alright?" She nodded and walked back to the place where the body lay. "Let's go Sergeant," he continued. They returned to the doorway and stepped out of the building as Avalon asked,

"I was told the place opens for business at nine, why was the body not reported until later?" They both noticed Ross coming towards them.

"Well, as I have just explained tae DS Ross here, last night the fencing contractors were supposed tae take some of the fencing away but the truck broke down on ets way. They asked the curator ef they could leave the fencing inside the grounds until the morning," he stopped and shrugged, "they said a driver would pick et up sometime around ten but the curator decided et was a hazard where et was and decided not tae open the Priory until the fencing had been removed. The body wasn't found until later."

"So where is the driver now?" asked Avalon and the Sergeant pointed and showed him the way. The driver was seated in a police patrol car in the square and he looked a little impatient rather than shocked.

"Mr Alan?" asked Avalon as he sat in the rear seat beside the man, "I'm Detective Inspector Avalon, I just want to clarify a few things before we let you go."

"Aye, get on weth et then, I wes supposed tae be at Achnagairn by half one, god knows whet time et es now." Avalon considered telling him he was a heartless bastard but he didn't. Instead he said,

"Tell me how you found the body?"

"Again? Thes es the third time."

"I could always take you down to the station at Inverness if you like," explained Avalon casually. The man glared at Avalon and then sighed.

"As a' keep sayin', et took me nearly an hour tae load them up, et's a two man job, et's bloody hard work doin' that yerself particularly en thes heat." Avalon's face showed no sympathy so the man continued. "When they was all loaded the guy weth the keys tae the Priory said he would go an' open the other gate so a' pulled the truck forward a wee bit tae clear the gates and then he came back. We chatted a bit an' then I said a' would get off but I would check around tae make sure none o' the fence clips had been left knockin' about," he paused as if he was thinking it through. Gradually Avalon could see his demeanour change a little, he wondered if it was shock giving him the bravado. The man sniffed and then looked down to his hands before he continued. "Tae be honest, a' went en there for a quick smoke, I did'nae expect to see *that*," he said the word as if what he had seen wasn't human, had never been human.

"Okay Mr Alan, we'll get someone to take you home and contact your employer, we may need to interview you again at sometime," explained Avalon as he climbed out of the car. The man suddenly turned and said,

"Et's a church, a church for Christ's sake, who does somethen like that in a church?" Avalon realised that he hadn't examined the body yet, it was quite obvious he needed to go and see for himself. Avalon and Ross returned down the path of the Priory and entered, there was still some activity near the body. They walked closer and it became obvious that the arms of the corpse had been bound behind the gravestone, the body slumped naked down the front of it. The victim's legs were sticking straight out in front with his head leaning forward and slightly to the left. Avalon stupidly considered that if the man had not been dead, it would have been a very uncomfortable position to be in. Sarah Underwood was close by the body, examining every square inch around it. Avalon looked beyond her to where a doorway lead out to the side of the transept which was the only part of the ruin with a roof. It was sealed off from the nave by an iron fence. He looked outside and followed a short path to a locked gate and then returned to take a look at the body.

"Jesus Christ," exclaimed Ross.

"This may not be consecrated ground now," said one of the white suited technicians, "but please give it the respect it deserves." Ross turned on the man.

"Respect for what, a god that allows this to happen?" he spat pointing at the body.

"DS Ross, can you go and find out where Detective Constable Frazer is?" insisted Avalon.

"Sir," replied Ross but he glowered at the technician as he left. Avalon said nothing else, he crouched and looked over the body. It was a mess, plain and simple and there were wounds that did indeed make it look ritualistic. Most of the body had wounds, some worse than others and there seemed to be lesions on the face too. The victim was in his mid to late fifties, balding with some grey hair. He was clean-shaven but bristle was showing on his chin. His face was covered in flies, and they were busy exploring his groin, armpits and features to the degree Avalon couldn't even make out the colour of his eyes. Several attempts had been made to waft them away but to no avail, they just returned. Avalon was thinking that this was something the TV dramas never showed, the invasion of the blowfly. It sickened him, it was a natural process he knew and forensic entomologists could tell so much these days by the activity of the myriad of flies and larvae on the body, but it still sickened him. He shook himself back to the job at hand as he heard footsteps coming forward. He looked up to see DC Frazer with Ross a few steps behind.

"Boss?" she said as a question nodding slightly. He stood.

"A bit of a mess I'm afraid," he explained but Frazer wasn't put off and she made her own calculations.

"Not killed here then?" she said, which prompted Sarah Underwood to look up.

"I wouldn't think so," she agreed and she too stood.

"Well there doesn't seem to be any blood here I admit but it's an odd position to dump a body I would have thought," frowned Avalon.

"The pathologist will tell you more when he arrives," added Sarah, "but to my mind he was seated when he died," she pointed to the souls of his feet, "there are signs of post mortem hypostasis on his feet and posterior."

"So death was probably some time ago?" asked Avalon. Sarah nodded and bent back down to continue her work. Ross stepped forward and whispered,

"Do you think this could be our missing person from a couple of weeks ago?" Avalon turned to him and nodded.

"I was certainly thinking that."

"What dae y' want me tae do Boss?" asked Frazer.

"I want you on this Megan, it's your area and local knowledge may come in handy," explained Avalon.

"But this may just be a dumping ground, if he was killed somewhere else then he could have been done away with anywhere," pointed out Ross.

"True, but why put the body here? There has to be something relevant here, just look at the way he has been displayed. This was meant to be public and this place was chosen for a reason," explained Avalon. He thrust his hands in his pockets and said, "let's see if we can get a cuppa, I'm parched."

A local cafe arranged to supply them with drinks and Avalon explored the grounds of the Priory with Ross in tow, Frazer was doing the door to door to see if anything had been heard the previous night. Avalon walked to the far end of the grounds where the boundary wall seemed lower, due to the ground rising at that point.

"If the body *was* brought here, this seems the obvious place for it to be put into the grounds if the gates were locked," mused Avalon sipping at a beaker of tea.

"It's likely and it would take at least two to lift a well built body over that wall, it's as tall as us," replied Ross and Avalon nodded his agreement. "I'll get some of the uniforms to seal it off," continued Ross as he hurried away. Soon police officers could be seen at the rear of the wall taping off a grassed area close to it. Avalon returned to the front and sat on a low gravestone minus his jacket, it wasn't sunny but it was fairly warm. It seemed ironic that sitting there in the lush grass, surrounded by blooms in such a peaceful setting, a horror of sickening proportions could be found just fifty feet away.

"Detective Avalon?" he turned to see Sarah coming towards him with a slight smile. She had removed her white forensics cover-alls and was carrying an evidence bag.

"Do you want a cuppa?" he asked.

"Love one," she said adding, "no milk." Avalon moved off to fetch her a drink, remembering she was a vegan, and returned to see her sitting where he had been. He handed her the beaker and sat at her side.

"Found anything?" he asked.

"Not much but what I did find is rather odd," she held up the evidence bag. It seemed to contain a scrap of crumpled paper, she had straightened it out before sealing it in the bag so it could be examined. It was bloodstained but on one side could clearly be seen writing.

"What the hell does it say?" asked Avalon straining his eyes.

"Language isn't my forte I'm afraid," she said with a slight shrug.

"Where was it?" he asked.

"In his left hand, though I think it was placed there after death," and she took a sip of the tea. Avalon handed the evidence back to her.

"It does look ritualistic I have to admit but this seems the last place in Scotland you would commit such an execution."

"Don't let first impressions fool you Inspector, underneath every community, lies some sort of history, some sort of secret," she insisted.

"I hadn't got you down for a social theorist," smiled Avalon.

"I'm not, it's just my experience," she smiled before continuing, "the coroner arrived a few minutes ago, I suppose he might have something to tell you soon." She stood, "thanks for the tea," and she handed him the empty beaker and returned to the building. Ross returned and sat.

"SOCO are having a quick break and then moving over to the wall area at the back," he announced.

"There was a scrap of paper in his hand," announced Avalon staring into space.

"Anything on it?"

"Yeah, some writing," he answered turning to Ross from his daydream, "it could be Gaelic I suppose, do we have anyone who speaks it?"

"I suppose so," nodded Ross, "I think there are a few back at the station who know the basics."

"It's difficult to read anything as it is but I would think forensics will be able to enhance it. I certainly couldn't make anything of it," explained Avalon as he stood. "The pathologist is here apparently, I better go and see him."

The pathologist was by the body and seemed to be speaking to himself. He was around fifty years old and had a full shock of hair that was almost white. His thick-rimmed spectacles looked large enough to be safety eyewear and were utterly out of date. Sarah Underwood and her photographer were close by watching the pathologist work.

"Detective Inspector Avalon," Avalon said, trying to attract the mans attention, it worked, he stopped rambling and looked around with a slight nod.

"I'll be with you in a moment detective," and he continued with his work. "So in conclusion, the rigid period has passed and the lividity gives an indication of the position at the time of death. As to that subject, I can only conclude at this point that the decease did not expire at the site and was already dead at the time he was deposited here," he hesitated for a moment then made a 'harumph' sound then continued, "pause recording," and then he looked at Avalon, "modern technology inspector, what a marvellous advancement," he patted his jacket as if explaining where a recording device was and gave a brief smile. He held out his hand. "Sandy Lennox," he added.

"Have you any idea of the cause of death yet Mr Lennox?" asked Avalon shaking his hand, wondering if he should have called him doctor.

"Well he had been brutally beaten before death and there are a few wounds that could have been fatal in themselves but, I would have to say, what most likely killed him is a small incursion into the top of the spine made by a pointed instrument." Avalon looked over to the rear of the neck of the body, he could just see a slight puncture mark. He frowned deeply then Lennox continued, "Of course, the autopsy may, or may not, confirm my theory."

"Time of death?" asked Avalon.

"Ah, that old chestnut," smiled the man. Avalon was surprised that humour could have any place in this man's repertoire, "I can't secure a time at the moment but I would guess between sixteen-hundred hours and midnight yesterday." Avalon nodded, it was plain that he was certainly brought to this spot but the reason for that seemed as odd as the manner of death. "I think we can move the body now, are you happy with that Miss

Underwood?" he turned to Sarah.

"Yes Professor, I have no issues with that," she smiled. Professor too? Avalon knew police pathologists were usually highly qualified, but the fact that Lennox had the look of a 'mad professor' made it seem ironic. Sarah then explained she would like some help moving the body in preparation for removal. Some of the SOCO team, plus the Sergeant, were on hand and Ross came in to help just after they had begun. Sarah examined the spot where the body had been as it was placed in the body bag but, before being closed, the pathologist took a few more tissue samples. Then the body bag was zipped up and taken to the unmarked van waiting near the gate. SOCO wound up the examination of the rear of the building and Avalon returned to the front of the grounds. There were very few of the public left and so, he and Ross returned to the car and Avalon loosened his tie for the first time.

"It's humid today, what time is it?" he asked.

"Six forty-five," came the reply.

"We'll probably have to keep the site sealed, I would think forensics will need more time for examination." Ross nodded and reclined his seat as he wedged open the car door with his foot. There was a silence of around two minutes, then Ross asked,

"So what are your first impressions?"

"About the case?" asked Avalon knowing what he meant but needing time to think, "well it looks like it will be a tricky one but at least we know it would have taken at least two strong guys to push a dead body over that wall and that's a bonus."

"I suppose so, more chance of one of them making a blunder," nodded Ross, but what do you think about the torture?"

86

"It looks like whoever did this wanted him to suffer, which means he had upset someone."

"I'm not sure how a wedding car chauffeur would get caught up with someone who would torture their enemies," added Ross.

"Who knows," sighed Avalon, "but we don't know that this is the missing man yet."

"I keep asking, 'why here?' and why in the Priory?" said Ross.

"I think that's clear, they wanted to send out a message, this could be the tip of a very large iceberg," replied Avalon just as Frazer returned.

"Nothin' Boss, I've been around all the closer houses except two where there was nobody en. No one heard a thing," she announced.

"Give the two addresses you missed out to the uniform branch, we'll get them to do a blitz of the town." She nodded and sat in the rear seat.

"What do *you* think Frazer?" asked Ross.

"I don't know, et's a bit 'big time' for Beauly so you can discount any local involvement but et's a good place for a bit of theatre," she said.

"What do you mean by that?" asked Ross sitting up and facing her.

"The old Priory has had its share of legends, mainly because there isn't that much known about ets early history, so ef y' want tae make a point, et's a good stage tae do et from."

"What sort of legends?" asked Avalon.

"Well there are a lot of references to Auld Clootie and there es even supposed to be his footprint on one of the door stones, but I never found et," she added.

"Old what?" asked Avalon, he too sitting up.

"Auld Clootie," she repeated and then looked

slightly embarrassed, giving a quick glance to Ross. Ross seemed to jump in with the answer very smartly as if covering something up.

"It's the Scottish version of Old Nick."

"The devil?" frowned Avalon puzzled by the two detective's reaction. "Every church in Christendom seems to have a legend tied to the devil, I suppose it was used to scare the locals to church."

"Aye maybe," continued Frazer, "but Beauly Priory has always had its folklore. When we were weans, we used tae dare each other tae go in there at night," she laughed as she remembered, Ross didn't think he had ever heard her laugh before, "it frightened the crap out o' me I can tell y'."

"Not as frightening as the bastards that did this," interrupted Ross, the mood changed.

"I better see how SOCO are doing," suggested Avalon, he got out of the car and tightened his tie but the jacket was swung casually over his shoulder. Sarah and her team looked busy in their cover-alls and masks, painstakingly checking the area.

"How are you doing?" called over Avalon. Sarah looked over and waved, she stood from her position and backtracked before walking to the boundary tape.

"Oh, nearly there," she admitted as she removed the paper mask.

"Found anything?"

"Not much," she shrugged, "and what we have found may not be connected, what about you?" Avalon looked around as if searching for inspiration.

"I wish I could say I had ideas but I don't, we have a missing person that would probably fit with the victim but nothing else," he replied as he adjusted the jacket over his shoulder, "I'm going to arrange for the site to be sealed until tomorrow at least."

"Yes that would be good," nodded Sarah, we'll wind up here and then come back in the morning to do a look around the rest of the Priory grounds." This time Avalon nodded.

"We'll get off in a while, I'll talk to the Sergeant and make sure there is a presence," he gave a weak smile and nodded then turned to leave. Sarah thought he was about to ask something else but he didn't and she watched him return to the far gate shaking her head a little. Recently she had been feeling a little uneasy when he was around but she couldn't work out why, he seemed pleasant enough and was easy to work with but there was something she couldn't quite put her finger on, something that wasn't there the first time she had met him almost four months ago.

When Avalon returned to the car, he could feel the air cooling and he decided to replace his jacket. Sergeant Morris had been helpful and there was to be some sort of presence at the site all night and through the morning. Avalon had also spoken to the curator of the Priory to explain that it would have to be closed until further notice. Ross was leaning on the bonnet of his car eating what looked to be the remains of an ice cream.

"Where's mine?" asked Avalon.

"It was melting so I gave it to Frazer," he replied finishing it off.

"I bet, where is she anyway?" asked Avalon looking around. Ross walked to a waste bin and threw a tissue away he had cleaned his hands on, as he turned he said,

"Gone, she said she had someone to talk to."

"It looks like I need to have words with her."

"I think it's relevant to the murder," insisted Ross. Avalon looked at him.

"I have two issues with that, one you are assuming again and two, she didn't ask me if she could leave," Ross raised his eyebrows and opened his mouth in disbelief.

"And I have two issues with *your* statement," demanded Ross with a deep frown, "one, even you can't put this down to anything but a brutal murder," Avalon looked into Ross's eyes, he was furious, "and two, you forget I am now DS, and that means *I* gave her permission." Avalon nodded slightly.

"Yes, sorry, I did forget," but the apology stuck in his throat and so he retaliated, "but I have to tell you, don't start arguments with the SOCO technicians, or anyone else for that matter. It isn't professional." Ross glared for a moment without any expression, then he just said,

"Kiss my arse Detective Inspector," then he turned and got into his car.

The journey back to the station was conducted in pure silence, Ross drove more slowly than Avalon had ever known, as if he was punishing Avalon with the tedious drone of the engine noise. Once back at the station they parted and Avalon went back to the office and found it empty, except for Mackinnon. He glanced at the clock, it was almost seven in the evening.

"Don't you have a home to go to?" he asked as he threw off his jacket and tie.

"Er no, I mean yes sir, I just thought I would get this finished," stammered the young man.

"What's '*this*'?"

"Sorry sir?"

"You said finishing *this*, what is it that can't wait

until the morning?" repeated Avalon sitting at the nearest desk and throwing his feet onto the top of it.

"Oh," Mackinnon hesitated, he didn't want to make the same mistake he had previously, "I'm just writing up what I have been doing, it always seems to take longer to write it up than it took to do it."

"Welcome to the world of police work," announced Avalon throwing his head back. The door opened and in walked Ross, as he passed Avalon, he placed an opened bottle of lager on the desk he was at. Avalon looked to the bottle and then over to Ross who pulled off his shoes and sat on his own desk in a crouched position looking out of the window to the fields beyond. He was drinking a similar bottle to the one he gave Avalon who picked it up and read the label. It announced that the contents were 'Budweiser Budvar Strong' and Avalon gulped greedily at the liquid. It wasn't all that cold but it was just what he needed. He looked back over to Ross.

"Accepted," he said. Ross looked back but he couldn't quite see Avalon so he spun slowly on the desk.

"It isn't an apology," he insisted. Avalon shrugged.

"So where did you get it?" he asked raising the bottle.

"I broke into Tom Murrey's locker, he usually keeps something in there." Avalon opened his eyes wider at the information. He took another drink and asked,

"So shall we kiss and make up?" Ross took another drink and nodded to Mackinnon who had been totally silent.

"Not in front of the children." Avalon smiled slightly, stood and reached over to Ross with his bottle,

"Sludge!" he announced, Ross smiled and tapped

his own bottle on Avalon's and repeated the word. Avalon looked over to Mackinnon.

"Go home Rory, Mrs Hamilton's terrier will still be lost when you come back in the morning."

~~~~~~~

The following morning, Avalon sat at his desk thinking his way through the scene at the Priory, trying to look at all angles of the case and seeing if there were any details that should be given his immediate attention. There was *one* thing, and he considered it would be easy enough to sort out. He stood and walking into the main part of the office and looked directly at Ross.

"I've got a theory I want to try out," Ross looked at him and waited for a further explanation but Wilson intervened.

"So do you thenk that the body is the missing man?"

"It looks likely," nodded Avalon, "but he must have been held hostage for some time as he hadn't been dead all that long," and that brought another consideration that would need some careful handling, "I suppose we ought to be ready to arrange a meeting with the family to let them know," he continued looking around at the faces in the room.

"Don't even think of asking me to tae do et," demanded Wilson, "that is the worst part o' this job in my opinion."

"I think Frazer should do it," smiled Ross looking straight at her, "she has the right attitude for giving people bad news." Frazer had already begun to form the letter 'F' on her lips as Avalon interrupted with,

"We'll sort that out once we know it's him for

92

sure."

"So what was this theory you wanted to try out?" asked Ross reminding Avalon of his earlier statement.

"Oh, just something I thought of," he explained, "can you get hold of some sand bags?"

"The sort they use during flooding? Yeah I suppose so."

"Right," added Avalon, "I want about two hundred pounds of the stuff then meet me up at the priory.

"I'm not putting sand bags in my car," he insisted with a deep frown.

"Well take my car and I'll go up with Megan," suggested Avalon.

"You bought one then?"

"No," replied Avalon shaking his head, "it's a pool car."

"You've got a pool car? How long have you had that?" asked Ross raising the pitch of his voice.

"Since the Mondeo died, give or take a day or two," explained Avalon.

"Why didn't you let me know?"

"You didn't ask," replied the DI with a shrug.

"And all this time I have been ferrying you about?" he paused, shaking his head, "I bet you don't have many friends," he added incredulously.

"Friends are overrated," winked Avalon and he tossed the keys over, "it's the Renault something or other, a sort of decomposing green colour. He then turned to Wilson. "Gordon, I know this is leaving you a little short handed but I need Megan on this, set young Mackinnon to work with Mack until we get back." Wilson nodded slightly. "Megan, see if you can find a spare forensics overall and some strong twine and then meet me in the car park," and then he left.

Once he was in the car with Frazer heading up to Beauly, he found himself trying to find a way to ask about her connection with Lasiter.

"When did you first meet DI Lasiter?" he asked. He saw her eyes flit towards him, but her head stayed facing forward as she drove.

"When I first came tae work for Inverness," she answered, "why?"

"Nothing really, I was just trying to find out more about the team."

"My old boss at Aberdeen knew him but I never bumped into him before coming here," she added.

"Do you get on okay with him?"

"Lasiter?" she asked with wide open eyes, "no not at all, we used to argue all the time." She changed gear and checked the rear view mirror then said, "tae be honest I thenk he's the reason I keep gettin' passed over for promotion."

"I doubt that," frowned Avalon, "he always speaks highly of you."

"Lasiter?" she asked again, this time glancing over to him, "trust me, I *know* he has stopped me gettin' on but don't ask how I know." Avalon was confused, he didn't know how to proceed now as this was throwing any theory he may have had into oblivion. Instead he changed tack slightly.

"So what sort of thing did you two argue about?" he asked. She seemed reluctant to continue and then in a quieter voice simply answered,

"My methods I guess," and she gave a slight shrug. He could see she was a little uncomfortable with the answer and he decided not to pursue it.

"Ross said you were involved with surveillance

at Aberdeen."

"Ross knows nothing except what I planted in that tiny mind of his," she then nodded, "that bit was correct though," she took a deep breath. "I ended up in a team that was using some pretty cool technical kit too, I enjoyed it..." she tailed off, Avalon could sense a change in demeanour and she changed the subject, she asked about *him*. He had never heard her ask anyone about themselves before. He decided to answer though.

"Me? There isn't much to tell, my career had hit a brick wall in the West Midlands so it was a good move for me coming up here." She didn't ask anything else however, and the rest of the journey was completed in silence, leaving Avalon more confused than when he had started.

Inside the Priory were two uniformed officers on duty and several of the SOCO team, minus Sarah Underwood. Avalon was informed she was at the lab making a start on the evidence they collected the previous day, he wondered if she was working on the paper she found in the hand of the body. When Ross arrived, Avalon told him to take the car round to the rear of the Priory, he and Frazer took the little pathway that followed the boundary. He unfolded the white forensics suit and placed it on the ground and as Ross reversed the car to his position, he removed his jacket and tie. It was a warm start to the day but it looked like the rain was close so they would have to work quickly. He popped the boot of the car and pulled out one of the sandbags and slit the top with his penknife and commenced to fill the suit with sand.

"Please feel free to help," he said as he threw another handful in.

"What are we doing?" asked Ross looking down.

"I'd say we are making a copy of the victim," suggested Frazer as she removed her jacket and begun to help. Ross simply walked off. He soon returned with a small shovel and removed his jacket and loosened his tie stuffing the long end of it in his shirt.

"Come out of the way," he insisted as he helped fill the cover-alls. When the garment was filled and the twine tied tight at the ends of the legs and arms, the white suit was fastened and it almost resembled a body without a head. The hood was folded back into the top of the suit to keep the sand in.

"I'm more interested in getting the weight right than the shape or size," insisted Avalon. Ross handed the shovel to Frazer and explained where he had borrowed it from and as she went to take it back the two detectives tested the body for weight and decided it was as close to fourteen or fifteen stones as they could estimate. They were hot and panting and sat on the grass under the lee of the wall.

"I'm sorry for yesterday afternoon," whispered Ross as he regained his breath.

"Forget it, it was a rough day for us all."

"I just find that these days the slightest thing gets me angry, and y' know what, I actually like it," added Ross with a slight look of surprise on his face.

"You've been through the grinder, it's to be expected," sympathised Avalon.

"It's like I said the other night, I feel like I've been let loose and all that crap of the fantasy of a happy life seems a nonsense," Avalon nodded as if he understood as Ross continued, "the neat lawn, the nice car, the 'just so' friends of the perfect couple," he shook his head, "it all seems so pathetic now." He stopped as Frazer returned.

"So what now?" she asked.

"Well," explained Avalon as he stood, "we need two, strong manly chaps to try to get this over the wall, any idea where I can find another?"

"No idea," said Frazer with a shrug. Ross stood.

"You don't know what manly is, I can get this over on my own," and he tried but he couldn't. In reality, the two of them struggled and, only with the last ditched help of Frazer, did the lifeless mannequin eventual fall over the wall into the grounds of the priory. Ross and Avalon once more plummeted to the ground out of breath and Frazer walked around to where 'the body' fell, to alleviate any concerns of the SOCO team seeing a chubby, headless snowman scramble over the wall and drop lifeless onto the grass.

"Three?" asked Avalon between gasps.

"At least three," nodded Ross wiping sweat from his brow. As they recovered, Avalon was the first to speak.

"Listen," he said, "if I can get the time off, I'm going to the house for a surprise party for Angie, you're quite welcome to come over, O-K is going too."

"When is it?" asked Ross.

"Sunday."

"Ah, I can't, I'm at the Rugby club if I can get time," sighed Ross.

"Rugby, I didn't know you were interested in Rugby?"

"I used to play regularly before I was married but with this job, any free time I had I spent with Lucy, so I sort of stopped playing." He looked at Avalon and continued, "last week an old mate said I ought to go down again and have a practice."

"Good idea, keeping busy is the best way in my

book," said Avalon standing and brushing himself down with his hands. "I'm guessing it's rugby union," added Avalon.

"Oh aye, it's almost national sport up here," smiled Ross also standing.

"Odd really," began Avalon, "I would have thought the Scots would have chosen a sport they could play well." Ross stopped and glared at Avalon.

"You mean like the English and football?"

"Point taken," conceded Avalon, "but let's be honest, Scotland have a better record in Elephant Polo than Rugby." As they picked up their jackets and moved off to join Frazer in the grounds, Ross explained,

"But you see, you are missing a vital part of the Scottish psyche,"

"I don't get you," frowned Avalon attempting to replace his tie as he walked.

"What happens to the fans when Scotland wins a match?"

"Well, I suppose they retire to the nearest pub and get blind drunk to celebrate," offered Avalon.

"Exactly," agreed Ross, "and what happens when they lose?" Avalon smiled and said,

"They all go off to the pub and get..." Avalon trailed off as he looked to Ross, "a win - win situation I suppose?" he smiled.

"We'll make a Scot of you yet," grinned Ross.

Inside the Priory ground the solemnity brought them back to earth as they joined Frazer at the place where the sand-filled suit lay.

"Shit!" exclaimed Ross in a whisper.

"What?" asked Frazer.

"I suppose we have to drag this thing back over the wall?"

"Well we could make it a little lighter by repatriating some of the sand, it's not exactly toxic waste is it?" suggested the DI as he slit the twine on one of the legs.

"So what's the conclusion boss?" asked Frazer.

"We reckon that unless the people who dumped the body were American wrestlers, there must have been three of them to get the victim over the wall," insisted Avalon.

"So et could be a gang related thing?" she added.

"It's possible but as you said yesterday, it's a bit hard-core for Beauly," she nodded and then said,

"I had a trip out tae a snitch I know who lives in the area, I asked him what he thought and he said there was absolutely nothing going on locally." Avalon nodded twice and sighed, then they decided to drag the 'body' back rather than carry it, but found a convenient, if small, pile of building sand near the gate. It was slightly larger by the time they left. As they tried to clean themselves up before climbing in their cars two young boys passed, one carrying a football.

"Hey mister," said the tallest looking at Ross, "are you the polis' up here for the murder?"

"Aye, get on with y'," replied Ross.

"Is it true he was mauled by a wild beast?" asked the child but the second one interrupted,

"A told y' et was the devil that had him not a wild beast."

"You know nothen'," cut in the other one and Avalon motioned that they should leave while the lads argued.

"They sound like you two," frowned Frazer as she got in the driver's seat of her car as it began to rain.

Chapter Four

"So it's going to be one of those days," thought Avalon to himself, he had already received two phone calls that were about to make his life difficult and it wasn't even ten o' clock yet. The first one was from the Procurator Fiscal's office, to tell him that there would be an inquest into the death of a young man who was fatally injured after falling down a staircase at a nightclub, DC MacDonald had attended and *he* was going to have to attend the inquest. That meant he would be missing for the duration of the affair. The second one had few details, but Avalon guessed it would have repercussions for some weeks. Avalon had dealt with Dr Phillip Cruickshank a few times previously and had found him similar to most pathologists, efficient, thorough and professional but that was about all Avalon could say about him. He seemed to tolerate humour without becoming involved in it but he was neither morose nor ebullient. If there was one overriding characteristic about him, it was that he had no overriding characteristics, so when the man rung him and explained that the body from the Priory was not Avalon's missing person, Avalon just sighed and thanked him for letting him know. The man also told him that he was on his way to the police station for a meeting and could deliver a copy of the report by hand if he wished. Avalon had thanked him again and said it would be a great help. After a few more sighs and the consumption of the last dregs of his coffee, he headed towards Ross's desk to tell him and Frazer of the news.

"He's not our man," he began and after short pause, "at the Priory, the coroner has confirmed that the cause of death of the now *unknown* man was probably the insertion of a pointed object into the spine but the body is not William Ewart, our missing person."

"Do we know who he is then?" asked Ross.

"Not as yet, his DNA isn't on the database so we have to wait to find dental records or someone else missing. Check the records to search for anyone who may match our body."

"That complicates things," said Frazer.

"It does, but something should show up soon. Maybe forensics will give us some good news," he offered.

"Or the door-to-door by the uniform branch," added Ross but they didn't really pin hopes on that, "oh and the press are asking questions about it too."

"Great, that's all we need," replied Avalon looking out of the window. It was another cloudy day and the sun struggled through the light grey cloud now and then, just to have the cloud rally and hide it. Ross had commented as he had arrived, that it was a 'record-breaking summer',

"Two consecutive days without rain, the longest Scottish summer on record," he had jibed, but out near water, the midges were gathering their armies for the day and Avalon knew it. Fifteen minutes later, his phone rang, it was the desk in the foyer announcing Dr

Cruickshank had arrived, Avalon went downstairs to get the report. Avalon thanked him for the file and asked,

"Is there anything in particular that may pique my interest?" The doctor thought for a moment and picked up his briefcase from the desk where the duty officer was standing.

"I think you already know most of it, very severe wounds, probably committed over a two or three hour period, with the coup d' gras from the stylus type instrument with a triangular section blade, into the top of the spine." Avalon held out his arm to lead the doctor up the stairs, he wanted to keep him talking as the report would contain fact, the 'horses mouth' almost always offered more.

"Sarah Underwood thought he probably died in a seated position," suggested Avalon.

"Yes, I'm sure of it, subcutaneous hypostasis usually leaves a dark colouration and this was present to varying degrees in the buttocks, the backs of the legs and the soles of the feet. There was also a lack of injuries in these areas. He was probably restrained with duct tape on an office chair or something with a light padding. I found light patterning consistent with fabric weave where the hypostasis showed on the buttocks. Traces of a substance that resembles the sticky surface on duct tape was found on his wrists, and there were very few hairs in that area which supports this, meaning, it is likely that the cord that bound the hands was applied after death as there is no evidence of it being there before." They had reached the top of the stairs where they would part company, but Avalon wanted a little more.

"And what about the time of death?" he asked.

"Well, that is a little odd," he placed his briefcase on the floor and thrust one hand in his trouser pocket and the other on his chin, "the time of death must have been around five or six in the evening, and yet, there is no insect activity on the body to support this," the man was clearly still not convinced he was correct and was still considering how it could be. He sprung his eyes wide open, placed his other hand in his pocket and continued with, "though I haven't suggested it on my notes, the only reasonable assumption I can offer is that the place he was killed was sealed, dark, or both and the body was left there overnight, insect activity shows that he was probably in the priory grounds by dawn," and he looked over to Avalon in conclusion. Avalon nodded slowly, he had more or less considered the body had been there from early morning but there was another question on his lips.

"Were there any injuries he may have received after death?"

"Yes," replied the doctor as if it was obvious. "the heels of both feet show abrasions and particles of mud and grass, I would think from being dragged, and there are multiple abrasions on the arms and front of the torso consistent with being moved over a very rough surface, such as stone or asphalt," Avalon nodded again, he thought his experiment at the priory had solved that one already.

"And just one final question," smiled Avalon, "was he in good general health?"

"For a man of his age, I would have said yes," nodded the doctor, "there are no signs of heart or liver disease and though he has probably seen manual labour in the past, I would think that he was either retired or had some sort of clerical position." Avalon thanked him and left him to go to his meeting and made his way back to the Cave. In the office, he dropped the file on Ross's desk saying,

"The report on the victim, I know most of the details, but it needs reading through, I'm off to have a word with forensics."

"Can't wait for the report, or do you need a Sarah Underwood fix?" grinned Ross.

"Just read the report Detective Sergeant."

~~~~~~

"Fancy a tea?" asked Miss Underwood, "I need a break," and she lead the way into the small office by the door. She filled the kettle and put teabags into two cups. "You know Detective Avalon, you could always wait for the report."

"I know," smiled Avalon, "but I'm always pushed for time and I like to get to work on it as soon as I can." The kettle clicked as steam thrust its way from the spout and she filled the cups to the top.

"Please, make yourself comfortable, it's just insta-tea, I don't have a china teapot I'm afraid," she said nodding to the cups and then taking her seat.

"I've had worse," he confirmed.

"So, I'm guessing you want to know what we have found?" Avalon almost smiled as he thought of what Ross had said earlier and he could find many reasons for being there but he just told the truth.

"Yes, I have had the coroner's report and could really do with some corroboration from what you may have found."

"Where to start then?" and she stood to remove the tea bags from the cups, "my colleagues may have some milk if you want me to ask?" she suddenly added pointing to the cup. Avalon shook his head and she

104

handed him what turned out to be a scolding hot cup, he quickly looked for somewhere to place it. The floor wasn't convenient but it got rid of the pain in his fingers. "Sorry, I bet that was hot," she said seeming not to notice how hot her own cup was.

"It's fine," he smiled, trying not to wince. She gave a slight smile and sat once more.

"I have to say, it's a bit of a mixed bag, evidence was slight, but what we did find may clear a few things up."

"What did you make of the slip of paper?" he asked.

"Well, the first thing is, it's not paper, it's vellum and not animal skin. It's a synthetic version made from plasticised cotton, which, I would suspect could be analysed further to maybe find the source," she stopped to sip her tea.

"Did you have any luck with the writing on it?" he asked.

"None of the team recognise it but collectively our language skills are limited, having access to English, a few words of Gaelic, the numbers from one to seventy in German and a basic smattering of Klingon. We know it's not Klingon however," she pursed her lips and formed a smile.

"Well I already knew that," said Avalon trying to keep a serious face and failing. She then lost the smile and continued.

"The blood on the parchment is from the victim and we have tried to clean it up around the lettering. We've also set it in a glass plate and photographed it, I can email that to you," he nodded and reached for the tea, which seemed a little cooler, "the cord used to tie him to the tombstone is being analysed but we have confirmed that he was originally bound with duct tape as there was residue consistent with tape glue found on his wrists," she stopped and looked at him.

"Is that it?" he asked.

"More or less," she nodded sipping the tea once more.

"More or less?" he asked.

"Well there is this," she said reaching for a sheet of paper and handing it to him. It was a very rudimentary drawing of a wall with circles of various sizes with numbers set against them. The numbers went up to about fifty. He studied it, looked up to her and back down to the sheet.

"I thought the idea of painting by numbers was to colour it in?" he said but regretted it, he didn't think he knew her well enough for that kind of joke. Fortunately she smiled.

"Those circles and numbers are the points of interest on the rear wall of the priory. Twenty-two of them had traces of genetic material consistent with that of the victim. Twenty of them were marks or other natural anomalies on the stonework."

"That figures, we think three or more people manhandled the body over the wall."

"Yes I heard about your experiment from my team," she admitted cradling her cup in her hands. He looked down to the sheet again.

"So what are the filled in circles?" he asked.

"They are points of interest on the back of the wall, just two there, probably as the body fell down the opposite side," she suggested. Avalon sighed a little, he had noticed circle number twenty-three had a small cross at the side of it, he had noticed it, but thought it must be a datum mark or something. His curiosity finally kicked in.

"So what is twenty-three?"

"That, detective, is your smoking gun," she said with a mischievous smile.

"Would you care to explain?" he asked.

"DNA material *not* consistent with that from the victim," her eyebrows lifted as she emphasised the word 'not'. He looked at the circle and the cross once more.

"One of them probably scuffed his hand on the wall as they tried to lift the body over it," he mused. She simply sipped her tea, watching him over the edge of the cup. "Any matches?" he asked.

"Not as yet," she replied.

"Brilliant work Miss Underwood," he smiled, "this should make the job easy if we can track them down."

"Over to you then," she replied.

~~~~~~

As Avalon entered the office, he saw that DS Wilson was in, and by the look on his face, had some bad news. Avalon headed to the booth and Wilson joined him in there.

"You look as if you have something to tell me, I suppose it's not good," he frowned as he removed his jacket and sat.

"Good and bad boss," replied Wilson, "we have confirmation that the warehouse gang are planning another job."

"So what's the bad news?" asked Avalon.

"Et's between midnight and one on Sunday night."

"Why can't crooks keep decent working hours?"

sighed Avalon looking through the glass into the Cave, "okay, you better get organised with the uniform section, I'll let the team know," he stood and walked into the main room.

"Listen up people," he called. When he had their attention, he told them, "DS Wilson has informed me that Sunday night is D Day for his sting on the warehouse gang. It looks like optimum time is to be between midnight and one in the morning and that means most of Saturday writing reports and processing what we find," he looked round at Ross for a second raising his eyebrows, a sort of apology for messing up his rugby plans. He also considered that Angie's party was a 'no-goer'. "Wilson is co-ordinating the uniform section, but he and Mack will lead the arrests, with DC Frazer as their back up. Myself, DS Ross and DC Mackinnon will be the support team. There will be a briefing in this office at twenty-hundred hours on Sunday night," he paused for a moment and then concluded with, "sorry to mess up any of your weekend plans, but this should be an excellent conclusion to DS Wilson's hard work," he returned to the booth and put his jacket on. There was something he needed to do, and after retrieving a small box from his locked draw, he went downstairs and straight to the front desk. He was told that PC Kirk was in the communications room so he called there and asked for a word. They walked down the corridor and into an alcove by a little used vending machine.

"What is et?" asked Kirk.

"I want you to do me a favour," answered Avalon.

"Aye, o' course ef I can," Avalon took a small, dark blue box from his pocket.

"Will you give this to Angie for me, we have a

108

job through Sunday night so it's unlikely I'll be at her party," he handed her the box, she smiled and asked,

"Can I take a look?" Avalon nodded.

"Oh et's lovely, she will just love et."

"You don't think it's a bit naive?" he asked.

"No, not at all, she might be of Italian stock but her heart es all Scottish," beamed Kirk still looking at the thistle pendant. "Do y' want me tae wrap it for you?"

"That would be kind, thank you," smiled Avalon. He returned to the office pleased with himself, Kirk seemed to think the gift was perfect and he really wanted Angie to like it. He wasn't too disappointed about not going to the party though, Kirk and Angie would be the only people he knew, and he disliked having to go through all the chit-chat and explain he was a detective. Then again, he would have loved some time off to christen his bike on Scottish roads, but that could wait. As he entered Ross called him over.

"What have you got?" he asked. Ross pointed to his computer screen and Avalon stood in a position to read it. It was a local press website and beside a photograph of the Priory was the headline, "*Victim Found Torn to Shreds in Priory Grounds.*"

"Wonderful, that's all we need, DCI Croker has some kind of phobia about the press," sighed Avalon as he looked out of the window.

"The local press don't get many big stories, it's obvious they're going to make a meal of it," explained Ross.

"What does it say in the editorial?" asked the DI. Ross scrolled through the text and began to read,

"*Locals have expressed concern that a wild animal could be responsible but Inverness police will only say that an ongoing murder inquiry is underway*

and would not be issuing further comments at this time."
Ross paused for breath then continued, "*The public's
fears have not been alleviated however and a few people
are worried that a dangerous maniac could be on the
loose. Other theories have been offered including
religious sects, devil worship and a legend over two
hundred years old about a witch coven.*" Avalon turned
to Ross,

"I think we will have to issue a statement or this
is going to get a little silly."

"And tell them what?" asked Ross.

"I'm not exactly sure but we probably need to
explain that it is nothing more than an ordinary murder
investigation." Ross nodded.

"Okay, shall I ring the press team?"

"Hang on, I better go and explain to Croker, I
don't want to give him an excuse to come down heavy
on us. Avalon went to speak to DCI Croker and he told
him about the story they had seen on the internet, but the
man seemed as if he just wanted to ignore it and, when
Avalon pressed his case for a statement, Croker
dismissed it out of hand.

"But if we don't say something they'll keep
making up their own 'facts'," insisted Avalon. DCI
Croker removed his spectacles and began to clean them
with a tissue, Avalon wondered what his aversion to the
press was. He certainly seemed on edge.

"Even if we do, they will still put their own take
on it Detective Inspector," replied Croker replacing his
spectacles, "but the point is, we have nothing to give
them, so I think it's best if we keep to a non-committal
attitude for now." Croker raised his eyebrows a little as if
to say, "is that clear?" and then continued, "and have you
made any headway yet?" Avalon was surprised at the

question, there hadn't been much chance for 'headway' and that would be put back even further with the Sunday night operation.

"We have the report from the coroner but I haven't been able to find time to read it all, it's still early and with this warehouse operation on-"

"I'd rather not have excuses DI Avalon, we are all under pressure and better time management is the key to success," cut in Croker in a matter-of-fact way. Avalon sat, silent, he didn't like being interrupted at the best of times, but to have it done with nothing more than an inane comment was sapping his patience. For a moment he considered just standing and walking out but he had to say something.

"I'll leave it to you to let me know when you think we should release details to the press then," and he stood.

"I'm sure you would love me to follow you around detective but I have my own work, so I suggest you continue with yours, and forget about the press," replied Croker.

"Well yes," replied Avalon as he opened the door to leave, "I have a great deal to do," he paused as he stepped through the door, "I have to look at better time management for a start," and he closed the door slightly more heavily than he should. Back in the Cave, Avalon told Ross to forget about a press statement.

"So I'm guessing the CI does have an issue with the press?"

"I don't know," said Avalon abruptly as he returned to his booth. Ross glanced over to Frazer, they could see he was angry and guessed Croker was to blame.

"Can anyone think of a good anonymous story to

send to the press?" he asked to the room in general.

~~~~~~~

Sunday night had the possibility of being both boring and exciting, the wait for all the suspects to turn up would be tedious for sure but there could be fireworks when the raid actually begun. Seated in the car in the dark, Ross had tried several ideas to hold the boredom at bay and keep himself awake but he was getting close to the end of his repertoire. He had finally asked who could think of the silliest Scottish place names but Avalon was an unwilling participant. After Ross had suggested 'Buttock Point' and 'Backside' he seemed to struggle for a moment,

"I used to know quite a few, oh, there's 'Brokenwind' and 'Dull'," and then he went quiet again. Avalon looked over to Mackinnon and shrugged a little before saying,

"I noticed a place called 'Ecclefechan' on my way up from England but that's me done," he said with a straight face and then Mackinnon looked round to Ross, and added,

"There's a settlement on Orkney called 'Twatt'," which caused Avalon to smile for the first time that evening.

"I thought you would have come up with that one?" said Avalon turning to Ross but he didn't give the DS time to reply, and quickly changed subject to discuss the Priory murder.

"So, have either of you two got any ideas on the Beauly case?" Ross made a 'hmm' noise and then said,

"I've given it some thought, but what puzzles me is why is it so public?"

"As I said," explained Avalon, "it's fairly plain

112

that whoever did this wanted to send a message out to someone."

"Yeah, I see that, but to my way of thinking it would have been easier to cut his hand off and send it to whoever they were trying to scare. It's easier, just as effective, and less risky."

"But not as threatening," added Mackinnon.

"That's my point," agreed Avalon, "they are sending a message to say, 'look, we don't care what the police do, we have this much confidence' which means these are not your average villains."

"I can see this making an impact in Glasgow or Edinburgh, but it's completely over the top for round here," insisted Ross, "it somehow feels," he paused to find the right word, "artificial." Avalon considered this point, it did seem a bit 'theatrical' leaving the body tied to a gravestone with a parchment in his hand. There was the manner of the final slaying too, a pointed, triangular instrument stabbed into the spine, was that also saying something that he couldn't understand?

"Maybe things will start to fall into place when we know who he is," offered Mackinnon, Avalon agreed but Ross seemed doubtful. In the darkness Avalon was sure he could *hear* Ross frowning.

"What is it?" he asked.

"I don't know, there is something that we could be missing," he sighed.

"Like what?" asked Avalon.

"What if this is cult or religious based, what if some group or sect are playing out some sort of sick ritual?" he replied.

"I agree that we have to examine every aspect of the case," began Avalon, "and I agree there are elements of ritual about it but that could be part of the deception."

The radio suddenly crackled into life.

"*Movement spotted, all teams sit tight,*" whispered the voice. "*wait for the command...*" there was a pause, "*go, go go!*" the voice called, Avalon started the engine and drove to their position.

~~~~~~

Avalon was back at work on Tuesday, after the cripplingly long shift on Sunday night through most of Monday morning. They would normally get some time off but not with a brutal murder case to begin work on. Sunday night's operation had been a success and five individuals were in custody, two of them thought to be the ringleaders and DS Wilson was reasonably happy with the result. There had been a great deal of processing and paperwork to go through on Monday, as well as a debrief to the DCI who was unusually upbeat about the affair. Avalon had managed to get finished on Monday afternoon but worked late because he didn't want to disturb Angie, particularly after missing her party. He eventually arrived home at ten past midnight, after a few sandwiches at the pub, and a walk in the chill air to help him think. He showered, went to bed and slept well. He was awake by nine-fifteen and was back in the office by ten-thirty, almost ready to begin. The only thing left to do was to open and read the note from Angie he had seen left on the kitchen table. She 'adored' the pendant and chain and even left him three kisses on the bottom of the note. He smiled and locked it in his drawer. Wilson and Mack were not in, they would be busy downstairs most of the day but Frazer and Mackinnon were there, Ross was missing and it seemed he was back to his old ways. Avalon had said 'don't be too early' but Ross would probably abuse that suggestion as much as he dare, then to his surprise, Ross walked in. He was holding a note and came straight into the office.

"Just arrived?" asked Avalon.

No, I have been tracking down an important lead," he frowned dropping the note on the desk with a hint of sarcasm. Avalon picked it up and read a name.

"What's this?" he asked.

"This, my ungrateful friend, is the name of a missing man from Elgin." Avalon decided to look more closely at the name, Alan Clacher, fifty-six years old and missing for six days.

"So what's the story?" asked Avalon as Ross leaned on the glass panel and folded his arms.

"He was reported missing when he didn't meet his business partner for lunch, his wife said he hadn't mentioned he was changing his plans, so she contacted the local police. They didn't think it was all that important but logged it all the same."

"Does he fit the body in the morgue?" asked Avalon leaning back in his chair.

"It's possible, I have contacted the local police to try and track down dental records or DNA profile," Ross shrugged, "but it's a bit of a waiting game to get a positive ID." Avalon nodded and then Ross added, "everything fits though, the description is close, he's a semi-retired haulage contractor, his business partner has been running things for the last ten months."

"Okay, we better get this up on the wall, let's hope more comes in." Ross picked up the note and headed into the main room where he began to put the pieces of the puzzle on a large 'whiteboard' near the door. Avalon thought for a moment and then followed. There wasn't much on the board, a photograph of the priory, a written description of what the murder weapon may look like, a small card with three blacked out heads and a question mark, the word motive written in black, also with a question mark and, in the middle, a circle with the word 'body' and yet another question mark by it.

"Not inspiring," said Frazer.

"Not yet, but we may have an ID for the victim and I had an email from forensics, it has an image of the paper found in his hand. I've asked PC Kirk to have it printed on a larger scale," explained Avalon looking at the sparse board, then he added, "right," and he rubbed his hands together, "let's make a start." He then sat on the edge of the nearest desk, which was Mackinnon's, and looked at his team, a team that seemed woefully small for the work at hand. He wasn't including Wilson and MacDonald, so his first orders went to Mackinnon. "Rory, get on the internet, I want everything we can find on the Priory, there were two orders of monks that held it over the years, see if you can dig up anything about them," he then paused, "oh and check to see if there is anything with a French connection, both orders were French and the name Beauly is also French." Mackinnon nodded and began immediately. Avalon looked at Frazer. "Megan, check through the door-to-door records that the uniform did, someone must have heard, or seen something, the damn place is surrounded by houses," and he sighed a little before turning to Ross, "we need to check if there are any records of a similar murder, anything that would connect this to any other case, and I mean anything, even down to the type of wounds or manner of dispatch, anything that resembles an MO. There must be something we can pick up with this triangular blade." He then looked back to the circle with the word 'body' inside, he knew that if the missing Elgin man was their victim, they would have more to work with but at the same time, it would bring horror onto the victim's family. Every dead body had someone left behind, well almost every dead body. He had known cases where there seemed to be no one that gave a damn. He wondered if anyone cared if *he* lived or died, or was he just feeling sorry for himself because Carol had a boyfriend? Probably, he must ring her sometime to let her know how things had turned out. 'Sometime'. Right, now he had a great deal to do and it wouldn't be long before Croker was asking for an update. He returned to his booth and began to examine every aspect of the coroner's report and hoped that the forensics document would soon arrive. Not long after, Kirk entered and she handed him the blown up image of the parchment.

"What es et if y' don't mind me asking?"

"It was found on the body at the priory," answered Avalon, then said, "I was going to ask if anyone downstairs could speak Gaelic but I can now see that this isn't even the English alphabet."

"Et looks like runes," she replied.

"What?"

"Runes," repeated Kirk, "you know like 'Lord of the Rings'." Avalon was clearly bemused by her statement and then it clicked, the language of the Dwarf characters in the book by Tolkien, were called runes.

"Is it a real language?" he asked.

"You're asking the wrong person about that, where I come from, we struggle reading English," she smiled and then, in her usual way, she turned and left. Avalon stood and stuck the image on the wall.

"Megan, do we know anyone who is good with languages?" he asked, she shrugged a little and replied.

"I think there is someone on the books, a

translator of sorts, what's the language?"

"Probably Dwarf," he answered as everyone stopped what they were doing and looked straight at him, "just joking, but I haven't a clue what it is, so we need someone with experience." Mackinnon was on his feet and looking at the blown up image.

"I have seen something like this and..." he began to smile a little.

"So what is it?" asked Avalon.

"When you said Dwarf I thought of the film franchise of 'Lord of the Rings' there were several examples of this type of lettering."

"Kirk said Tolkien as well," frowned Avalon.

"It's got to be a wind up," insisted Ross. Avalon spun around to him.

"Wind up or not, we have to find out if this actually says something," and he turned back to Mackinnon. "Well this is sort of your field Rory, see what you can dig up, an alphabet would be good." Mackinnon nodded and sat back in his seat.

"Why would someone strip a body but leave something like this in his hand?" asked Ross still unconvinced.

"Why would someone torture a man tae death and tie him to a gravestone? I don't think we are dealing with a well adjusted individual here," answered Frazer, with a hint of sarcasm in her voice.

"Sarah Underwood thought that the paper had been placed there after death," frowned Avalon and wondering about it, added, "I'll give her a call," and he walked back to his phone.

"Et's Sunday boss, she probably won't be there," called Frazer.

"They're almost as busy as us, I bet someone is

118

there," suggested Avalon.

"Miss Underwood?" he asked as a voice answered.

"*Yes?*"

"It's Avalon, Detective Avalon, look I was thinking about what you said about the parchment found on our priory body."

"*Oh right, what can I help you with?*" she asked.

"You said that you thought that the parchment was placed in the hand after death, do you still think that?"

"*I can't be sure detective but I would say it was, it was pushed into the fist over the thumb and there was blood on the palm, the paper hadn't stuck to it,*" she explained, "*but I can't be one hundred percent sure.*"

"Yes I understand, but it does make a difference to the case," Avalon said.

"*I'm sure it does detective but I simply couldn't pin to down either way, it's just my opinion.*"

"Which I value Miss Underwood," replied Avalon, trying to make his voice sound as friendly as he could, "but if you find anything to confirm that, it would be very helpful," he thanked her and returned to the main office where Ross and Mackinnon seemed deep in discussion.

"What's going on?" asked Avalon.

"Mackinnon thinks the devil did it," said Ross, with a slight grin.

"With respect DS Ross, I said nothing of the sort," frowned Mackinnon.

"So what do you think Rory?" asked Avalon taking a seat near the door.

"I simply pointed out that this case reminds me of an old British 'B' movie."

"Go on," prompted Avalon. Mackinnon glanced over to Ross, before explaining.

"It was called Night of the Demon, the story goes that a satanic cult had the power to bring death to anyone by giving them a slip of paper with arcane text written on it," Mackinnon paused for a moment, as he thought he heard Ross make a noise, "the film is based on an earlier book by M. R. James called 'Casting the Runes'," he added.

"There's that word again," interrupted Avalon.

"Arcane?" asked Ross.

"No, runes," frowned Avalon knowing exactly who Ross was getting at, and he asked, "you seem to know a great deal about this Mackinnon?"

"It's one of my favourites sir, a real classic of the cinema," he smiled, and then continued with the plot of the movie, "once the runes were secreted on the victim, the person was cursed to be destroyed by a demon."

"But just a minute," said Ross, "are we giving up police work in favour of exorcism?"

"No one is suggesting we go looking for a wizard with a ninety foot demon on a chain," insisted Avalon, but we do need to consider what our killers are trying to get out of this."

"You saw the film then?" smiled Mackinnon.

"Yeah..." Avalon paused, "and it scared the crap out of me when I first saw it as a teenager," and then he stood, "this goes back to the runes, we need to find out if these *are* runes and if it means anything," he tapped his finger on the image of the parchment, "or if it's just a load of cobblers," and he headed off back to the booth.
Avalon thought deeply, there was so much of this case that seemed crazy. No matter why the sliver of parchment had been left at the scene, why the hell would

anyone risk being found out by leaving something that could be traced? The area around the site had shown no real forensic evidence, so why be so careful and then leave something so obvious? Avalon could think of one reason and that didn't make sense either. What if it had been planted to implicate someone else? It seemed too corny but he would keep it as an option. Then there was the actual killing blow, there must be a thousand ways to kill someone, particularly as the victim had been brutally tortured but they had decided to use a method that was unusual and gave possible clues, if not directly, it told you the type of killing this was. No matter how much Avalon didn't want to think it, the murder looked ritualistic, and that bothered him. Someone bound to ritual or religion wouldn't think like the normal crazed killer, there would be rules, methods, and a formula. More than that, there would be planning, lots of it, to perpetrate the crime and to cover it up. Then Avalon came back to his immediate problem, lack of staff. There were hardly enough of them to run a day-to day-office and here he had a major murder investigation with all the man-hours that would entail. He decided to go back to reading the coroner's report.

It wasn't long before Frazer knocked on the glass as she entered the booth.

"Got something?" asked Avalon as he looked up from the computer screen.

"Not sure, but I think et may be of interest,"

"I'm all ears," he smiled.

"Looking through the reports from the uniforms that did the door-to-door, I found something that sort o' made me wonder," Avalon kept his gaze on her, "one chap had informed the officer questioning him he had seen and heard nothing but he was insistent that the area was having a crime wave. To humour him, the PC recorded that a flower display had been vandalised and the container was missing, he lives on Riverside Drive, not far from the priory," she stopped and waited for a reaction.

"A wheelbarrow?" questioned Avalon.

"How the hell did y' know that?" she asked folding her arms.

"I had already thought about how the body was moved, but discounted it, phone the man up," he insisted, "you and Ross go and question him and see if you can find the barrow nearby, though I doubt it." Just as Ross and Frazer had left, the phone rang.

"Avalon."

"*Hello detective, it's Sarah Underwood, I have something you may be interested in.*"

"I could do with something, anything would be great," he answered.

"*It's probably not the breakthrough you were looking for, but the tests have been done on the twine around the victim's hands, it's nylon cord that has been unwound from a larger rope.*"

"And now you're going to tell me it's as common as..." he paused, he was about to say a 'Brummie whore' but he thought better of it. She took the pause as her cue.

"*Sort of, it's the type used on camping tarpaulins and items of that nature. I've asked the team to keep digging to see if we can narrow it down, but I doubt it.*"

"Well thanks anyway, how about the rogue DNA sample found on the wall?" he asked.

"*Well we have a full result but there are no matches in the database, it looks like this is probably his first offence,*" she answered.

"Or he's never been caught," added Avalon, "well

thank you," he said and he put down the phone. It wasn't going very well, but he knew it was early days.

Avalon had just finished reading every scrap of the coroner's report, when his phone rang again.

"Avalon," he said.

"*It's Ross, the wheelbarrow went missing the same night,*" confirmed Ross.

"Have you had a look around?"

"*Better than that, we've found it, it seems it was thrown in the river from a wharf close to the priory. The current took it downstream but it snagged on a tree.*"

"Okay, can you get it?" asked Avalon.

"The bank is steep here, so we have asked for a team to come to recover it."

"Fine, get it down to forensics as soon as, but I'll bet a golden haggis we find nothing on it," replied Avalon and he leaned back in the chair. If this case was to be solved quickly, they would need more leads than a theft of an old wheelbarrow. He went to see how Mackinnon was doing.

"Found anything?" he asked. Mackinnon was so engrossed he didn't notice Avalon at his side.

"Oh sorry sir, yes, well no actually," stuttered the DC.

"Spit it out Rory, have you or have you not?" demanded Avalon.

"It's much more complicated than it first seems, Tolkien wrote English words in old English runes, well sort of but there are several systems used for some of the special characters," answered Mackinnon, then he pointed to his computer screen. "I thought I had struck gold when I found this website that translates English into Tolkien Runes but it's quite different to ours."

"Cut to the chase," nodded Avalon, "can it be read, or not?"

"Not by me sir, it would take a week or so to study it, I can do it at home I suppose but looking at this website it's probably not the same script."

"We'll have to find someone who can read this stuff, an expert if there is such a thing, god knows where though," frowned Avalon and then added, "pity it's not Klingon," and he returned to his booth patting the young man on the shoulder.

~~~~~~

Avalon slumped in his chair, pulled off his shoes, and wondered if he could be bothered with food. He looked around the sitting room and saw the television but resisted the urge to turn it on. It had been yet another long day and here he was, home just under an hour before midnight. It hardly seemed worth doing anything at all and he considered going for a shower and straight to bed. The shower helped relax him a little and he thought more about the case. The wheelbarrow had been taken to forensics but in the back of his mind, he knew it was nothing to do with the crime. He dried himself and dressed in a pair of shorts and a tee shirt, then went to the kitchen to see if there was anything that would make a simple snack. He filled the kettle and switched it on and tried to review the details of the coroner's report to see if he had missed something, but no matter how much he threaded his way through it, he was still staring at a blank wall. The click of the kettle brought him out of his thoughts and he poured water over the tea bag and left it to brew. He decided that beans on toast would make a reasonable supper and he popped two slices of bread in the toaster and reached for the cupboard above the worktop. As he scanned the paltry items on offer, he saw there was just one tin of beans left so he would have to make a real effort to do some shopping, but then he saw it. Just behind the jar of sweet pickle, was a sight that took Avalon by surprise, a tin of spaghetti hoops. Just for a moment, he glanced around the room thinking he had been 'set up' but he was alone and the tin of spaghetti hoops was really there. He knew damn well he hadn't bought them, so how the hell had they got there? He suddenly wondered if this was the same tin he had left on the television back in Wolverhampton that had somehow gone through yet another temporal rift and followed him here. He gave a slight grin to himself, that was just too stupid to imagine and he picked the tin up to examine the 'best before' date. To his relief it wasn't the same tin, so how had it arrived here? Maybe it was Angie who put it there by mistake, so he looked in her cupboard but there were no tins whatsoever in her side. He was baffled, no one in Scotland even knew about his aversion to spaghetti, so what was going on? Then it struck him. Ross! The DS had overheard him talking to his ex-wife some months ago and he had mentioned spaghetti hoops then, but how did he get the tin into the house? He thought he knew the answer to that too. This had all come from a conversation with Carol. That reminded him, he needed to phone her. He looked at the clock, it was probably too late, but then again, she had never been one to go to bed early. He thought better of it and he put the tin back in the cupboard and buttered the toast instead. Then, with an uncharacteristic determination when dealing with his personal life, he phoned Carol's number. Her phone would be switched off anyway if she *was* asleep.

"*Hello?*"

"It's me, James."

"*Oh my god, I thought you had left the country,*" she said.

"I have," he smiled.

"*Well, yes you have, but you know what I'm getting at.*"

"Can you talk?" he asked, feeling quite calm about the call.

"*I was just thinking of going to bed, but this is so rare I will cope.*"

"I know I should have called earlier, but I never seem to get any time to myself," he explained.

"*Nothing changes,*" she said, "*so how are you?*"

"Fine, I thought I would tell you what has happened recently," he began and tried to picture her lounging on the sofa with her feet up, "it's all change for me. I have been set on permanently."

"*Oh great, well done,*" she replied.

"And..." he paused wondering how to word it, "I was promoted, Detective Inspector with my own team."

"*You see, it all worked out good in the end,*" but Avalon wasn't sure that was accurate, and he didn't think she sounded as happy for him as he had expected.

"How about you?" he asked.

"*Oh I'm fine, still working at the same place,*" she replied.

"And your friend, are you still seeing him?" Avalon was still uncomfortable with 'boyfriend'.

"*Graham?*" she said, Avalon didn't know his name, didn't want to know it, but he made an effort to be interested in him, for her sake, "*yes, I still see him.*"

"What does he do?" he asked, still not even slightly interested.

126

"*He's a fireman*," she said, Avalon wanted to ask if she was working her way through the emergency services, but he didn't.

"Oh," was all he actually said.

"*Well you know me, I like a man in uniform*," she replied, but Avalon noticed she sounded slightly embarrassed at the end of the statement. "*Did you get the note I put in the box with your bike kit?*" again there was hesitation in her voice, he was silent for more time than he ought to have been

"Er, no," he lied, "I haven't had chance to..." he paused, "yes I saw it," he then admitted, "but I haven't felt brave enough to read it all." *She* was silent now. "I'm guessing it was important," he eventually said to break the quiet, "I started reading it, but you know me, I'm not very good at dealing with that sort of thing."

"*You don't make it easy for me do you?*"

"What do you mean?" he asked with some trepidation.

"*I wrote to you because I thought it would be easier than telling you on the phone, cowards way out I know, but...*" Avalon swallowed, he had been right not to read it, somehow he knew it had been bad news, "*I'm thinking of moving in with Graham, he's moving to Rugeley with his job and buying a house over there.*" Avalon just didn't know what to say, he had always known it was coming, but it was still going to hurt. He knew he was a fool, he had no say over what Carol did, or didn't do with her life, but he still wanted to protect her. He tried the 'brave face' routine when he eventually got back his power of speech.

"What about your job?" he asked.

"*I can another job like that anywhere, I'm well qualified*," she replied.

"Are you sure you aren't going down the same route again, I mean a fireman works long hours and it's a tough job?"

"*Look,*" she began, "*I don't think he will be working thirty hour shifts or having mood swings due to the case he's working, or even waking up in the night in a cold sweat shaking,*" she paused, and then said, "*sorry, I shouldn't have said that.*"

"No," insisted Avalon, "it's fine, I know it was tough, but I just don't want to see you make mistakes in your first serious relationship." He heard her sigh.

"*I know you think you were in the wrong, and you still insist on raising me on a pedestal, but the point is, this isn't my first. I'm no angel, I moved on even if you didn't,*" then came a silence, a silence that seemed to have no end, and then Avalon could hear her talking, but nothing went in. It was as if he had been punched and was seeing stars, his vision seemed to blur and then clear and he could hear her voice again. "*and if you had read the note it explains all that... are you there? James?*"

"What? Er yes... I'm still here."

"*I still think a great deal about you, I always will but you have to understand...*"

"Yes, yes, I do understand," he really did. A great deal of things now made perfect sense, "look, I have to go, I'm not sure how to continue this conversation at the moment," he felt he was staring into space but there was a clarity, there was also something else too. Sadness, loss, yes, but a feeling he couldn't quite put his finger on.

"*I'm sorry you had to hear it like this but-*"

"Carol," interrupted Avalon, "I'm fine with it really, but I do have to go," he said with a voice that seemed a little too firm and he cut the line and switched his phone off. He walked over to the kitchen sink and

128

looked out of the window into the darkness, but all he could see was his reflection and the kitchen behind him. To his surprise, he was feeling reasonably good considering how tired he was, and the kick in the truth gland he had just received, but he couldn't shake the other feeling, what the hell was it? And then it came to him. Realisation. Everything can be interpreted in any way you want to see it and it clouds the judgement because you aren't expecting it, but Carol tipping his world off its axis by a few degrees had made him see a little clearer, and he could suddenly see things that he wasn't expecting were there.

~~~~~~

Ross brought his car to a stop and got out, Frazer pulled herself from the passenger seat and the two of them walked back up the road to where Avalon was seated on the stump of a sawn off tree by a road sign, reading something. Ross thought it was an odd image, his lone, hunched figure on a stump by a road junction, it seemed to him he remembered the image from somewhere, he then recalled that image and looked over to Frazer.

"He's at the crossroads," he grinned but Frazer just rolled her eyes.

"We got the message, what's wrong?" asked Ross. Avalon seemed to jump from his thoughts.

"Oh, you got the message then?" he said.

"Yes, I just said so," insisted Ross looking over to Frazer.

"Sorry, I was deep in thought, I couldn't recall if I had left where to meet in the message," he said with a shrug.

"You just said Riverside Drive but you are hard

129

to miss sitting here, staring at the river," insisted Ross, "what are you reading?" Avalon looked down at the sheet as if it was a surprise to him.

"Oh, it's a copy of a poem,"

"Does it say who did it?" asked Ross flippantly.

"Sort of, I never rated the poem until I sat here and read it, I understand what it's about now,"

"So I'm guessing it's the one about the Priory?" asked Ross remembering Avalon speak of it before. Avalon nodded slowly looking wistfully over the river.

"Right," announced Avalon, jumping to his feet and walking off towards the Priory, "yes, it's the one by Keats and Brown, but something came to me last night, something I hadn't really taken into consideration."

"What's that?" asked Ross, following on and giving Frazer a quick, questioning glance.

"The wheelbarrow, it doesn't fit into this case."

"We don't know that yet boss, not until the forensics are done with et," said Frazer. Avalon glanced round at her.

"I'm sure it hasn't anything to do with moving a body."

"Well are you going to explain your thinking?" asked Ross, still unsure what he was getting at. Avalon stopped and turned to them.

"Think about it, a wheelbarrow is a great tool to move a body, but one that was being used to display flowers in on one of these gardens?" he pointed to the closest houses, not knowing the exact address.

"But et could have been spontaneous, they see et and think et's a useful bit of kit?" offered Frazer, "so they empty et out and Bob's your close relative."

"But think about what you just said, 'spontaneous', a word that comes easier to my lips in this

130

case is meticulous." Avalon noticed Ross nod slightly, and he looked down the road.

"I'm not sure I follow," added Frazer.

"There is only about fifty or sixty feet of grass from the road to the rear wall of the priory, why risk trying to move the body in a wheelbarrow that had stood as an ornament on a garden? It may have a squeak, it may even fall apart when you get the corpse in it." Frazer raised her eyebrows, Avalon continued, "there are probably at least three people to be able to lift the body over the wall, so they have the manpower," and he continued walking down the road.

"So you're saying that these people wouldn't take the risk with the wheelbarrow?" asked Frazer as she followed.

"Exactly, they're too organised."

"So how do they quickly get the body to the wall? I would think they would want to do it as quick as possible," she inquired.

"Hopefully with DS Ross's help, I can show you," said Avalon giving a quick glance to Ross. As they reached the part of the road opposite the wall of the priory, Avalon stopped.

"They would probably park the vehicle a little away from the wall to stop any suspicion... say, here..." and he pointed to a slight pull-in, "and then, they would load up the body."

"On what?" asked Frazer.

"What do you weigh roughly?" asked Avalon to Ross.

"I would think about a hundred kilos," shrugged Ross.

"We have just voted to come out of the EU so can we have it in British money please?" asked Avalon raising his brows a little.

"Fifteen... fifteen and a half stones..." considered Ross.

"So," continued Avalon, "they pull the body from the vehicle, one or maybe two, lift the body to a standing position and then, the third one does this," Avalon raised his eyebrows and asked Ross, "ready?" and he removed his jacket and handed it to Frazer, Ross nodded and Avalon lifted the DS over his shoulder and then turned and made a spirited jog with Ross over his shoulder up to the wall. He was clearly out of breath when he released Ross and gasped at the air.

"Well, I'm impressed, you don't look that strong," smiled Frazer. Avalon was resting on the wall and leaning over with his hands on his knees. In stilted gasps, he said,

"Either gravity is high today, or you are nearer seventeen stones."

"There you go again with my weight, just stop it," replied Ross, "it's more likely to do with your age."

"Where I'm from, they call this a 'fireman's lift' and it works really well.

"So," began Frazer, "the wheelbarrow was nothing tae do with this particular crime?" she asked, handing back his jacket.

"Yesterday I would have said yes, but last night..." he paused and made out he was still short of breath, but he was also thinking through what Carol had told him, "I saw how we could be convinced of something because it seems difficult to see another reason for it."

"I'm not sure that makes sense, but I think what you are saying is, that we are being played?" Avalon just nodded.

132

"So if that barrow was just thrown in the river to make it look like they used it, the same could be true of the parchment with the runes on it?" offered Frazer. He nodded again.

"Whoever is in control here, is clever, has some knowledge of how crimes are processed, and likes to play games," he stopped for breath, "but we have to retake control from him and take heed. All the evidence we find has to be double checked by everyone on the case and nothing can be left to chance."

"This es going tae be an interesting case," shrugged Frazer.

"A difficult one too, whoever organised this, is throwing confusion where ever he can, he wants to play witches, demons, the devil, but he didn't vector C Section into his calculations," smiled Avalon as he replaced his jacket. His eyes shone with fire and an expression of controlled ferocity, for a moment Ross could see that Avalon had a new purpose, an energy, even tougher and stronger, but he began to wonder about his boss. Had he succumbed to the pressure of the job and was slowly going mad, or was this 'charged aura' real?

"But we still have nowhere to go yet," insisted Ross, "and until we have more to work with, no amount of enthusiasm is going to solve this." Avalon pulled the crumpled sheet from his pocket and searched through it, then read out aloud,

> *"Here's a true Churchman he'd affect,*
> *much charity, and ne'er neglect,*
> *to pray for mercy on the elect,*
> *but thought no evil,*
> *in sending heathen,*
> *Turk and sect,*

all to the Devil."

He looked up to Ross as he folded the paper and placed it back in his pocket.

"So what's that mean?" asked Ross, but Avalon walked off.

"Let's find that cafe and get a drink," suggested Avalon, "I'm spitting feathers here." Frazer shrugged and followed.

"Yes, quite mad," thought Ross to himself.

Chapter Five

Ross was daydreaming about the possibility of some time off and an idea of a holiday somewhere, dreaming was about as close as it got though. He couldn't remember the last time he had taken more than a single day off work. He was sitting by a pool sipping a long drink, looking out over the sea and noticing two lovely creatures in bathing suits, when the phone in Avalon's booth rang and washed the whole image from his brain.

"There's no point in ringing the DI anyway," he thought, Avalon was out at a meeting with the coroner about the identity of the body at the Priory. The phone continued to ring and he looked over to Mackinnon who didn't even seem to have noticed it. Ross looked at his computer screen and considered getting back to his report just as the phone went quiet. The return to silence, all except for the clicking of Mackinnon's keyboard seemed a far cry from some foreign holiday resort and he wondered if he could slip back to where ever it was, then *his* phone rang.

"God damn it!" he hissed as he reached for the receiver, "DS Ross," he announced sharply.

"*Ah, Ross, it's Superintendent Price,*" Ross

almost recoiled from the phone, the Superintendent ringing him? "*is DI Avalon about?*"

"Er, no sir," gasped Ross, "he's with the coroner."

"*Oh, okay, you may be able to shed some light on this then,*" Ross was sure he couldn't, not for a 'Super' but he listened anyway. "*I've just been informed that there has been no updated press release about the death at Beauly Priory, is there any reason for this?*" The first thing that struck Ross was, why a Superintendent would soil his hands with something as lowly as a press release.

"We're under orders sir," answered Ross.

"*Orders, from whom?*"

"From the DCI sir, DCI Croker," replied Ross.

"*Do you know why?*" asked the Superintendent.

"Not really sir, DI Avalon intended to do it but the DCI countermanded it." There was a slight pause.

"*Hmm, okay Ross, I'll contact DCI Croker,*" and the phone went dead. Ross didn't know whether to sprinkle holy water on the phone or make the sign of the cross, he didn't think he had ever spoken to the man previously. He looked around the office, Mack and Wilson had their faces buried in their work, and Mackinnon was still oblivious to his surroundings. Ross thought about telling them all what had just happened but he thought ten more minutes at the holiday resort was more attractive. It wasn't to be, Avalon's phone rang once more, but this time he walked over to answer it, just in case it was Croker or even the 'Super' again.

"DS Ross," he announced.

"*Es the boss en?*" it was Frazer.

"No he's out, what's up?" asked Ross.

"*Well, et might be nothin' but I just heard that a truck has been nicked, and he wanted to know about anythin' like this.*"

"Okay I'll let him know, where was this?" asked Ross.

"*Down the A9, et may be worth asking O-K to check on it, I'll be back in an hour or so.*" Ross immediately called downstairs to ask PC Kirk if she could track down the details of a stolen truck and it didn't take her long. Ross returned to the Cave and saw the email arrive soon after and he quickly read the details then did some more phoning around. By the time Avalon returned, he knew enough to tell him exactly what had happened.

"So let's hear it," said Avalon pouring himself a coffee.

"Straight forward truck theft it seems, the driver was in a lay-by overnight and when he got out for a pee he was attacked and threatened. Three attackers, two held him and beat him while the other got in the truck."

"Sounds like they were waiting for him," replied Avalon sipping his coffee and heading back to his booth.

"Probably," agreed Ross, following on. Avalon sat and asked,

"Where was this did you say?"

"On the A9 near Tomatin, the driver was shaken up but he said the truck headed north and a car followed it."

"Is there a description of the truck and the car?" asked Avalon. Ross pulled out his notebook and read from it.

"The truck was a light blue DAF with basic graphics stating it belongs to Crisp Brothers Haulage. The trailer didn't have any graphics though, and was plain white, but we do have its make and number. The car was either a grey, or a blue, Volkswagen Passat."

"The car will be stolen," nodded Avalon, "did the

truck have a GPS tracker?" Ross nodded.

"But apparently they are easy to find and disable, the trailer has one too and the haulage company say it's solar powered so it should keep online even if it's uncoupled," he explained.

"So I'm guessing they are tracking it at this moment," added Avalon taking another sip of his coffee.

"They were, but the truck had stopped just outside Inverness on a back road, the B9177. The uniforms sent a car to find it. The trailer seemed to continue north until its tracker went offline somewhere near Duncanston." Avalon nodded again and then sat upright.

"So what was it carrying?"

"Chemist shop supplies and pharmaceuticals," replied Ross.

"Well, it's not likely to be of interest to us, but we'll keep our eye on how it works out," then he stood and walked into the main room. "Rory, I would normally give this one to Mack, he's the truck roadie, but he's a bit busy." Mack looked over and rolled his eyes then got back to his work. "We are watching how this stolen truck evolves, I want you to keep an eye on what's found. Ross has the details and the incident number. If they bring it to us, fine, but for now just track it covertly, if you get my drift?" Mackinnon nodded and took the details from Ross, then Avalon looked at Ross, and said, "we'd better have another look up on Windy Ridge just to be on the safe side."

"Okay," agreed Ross, then added as an afterthought, "oh and we had a phone call from the Superintendent earlier on." Avalon looked surprised and after a moment he nodded sideways to the booth. Once inside, the two of them sat.

"What did he want?" asked Avalon continuing his almost cold coffee.

"He wanted to know why a press update hadn't been issued."

"Odd?" mused Avalon, "why would he get involved?"

"No idea," replied Ross but when I told him that Croker had stopped us, he said he would speak to him about it." The phone rang again and Avalon reached for it.

"Avalon."

"*Have you spoken to the Superintendent DI Avalon?*" it was Croker and he sounded agitated. Avalon pointed to the handset with his free hand and raised his eyebrows to Ross.

"No sir, I don't think I have *ever* spoken to him," replied Avalon.

"*Oh, er, I see,*" Croker sounded crestfallen and seemed not to know how to continue. "*Did anyone else in your office speak to him?*"

"I doubt it, though I can ask, I have only just got back from the coroner's office," explained Avalon.

"*No, no, that's fine,*" and he rang off. Avalon replaced the handset on the phone and looked to Ross.

"It looks like the Superintendent was true to his word, DCI Croker seems out of sorts," smiled Avalon.

Soon after, Frazer returned and she was carrying a file.

"He's our man," she said as she dropped the file on Avalon's desk.

"Alan Clacher?" he asked. Frazer nodded.

"Dental records confirm et, they're checking DNA but the odontologist says there's little, or no, doubt." Avalon tapped on the glass and motioned to Ross to join them and after Avalon showed him the file, Ross shrugged and said,

"Well we knew it was likely."

"Yes but we can put some work into Mr Clacher's background and let's hope there is something there for us to find. Has the family been informed yet?"

"I don't think so," replied Frazer.

"Okay, this is yours I'm afraid," said Avalon looking at Ross, "take Mackinnon with you, let him get a taste of the shitty part of the job." Ross nodded solemnly and went to talk to Mackinnon. "Christ we are so understaffed," he spat as Ross left the booth.

"We're gonna have tae deal with et for now though," frowned Frazer. Avalon sighed and leaned back.

"Oh and as we thought, forensics say the wheelbarrow was clean."

"Et could just have been a few drunk lads walking past and deciding to arse about. Et might not have been anything tae do with the murder," insisted Frazer.

"To be truthful I think that's more likely but we have to keep digging." Frazer nodded and walked back to her desk as Ross and Mackinnon left the Cave.

~~~~~~

Mrs Clacher was distraught, not just to hear that her husband's body had been found, but that her husband was the actual victim the local press were calling '*A torn up mess'* found at Beauly Priory. Ross waited for her to calm a little, as did her sister who was there to support her.

"I'm sorry Mrs Clacher, but we need to ask you some questions when you are feeling up to it," said Ross quietly and then he added, "we have some details from

140

when you reported your husband missing but we need more information about his movements prior to that." The woman nodded through the tears.

"I'll do what I can," she sobbed, "when would be best?"

"When you feel up to it Mrs Clacher." She nodded again and her sister embraced her. Ross gave her his number and he and Mackinnon left and got into the car.

"Wow, that's awkward," sighed Mackinnon.

"Yep," was all Ross said.

"Do you have do go through this a lot?" asked the young DC.

"Fortunately not but it's not pleasant, and if the surviving relative saw the death it gets really difficult as we have to try and interview them as soon as we can, just in case they forget something," explained Ross.

"How are they going to forget something like that?"

"It's a reaction to shock with some people, best to get what you can, when you can." The rest of the journey back was relatively quiet.

~~~~~~

The phone rang.

"Avalon," he said, still looking through the forensic report delivered that morning. It was the press office wanting material to send to the local papers on the Beauly body. "Has anyone sanctioned this?" asked Avalon.

"*I don't know what you mean,*" said the woman on the other end of the phone, "*I was just asked by DCI Croker.*"

141

"Are you sure it was from the DCI?" asked Avalon.

"Well I assume it was, it's the first time I've met him." Avalon was taken aback, Croker had actually walked to the press office to tell them to ring *him*. He smiled slightly. It made sense that the Superintendent had found out about the lack of press details, probably from one of his golfing friends, and he had put pressure on Croker, but, Croker being Croker, hadn't got the guts to directly approach C Section. If Avalon had little respect for Croker before, he was now beginning to actually loathe the man. He sent the prepared press release, adding the name of the victim, to the press office. He then saw PC Kirk enter the Cave and come straight over to him.

"This one's for your section I believe DI Avalon," she said handing him a case sheet. He quickly read the top, it was the truck theft, and Avalon nodded.

"Thanks O-K, I expected to get this one," and he looked through the glass at the team hard at work.

"How did you go on with the parchment, did y' find out what et was?" she asked. Avalon looked up to her and shook his head.

"No, DC Mackinnon has been working on it as and when, but we are pulled out as usual." Kirk shrugged and went to have another look at the blown-up image and stared at it for some time before leaving without another word. As Avalon went back to the forensics report, he noticed that it mentioned the twine used to bind the hands of Alan Clacher had been analysed further and was a close match to heavier rope usually found on tarpaulin covers, but that was all they could confirm, they had however, kept a sample for spectroscopy testing. He leaned back a little and thought about the wheelbarrow again, if the barrow and the parchment were red herrings meant to cover their tracks, this twine could be too. He was getting nowhere, it had been over a week since the body had been found, and all they knew was the name of the victim and maybe how he died. It was a shambles, with so few staff, there was little hope of solving this quickly, if at all. Failure hadn't been something he had ever contemplated before, he had always assumed that if he kept down a methodical and logical route, then all crimes could be solved. At first glance, this one looked like it could be cracked, but Avalon thought that whoever was responsible for this one was no amateur, neither was he stupid. He sighed deeply, picked up the report on the truck theft, and quickly read through it, he then stood and joined the others in the main room. Wilson and Mack were out but all the others were present.

"We've got the truck theft too," he announced holding up the sheet and he sat on the front desk by Mackinnon.

"So who's going to work that one?" asked Ross. Avalon shrugged.

"Whoever, whenever," he replied.

"I'll give it a go," replied Mackinnon.

"So," began Avalon turning to him, "you're not happy sorting the rogue paperwork, checking lists of suspects and translating dwarf runes, you want to solve crimes too?" Mackinnon thought the DI was joking so he gave a weak smile. Avalon looked at the sheet and said to the room,

"So we have a truck taken in the very early hours of the morning on the A9 near Tomatin, driver had been resting at a spot he has used before. He was attacked and beaten as he exited the cab to relieve himself and

143

abandoned at the side of the road. Just three 'perps' as far as we know, with a car as backup. Both car and truck headed north up the A9 to a quiet spot by a pull-in on the B9177," he stopped to check on the notes, then continued. "The truck and the trailer both had GPS trackers, but because of the early hour and the driver being left at the side of the road, the gang got a two-hour start. Officers were sent to where the tracker said the truck was and they found it abandoned but there was no sign of the trailer. Tracks in the mud showed another vehicle was probably waiting to take the trailer away," he looked up, "nothing else was found at the scene." He looked over to the coffee machine for a moment but it looked like it needed refilling. He continued. "Records from the tracking company show the trailer, which had a solar powered tracker, continued north over the Kessock Bridge and the signal went dead near Duncanston, they later confirmed that the tracker had been removed from the trailer as it registered a tampering alert before it went dead. Police officers issued a BOLO for the trailer, but it's plain white with no markings, and we don't know what make or model the truck unit is. Local officers have been out scouting the area all up the A9 and at the ferry port at..." at this point he looked down at the sheet, "Scrabster, just in case they tried to unload it there." He stopped for a second. "The trailer contained chemist supplies and a certain amount of pharmaceuticals but as of yet, we have no breakdown of exactly what. Any question or ideas?" he concluded. Frazer was the first to speak.

"Et sounds like someone knew he would be there, so I would say an inside job." Avalon nodded then Ross said,

"Which direction was the truck supposed to be

going?"

"South I believe," said Avalon checking the details, "yes, Inverness to Glasgow." Ross shrugged and said,

"Makes me wonder if they moved it north because they knew it was being tracked, then disabled the tracker and turned it around."

"It's possible," agreed Avalon.

"Not tae me," cut in Frazer, "I would have thought they wouldn't risk coming back south with et, not unless they are stupid."

"But it's unmarked and they had a two hour start," insisted Ross.

"So, if we consider they *are* returning south, *why*, has to be the question?" Avalon asked.

"Simply to throw us off the scent, we'll be looking north while they take it to Aberdeen or somewhere to empty it," offered Ross.

"Okay, we'll put a wider area on alert but I can't see most traffic sections being arsed with a stolen trailer," said Avalon with a slight frown. He looked at the sheet once more then added, "neither can I see the point in having the place where the trucks were swapped checked over as it's a regular pull-in by all accounts, but we ought to ask the local hauliers if they saw anything," he looked up to them again. "I'll ask forensics to check the truck over though, okay, let's crack on, Megan I want you to check records for anyone in the area that has 'previous' for this type of crime, I'm going to have a look at the address Scobie gave us," he looked at Mackinnon, "Rory, you're with me," the two of them left for the car park.

Avalon set the satnav for the address that Frazer had given him and set off for the Scorguie area. Mackinnon was quiet in the car and Avalon wondered if he should break the ice.

"What do you think of it so far?" he asked.

"Good, it's what I expected but I didn't think we would be quite this undermanned," he replied.

"It's not always this bad, but most stations have some shortfall these days." Mackinnon nodded but offered no further observations, Avalon thought he must just be the quiet type, not like Mack, he could talk until doomsday once he started. As they closed in on the place marked on the satnav, Avalon decided to drive past to check what was there, but he saw nothing out of the ordinary. A car was parked on the drive but no sign of any activity or a missing truck trailer. He jotted down the registration number of the car and then decided next time he bumped into that weasel Scobie he would kick his criminal arse for him. He had another look around and then decided it was a waste of time so headed off back to the station. Avalon tried to think of something else to say to get Mackinnon talking but nothing came to mind, he then asked a question about something that had puzzled him some days earlier.

"What do you know about the phrase "Old Clootie?" Mackinnon glanced at him for a second and then said,

"Auld Clootie is the Scottish name for the devil, I think it means 'cloven foot'."

"I know it's the devil," said Avalon, "but is there anything else?" Mackinnon shook his head.

"I don't think so sir, why?"

"Oh, I was talking to someone the other day and one of them mentioned Old Clootie and just for a moment..." Avalon paused to think, what exactly he had thought? "maybe it was my imagination," and he

146

concentrated on driving. Mackinnon said nothing, was this one of those moments Mack had warned him about? He thought it better if he kept quiet.

"Tell me you've got something," announced Avalon throwing his car keys on the nearest desk. He was reacting to what he thought was a 'buzz' in the room.

"Probably nothing," said Frazer, "but I've found two names that fit the bill when et comes to truck thefts.

"Tell me more," said Avalon pouring a coffee, Mackinnon returned to his seat and began working at his computer.

"Toby Cheeseman and Bobby Cotter, both done time for similar robberies and both out at the moment," she elaborated.

"Tell him about Cotter," added Ross.

"Well, I know him of old, I once used his information on a sting, the problem was, he was lying and we found nothin', while we were busy, a gang hit somewhere else," she explained, Avalon could see she had a score to settle with him.

"He was caught though and was found guilty, all counts were van and truck robberies," added Ross.

"But this is different, they took the whole thing," pointed out Avalon.

"They may have changed tactics, you learn a lot in prison," added Ross. Avalon sighed and sat on a spare chair.

"The other thing es," added Frazer, "when we rang up the haulage company to ask about these two, et seems Cheeseman used tae work for them cleaning the trucks but they let him go as he was suspected of stealing from some of the drivers."

"It sounds like we need to speak with him then,"

suggested Avalon.

"There's no address for Cotter, but we do have a 'last known' for Cheeseman, from the haulage company," explained Ross. Avalon nodded and then asked,

"Any movement on the murder case?" Ross shook his head slowly.

"Nothing yet, but I'm interviewing his wife in the morning," said Ross.

"Er, sir?" came the tentative voice of Mackinnon, "I put a message on a Tolkien forum about the runes on the parchment and someone has answered that he can read them." Avalon looked at Ross and Frazer and then back to Mackinnon.

"Good move Rory, see if you can get him to come in for an interview," said Avalon.

"Er, problem is, he lives in Canada," replied the DC. Avalon smiled a little and then shook his head.

"Okay Rory, send him a low resolution mage of the lettering but don't tell him what it's about. Make up some story."

"Yes sir," nodded Mackinnon.

"Oh and check on the registration number of the car we saw up at Scorguie," he added. The phone rang in the booth, Avalon made steps towards it.

"Avalon."

"*You got a minute?*" it was Lasiter.

"Yeah, your place or mine?" asked Avalon.

"*Mine, et's more private.*" Avalon put down the phone and left, saying he would be back in half an hour. As Avalon turned the corridor, he saw a face he recognised coming towards him.

"DI Davies," smiled Avalon and he held his hand out.

"Hello James, how are you?"

148

"Fine, fine, but how are you, are you coming back soon?" Avalon felt that the handshake wasn't as vigorous as it used to be, Davies still looked tired, he had lost weight, but there was something very different about him, something inside that Avalon couldn't quite grasp.

"No, not for some time, anyway, nice to see you again," and he turned and walked away. Avalon was shocked, it was almost as if Davies was embarrassed to see him. He continued to Lasiter's office, knocked lightly, and walked in.

"What is it?" he asked. Lasiter pointed to the seat opposite. "Oh, I just passed Davies in the corridor, he didn't seem very pleased to see me," added Avalon as he sat.

"Not surprising es et?" replied Lasiter, raising his brows.

"What, because of the security van case?"

"Of course, you blew his investigation out of the water, if I had been Davies I would have had you marching back to Wolverhampton," Lasiter looked very serious about his comment and even raised his voice a little.

"I know he was angry, that was to be expected but-"

"No buts," interrupted Lasiter, "you overstepped the mark, as I told you at the time," he lowered the volume as he continued, "anyway, that's water under the bridge." Avalon was still reeling slightly from Lasiter's outburst, they were equals in rank now, but Avalon still considered him senior.

"So why do you want to see me?" he eventually asked.

"Et seems that Croker has a past, we don't know

149

what et es but something happened that stopped his career dead en et's tracks."

"Oh?" said Avalon as if it was a question.

"Up until this event, his career was that of a model detective. High solve rate on some high profile cases, he was tipped to get a superintendent's job. Then suddenly, wham!" Lasiter slapped his fist into a cupped hand for effect, "posted off to Newcastle as a DCI, where *they* spent two years trying to get rid of him."

"I see," nodded Avalon, "we drew the short straw then?"

"Just bad luck," shrugged Lasiter, "Anderson moved on just at the wrong time."

"Well thanks for the heads-up," and Avalon began to rise.

"There's more," insisted Lasiter. Avalon let his body sink back into the chair. "The Superintendent and the Assistant Deputy Commissioner know him of old and he isn't liked."

"How do you know all this?" asked Avalon with a deep frown.

"A friend I know plays golf with one of them and tipped me the wink," smiled Lasiter. Lasiter's smile was never something you could forget and Avalon was positive he had never seen it before, neither was he sure he wanted to see it again. It was like a mixture of trapped wind and toothache.

"A friend of yours?" squinted Avalon, "Davies isn't it?" insisted Avalon. Lasiter's smile vanished and he nodded slowly. Avalon thought about this for a moment, so Davies played golf with some high ranking officer, Davies, the same man who arranged for him to be seconded, the same man Avalon now knew disliked him. The man, whose career, Avalon had probably ruined. He swallowed.

"So why would Davies tell you this, what's in it for him?" he then asked.

"I know what you're thinking, Davies wants his job back and you are en his way," asked Lasiter with a straight face.

"The thought may have crossed my mind."

"Davies is'nae like that, anyway, I don't think he *wants* his job back. He just wants to help out."

"He can't do that, even if he had the ear of the Queen of England, he couldn't circumnavigate the police process," insisted Avalon.

"No, but ef the proper working of the CID es compromised, someone will have to act."

"I won't have anything to do with sabotage, even if it is to get rid of Croker, anyway, we could end up with someone worse, like you." Avalon didn't smile, he let Lasiter figure it out. Lasiter pursed his lips and dropped his head.

"I'm not suggesting anything of the sort but I told Davies about the demarcation that Croker has instigated and *he* thinks et goes against policy." Avalon thought for a moment.

"All I want is more staff," insisted Avalon, "nothing more and nothing else really matters to me. I can deal with the likes of Croker in my own way."

"Staffing is one thing I brought up with Davies, he came to tell me that there are to be changes in that area," nodded Lasiter. Avalon looked considerably brighter at this prospect, "the brass are as concerned as us about it but don't expect a flood of new blood, it will be a trickle."

"Anything is better than no flow at all," he admitted.

As Avalon returned to the Cave, he wondered if anything would come of what Lasiter had been saying, more staff would make such a difference to their work. He then wondered if his name was being spoken of in high circles, as the man that ruined the career of the popular DI Davies. He made the decision not to mention any of the conversation to anyone else.

~~~~~~~

Ross wasn't the obvious choice of character to interview a recently bereaved woman, particularly one whose husband had been tortured in such a savage way, but as usual, Ross seemed to be able to adapt under adversity. He had hidden sides to him that Avalon had experienced at first hand.

"Just take it steady Mrs Clacher, there's no rush," said Ross in soft tones but no matter what he said, he wanted out of there as soon as he could. Mackinnon was taking notes as she spoke.

"If I can help I'm happy to, anything to find the disgusting people that did this," she said holding onto her handkerchief. She had obviously been crying earlier as seen by her red, puffy eyes, but for now, they were dry. Ross wanted to make the questions as easy as he could, so they could be off as soon as possible.

"Do you think your husband had any enemies or any associates that may bear any grudges?" he eventually asked.

"No," she said shaking her head, "I don't think so, but I didn't know any of the people he dealt with in his business," she paused, "you would have to ask his business partner about that."

"That would be a Mr Gary Hunter would it not?"

"Yes, she nodded, "Alan knew him for many years, he started as a driver but he has a very good business brain Alan always said."

"I understand he left the running of the business to Mr Hunter in recent times," said Ross. The woman nodded again and explained.

"He wanted us to see some of the world and we were reasonably comfortable, so Alan spoke to Gary about it and they decided that Alan would take a back seat and let Gary handle most of the running of the company."

"I see," said Ross, "were you happy with that?"

"Oh yes, I told Alan he had worked hard over the years and it was time he spent some time off, you know, enjoy early retirement and then this..." she began to cry again.

"Well, I think that's all Mrs Clacher, oh and did you find a recent photograph of Mr Clacher for us as I asked?" She nodded between the sobs and lifted her handbag. She pulled out a colour photograph of the man with a big smile standing by a truck. "Thank you for your help Mrs Clacher, we will be in touch as soon as we know anything," and they left the house.

"Is it just me," asked Ross when he and Mackinnon were back in the car, "or does anyone else see a connection with something here?"

"You mean the truck connection?" smiled Mackinnon.

"Oh, so I'm not going crazy? An owner of a truck company is murdered and a few days later a truck goes missing," sighed Ross.

"Coincidence?" offered Mackinnon. Ross just shrugged and started the engine.

"Let's go and talk to Gary Hunter," said Ross.

Frazer put down the phone and walked into the booth.

"Toby Cheeseman es still at the same address, et's been confirmed. Do you want me to go and talk to him?" Avalon thought for a moment.

"What, and leave me here all alone?" he replied without a whiff of a smile and then added, "we'll wait for Ross and Mackinnon to get back before we decide on that one." Frazer nodded and went back to her desk. Avalon soon followed and went to look at the whiteboard on the wall of the almost empty office. He looked at the detail, all that had been added was the name of the victim and some small items of forensics. Avalon felt as if the board hadn't changed for days and it was beginning to get to him. Frazer, the only other person in the room, said,

"I suppose you've noticed the truck connection?" Avalon turned his head towards her as he folded his arms.

"Yeah but I think it's just odd timing, it would be easy to read something into it that isn't there," and he turned back to the wall. For several moments he pondered the items, then unfolded his arms and sat in Mackinnon's seat returning his gaze to the whiteboard.

"So what're y' thinking?" she asked.

"I don't know, probably nothing, I just can't see we've missed anything and yet, as it stands, there's nothing here to make any sense of the crime." He folded his arms again.

"Start from the top? A colleague many years ago once told me, ef you can't see anything you're not looking hard enough." Avalon turned to her with a slight smile.

"Yes, a few of the 'elders' I have come across

154

have said that same thing," he paused and nodded, then turned back to the wall, "tosh though. If you can't see it, it's usually because it isn't there." Frazer shrugged then stood and walked closer to the wall.

"I don't always agree with that," she studied the items on the wall and then began to list them. "So, body was found, tortured, and mutilated. He had been murdered and then moved to a public place and left for someone tae find." Avalon nodded slightly then replied.

"It was made to look ritualistic but placed to ensure that everyone would know it had happened."

"So," continued Frazer, "what possible motive could the bad guys have for that?"

"A warning, plain and simple. They are setting an example, saying 'you could be next'."

"Unless it really is ritualistic," insisted Frazer.

"I discounted that because it seems too obscure," replied Avalon shaking his head.

"Okay, then we come to the fact that et isn't an easy place tae get the body to," Frazer continued, "which means they took risks." Avalon nodded once more.

"Which means the actual place is relevant to who the message may be directed at, or there is a connection with the victim," insisted Avalon. Frazer became quiet, she leaned on a desk and glanced over the details once more.

"Well, nothing comes to mind, unless the victim has some hidden past, we're still fumbling en the dark," she admitted. Avalon was silent, the parchment seemed unrelated to anything, the runes could just be 'smoke and mirrors' and the wheelbarrow was just a nonsense. He sighed.

"We need more damn staff," he hissed just as the door opened.

"Not this side of Christmas," said Frazer as Ross and Mackinnon came in.

"Anything?" asked Avalon. Ross shook his head.

"Not much, if the victim was involved with crime, the wife doesn't know about it," and he placed the photograph of the victim on the wall at the side of his name, "and we've also been to talk to his business partner, he seems in the clear. He almost lives at work, so he has an alibi for the whole period from the drivers." Avalon looked at the picture of Mr Clacher, it was in such a contrast to the last time he had seen him. "What about the truck connection?" added Ross.

"We've just been talking about it but it could just be pure coincidence," informed Avalon.

"I'm not so sure, the business partner says they had two trailers stolen about a year ago and they have also had their share of vandalism to the trucks." This made Avalon stand, then, he looked at Ross.

"Vandalism? Did you get details?"

"Yes," replied Ross, "Hunter thinks it may have something to do with a court case Mr Clacher was involved with last year."

"We better check on that then, where are the details?" asked Avalon.

"Flicks has it in his notepad."

"Flicks? I assume this is Mackinnon's new nick-name?"

"Probably, we can't decide yet," smiled Ross glancing at Mackinnon, "so we better get started typing these notes up then." Avalon nodded.

"I want all the details of the vandalism on the wall too, stolen trailers are one thing, but if someone was vandalising the trucks, it may well be related to this previous court case, which we also need to know about."

156

Ross gave a single nod and then Avalon added, "Me and Megan are off to see Toby Cheeseman if we can find him. Do some deeper digging into Alan Clacher."

Cheeseman's wife wasn't pleased to see detectives on the doorstep but she confirmed he was home but was busy. As Avalon stood on the doorstep trying to convince Mrs Cheeseman that they would need to talk to him, even if it meant taking him to the police station, he noticed movement behind her.

"Et's alright Karen, I'll talk to them," and reluctantly she moved back into the house as he came to the door. "What's thes about?" he asked folding his arms in a challenging manner.

"Mr Cheeseman, I'm Detective Inspector Avalon this is DC Frazer, we would like to ask you a few questions, that's all," said Avalon.

"What about?"

"Can we come in, it would be easier?"

"No," replied Cheeseman. Avalon looked down and nodded slightly.

"Very well, we understand you know Robert Micheal Cotter," said Avalon.

"Aye, what of et?"

"When did you last see him?"

"When I came out of Gateside, I hav'nae seen em since," frowned the man.

"Gateside?" asked Avalon looking to Frazer.

"It's the old name for Greenock," explained Frazer.

"Still wet behind the ears es he?" asked Cheeseman, looking to Frazer, but nodding at Avalon. She gave him a neutral stare.

"Where were you on the 20th and 21st of July?" asked Avalon without emotion.

157

"Not sure, I thenk I was here with the wifie," sighed the man.

"I'm sure she'll confirm that?"

"I'm sure she will," smiled Cheeseman.

"We understand that you used to work for Crisp Brothers Haulage?" asked Frazer. The man gave a muted chuckle.

"And I bet they told you porkies about me did they?"

"They said they ended your employment due to complaints from the drivers," explained Frazer.

"Et was all bullshit, they found out I had been en the nick and that was that, they sacked me," insisted the man, unfolding his arms.

"Well that's all Mr Cheeseman," Avalon left quite a pause for effect, "for now, but if you do hear from Mr Cotter I'd appreciate a call," and he handed the man a card. He slowly took it from the detective and glanced at it. He then smiled at Avalon and skimmed the card down his short drive.

"Are you Megan Frazer?" he asked looking at her.

"Good day Mr Cheeseman," said Avalon and he turned noticing that Frazer had been affected by the comment, and just for a second, he thought she was going to say something, but she followed him down the path. Back in the car he started the engine and drove away then asked,

"What was that about?"

"I've no idea," she replied but he could see she was still angry.

"Two things tell me that isn't true, firstly why did he recognise your name, and secondly, you are fuming?"

"Come on boss, you know cons talk about who

158

was on their case, et happens and I've helped put a few away in the past believe et or not," she explained, and then with a sudden intake of breath, she continued, "and yes I'm fuming, I just wanted to slap that grin off his face."

"I thought you were going to at one point," said Avalon quietly.

"It's taken some years tae stop myself but when you come across a lowlife like that et pushes the limits of my patience." Avalon shrugged.

"It's part of the job, you know that."

"Aye, et es," she admitted, "but et doesn't make it right." Avalon was beginning to see why Lasiter seemed concerned about her, she had a hot temper and certainly struggled to control it. "We put 'em away for some petty crime," she continued, "and where do we send them?" she shook her head, "to places like Greenock. They're called prisons but they're higher education centres for criminals, they go in small time crooks and come out with the best vocational training the tax payer can afford." She folded her arms and looked out of the side window.

"As much as I agree with you, there isn't much option, community programs don't work very well and apart from cutting a hand off, or branding, I don't see other routes," frowned Avalon as she turned to stare at him. "The bit about cutting hands off and branding was a joke," he insisted returning the glance. She looked back out of the side window. Yes, Avalon could see exactly what Lasiter was worried about, Frazer was a time bomb and the fuse was short. He would have to reconsider how she was used in the future.

When Avalon returned to the office, Ross had more

news, it wasn't exactly bad, but it was just that it would stretch their resources even further.

"The Sneaton brothers have been arrested in Glasgow," he smiled.

"It's about time," replied Avalon, as he poured a coffee, "the only problem is, most of this section may be called to the trials and there's loads of paperwork to prepare for it." The Sneaton brothers had taken major roles in the security van robbery earlier in the year and, though they were not apprehended at the time, there was plenty of evidence and witness statements to ensure that the robbery would add extra sentences to whatever Glasgow had on them.

"I can't see them going to trial until later in the year, with their reputation it's going to be a big deal," insisted Ross. Avalon nodded, and then, as an afterthought said,

"Maybe this is an excuse to go and see Scobie to give him the good news," said Avalon with a slight smile, "and to find out why he spun us the crap about Scorguie?" Ross raised his eyebrows.

"Yeah, we could do."

"Take Mackinnon with you and see what our favourite weasel comes up with, he'll probably crap himself when he realises he will finally have to testify against the Sneaton brothers," grinned Avalon. Ross nodded and stood, then called over to Mackinnon.

"Get your reflective underwear on Flicks, we're off out."

"Me again?" smiled the young DC.

"You can stay here with your paperwork if you like," added Ross.

"I'll get my jacket," nodded Mackinnon, "oh, the car up at Scorguie checks out with a chap that has lived there for years, no prior convictions." Avalon gave a nod as if it was what he was expecting then as an afterthought Mackinnon added, "I also got a reply from the Canadian runes chap."

"And could he tell us anything?" asked Avalon, assuming he couldn't.

"Well he said that there are nine separate characters but not all of them are from the alphabet he knows, he says it could be from two character sets."

"Oh," replied Avalon.

"But he did say that he tried lots of permutations but it didn't make any sense," added Mackinnon.

"So it could just be gobbledygook," put in Ross.

"Yes, it's possible," replied Mackinnon with a shrug.

"Okay, it was worth a try," conceded Avalon accepting more proof that the parchment was just another red herring and Ross led them from the office. As soon as they had left, Avalon called Frazer into the booth.

"Yes boss?" she asked with a neutral look.

"Have you got something on your mind?" he asked, pointing to the seat for her to sit.

"You mean about this mornin'?" she asked with a dark look.

"Well, you have to admit, you let yourself get taken in with his question." She was silent for a moment staring down at the desk, then looked up and said,

"I probably got angry but I was completely under control."

"I hope so Megan because I didn't think that myself."

"It won't happen again," she insisted.

"Is there anything you need to tell me?" he asked

in a softer tone. She shook her head and tightened her lips, then stared at him. He knew there was something going on in that head and he hoped with all his heart that it wasn't something destructive. He raised his eyebrows and nodded slightly, then said,

"Okay, we need to go through the Beauly case again, from top to bottom. There may be something we are missing, at least I hope there is, I'll have a look through the door-to-door statements, you concentrate on the forensics reports," he said and Frazer returned to her desk. Ten minutes later he stood and walked over to her with the statements folder. "Did you notice this one when you looked through them?" He placed the folder on her desk and tapped his finger on the sheet. Frazer read quickly through the statement and then said,

"Yeah, the man told one of the PCs that he saw three drunks on the night, but when he was interviewed later, he said he had got the wrong night," she nodded and then looked up to him.

"Does that sound fishy to you?"

"Aye et did and I rang him, but he still maintained he was in error," she explained. For a second, Avalon looked blank and then he looked at the sheet.

"You know the place better than me, would he be able to see the Priory from that address?" Frazer looked at the name and address, and thought for a moment, gradually, she began to nod.

"Yes, I would think so, but I doubt et would be a clear view, the problem es he could be lying but we can't do much about et ef he doesn't want tae help can we?"

"We can go and talk to him and try to poke holes in his story," replied Avalon, "assuming he *is* lying," he added as he reached for a phone. He picked up the sheet with the contact details. "How old is he?" he asked as he

162

dialled.

"He sounds about retiring age on the phone," she shrugged.

"Hello, is that Mrs Tedder?" he asked as the phone was answered by a thin female voice.

"*Yes*," said the woman.

"Can I speak to Mr Tedder please?" and she went to find her spouse.

"*Hello*," said the male voice in a clearer dialect.

"Mr Tedder? This is Detective Avalon from Inverness, I'd like to ask you some more questions if that's possible."

"*As I already said Detective, I got the night wrong.*"

"Yes I saw that, the thing is Mr Tedder, we now think that there is a connection between your sighting and the murder," Avalon said, and he glanced over to Frazer to see how she was reacting to the DI telling a lie.

"*Aye, that as well might be but I'd rather not get involved,*" the man insisted.

"I'm afraid you are already involved, can we come over and sort this out?" The man tried every excuse, but Avalon made sure he knew he wasn't going away, in the end, Tedder agreed. It was late in the afternoon by the time Avalon and Frazer were let into the house and they sat on the sofa with Mr Tedder in an easy chair. The little wife went off to make tea. They were both in their late sixties Avalon thought, and the house and its ornaments seemed to confirm this.

"You see Detective," began Tedder, "after you called, I realised my mistake. I was saying to the wife, it was the night I took a sleeping pill and I thenk I imagined the whole theng."

"And it's taken you this long to realise that?"

asked Avalon.

"Yes, exactly, I've not been sleeping too we-"

"Why are you lying to us Mr Tedder?" interrupted Avalon tired of the vacillating man.

"It's not a lie Detective, I was confused," insisted Mr Tedder.

"It could be construed as hindering the police in an investigation," said Avalon, raising his eyebrows slightly theatrically. The man baulked a little at this and pondered a while.

"I wanted tae help, I really did but I'm scared now," he eventually admitted.

"Why are you scared Mr Tedder?"

"Well, when I heard there had been a murder, I thought that the people I had seen were possibly involved and I should report et, but after hearing stories about what happened tae him, I wondered ef et was any o' my business," he paused as the wife entered.

"We don't get many police officers here but we've had loads in the last few days," she smiled placing the tray on a small coffee table. It was clear Mr Tedder wanted her out of the room quickly, so Frazer made a move.

"Well Mrs Tedder, with a murder on the doorstep that's tae be expected," she said.

"I know," smiled the aging woman, "it's exciting. Did Ernest tell you he saw it all?"

"That's enough dear," he replied and made a sign with his hand to indicate she was losing her marbles. She probably had dementia thought Avalon, but that put more importance to the statement she had just made. Tedder ushered her out of the room and then returned to his seat looking up at the two stone gargoyles that Avalon and Frazer had become. It worried the man.

"As I was sayin', I... I wanted to tell but after I heard he had been ripped apart by some crazed sect I... I panicked, I did'nae want tae get involved with such a thing," he stuttered.

"As I said, you are already involved and withholding evidence is very much frowned upon as you know." The man looked down at the coffee table and began to ring his hands. "You need to tell us everything you saw Mr Tedder," demanded Avalon.

Chapter Six

A new day always brought new opportunities and new hope, though James Avalon wasn't the most optimistic person when it came to his personal life, he did feel much better about himself of late. He was beginning to see the flaw in his thinking, and rather than just winding up Ross about the way he put his detective logic into all things, he actually started to believe it was indeed the way forward. He was a little early this particular morning as he knew he had much to do. It was raining of course but he was out of the house and in the car before there was any sign of Mrs Pink, true, having a murder case that was going nowhere wasn't conducive to good sleep but he had plans, some of which would have to wait until later. Once at the station he went straight to the office and brought the coffee machine to life, then checked emails. With nothing to pique his interest, he pulled out his mobile phone and ordered a sizable bouquet of flowers to be delivered to his ex-wife, which was to go with an extended note, apologising for being a fool. It wasn't a rushed note, he had composed it in his head the previous night. It was honest and forthright but it told Carol he totally understood her feelings and he had been blinkered and idiotic. He stressed he hoped they would remain good friends and she might someday forgive him for being a thorn in her side. He finished with a simple line.

"*If EVER, for WHATEVER reason you need my help, to talk or to complain to, I will ALWAYS be there for you.*"

He still loved her, he always would, she was everything he wanted, and without her, he knew deep down, he would never feel complete. He emailed the note to the florist and asked that it be put into an envelope.

He then went down to see one of the traffic unit officers who was something of a car expert, Ross referred to him as a 'petrol head'. Avalon was eager to pick his brains about what might be an ideal car for him. Unfortunately, they said the officer wasn't in, but they would pass on Avalon's message when the officer started his shift, so he returned to the office and found his team were gradually arriving and starting their first work of the day. Usually that was paperwork, it was endless and constant, like a poison, it seeped its way into every aspect of the job, but then again, it wasn't the only poison in the police force. The draconian, 'stop and search' laws were turning what little faith the public had in the police, into global hatred and in recent years, the changes made to Police Scotland had thrown up critical flaws in the whole system and, in a few cases, people were being seriously let down. What the public didn't seem to understand was that many officers were also against these changes but could do nothing about them. Just because policy seemed to be issuing from the mind of a six-year old child didn't mean that the average copper on the beat thought it was a good idea. That average copper had to implement it of course. Avalon stood and walked over to Ross who had just arrived, he looked out of the window in contemplation, watching the drizzle fall from beneath antagonistic clouds. When Avalon had returned the previous evening, Ross had told him that Scobie had been nervous about the idea of testifying against the Sneaton brothers, but he realised he had no choice, on the matter of the tip-off he had given DI Avalon, he insisted it was reliable but he would only discuss it with the DI himself. Ross had made arrangements for someone to bring him to the station when Avalon would be available.

"When do you want Scobie bringing in?" asked Ross removing his jacket and taking his seat. Avalon turned from the window.

"Later," he shrugged and then turned his attention to the previous evening's meeting with Mr Tedder, he took a marker pen from Ross's desk and went over to the whiteboard and noted his findings.

"What's that?" asked Ross looking at the board.

"A sighting by an elderly resident of Beauly," he replied as he completed the details. He placed the cap back on the marker pen and used it to point to the words he had just written. "A *Mr Tedder* says he saw what he thought were three drunks staggering towards the rear wall of the Priory on the night the body was taken there. He says it was three-twenty in the morning as he remembered glancing at his bedside clock after returning from the toilet. He says he checked the time as he considered it was late for drunks to still be out and about."

"So we think this was them moving the body?" he asked.

"Probably," nodded Avalon, "either way, if it wasn't them, we need to speak to these three," and he tapped the words on the board to emphasise the point.

"It does seem tae fit," added Frazer, "they seemed

168

tae be having trouble keeping the centre man on his feet and one of them ended up carrying him."

"Any other details?" asked Ross.

"Nothing case breaking and I'm not sure the man is a reliable witness, but he says there was a vehicle parked just off the drive under a copse of trees," frowned Avalon, "probably a small van and probably white, but could have been silver."

"He did say that he saw movement near the wall of the Priory but et was too dark tae make out detail," added Frazer, "he thought they were probably relieving themselves by the wall and so he went back tae bed." Ross nodded and after a few seconds of consideration, he shrugged and said,

"As you said, not case breaking."

"No, but if it was the people who dropped off the body, two things come to mind," stated Avalon, "firstly, just two men must have got the body over that wall, which seems a Herculean task. Secondly, Mr Tedder thought that the man in the centre of the three was clothed and that doesn't fit with what we know."

"Maybe they dressed him for the move," suggested Frazer.

"That's possible," nodded Avalon, "but not likely." He leaned with his back on the wall at the side of the board and folded his arms. "It would take time to remove the clothing afterwards and in any case we know from forensics that the body was naked when it was pushed over the wall."

"Then we have to discount the sighting," insisted Ross.

"Not discount it, just put it to one side," concluded Avalon returning to the window. He held his hands behind him, cupped in the small of his back, as he

169

watched the traffic roll past the building and then his phone began ringing. Making his way back to the booth, he wondered if there might be any CCTV cameras in Beauly town that may show a light coloured van on that night though it was likely it would be stolen even if it did.

"Avalon," he said into the phone.

"Oh, DI Avalon, you wanted tae have a word with me, it's Sergeant Collins from traffic?"

"Oh, yeah," replied Avalon, he had forgotten about that, "yes it's nothing urgent, I'm thinking of getting a new car but I know nothing about them and wanted some advice."

"Yes certainly, pop down if y' like and we'll see what you're after," replied Collins.

"I'm a bit busy at the mo, can we do this a bit later?"

"Aye, you could always send me an email with what you're looking for and I could tell you what I think."

"Excellent idea, I'll send you an internal mail," he thanked the sergeant and went back into the Cave. "Rory, can you find out if there are any CCTV cameras in Beauly town, if so, see if we can get access to any footage for the night of the murder?" Mackinnon nodded and started ringing around. Avalon turned to Ross and said, "We better get Scobie over and look at this trailer robbery too." He looked over to the whiteboard, it was filling up, or rather it didn't look quite as 'white' but without more information, they were getting nowhere.

He returned to his booth and listed the criteria he had for a car to Sergeant Collins, then he began to check through the written reports of his team for the last two days. It wasn't long after when the door to the cave opened and in walked the recognisable face of PC Dowd, he came to the booth and knocked politely on the frame of the wall being no door for the purpose.

"Dowd," smiled Avalon, " what can we do for you?"

"O-K... er PC Kirk asked me to bring this up for you to have a look at," he held out a copy of the local newspaper, "she said page seventeen is particularly interesting."

"Tell her thanks and will you pass it to DS Ross, he's our fantasy expert?" asked Avalon with a wry sort of smile. To Avalon's surprise, Ross was soon at the booth with the paper.

"Have you read this?" he asked. Avalon shook his head dismissively. "It's..." he paused to find the words, "interesting," Avalon looked up.

"Okay, I suppose we all ought to hear it if it's that 'interesting'," shrugged Avalon rising to his feet. In the main room, Ross rested his backside on his desk and read while everyone who was there listened.

"The main part is the press release we sent out but they have run something at the side of the main article," began Ross. "The title reads, *'Satanic Cults growing in the area,*' and then below it," Ross stopped to fold the paper over to make it easier to handle, "*Devil worship and satanic cults are growing throughout Scotland and the Aird and Loch Ness ward is no exception.*" Ross looked over the top of the paper for a second. "*Our area is becoming a centre of this kind of activity according to spiritual medium, Adreanna Leslie.*" There were audible sighs at this. "Come on people, give me a chance," smiled Ross and he went back to the article. "*Miss Leslie, a well known local medium, says she can feel the negative energy and she*

171

believes that incidents like the horror at Beauly recently are just the start of a 'crusade' of the Satanists."

"What a load of shite," interrupted Frazer, "how the bloody woman has the gall tae bang a drum about Satanists when she claims to talk tae the dead es beyond me."

"Go on DS Ross, let's hear the rest," smiled Mackinnon. Avalon noticed that Rory was still calling Ross by his title, he wasn't sure if that was good or bad. Ross looked down at the article again and continued to read.

"She claims that local activity is so strong that it is making her job of contacting the spirits almost impossible. She is insistent that the police will never solve it, because it is unsolvable. She also says her spirit guide has told her of another body connected to the death that has not been found."

"I can't believe the papers are printing crap like this," interrupted Frazer once more.

"Lack of anything more interesting I would think," replied Mackinnon. Avalon had been quiet and had a reflective expression on his face.

"We may as well hear the rest of it," he said. Ross continued from the paper.

"Over the last few days, she has seen many disturbing images from spirits and says it could be the start of something much bigger. She says the old stories that surround the Priory mean that it has been a 'channel' for this sort of activity for hundreds of years and the place is closely connected with Auld Cloot...ie." Avalon noticed a slight pause in the word 'Clootie' and, instinctively, he looked at Frazer, but she gave nothing away. Ross quickly continued, *"and Beelzebub,"* he concluded.

"That's clinched it for me," said Avalon suddenly, "Rory, ring the paper and get her number, we need her on the case." Mackinnon nodded, picked up the phone but looked up at the others and stopped.

"Joke right?" he asked as Avalon nodded to him. Ross's desk phone rang, he picked it up with his free hand, whilst still reading the paper.

"DS Ross," he said, and he placed the newspaper on his desk. "Right, okay, we'll be down." He replaced the phone and looked at Avalon. "Scobie is here, interview room two." Avalon nodded.

"Okay, let's go and have a word," said Avalon, he and Ross went downstairs. As they reached the ground floor, and made their way down the corridor, Avalon asked,

"What's with the 'Old Clootie' then?"

"What do you mean?" asked Ross.

"I had never heard it before coming to Scotland and now each time it's said, you hesitate, or seem distracted when it crops up."

"I've no idea what you mean," said Ross opening the door to the interview room.

"Mr Scobie," said Avalon flatly as he sat opposite the man.

"Mr Avalon," smiled Scobie, "or should I offer my congratulations Detective Inspector?"

"Quite," said Avalon and then continued, "down to business, you gave us a tip on an address but we checked it out and nothing seems wrong." The smile left Scobie's face.

"I did say Mr Avalon that ef y' went snoopin' afore anythen happened they might scare off."

"Something has happened and we have still seen nothing," insisted Avalon. Scobie looked up to Ross leaning against the wall behind Avalon, and then back to the DI.

"I don't understand that Mr Avalon, I really don't, the information looked good," frowned Scobie.

"What exactly were you told?" asked Ross.

"Well Mr Ross, I wes in a pub having a drink weth an associate and one theng got tae another, then he asked me ef I knew anybody who could drive a truck, an artic ef y' know what I mean?"

"Go on," insisted Avalon.

"A said I did'nae an' he left et at that but later another guy came en that *he* knew, but I did'nae, an' he asked hem." Scobie looked up to Ross again and then down to the table. "I suppose a could o' got et wrong..." he tailed off.

"Got what wrong?" asked Avalon.

"Thes other guy said he knew somebody who could drive a truck and he lived out at Scorguie and he drew a wee map o' where tae go. I tried tae remember et and sort o' drew it out for y's on that note a sent but thes guy had a foreign accent, so I might have got et wrong."

"Who's the associate?" asked Ross.

"I dunna know es real name, a just know em as 'Parky'." Avalon looked at Ross but he just shook his head, it wasn't anyone *he* knew.

"We need more on this Scobie," insisted Avalon.

"I'll do ma best Mr Avalon but I have tae keep a low profile these days as y' know." Avalon narrowed his eyes to Scobie, then asked,

"Do you know someone called Bobby Cotter?" Scobie seemed to think about the name for a moment than said,

"No, a don't thenk so, what's hes angle?"

"Truck thefts," Avalon replied, staring at Scobie,

who raised his weasel eyebrows a little.

"I see," he replied, "a can ask around ef y' like?" Avalon nodded.

"Keep me posted if you hear anything," he placed a card with his mobile number on in front of Scobie, and stood to leave.

"I've been straight Mr Avalon," said Scobie with a little urgency, Avalon turned at the door, "since you gave me a chance I'm meaning. I've turned over a new leaf ef you know what a mean?" Avalon replied but was looking at Ross when he spoke.

"You and DS Ross both then," and he allowed a slight smile and left.

~~~~~~

"So did you find anything from the criteria I gave you?" asked Avalon. Sergeant Collins was quite a large man, tall, with a strong frame and Avalon considered that he may not favour small cars for that reason, which was good, neither did he.

"Well, I've come up with a few options that sort of fit, but it's always gonna come down to money," he smiled, his deep voice suiting both his size and his Inverness accent.

"Doesn't everything?" replied Avalon. Collins took out his notebook and scanned through the page with Avalon's details and approached each entry with an explanation.

"The first criteria was cost, so I looked at cars no newer than 2010," he began, "then you said it had to be medium or large, so that put quite a few out of the contest."

"I hired a small car a few years ago and hated it,"

175

explained Avalon. Collins nodded.

"Well you said you wanted room but didn't say anything about comfort, 'ride' or performance."

"I used to have a Mondeo," shrugged Avalon and Collins smiled.

"So," continued the sergeant, "we come to the last part of your list, you said you didn't want the same car as everyone else on the street and, to be honest, that is where I struggled."

"I can see that," grinned Avalon.

"Yeah it was difficult, I would have said the Skoda until I saw that part," nodded Collins.

"I grew up knowing the Skoda as a butt of all car jokes and they still have a stigma attached to them for me," explained Avalon with a shrug.

"Okay," sighed Collins, "well I have a colossal list of three, with a bonus car if you really want to spend a little more." He tore out the page and handed it to Avalon who raised his eyebrows a little. It was for effect, as he had no idea what two of the cars on the list looked like. He thanked Collins for his help.

"Glad to be of service and if you see something you like, give me a shout and I'll try and arrange to look it over for you." Avalon thanked him again.
Ross came to the booth as soon as Collins had left, he asked,

"So what did he suggest?"

"He gave me a list of three cars that might fit my criteria, but to be honest I'm still not sure," shrugged Avalon.

"I bet there was a BMW on that list, his patrol car is a Beemer."

"Nope."

"No?" said Ross incredulously, "he probably

doesn't know as much as people say then."

"It wouldn't have made any difference if it was, I wouldn't buy one," shrugged Avalon.

"Why? It would be ideal for you."

"When I was back in Wolverhampton, all the drug dealers seemed to aspire to them, so I got used to thinking that if I saw a BMW, there was probably a low-life behind the wheel," explained Avalon.

"None taken," replied Ross with a frown.

"Well, obviously not *all* of them are, but you get my drift."

"There's no point in back peddling, I'm severely wounded," sighed Ross.

"What's a Lexus look like?" asked Avalon with a flat tone.

"A Lexus?" asked Ross almost choking, "he put Lexus on that list?"

"I don't think I said that," frowned Avalon, "anyway, when I get home I'll have a look at his suggestions on the Internet and get back to you." Ross shook his head and walked dejected from the booth. Avalon felt a little guilty for teasing him, he was, after all, trying to help him get the right car, he maintained that his private life could be 'tuned up' a little and maybe the car was the start he needed. Avalon knew that wasn't the case, if there was any tuning to be done, it was from the inside and had nothing to do with material things. He appreciated Ross's interest though and was beginning to see him as a friend as well as a colleague, they got on well and their humour was similar, even if Ross didn't always know when Avalon was joking.

Mackinnon came into the booth carrying his notepad.

"I may have found something boss," Avalon had told Rory not to call him sir in the office, so he had copied some of the others calling him 'Boss'.

"Go on," Avalon said.

"I have done a check on the houses at Scorguie and one of them is a rented property."

"Which one?" asked Avalon.

"It's neither of the two we looked at previously, it's just round the corner from the ones on Scobie's map," he explained.

"Well maybe Scobie's map was a bit out, who's the landlord?" Mackinnon looked down at the pad and said,

"Someone called George Barber," Mackinnon looked back at Avalon, "he has a record, nothing recent but he was sentenced five years ago for small-time cheque fraud."

"Address?"

"I checked with the council, he lives on the Raigmore Estate?" he said it like a question and though Avalon knew where it was, he didn't know many of its road names, "Mackintosh Road," added Mackinnon.

"We probably need to do more digging into his affairs then as we've no real reason to question him." Mackinnon nodded. "See if you can find out who is renting the house from him, I think that's our only course for the moment," asked Avalon and Mackinnon left to continue.

Late in the afternoon, Avalon got a call from DCI Croker, who asked to see him, so Avalon straightened his tie and made his way the office.

"Sit down DI Avalon." There was an air of expectancy in the room, Croker seemed calm, he even sounded fairly civil, he was writing something in a folder and then he closed it and looked up. "I have good news for you and your section," Avalon doubted it coming from the DCI. "Two new personnel have been sanctioned, one officer is from outside but the other has been working in the Community Investigation Unit." Croker pushed a thin file towards him. If Croker was expecting Avalon to thank him, he was sadly mistaken, Avalon knew, from what Lasiter has told him, that if they were getting more staff it was coming from a higher echelon than the DCI.

"It will help sir," he said without any enthusiasm in his voice but he was upbeat about it inside.

"How is the Priory murder going?" Croker asked.

"Slowly, but we are starting to make a little headway." It wasn't a complete lie, they had ruled out the use of a wheelbarrow and discounted most of the statement of a Beauly resident but Croker didn't ask if they were going forward with the case. If he had, the answer would have needed to be utterly different.

"Good," nodded Croker, "we need to put this one to bed as soon as possible." Avalon thought the phrase "to bed" just didn't suit him, he would rather him be antagonistic than use terms to make him sound more 'human'. "I won't keep you then DI Avalon."

"That was more like it," he thought, it was as if Croker had said "sod off and get back to work", he could cope with that from the man but not anything that resembled niceties. Avalon picked up the file and left.

The rest of the day was a mix of going through reports and recapping details from the Priory murder, he had also had a quick glance at the file with the details of the new staff but left it for later, so when a call came in to break the monotony, Avalon was relieved. It had been Ross who had answered the phone as he and Avalon were looking back through the forensic report.

"Oh, why do they think it could be ours?" asked Ross into the phone. After a pause he pulled a sheet of paper towards him and picked up a biro. "Right, go on," he said and he jotted down some details. Ross was nodding and saying, "got that," and "right, yes I understand," and for a moment he glanced at Avalon and then wrote some details down feverishly. "Okay, that's great, thanks for the info," he concluded and put the phone down. "That was interesting," he said as he added a few details to his scribblings, "it looks like our stolen trailer has been found."

"Oh," said Avalon, raising his eyebrows.

"It seems that a driver for Crisp Brothers Haulage saw what he recognised as one of their trailers on the A1 south of Edinburgh. He knew it was one of theirs, as it had a slight scrape down the side of it, so he phoned through to the yard and they gave the police a description of the truck towing it." He stopped and looked for the details on the sheet. "A red Iveco on Polish plates. They sent out a BOLO to their patrol cars but couldn't find it. Later, it was spotted on CCTV at the Newcastle ferry terminal but the ferry was disembarking, so they got on the blower to the ferry."

"Newcastle?" asked Avalon frowning. Ross nodded and continued.

"They then phoned ahead to Amsterdam police who impounded the truck but the driver did a runner," concluded Ross.

"Have the Dutch police found anything?"

"It seems the trailer was empty," answered Ross. Avalon tapped the desk with his index finger.

"Then it looks like whoever took the trailer emptied the contents on the mainland and then moved the trailer on, which also means that maybe two scams are taking place here," he insisted.

"One gang nicks the trailer and takes the spoils from inside and then sell on the trailer for use on the continent?" said Ross wondering what the worth of a trailer was. Avalon was thinking the same thing and had a quick look on the Internet.

"There seems little sense in that, they aren't that expensive, you can buy a second hand trailer and the truck for the price of a new family car," he pointed out.

"Then was there anything special about this trailer I wonder?" asked Ross. Avalon shrugged.

"Could be, get in touch with them and find out." Ross got on the phone and rang the haulage company who said, although the load it was carrying wasn't perishable goods, the trailer was a refrigerated unit. They were more expensive to purchase but neither Ross nor Avalon could see that it would be a very profitable business to go into. By the time he left for home, he still couldn't work it out.

Once he had eaten a light tea, he sat at his laptop and looked at the details of a refrigerated trailer but after several minutes he gave up and decided to relax by checking the list of cars given to him by Collins. Of the three cars listed he didn't like any of them, he considered that none of them were quite 'him'. They all looked like every other car he could see out of his window and that just wasn't his style. Ross had tried to get him to look at a BMW and he did think that a couple he saw on ebay looked okay but they were more expensive than he was willing to pay. He wondered off, looking at other cars instead, cars that he liked the look of, but the cheapest that he saw that he really liked was almost thirty grand. He gulped and went back to reality. The Corvette, he decided, wouldn't be the ideal car for a detective anyway. He heard a noise, it was his phone but it was faint, he reached for it in his jacket pocket and looked back at the screen of the laptop as he answered.

"*Hello, it's Carol.*" It took Avalon back a little as he returned to his seat.

"Hello, I didn't expect to hear from you," he said, "but it's a nice surprise."

"*I got your flowers and the note, it wasn't necessary,*" she insisted.

"I wanted to do it, I was a bit of an arse the other night so I thought I would say sorry," he said, glancing at options on the PC.

"*Well, I better go, I know you must be busy, I just wanted to say thank you, they are lovely.*"

"It's okay, I've just got in, from work, I mean."

"*Oh, right, so how are you?*" she asked.

"Great, I'm just looking for a new car as it happens."

"*New car?*" she said with a little surprise, "*I didn't think you'd ever release your grip on that old Ford.*"

"It released its grip on me actually, I had to have it shot some weeks ago," he smiled.

"*So I'm guessing you've settled in by now?*" she said with a little doubt in her voice.

"Very much, I'm still renting but I'll probably buy something when the house sells."

"*I meant with the job,*" she added.

"Oh, yes, it's fine. It took a little bit of getting used to the differences, particularly with law and the social aspects but I already feel like a native." He didn't want to sound too upbeat but in many ways it was true, he did think it was the best move he had made for years.

They chatted for a while until everything seemed to be said, they agreed to keep in touch and ended the call. Avalon didn't feel as bad as he expected to and he wondered if his change of attitude was working.

He went back to scrolling through images of cars and after a few minutes, he decided to abandon his search but he saw something that caught his eye. It wasn't something he would normally look at and it wasn't on the list, not even the 'bonus' car but he thought that he could live with it. The price made him heave slightly but he could afford it, why not? He then looked for local dealers who may have something like it and he found one, just one but it was a good colour. Dark and moody, not quite the gunmetal grey of the Ford Focus he had looked at on Harbour Road, but black with black and grey trim. The dealer was close by too. He decided to email Sergeant Collins about the car in the morning and then, when he could find time he would go and have a look at it.

~~~~~~

As Avalon set himself down on his seat, he looked out into the Cave and saw everyone hard at work. DS Wilson and Mack had just about wound up their warehouse case and though they had paperwork to finish off, they were now available for other duties. Avalon decided to have another look through the files of the possible new recruits to C Section. The first one was a local officer. He had been working in the Community Investigation Unit, which did a great deal of work in the anti-drug field. Avalon considered someone with that sort of experience would be a real asset to the team and looking at the file of DC Ewan Pottinger, proved him to be quite experienced even though he was still a DC. Though he had been a police officer for ten years, he had worked in civilian capacities for the police force before that. At thirty-four years old he had been a detective for five years and seemed to move around departments quite a bit, his last tenure, with the CIU, for just fifteen months. Avalon thought he was likely to be impatient but quick thinking. The second recruit was a different matter. DC Alison Boyd was thirty-nine years old and though being a police officer for almost twenty years, had only been a detective for the last two. Avalon considered that the two officers were opposite sides of the coin but time would tell. He placed the folder in his drawer, turned on his PC screen and began work in earnest. It wasn't long before his mobile rang.

"DI Avalon," he answered.

"*Mr Avalon, et's Antony Scobie,*" said the quiet voice, Avalon wondered if it had been wise giving him the number.

"What do you want?" he asked.

"*Y' asked me tae find out about a Bobby Cotter.*"

"So have you got something?" asked Avalon, sounding a little impatient.

"*Aye, sort of, he's living weth hes girlfriend en the Muirtown area,*" said Scobie, "*someone a know says he talked to hem last week an' he wes still living there then.*"

"An address?" asked Avalon reaching for his pen.

"*The theng is, they're livin' on a boat, an tae tell the truth Mr Avalon, a can'nae find the name of et.*"

"It can't be that difficult, I don't imagine there are that many boats there."

"*There are a few a would say, but the theng is, I heard he's still married an' this girlfriend does'nae know about hes past, so I'm thenken that she does'nae know about es record, ef y' know what a mean?"* said Scobie.

"I can see a cruel side to you Scobie," said Avalon.

"Ah, he means nothen tae me, I'm just doin' my bit," explained Scobie. Avalon considered it was time to try and groom Scobie, he may prove useful in the future.

"So if we pick him up, could this come back to you?" he asked.

"Thanks fer askin' Mr Avalon but a doubt that, the guy that gave me the info hates the little shite." Avalon told him to keep his ear to the ground about truck thefts and rung off. In the main room, Frazer and Mack were out so Avalon called over to Ross. "Do you know what Bobby Cotter looks like?" he asked. Ross shrugged and shook his head. "Can you pull a picture of him then, we need to ID him and ask some questions?" Ross inputted the details into the computer and then read out the result as he sent the image to the printer.

"Robert Timothy Cotter, thirty-eight years old, dark-red hair, blue eyes, five feet six tall weighing around..." he tailed off working it out, "ten and a half stones."

"He should be easy to spot then, a little guy with ginger hair," grinned Avalon. The printer spewed out an image of the man, it was black and white but would suffice. "Fancy a ride out?" he asked.

Muirtown Basin took some finding and Avalon went to see the harbour authorities to find out where they might find the boat and get access. They had forgotten it was Sunday and there was no one there but the security guard was helpful. He told them that he had seen the man he described but wasn't sure which boat he was on. It didn't take long, not being difficult to spot anyway. Ross couldn't believe his luck when a Transit van stopped at the gate and the driver was Bobby Cotter.

"Bobby, can we have a word?" asked Ross and Avalon walked over.

"Coppers, I can smell you a mile off," frowned the man.

"We need to ask you some questions."

"No, so unless you're arresting me, piss off." Avalon stepped forward.

"We could always come down to the boat, I'm sure you've told your girlfriend about your past," he said. The man began to shake his head slowly.

"You lot are a real set of bastards, you know that?" he spat. Avalon just tilted his head slightly like a kitten watching a spider climb down a wall into its reach. "Okay," sighed Cotter, "a few questions but we will have to go to the station, I don't want the girlfriend seeing me talking to you," and he got out of the van. He said nothing during the journey but once they were in the interview room with a cup of coffee, he said,

"So what is it?" He had a similar accent to Ross, not at all broad and he seemed fairly articulate.

"We have had a truck stolen and we are following all the natural routes of investigation," said Ross sitting opposite him at the table, Avalon stood with his hands deep in his pockets.

"You lot never let us go do you, once we are on your books we stay on them?"

"As we said, just questions, such as can you tell us where you were during the early hours of the twenty-eighth of this month?" Ross asked the usual questions and Cotter gave the usual answers but Avalon was watching reactions and he could see something building

186

up in Cotter. His natural, internal polygraph machine was telling him that the man was lying. As Ross wound up the questions, Avalon could see Cotter was agitated and he would probably open up if pushed a little.

"I don't think you are telling us the truth Mr Cotter," he said.

"To be honest I don't give a shite what you think, I didn't do it and I can't do anything to get it through your thick copper skulls that I have gone straight," he replied, raising his voice a little. Avalon pulled his hands from his pockets and paced the room a little.

"Thick?" he said, "well, I'm not sure about that, you see both myself, DS Ross here and many other officers have been to college, even university, some have degrees," there was slight pause before he spun around to the table and banged his hands down with force, "whereas you, *Mr Cotter,* just steal things from people." The man visibly jumped. He tried to calm himself and then said,

"Either charge me and send for a solicitor, or I'm off." Avalon retuned to the door, glancing down at Ross for a second and raised his eyebrows. They couldn't do anymore, he wasn't going to say anything, so they would let him go but the pressure may work, maybe he would make a mistake, maybe not. It was possible he knew nothing about the case but Avalon's instinct said otherwise. Ross sighed and stood.

"Maybe we should have let Frazer interview him," he said in a quiet voice but the reaction from Cotter was dynamic. He stood knocking over his chair and called out,

"Frazer! Megan Frazer! is she still here?" he spat with wild eyes, "you keep that crazy bitch away from me." Avalon and Ross turned to face him but couldn't

187

find any words. The man looked in a panic and Avalon tried to calm him down.

"What are you talking about Mr Cotter?" asked Avalon.

"I told *him* and I'm telling *you*, if I was pushed I would squeal and that's the truth," he called with wild eyes.

"Please sit down. DS Ross, fetch another coffee will you?" Ross looked at Avalon, he clearly didn't want to leave but Avalon's gaze was very determined, he understood and left. Once Cotter was seated and calmed a little, Avalon sat opposite and spoke. "I'm not aware of anything that passed between you and DC Frazer." Cotter lit a cigarette but Avalon considered he needed to give Cotter some space, so he allowed it.

"I told him I would squeal and I meant it," he repeated nervously.

"Told who?" asked Avalon.

"She's bloody mental you know that," he said, his eyes still looking wild. He was clearly agitated as if something tucked away in his memory had come back to haunt him.

"What happened between you and DC Frazer?" he asked calmly. The man lunged forward suddenly putting a finger up to his cheek, pulling the skin taut.

"You see this," Avalon noticed an old scar, about an inch long, "that's where she hit me with a pair of handcuffs." Avalon began to see something, something he had missed, but then again it had been far from obvious.

By the time Ross returned with the coffee, Cotter was calm and the room stank of tobacco smoke.

"Can you arrange for a car to take Mr Cotter home?" asked Avalon as he stood and left the room with

Ross.

"What was that about?" Ross asked. Avalon looked at the floor and back up to Ross.

"It's not that I don't trust you, but what I have heard needs to be thought over before I make any decision," he paused, "but either way, I can't tell you and I need you to keep this quiet," and he walked off.

~~~~~~

"Where's the boss?" asked Wilson as Mackinnon returned to the Cave.

"He's gone to pick up his car," he smiled.

"*His* car?" asked Ross with surprise.

"Well, that's what he said, he asked me to take him to pick up *his* car," repeated Mackinnon.

"Okay," chirped in Mack, "let's run a book, fiver a go tae see who can guess what he buys."

"And what ef nobody guesses it?" asked Frazer. Mack thought for a moment.

"Well, everyone put down a colour too, there aren't that many colours." Frazer was reluctant but she eventually added a fiver and they wrote down their choices. When Avalon came back, the room was quiet and Avalon suspected something. He usually threw down his car keys on his table but this time he didn't. Ross was suspicious, he didn't look like a man who had just picked up a new car. Avalon removed his jacket, hung it on his chair and then walked into the main room.

"Have you got it?" asked Ross with a slight grin.

"Got what?" asked Avalon pushing his hands into his pockets.

"The car," he replied, "because with a modicum of superior detective work we have deduced that our DI

189

has purchased a new vehicle."

"You mean you asked Rory where I've been," he looked at them one by one, "so why the expectant stares, it's just a car?"

"Just a car but one that offers monetary rewards," grinned Mack holding up a sheet of paper.

"You have run a book on which car I've bought?" he asked with surprise. There were no answers, just stares, except for Frazer who seemed disinterested.

"It's no secret," shrugged Avalon, "it's a-"

"Hang on," called out Ross, "is there a window we can see the car park from?"

"Aye, the corridor down to the rest room," replied Mack.

"Okay, I want to have a look, I bet I can find it." As he left, Avalon shrugged and decided to follow him. Ross was by the window in the corridor looking out into the car park.

"You haven't spoken to Frazer have you?" asked Avalon quietly.

"No course not," frowned Ross before looking back down to the cars. "Well, I can't see a Mondeo, so you have broken with tradition but neither can I see a V-W camper van."

"You are telling me someone put that down on the sheet?" asked a doubtful Avalon.

"And neither can I see a thirty year old Ford Fiesta," continued Ross and then said as he pointed, "got it, over there, the white Nissan Micra. Voted worst car of the year for thirty-eight consecutive years and it's only been produced for thirty-four."

"Not guilty," said Avalon and he turned to leave.

"So which is it?"

"You're supposed to be a detective, you work it

out," called back Avalon.

In the office, he agreed to look at the sheet and see if anyone had won. Avalon looked at the suggestions.

"Mack, you said a Mercedes and your colour was red," Avalon smiled and shook his head. "Oh come on Wilson, a Jag?" Wilson shrugged, "and Megan, I don't think I would drive a Skoda under *any* circumstances, and thanks go to Ross for suggesting," he paused, "a Mondeo." He turned to Mackinnon. "Range Rover in black?" Rory smiled and said,

"I thought of those movies where you see the CIA in convoy with four-by-fours with blacked out windows." Avalon gave a smile at this.

"So we are guessing it's none of those?" asked Mack. Avalon looked around and theatrically said,

"Ladies and gentlemen, the winner is," and he pointed to Mackinnon, "Flicks Mackinnon."

"Range Rover?" asked Ross.

"Don't be ridiculous, *black*," frowned Avalon.

"Figures," replied Ross, "suits your humour."

"So are we going to do any work today?" asked Avalon.

"So what's the car then?" asked Ross once more.

"I forget, but it's black," and he turned and walked to the booth, just as the phone nearest the door began to ring. Avalon stopped and looked at it.

"I didn't think that line worked."

"It used to be the incident phone, there must be someone new in the exchange," said Ross as he approached it.

"C Section," he announced and stood for several seconds, "okay, can you give me some details?" said Ross, trying to get his notepad out of his pocket with one hand. Mackinnon helped out and held his own pad for

Ross to use. As Ross scribbled something down, Avalon could see the expression grow, he knew that expression well by now. Something was wrong and the slight glance that Ross threw Avalon made him somewhat concerned. "Right, yes got that," continued Ross. He stopped writing and nodded to Mackinnon to relax with the pad. "Okay, thanks," he said and put the phone down. "Another late one folks," he said and looked up to Avalon, even before he spoke, Avalon knew what was coming. He had considered it through the past few days and with what he had just seen of Ross's expression he wasn't wrong.

"Another body," Ross said.

Chapter Seven

Avalon and Ross hurried downstairs and jumped into one of the pool cars. Avalon had requested it, as Ross had pointed out that the siren and flashing lights fitted would allow them to get through the traffic much faster. The car would also have equipment that they may require. They needed to move fast, as they had some considerable miles to drive, the location being quite a way from Inverness. Several other uniformed officers had been diverted to the spot to protect the scene, and Frazer would follow as soon as she could with Mackinnon.

"Where is this place did you say?" asked Avalon.

"Glen Affric, it's quite a way from here," he replied, speeding out of the car park.

"I hope you've had the training to drive this fast," said Avalon nervously, gripping the sides of the seat, as Ross switched on the siren and raced past a line of traffic. They had little, or no, information about what to expect, so there was not much to discuss along the way, Avalon tried to focus on the road ahead but was finding the journey somewhat hectic. "How did you know which car had all the emergency equipment?" he asked.

"All the pool cars have," he replied swerving a

little to weave out of the traffic.

"The one I was using didn't."

"I'd be surprised if it didn't, it's a bit of a scam. If a car has sirens and lights, it is classed as an emergency vehicle, and in the eyes of the HM Customs and Excise, it doesn't cost much to keep it on the road."

"Really?" replied Avalon, a little surprised, "I suppose the public are going to hate the idea that the police are using a legal loophole to save money."

"Probably but they shouldn't, after all, it's saving the taxpayer cash," replied Ross settling down to a bit of clear road.

"That's a flawed argument, seeing as HM Customs are collecting *for* the tax payer." Ross frowned a little and shrugged.

"I suppose so, I never really considered that." Avalon watched the world whiz by and tried to relax but then thought it quite stupid, how could he relax when he was in the middle of a murder case that was driving him to despair and now another body had been found? He could only hope that this time it was a natural death.

They travelled for over an hour, down the side of Loch Ness, through Drumnadrochit and up into the hills. The scenery began to change, and the forested hillsides became more prominent on both sides of the valley. The road began to climb and as they continued, the overcast sky seemed angry. It was a windy day and the mottled clouds were in a hurry to be somewhere else. Cumulus clouds gathered over the hilltops and Avalon was wondering if the car's emergency kit included any waterproofs. Eventually, the road began to incline down a little and Avalon looked at the valley stretched out in front of them. He began to wish he was sightseeing, rather than going to the scene where a dead body had been found.

"How much further is it?" he asked, becoming sick of the expectation.

"Quite a way yet," smiled Ross. After a few more miles, the road turned sharply right and over a bridge, spanning a good-sized river and Avalon thought what a lovely place it was. He decided to remember the route, it looked like an excellent place to come for a ride out on his bike *if* the sun ever came out again. There was a long, straight road that stopped at a junction and they turned left at a place called Cannich, he noticed they were only seventeen miles from Beauly.

"The road is narrow from here, so I better take it steady," informed Ross as he slowed to keep within the speed limit. The road was narrower and the river now seemed to be ever present until they forked right onto an even narrower road that climbed up the valley side. Higher they went and through the trees, Avalon looked down at the severe drop right at the side of him. His nervousness returned as they continued along the winding track.

"It's a bit out of the way isn't it?" he asked.

"Yeah but the road is usually fairly busy, it's quite a touristy area," explained Ross.

"You've got to like your scenery to come this far out though, and this road..." he went quiet as he noticed yet another almost sheer drop, there was nothing to stop a car coming off the road and plunging down the hillside. There was a car up ahead, but it pulled into a passing place when it saw the flashing blue lights. The road then dropped, or the land came up to meet it, Avalon wasn't quite sure which and then Ross pointed to the left.

"Not far now, that's Dog Falls," Avalon looked at

a small pull-in area and said,

"It's probably tired."

"What?" asked Ross.

Nothing," replied Avalon, not sure if the current situation warranted levity. Not far up the road from there, a marked police car was blocking half of the road near a pull-in. When the officer standing by it saw Ross approach, he quickly waved him past. Avalon liked the idea of the flashing lights, it meant he didn't have to stop to explain who he was. They continued on, it seemed like the journey wasn't going to end, and now Avalon could see why Ross suggested a pool car, they had travelled for at least an hour and the day was growing long. A wonderful sight then met his gaze, the sun peeped through, low, under the clouds for just a second and then as if it was embarrassed, beat a hasty retreat, but to the left, was an expanse of water to behold. Avalon was getting used to the amount of lochs he came across, but this one was regal, like a painting, and it contained islands and headlands. Then, just ahead, he saw several cars, some of them police cars, and a few uniformed officers milling around. There was a rough car park and a road that seemed to head down towards the loch. They pulled up near a patrol car, to where three officers were looking at a map, one of the officers was a Sergeant. They got out and Avalon stretched his legs, saying,

"I feel like we've just driven up from Wolverhampton, and where are all the midges? I expected to be gang raped by them out here."

"It's too damn windy up here," replied Ross and they walked over to the officers.

"Sergeant," said Ross with a brief smile, "DS Ross," he nodded to Avalon, "and DI Avalon, what have

196

you got?"

"Et's pretty bad down there, a male body and et's been there for some time." The sergeant was wearing a frown that said it all, it had been warm and wet, so there would be some decomposition, that was to be expected. Avalon came forward.

"Who found the body?" he asked.

"Three walkers out from Cannich, they decided to stop for a bite to eat and stumbled across et," he folded his arms and leaned on the police car, "we've taken all the contact details, but we took them back to Cannich, they were a bit shaken up. A couple of our people are looking after them." Avalon nodded slowly,

"We better take a look then," he said to Ross, and they asked the sergeant to point the way.

"Et's down the track, follow the blue tape and then your nose," he explained raising his eyebrows. As they walked, the track headed downhill as if it would end at the side of the loch, and then, the stench hit him. Avalon could never explain the smell of a decomposing body to anyone. There was no way to describe it, particularly when it was as thick and pungent as it was there, even with a strong breeze under the protection of the trees. They were still a hundred yards from the source, and he wanted to cover his face. Ross was taking out his hanky and Avalon considered it was a sound idea.

"Well, we know why there are hardly any midges, there's no room because of all the flies," said Ross. There seemed to be thousands of them, constantly battling against the breeze to stay close to their quarry and they began to explore the two warm bodies newly arrived. It seemed almost pointless trying to waft them away, but they tried none-the-less. As they got nearer, they saw what was probably the body, but going further

197

may have compromised the scene, it was a daunting task and the smell was so strong down wind, it was almost like mist. Avalon caught hold of Ross's arm and said through his hanky,

"We better go back and arrange for some lighting, it's going to be dark soon and this is going to take most of the night." Ross simply nodded, he didn't feel at all like opening his mouth, even behind the fabric of the hanky. Avalon had a problem arranging for lighting to be delivered to the site because there was no telephone reception in the valley, but one of the uniform officers was sent down to Cannich to use the radio in the car there. By the time the arrangements were complete, the area was totally cordoned off and they returned to the car.

"What do you want to do?" asked Ross.

"Well I don't want to spend anymore time in there than we need to," explained Avalon, "so I reckon we can take a look when the SOCO team arrive, they will probably put a tent over the place while the body is examined on site." The scenes of crime team did indeed place a white tent over the scene though the wind tried to blow it into the woodland a couple of times, and when Sarah Underwood arrived, she went over to Avalon.

"It's been there a while I understand?"

"Yes," he nodded, "we didn't get too close as we didn't want to compromise the area, and it's a bit ripe down there." It was probably the biggest understatement he had made that year, he knew they would have to see the scene, so he was hoping to get a forensics suit and mask from her team. It certainly wouldn't filter out the stench, but it may make it easier to breath. She looked around the area and turned to leave but before she had gone half a dozen steps, she called back,

"Has the coroner been informed?"

"Yes," called Avalon, " the pathologist is on his way," then she continued towards her team who were 'suiting up'. Soon after, Frazer and Mackinnon arrived and parked close to the pool car, Avalon went over to Frazer.

"Megan, see if there is anyone still about at the Forestry Commission and try to find someone who can tell us how often this area is checked," he asked and she nodded then walked off to try and get a signal on the phone. "Rory, take the pool car and go back to Cannich, find the people who found the body and get full statements from them." Mackinnon got straight to work. Avalon then turned to Ross. "You said that the road is usually busy."

"Well yeah, it's a popular tourist area, people come from all over the world to see the Glen and the lochs."

"So how come this body hasn't been spotted earlier, I mean there's a pull-in for parking so it must be an obvious place to stop?"

"What, you mean you are thinking it was dumped here more recently?" asked Ross with some doubt. Avalon glared at him for a second.

"I know there are some seriously deranged people about, but I can't imagine anyone sticking a badly decomposed body on the back seat of their car and taking it for a spin to a tourist spot can you?" Avalon seemed angry, Ross had seen him like this before, he just sighed and walked away, saying,

"Nope, I don't suppose I can." Avalon *was* angry. He was angry that they already had *one* dead body, another was going to make things much harder with staff numbers so low. He knew they were going to get new personnel but when, and how long would it be before they could be sent out on their own cases?

"New staff!" called out Avalon. Ross turned and saw Avalon staring right at him.

"What?" said Ross.

"New staff, I forgot to tell you, we should be getting two new members to the team."

"How so?" asked Ross with a deep frown.

"It's a long story," replied Avalon, looking out over the water of the loch, "but we are getting them fairly soon, one is based at Inverness, so he should know the area." Ross nodded, more staff would help out for sure, even if it was too few. Avalon noticed the wind was abating and as he looked up at the scudding clouds, he saw that they were breaking up and that meant less likelihood of rain.

The pathologist arrived just before the lights, so with some daylight left, Ross and Avalon dressed in forensics suits to accompany him down the track.

"Hello again Detective Avalon," beamed Sandy Lennox, as he readied himself by his van.

"Hello Professor," smiled Avalon, remembering the title Sarah Underwood had used.

"I have to say," said Lennox, as he struggled with the forensics suit, "it's one of the more salubrious spots to find a dead body." Avalon just didn't have him down as the humorous type and maybe it wasn't humour, maybe he was just always happy. It seemed strange in a profession like his.

"You may change your mind when you go down the track," frowned Avalon.

"Been there a while I heard from one of the uniform officers," he said a little less upbeat, "but no doubt he will still have a great deal to tell us." Avalon couldn't quite get to grips with the man, sometimes he seemed as if he was absent minded, yet, he was totally aware of his surroundings, and he seemed to notice everything. He placed his recording device around his neck and into his inside pocket, then ran a cable down the sleeve of his white suit. "All ready," he confirmed, with a slight smile and he closed the doors of his van. Lennox began to walk down the track, so Avalon and Ross followed him. As was to be expected, as they neared the perimeter of the area, the stench of the rotting corpse made its way through the mask that Avalon had over his face.

The SOCO team were milling around the white tent and surrounding area, making it look like a scene from a science fiction movie, or a nuclear accident. Sarah Underwood was there and a corridor had already been cleared to the tent and the body. Avalon steeled himself for what he would see in there and followed Lennox into the tent. There was a photographer just inside and there, on the floor, lying face up, seemingly naked, was a badly decomposed body. Immediately he saw similarities to the body in the Priory, and his worst fears seemed confirmed, there could be a connection. Flies still buzzed around, but the tent seemed to help with that score, if not the smell. As Avalon looked over parts of the body, it was clear the corpse had been there some considerable time, and identification would have to be done at the mortuary, the body was probably male, but Avalon couldn't be sure on that particular subject. Lennox had begun and was already talking into his recording device, systematically looking for forensic evidence with Sarah Underwood assisting. He stopped recording for a moment to collect specimens and Avalon took the opportunity to speak.

"Do you think he was killed here?" Lenox looked over the body and shook his head slightly.

"I wouldn't like to say at this stage, it's possible but it could be difficult to pin down until later."

"I'll leave you to it then," said Avalon. Lennox nodded and Avalon walked outside. Over near the rear perimeter, Ross was talking with a uniformed officer slightly upwind, and so, he joined them.

"What do you think?" asked Ross.

"I think it could be connected to the Priory murder," replied Avalon, "I couldn't really make out any wounds but I just have a feeling it is connected." He then noticed the tech's setting up the lighting under the trees, it was already becoming a little gloomy. Just up the track, they could see Frazer making her way towards them, so they moved out of the cordoned area and found a better spot further upwind of the tent as Frazer wasn't wearing a suit or a mask.

"Anything?" asked Avalon. Frazer shook her head.

"There's no reception for the phone out here, so I had tae go through the radio at Cannich but there was no one at the Forestry Commission office who could tell me about visitor numbers but, one o' the uniform lads says he lives en Cannich and didn't think this spot was the best place for photographers, they go further up where there es a better view." Avalon nodded as she continued, "et's probably not visited that much, even though et's a good spot tae stop." A small generator started up somewhere on the track, and two of the lights flickered into life, several others came on soon after and the tech's placed them where the SOCO team pointed. Avalon looked towards the water, he saw a table and seat near the shoreline, as he headed towards it, he removed his

202

mask. The air was a little clearer there and he took a few breaths before turning to Ross.

"In some ways, I hope this *is* connected to the Priory murder." Ross nodded, he knew why.

"You're thinking there might be a connection between the victims?"

"Well, it's a hope," said Avalon opening his eyes wider at the thought. Ross replaced his mask and went to have a look in the tent, leaving Avalon to try and clear his nostrils of the pungent odour. Ross soon returned and sat on the seat.

"I can't make much out, it seems too badly decomposed to see any detail and the pathologist is still busy, but you may be right. There doesn't seem to be any clothing there, so that could be an indication."

"Is it male?" asked Avalon.

"I asked the professor about that, he says definitely male," replied Ross, "he's coming out soon anyway, he may have more info." Avalon turned back to look out over the loch again, twice he had attended a body and considered the contrast of such horror set against such a peaceful backdrop. Here was an exquisite landscape, and yet, such a terrible tragedy just yards behind him.

"Admiring the view detective?" It was Lennox, "Ah just smell that cool freshness gliding across the water surface," and he took a deep gulp of air, dropping his mask on the seat by his side. Ross had walked back to the tent and was talking with Sarah, he couldn't see Frazer. Avalon looked back to Lennox, taking another gasp of air, and made a sigh. How the hell the man could separate the funk of a corpse from the crisp air of a Scottish loch was completely unknown to Avalon, he doubted he would shake the smell from his nose for the rest of the month.

"DS Ross tells me you think the body is male."

"Yes, without doubt male, though I have no idea of his age yet."

"What about cause of death, is there any clue to that?" asked Avalon.

"I'm afraid that will have to wait for the autopsy," explained Lennox, taking yet another lungful, "though it does look like foul play."

"Ah, that was to be expected I suppose, being totally naked." Lennox smiled and looked at him.

"Why so detective, he could have just taken a dip in the freezing water of the loch and expired from the shock as he climbed ashore." Avalon nodded slightly.

"And I suppose an unfriendly salmon cut him several times with a sharp implement?" asked Avalon with slight sarcasm.

"Ah," nodded Lennox, "you noticed that?"

"Well," explained Avalon, "from what flesh is left, it seems there are injuries consistent with some sort of attack." Lennox sighed.

"It does look like we will find several injuries possibly pre-mortem," agreed Lennox.

"I really need those results professor, particularly as it looks very similar to the Priory murder."

"It does," agreed Lennox," but these things can't be rushed," and he looked round to Avalon with a smile. "All detectives are so impatient, I think it comes from lack of free time," he added as he picked up his mask from the seat.

"You're probably right," replied Avalon trying to humour him.

"I'm sure of it detective, maybe you need to take up a relaxation hobby, there is a wonderful Scottish pass-time that would be ideal," suggested Lenox taking another sniff of the air.

"Smoking you mean?" asked Avalon. Lenox laughed as heartily as he could under the circumstances.

"Yes, it does seem to be a popular Scottish distraction I agree," he chuckled. Lennox reminded Avalon of the English film actor Jim Broadbent playing one of his 'dotty' old men as he continued, "but I was thinking more of golf."

"I'm with Gladstone on that subject," shrugged Avalon.

"Sorry?" asked Lenox.

"Golf is a good walk spoiled."

"Oh right, yes," and the man laughed again. Avalon noticed Lennox preparing to move.

"Well I should continue and get the body ready to be removed," he smiled and replaced his mask, then headed back to the tent, which was now fluorescing in the glow of the lights, a contrast to the darkening woodland.

By the time the body was being moved to the coroners van, it was fully dark and Avalon walked across to speak to Sarah Underwood.

"There is a possibility that this could be connected to the Priory murder, so if there was a parchment in his hand, we really need to find it," he said.

"If it's here, we'll find it," she insisted and then added, "if it's any consolation, I agree, from what I have seen of the body, there are many similarities." Avalon looked at her inquisitively.

"My goodness, did I just hear a forensics expert make a guess?" There was a hint of a smile in the corners of his mouth.

"No DI Avalon, you didn't, you heard Sarah Underwood make a guess, the forensics expert says 'wait for the report'." She raised her eyebrows and returned to her team who were still working under the lights.

Back where the cars were parked, Avalon and Ross returned to find both Mackinnon and Frazer drinking something hot from plastic beakers.

"Et looks like this pull-in isn't used all that much," began Frazer, "not by tourists anyway."

"What's that supposed to mean?" asked Ross.

"Et's a bit of a 'dogging site'," she raised her eyebrows.

"Who the hell would come all this way to go dogging?" said Mackinnon, his teeth shining in the electric lights.

"Well if you're some sort of expert Rory, enlighten us to what is considered a reasonable distance for that sort of adventure," insisted Ross as Mackinnon looked at the floor.

"Maybe dogging es the wrong term," interrupted Frazer, "anyway, et's used for casual sex sometimes."

"Then someone ought to have noticed a dead body you would have thought?" added Avalon.

"Maybe they did, but in the dark, they may just have thought the smell was a dead deer or something," suggested Ross.

"Well, we first need to establish how long it's been here," said Avalon, "in the mean time, Megan, you and Rory get back to the office and start work on the statements that Rory has from the witnesses who found the body," he noticed Ross glance at his watch. He had forgotten the time, he looked at his own wristwatch. It was ten minutes to eleven, where had the time gone?

206

"no, belay that, do it in the morning. We all need to get some sleep."

As Frazer and Mackinnon drove off, Ross turned to Avalon and asked,

"Are you not taking your own advice?"

"What?" he said looking back from the track, "oh no, I'll stay until the forensics are done, you get off, I'll get one of the uniforms to give me a lift back."

"I'll keep you company then," said Ross, removing his white suit, "I know how grumpy you get on your own."

~~~~~~

Ross had made decisions in his life, in an effort to change his habits, he had decided to move to a flat. He had emailed his wife to tell her that the house was available to remove anything she wanted, and that he had put it up for sale as she had requested. He had packed two suitcases and a box of bits, loaded them into his car, and gone back for his stereo and CDs. He then turned his back on his old life and looked forward to a new one, deciding to sink more effort into the job. The previous night, as he and Avalon returned from the scene of the body, Ross had told Avalon about his change of address and explained he was feeling better about his prospects. Avalon hadn't said all that much, Ross assumed he was still fighting his own demons and just wanted to forget about it. The flat Ross had rented was part of a house on Highfield Avenue, which was close enough to the police station, but not too close to the town centre. It suited him and as he readied himself for work, he began to place his things where he thought they ought to go. He then realised he hadn't brought any food and would have to call somewhere, or eat out for a while. Yet another long shift had stopped any plans he had entertained of settling in and as he got into his car and drove into work, he wondered what the day would bring. As soon as he walked into the office, he could see that Avalon was missing.

"The boss not in?" he asked. Mackinnon and Frazer were the only two already there but as the door to the Cave opened, in walked Mack.

"He's been called into DCI Croker's office," replied Mackinnon.

"Ouch, sounds painful then," frowned Ross, as he sat at his desk. Wilson entered and called out his usual greeting.

"Mornin' all." Lasiter had once explained that Wilson's greeting was 'tipping his hat' to an old television programme called 'Dixon of Dock Green' but Ross had to research it on the Internet to find out what it was. "The boss not here yet?" asked Wilson.

"Mackinnon," began Frazer turning to him, "you're gonna have tae write et up on the whiteboard or we'll get nothing done today." Mackinnon grinned and nodded, but Wilson was less forgiving.

"Got out of the wrong side of the grave thes mornin'?" he called as he sat. Ross gave Wilson a quick glance, at one time he would have joined in goading Frazer, but something felt different, he considered Wilson's remark slightly unwarranted. He was just wondering if he should visit a doctor to get his sense of humour checked, when Wilson noticed Ross's reaction.

"What?" he said holding his arms wide. Ross ignored the gesture, and continued working. Frazer very slowly spun around on her seat to face DS Wilson and stared at him for a few seconds. Wilson stared back and then relented.

"I was merely pointing out, that you're not your usual happy self." Frazer, just as slowly, spun back to face her computer screen, but said nothing. There was a slight knock at the door and it opened, revealing a male about Ross's age.

"DI Avalon?" he asked, raising his eyebrows.

"He's out, have you come about the noise from next door?" replied Ross with a straight face. For a second the man hesitated, then said,

"No, I'm Pottinger, DC Pottinger." Ross looked over to Frazer who raised her eyebrows a little. Ross looked back to the man.

"I think you're too late," added Wilson, "the vacancy has been filled but you can take a seat and wait for him," and he pointed to a chair that didn't exist. The man looked to where he had pointed and then back to Wilson.

"It looks like this is the comedy club, I'm sorry I was looking for C Section?" he frowned and turned to leave. It was clear he was slightly agitated. Ross would have let him go normally, but something made him do the job that maybe Wilson should be doing. When the DI wasn't there, Wilson, being the most senior DS, should take command, he wasn't doing that, and so, Ross decided *he* was the one to take over.

"DC Pottinger," called Ross as he stood, "you need to wear a badge saying 'no sense of humour', you must be the new face for C Section then," but Pottinger just stared at him. "I'm Ross," he continued and held out his hand, but Pottinger looked at the hand, then back to his face but still stared, "*DS* Ross," added Ross emphasising the title.

"I would have thought, *DS* Ross, that you would

run a tighter ship," replied Pottinger. Ross let his hand drop, he was sick of the man already and he could sense the others in the room oozing dislike for the newcomer.

"Have it your way," he said, and returned to his desk as Pottinger left.

"Who is he then?" asked Mack.

"The DI says we are getting some new people, I'm guessing he's one of them," explained Ross.

"He's got no chance in this section," smiled Mack, shaking his head.

"I like him," smiled Wilson leaning back in his chair. Ross continued with his report for the previous evening, and now and then, stopped to consider how he felt when he first came to the section. It was hard, but he accepted the jibes and jokes. Mack was probably right, he wouldn't last long with that attitude.

When Avalon returned, Ross could see by the look on his face and his body language, that the meeting with Croker had not been a good experience and he stood and walked to the booth, following Avalon.

"Problems?" he asked as he leaned on the wall. Avalon shook his head.

"Nothing but," sighed Avalon, "the DCI thinks we are all sat on our arses over here," he continued.

"I'm guessing he's expecting quicker results?" asked Ross.

"Well yes, all chiefs do, but it's the way this man goes about it," replied Avalon as he stopped fussing with his desk, and looked into space. For a second, he looked as if he was going to say something else but then looked up to Ross and asked,

"Any updates while I've been out?"

"Not much, well nothing really," shrugged Ross, "oh except one of the new people arrived, but he left

210

soon after."

"He left, what do you mean he left?" asked Avalon with a deep frown.

"I don't think he likes us," grinned Ross. Avalon wasn't quite sure he knew what Ross meant, but he would return to that subject later.

"Okay," he announced with determination as he stood, "let's see if we can solve a murder," and he walked past Ross into the main room. Ross followed, and as Avalon perched on the front desk, Ross stood to one side.

"I'm getting flak from above about the Priory murder," announced Avalon, looking at the rest of the section, "and now with a second body, that may or may not be connected, we are under some pressure you could say."

"Ross says we've got some new staff, is that right?" asked Wilson.

"Yeah," added Mack, "we got a humourless DC in here earlier saying he was looking for you." Avalon nodded.

"We are supposed to be getting two new members, but it looks like you ugly lot scared one of them off," replied Avalon, "but don't get too excited, with two new staff we have extra problems."

"Such as?" asked Ross folding his arms.

"Such as..." Avalon paused, "we will have to go back to standby cover, two of you will take turns to be on rota each week to cover for callout." There were a few frowns, but it was probably better than the system they had at the moment, which meant everyone was *always* on standby. Avalon continued. "The second issue is we will have to team up," there were audible sighs at this, "you will be paired up to make things a bit easier,

211

rather than the free-for-all we have at the moment."

"So I'm guessing two o' us will have tae pair up with the new faces?" asked Wilson. Avalon nodded.

"Unfortunately yes, one of them is local enough to know the area, but we don't know them and so we'll have to hold their hands for a while."

"Ef I get the DC that came en earlier I'm handin' my notice en," insisted Wilson.

"I'll try to balance it, but both the new people are DCs," explained Avalon, "so you'll have to trust me on that score, but if you keep scaring them off, we are never going to get anyone in here." He turned to the whiteboard. "So, back to work," he sighed and looked at MacDonald, "Mack, will you look at this trailer theft, I think new eyes may see something we can't?" Mack nodded, Avalon turned his attention to Wilson. "Gordon, work with Megan, and go over the little we know about this new body, it looks like foul play and though we don't know his identity yet, it's likely this is the other missing person."

"Do you thenk et's connected?" asked Wilson.

"I'm not sure," replied Avalon, shaking his head a little, "there wasn't much to see with the naked eye up there, but forensics are going over the site again this morning." He then looked at Mackinnon.

"You are with Ross, I want the Priory gone over again, but this time look at anything that could tie this in with the body at..." he looked at Ross, "what's the place called?"

"Glen Affric, it's above Dog Falls, at the side of the loch." Avalon nodded, then continued.

"I want a deeper search into the background of Alan Clacher and while we are at, it we need to see if there is any connection with Willam Ewart." He then remembered something. "Rory, the credit card found in Stirling?"

"Yes boss?" said Mackinnon looking up.

"Your little hunch may come back to bite us, get in touch with them and ask for fingerprints to be checked on that card. If they give you any crap, get them to send it to us with the dabs of the reporting officer," he paused, and then continued quietly, "just in case."

The office was just beginning to buzz with feverish activity, when there was a knock on the door and Pottinger walked in. He assumed the man in the booth was the DI, so he made his way there.

"DI Avalon, I'm DC Ewan Pottinger?" he held out his hand and Avalon gave it the briefest of shakes.

"Please, take a seat," said Avalon.

"I came earlier but you were out," explained the DC.

"I heard, why did you leave?"

"I considered I was being made fun of," he replied.

"It's a hard life, some of them use humour as an anaesthetic," explained Avalon, glaring at the man.

"I realise it's hard DI, I have worked in this environment previously, but I couldn't see the point of standing around to be the butt of their jokes." Avalon sighed and put his head in his right hand.

"My thoughts are, Detective Constable, that if you buckle under the humour of C Section, you don't stand a chance against the likes of Harry 'Mad Axe' Halford, and yes the name is made up, because I use humour too." The man looked uncomfortable and Avalon leaned back in his seat. "Honestly," Avalon continued, "I can't use you, I'm desperately short of personnel, but you will never fit in here."

"But-" began the DC. Avalon cut him off,

"Sorry and all that, but we are trying to solve a brutal murder, we may have another one on our books and I haven't got time to arse about with moody, temperamental officers, so try B Section, they may give you a chance."

"But I was assigned by DCI Croker."

"I don't give a toss if the Home Secretary sent you. Look out there," he said pointing to the main room, "they all have their problems, they are doing up to eighteen hour shifts most days, three of them haven't had a day off in almost four weeks, Wilson has to look at a card in his pocket to remember his children's names before he walks in his house," his voice was loud enough for Ross to hear now, "and you come in here saying they made jokes about you?" The man was open mouthed. "Get out," insisted Avalon, and he began to type. The DC eventually stood and slowly left the room. Avalon looked up casually to see Ross following, he continued typing.

"Pottinger!" called Ross in the corridor. The DC turned with an almost blank expression. "He's a bit fiery sometimes, but he'll calm down," he explained.

"I don't know what to say, I almost feel like I just got the sack," said Pottinger, still in shock.

"Yes," laughed Ross, "I get the sack at least once a day."

"But now I've got to go to the DCI and tell him what happened and I don't like that prospect."

"Look," suggested Ross, "go and get a cuppa somewhere and come back in an hour, I'll have a word with the boss."

"Why would you do that?" asked the man.

"We need staff, but just don't come back with the

same attitude you had earlier," insisted Ross. The man nodded.

"I'll think about it," he said. Ross returned to the Cave and went to see Avalon.

"What was that about?" asked the DI. Ross looked down at him and leaned in his usual spot on the wall.

"I told him you were on medication," explained Ross with grim face.

"Has he gone?"

"I told him to come back in an hour after we had given you some more electric shock treatment."

"Thanks for that," said Avalon with a frown.

"We need him," insisted Ross.

"I know, but I won't have some prima-donna coming in and causing more problems than he solves, we have too much at risk here."

"Croker will overrule you anyway."

"Well I realise that, but not before I get chance to make my point that Pottinger is a waste of time."

"We don't know that, it may be a bad day for him," sighed Ross.

"Well this is new for you, benefit of the doubt was never on your list of 'most used idioms'," frowned Avalon. He then sighed deeply and leaned back, placing his hands behind his head. "We do need staff," continued Avalon in slightly more relaxed tone, "but not at the cost of someone upsetting what we are building in this room."

"That's not going to happen," smiled Ross, as he turned to leave, "this is C section remember."

By the time the new detective had returned, apologised to Avalon and was introduced to the team, a desk had been sourced and was on its way to the office, but they needed to find room for another one. It was going to be cramped, but they would make it work. Avalon had to do something that had been on his mind and had to be resolved, so he thought about an excuse to get to the bottom of it.

"Megan," he said, walking into the Cave, "we need to go and find some kit for the new desk, come with me and we'll see if PC Kirk can sort something out." She nodded and followed him down the corridor but instead of going downstairs, he carried on to the rest room. It was usually empty in there, and he considered it a reasonable place for what he had to do. There were two young women police officers at the far end, so Avalon sat near the door and asked Frazer to take a seat.

"Why have we come en here?" she asked as she sat.

"I need a word about something before we continue." She could sense he was in a dark mood.

"Oh aye, what's that then?"

"Bobby Cotter," he said. She shrugged and glanced around the room.

"What about him?" she asked.

"I know about the incident with the handcuffs," he said calmly. Her eyes dropped to the floor and she leaned forward in the chair.

"I suppose he blabbed when you put the pressure on him?"

"No, actually, he went into a cold sweat when we mentioned your name."

"Aye, he's a snivelling little shite and no mistake."

"Probably, but that doesn't make him a target for an assault," insisted Avalon, "so what is it about?" he

216

added, then, he took a deep breath and waited for a reaction. She looked up for a moment, and then returned her gaze to the floor.

"He had been winding us up, false information, red herrings and the like, so we picked him up and put some pressure on him."

"Who did?" asked Avalon.

"There was me and Callum, er..." she paused, "DS McGill." Avalon knew McGill was now retired, so he asked,

"Who was the DI in charge?"

"DI Lasiter."

"Well I've heard Cotter's version of the events, so what's yours?" Frazer looked up to Avalon without any obvious emotion.

"We were interviewing him, as I said, but he was taking the piss all the time and we were getting nowhere. McGill went to see Lasiter to ask ef we should let him go and he took that opportunity tae threaten me."

"A physical threat?" asked Avalon.

"No, not exactly, more like improper suggestions, I lost my temper and struck him." Avalon looked surprised.

"That's it, you hit him because he made a comment to you?" he asked, raising his voice a little.

"Aye, a know et was stupid, but et's done and I'm sorry you had tae find out," she said impatiently. Avalon looked at the two female officers, but they didn't seem to take any notice.

"So how did you get away with that?" he asked.

"I don't know," she admitted shaking her head, "DI Lasiter went ballistic and said that was the end of my career, but two days later, I had heard nothin' an' I went tae see him. He said someone had smoothed things

217

over, but ef I ever stepped out of line..." she paused, "well you can imagine with Lasiter." Avalon looked into her eyes, she was now facing that very same threat again, only this time, it was Avalon, and he wasn't so forgiving of that kind of mistake. He had seen something of her temper at the home of Toby Cheeseman, but he never imagined that this was the sort of thing that brewed up inside her. "So what now?" she asked looking him in the eye. Avalon shook his head but said nothing. For a moment, she relaxed, as if she was glad he had found out, but then she tensed up, and said, "I wish Davies had kept out of et, I could have happily taken a hit then and left the force," she seemed to calm a little, then continued, "but in the last few months I have really begun to get back to..." she trailed off.

"So you think it was DI Davies that bailed you out?"

"Probably," she nodded, looking at the floor again, "I was told that a deal had been made with Cotter and I had to stay out of his sight, that was all I heard about it, well, except for another round of shouting matches from Lasiter."

"Why Davies, it could have been DI Lasiter, or Chief Anderson?"

"Et wouldn't have been Lasiter, he hates my guts for gettin' him into that situation and why would Anderson get involved, he hardly knew I existed?"

"It doesn't mean he didn't sort it out, good 'Chiefs' know everything that's going on." insisted Avalon. She shook her head again.

"Et doesn't matter now does et?"

"Not to you, but it does to me," insisted Avalon, "and I don't think it was DI Davies who got you off the hook."

Back in the Cave, Mackinnon was writing something on the whiteboard as Avalon and Frazer returned. Avalon went over to him.

"What's this?" he asked. Mackinnon looked visibly excited.

"It's only a tenuous link, but I have found a slight connection between the man found at the Priory and the missing man," he smiled.

"If the body by the loch," cut in Ross from the other side of the room, "turns out to be William Ewart, Flicks has cracked the whole case."

"I wouldn't go that far but it may prove of some significance," he beamed.

"So, what have you found?" asked Avalon expecting Ross to be vastly exaggerating.

"Well, both Alan Clacher and William Ewart attended a transport trade fair on the same day in Aberdeen, back in May of this year," he explained.

"You're right, it is tenuous."

"But," cut in Ross again, "it could mean they knew each other."

"It could," agreed Avalon, "but it's a trade fair which means anyone in that industry would probably be there, it doesn't mean you know everyone. I went to a conference in Edinburgh earlier in the year and didn't know a single soul out of two and a half thousand people."

"But you're antisocial," grinned Ross.

"Got et," called out Wilson suddenly, reading from his computer screen.

"Got what?" asked Mack. Wilson put his hand up to stop further questions as he read details from the screen, and a smile grew on his large face, as he silently mouthed what he was reading.

"I've got the details of William Ewart's driving license, he may have run a wedding car business but he was licensed for HGV vehicles."

"And there's the link," announced Ross, pointing to Wilson.

"Before we open the Champagne," frowned Avalon, "this body may not be the missing man."

"But et's looking good if et es," smiled Wilson.

"I'll give you that, it is," nodded Avalon.

Chapter Eight

"Avalon," said the grim voice into the phone.

"*Good morning Detective Avalon, it's Sandy Lennox here, I thought I would give you a call about our progress.*"

"Oh right, thanks professor, I was just wondering how you were going on," Avalon exaggerated. It was true, he had been thinking about the autopsy but that was an hour ago when he was discussing the variables with Ross, "so do you have anything?"

"*Indeed we do, the dental records of the pour soul on the slab match those of your missing person, William Ewart,*" he paused for a second, "*I'm not sure if it's goods news or not for your case though, we will confirm DNA matches when we secure a sample from the family, the odontologist however, says he has no doubt.*"

"Well thanks for letting me know but do you have a cause, or a time of death yet?"

"*Is see the impatience is still there Detective, but then again, I would worry if it wasn't,*" Avalon could picture his smiling face in his mind's eye, "*but as much as I would like to help, I'm afraid the cause of death may not be possible, though the coroner may find something I have missed. As to the time of death,*" he paused as if he was trying to recalculate it, "*I would have to say between ten days and a month.*" Avalon was silent for a few seconds.

"That's a wide margin of error Professor."

"*It is and I'm sorry, but looking at the rate of decay, I suspect the cool air around the edge of the loch was at play here, if you could get some temperature readings from the area, it may be easier to make a better guess, but that's all it would be, a guess.*" Avalon sighed a little, then as if Lennox heard him, he continued. "*The smell of putrefaction at the site was still strong even though parts of the body were badly degraded, so I suspected that the underlying tissues had not decomposed as quickly as the ones exposed to the weather. Certainly, that looked likely during the autopsy and I can only imagine a cooler temperature held back the process, so to speak. That's why a temperature reading would help.*"

"How would I go about that?" he asked.

"*Well the easiest way would be to purchase two thermometers exactly alike and place one where the body was found, and the other a few hundred metres away from the water. Both in shade of course,*" explained Lennox.

"Will any thermometer do?"

"*Oh yes, as long as they are identical, a decent instrument from a garden centre would do as long as they read the same before you begin.*"

"Right, I see what you are getting at, confirm any disparity between the two and that would indicate a reduction in decomposition."

"*Exactly,*" replied Lennox, "*and that would help us make a more accurate time of death. Of course there will also be the results from the forensic entomologist*

too, but the temperature readings would certainly help."
Avalon thanked the professor and returned the phone to the desk, he then walked into the main part of the Cave and looked around the room. He made a quick glance over to the coffee pot and wondered if they were going to need a larger machine, the thing always seemed to be empty these days. He noticed Mackinnon look up to him, so Avalon raised his eyebrows questioningly.

"I've got the results back from Stirling police station," said the young DC. Avalon walked over and asked,

"What have they told you?"

"They found only the prints of the reporting officer and those of the person who handed in the card. He turns out to be a local minister," frowned Mackinnon.

"Don't look so glum Rory, that's what I expected," he replied.

"Expected?" asked Mackinnon with a doubtful expression.

"Yes, not the part about the minister of course," smiled Avalon, "but I expected there to be no connection with the area, so why would it be found so many miles away and wiped clean of prints except those that handled it at the police station?" Mackinnon's eyes showed he was seeing Avalon's theory.

"Because it was another red herring to throw us off track?" mused the DC.

"Could be, drop the card and either some miscreant hacks it and starts using it, or some passer-by hands it in, either way we put resources into following the lead," explained Avalon, as he looked into Rory's expressive face, he added, "so you were right to question it after all," and walked over to Ross.

"Fancy a few hours out?" he asked. Ross looked

223

up from the keyboard and out of the window, it wasn't raining and the cloud wasn't as heavy as it had been of late. He shrugged and said,

"Yeah, why not. I'll start with a trip to the massage parlour and then over to one of my mistress's houses. I think then I'll go for a cocktail-"

"I wasn't thinking of anything so extravagant, I was thinking more of a stroll by the banks of a beautiful loch." Ross thought for a moment, then replied,

"Okay, but I want more than you usually offer on the first date, I've heard about you and your Highland Tours of local crime scenes," he stood and picked up his jacket. As they reached the door, Avalon turned to Wilson.

"Gordon, I'm out for a few hours, but you won't be able to contact me, so I'll give you a call to check in later." Wilson stuck a thumb in the air to confirm he got the message.

"And we're going in your car," insisted Ross with a grin.

"We'll have to call and purchase a couple of thermometers so we could do with finding a garden centre or something," explained Avalon.

"Sounds interesting, I can think of somewhere we might get them," nodded Ross.

In the car park, Ross walked straight up to Avalon's car.

"What makes you think this is it?" he asked.

"I'm a detective, that's what I do remember, work things out by clues." He then looked around the car park theatrically and added, "this is the only black car that isn't a pool car, plus it's an estate which I would expect and..." he paused for a second, "it's an old man's car."

"A Saab isn't an old man's car," insisted Avalon,

as he pressed the key fob to unlock it. Ross got in, Avalon followed suit and started the engine.

"Well, *I* think it is," Ross insisted fastening the seatbelt. Avalon drove out onto the main road and made an attempt to follow Ross's directions.

"I really don't see how you can say that, this is a nice car, I'm quite pleased with it."

"Yes, but after your old Mondeo, a Russian armoured personnel carrier would seem like the height of luxury," replied Ross, looking around the car and feeling the quality of the finish, "to be fair, it's not bad inside but I thought you were expending your horizons?"

"What do you mean?" asked Avalon glancing quickly over to him.

"I just thought with that BMW I told you about, some advice about your wardrobe and a few CDs that don't sound like a dying Minke whale, you would be all set for your new life." Avalon smiled a little at the insult to his music taste, Ross was probably correct that it was time to archive his CDs. "As it is, you really can't impress a girl with a car that sounds like the Arabic name for 'master'."

"Not all of us measure success by your criteria," smiled Avalon.

"I don't think I was speaking of success, just fun."

"So when are you thinking either of us will have time for fun?" asked Avalon.

"Point taken," nodded Ross.

After collecting the thermometers, they set off towards Glen Affric but Avalon was quiet, he seemed deep in thought. Ross broke the silence.

"What do you think about Wilson?"

"That's an odd question, you know him more than I do," insisted Avalon.

"I just wondered, I mean I rate him as a detective, he's thorough but he should be a sort of 'second in command' don't you think?"

"I suppose he *is* senior to you but to be honest, I would think that most of the team are capable," replied Avalon, "why, are there problems?" he added.

"No, not at all, I just think that when Pottinger arrived, we were a bit off handed with him, and it got him into trouble just because he's humourless." Avalon looked at Ross again.

"You *have* changed," he grinned, but added no further comment.

When they arrived at the scene where the body had been found, the forensics team were just about finished, so they parked up and walked over to them as they were loading their vehicles. Avalon asked them if they had found anything significant and if a parchment had been found, but the answer was in the negative to both questions. As the team drove away, Avalon and Ross walked down to the spot where the body had laid. There was a dark stain on the ground that marked the spot and Avalon could still smell death there, nothing like two nights previous but there, none-the-less. He stripped the two thermometers out of their packaging and place one at the base of a tree about six feet from where the body had been, he then retraced his steps back up the track for about two hundred paces and laid the other instrument at the base of a similar tree on the opposite side of the road and returned to where the car was parked.

"What now?" asked Ross.

"Well, there's the thing, we have to wait for about

226

an hour, so apart from enjoying the view, there's nothing else to do." Ross decided to look around Avalon's car but Avalon went down to the side of the track, he sat on the trunk of a fallen tree and scanned the loch. It was quiet and peaceful, with just a few sounds of nature here and there. It wasn't sunny but it certainly was pleasant and the midges weren't all that numerous. As he sat there and thought, he realised this was one of the few times since he had been in Scotland that he had just sat and looked at it all. The water reflected the horizon perfectly, it was like polished steel, and he was sure he could feel the relaxation entering his body, soothing all his discomforts. He didn't even hear Ross come up behind him.

"Penny for them?" he said.

"What?" Avalon asked, looking up at Ross, he blinked a few times and then admitted, "Oh, I wasn't thinking much, I was just taken in with this place, it's truly gorgeous." Ross nodded.

"If landscape is your sort of thing, I can show you something better."

"Where's that?"

"Just up this road, we can leave the thermometers to do their thing, it wont take more than an hour," explained Ross. Avalon thought for a moment, there was nothing else to do and why not? He was feeling relaxed, so he was happy with Ross's suggestion.

They continued to drive a few miles further up the single-track road until they came to a larger parking and picnic area.

"Just pull in here," said Ross pointing to the car park and Avalon did as suggested. Ross exited the car, removed his tie and jacket and placed them in the car.

"Are we going running?" asked Avalon.

"Believe me," smiled Ross, "you won't need your jacket," and he set off walking to the tree line opposite, just over the road. Avalon locked the car and followed, looking up at the hillside. It didn't look that high, maybe Ross wasn't as fit as he looked. By the time Avalon had caught him up on the steep footpath, he was almost gasping for breath.

"Bloody hell," swore Avalon, what's the altitude? I feel like I'm breathing pure Mercury." Ross turned and grinned.

"Come on, if you want to be a Scotsman, you have to keep up."

"I don't think I ever applied to be a Scotsman," gasped Avalon. Several times he thought about giving it up, it didn't look high and it didn't look steep, but Avalon was getting a lesson about what fitness really means. Obviously a trip to the bar in the pub now and then hadn't been beneficial and occasional walks around the local supermarket were clearly not what people meant when they said 'get plenty of exercise'. He gave up trying to keep up with Ross and slowed the pace, he eventually saw Ross standing at the top. He struggled the last few paces, it didn't help that he was breathing more slowly to try and hide how exhausted he really was. Ross turned and looked at him.

"Shit, I suppose I shouldn't have brought someone your age up here." Avalon tried to swear at him but all he managed was an extended wheeze. Avalon sat on a low wall trying to recover and wondering if what he was feeling, was the same as a heart attack. He focused on a small shrub and tried to control his breathing, it worked and he began to feel slightly better. He noticed the wall he sitting on was some sort of viewing point, so he stood and turned, the sight he saw took his breath once more, but in a different way. Avalon had been around the world a bit, he had seen sights, that was for sure, but what he saw just pulled his eyes out of their sockets. Ross was rambling on about it being one of the most photographed places in the country but Avalon was oblivious to him. He stood and looked, trying to imprint that image onto his retina, he never wanted to have to look away from it. The sky was a mass of broken cloud and there was a slight breeze, it was exhilarating and spectacular. Eventually, he looked around to Ross with a slack jaw, he looked back to the view, and then brushed both hands over his head. He looked back to Ross who was now seated on the wall, and just said,

"Wow, that is something else."

"I didn't know if it would be your sort of thing."

"It's like a living painting, I don't think I've ever seen anything so sublime. Not in landscape anyway."

"Get a shot of it with your phone," suggested Ross.

"No point," replied Avalon, shaking his head slowly, "the best camera in the world can't capture this, I'm not going to corrupt it by taking a crappy snapshot of it." He sat and looked around, most of the three hundred and sixty degrees of vision was beautiful, nowhere was ordinary and Avalon just looked in awe. "I need to see more of Scotland," he said, "there isn't much point in coming here to try and protect the country and its people if I don't know what I'm protecting and why." Ross laughed.

"It's a nice view, but I didn't think it would have this sort of effect on you," and he laughed again.

"Pass me the form," said Avalon holding his hand out to Ross but looking down the glen.

"What form?" asked Ross.

"The one to apply to become a Scotsman." Ross laughed once more.

They made their way back down the road to pick up the thermometers, when they reached the spot, Avalon read the temperatures and Ross jotted them down in his notebook. As they recorded the second one, and the time, Avalon looked at Ross and said,

"There is a difference of two degrees."

"Is it significant?" asked Ross.

"I simply don't know, I'll let the Professor and the coroner decide that."

As they began the journey back to the station, Avalon once more became quiet, Ross had been watching him, and knew something was wrong.

"So what's distracting you then?" Avalon blinked and glanced over to him, then shook his head.

"Nothing, why?"

"Well, you keep going into some sort of trance and I know you well enough now to know something is on your mind," insisted Ross. Avalon stared forward and thrust his tongue over his teeth to bulge his lips, Ross could see he was thinking out an answer. He finally shrugged and said,

"It's internal and I can't tell you about it."

"So it's about Frazer?" Avalon turned quickly, then looked back to the road ahead.

"Why would it be Frazer?" he then asked.

"Well unless you are about to make a 'hit' on 'The Toad' then it has to be her."

"The Toad?" asked Avalon, "is this some Scottish euphemism I have never heard about?"

"The DCI," explained Ross.

"I hope that nick-name didn't originate in C

230

Section?" and he hesitated before continuing, "and why Toad?"

"Oh come on," replied Ross, "his bottom lip flaps as he speaks, and his name is Croker." Avalon wanted to smile but he resisted, the description was fairly accurate, but it was difficult enough trying to take the man seriously, knowing the station were calling him 'The Toad' behind his back, wasn't going to help. There was more silence and then Ross added,

"So it is Frazer?" he paused, "and something to do with Bobby Cotter." Avalon said nothing for a few seconds and then changed the subject completely.

"We have to put some thought into who will team up with who," he said, as if they had already been discussing it. Ross looked out of the window.

"That's your call," he said.

"Ultimately yes, but there's no point in teaming people up with a partner they can't work with." Ross nodded.

"Well, tell me your thoughts and I'll give you my opinion," he replied looking back to Avalon. There was nothing said, and the pauses seemed to be getting longer, but eventually, Avalon answered.

"Okay, I think Wilson and Mack work well together but Mack has come on a great deal lately. We could put the new man with Wilson, he'll hate it but he's a good mentor."

"Sounds reasonable, Wilson will keep him on his toes for sure," nodded Ross.

"That means you, as the other DS, should partner the other new face," continued Avalon.

"Oh great, I hope he's more flexible than 'Potty'."

"Well I suppose it was inevitable that Pottinger would be an easy subject for a nick-name."

231

"That's probably one of the more repeatable ones," smiled Ross, and then he added, "so the other new chap, what's his name?"

"Her name," replied Avalon.

"Pardon?"

"*Her*, female of the species," explained Avalon. For a moment Ross was taken aback.

"I assumed..." he began and then stopped.

"Boyd, Alison Boyd," added Avalon.

"Okay," said Ross eventually, "I suppose I can live with that, so who else?"

"I was going to put Frazer and Mack together." Ross shook his head.

"I don't think Frazer gets on with Mack," he hesitated, then continued, "but then again, Frazer doesn't get on with anyone."

"That creates a problem then, I can hardly put Mack and Rory together."

"Like I said, it's your call, I wouldn't want to sort it out," said Ross folding his arms.

~~~~~~

As Avalon and Ross entered the Cave, Wilson was in Avalon's seat and was speaking to someone on the phone. Avalon quickly turned, and flashed Ross a smirk, Ross raised his eyebrows. It seemed Wilson *did* take control when the DI was out. Wilson gave Avalon a quizzical look, and then spoke into the phone.

"Aye, that's right..." there was a pause, "okay, if you can send it to DI Avalon at the station, that would be great," and he put the phone down.

"What's that?" asked Avalon, removing his jacket and straightening his tie in the reflection of the glass.

"That was an employment agency," replied Wilson pointing at the phone, "Rory and Mack have been busy, they did some diggin' around tae try and find out who this 'Parky' was that Scobie mentioned. The trouble was, they found one hundred and twenty three names with Park en them that were on our records," explained Wilson.

"The man could have been a park keeper in his former life, it doesn't mean the 'handle' came from his actual name," suggested Ross.

"Aye, he could," admitted Wilson, "but he was'nae, Rory piled through the records and narrowed et down to three possibles, one es en hospital with a broken hip after a car smash an' o' the other two, one of them goes en the same bar as Scobie," and he looked at a name in biro on the back of his hand. "Alistair Parkes, previous for breaking an' entering. I sent Frazer and Mack tae go and talk to him."

"So where's the employment agency come into it?" asked Avalon reclaiming his seat, "or is Rory sick of the job already?"

"Well that's Rory again, he found telephone numbers of the neighbours of the house up at Scorguie and asked them ef they knew who lived there. They all confirmed that et es usually rented out to foreigners and I can't see that this George Barber es a humanitarian towards refugees, so we asked local employment agencies ef they had foreigners on their books."

"And?" asked Avalon.

"They're sending details over, they can't disclose anything on the phone," shrugged Wilson.

"So your theory is that the driver that the contact knew, was a foreign truck driver?"

"Well, with an accent at least," replied Wilson.

Avalon looked over to Mackinnon, he was still busy with something, he certainly put everything into the job.

"Okay, it's a bit of a long shot, but it may go somewhere," nodded Avalon. Ross and Wilson returned to their desks.

It wasn't long before Frazer and Mack returned from their visit to Alistair Parkes, and Avalon wondered how she had coped. He looked into her face but couldn't read her and she was noticeably quiet.

"So did you find out anything?" he asked.

"He didn't want to talk to us," replied Mack, "but after we put a bit of pressure on him, he was surprisingly chatty," and Mack pulled out his notepad to read his notes. "He said he was asked by someone he didn't know if he knew of a HGV driver who didn't ask too many questions as there was fifty quid en et for a name," and Mack looked up to Avalon, Frazer looked on quietly. "He says, that's why he was asking around, to make a bit of money. He also says that the man in the bar who told him about the driver had a foreign accent."

"No idea what nationality?" asked Avalon. Mack shook his head and Avalon gave it a little thought then said, "So who would he collect his fifty quid from if he didn't know the man?"

"Parkes says that the bloke that was asking goes in the betting shop on Baron Taylor's Street on a regular basis," explained Mack. Avalon tilted his head a little, and then said directly to Frazer,

"Could you get someone in the betting shop to try and ID this person?" she shrugged and then said,

"Aye, probably but we'll need a hidden camera."

"I was thinking of Pottinger, being new he shouldn't be recognised," suggested Avalon.

"He's untested, we don't know anything about

him," she replied.

"Give him a go then, or find someone else, I'll leave that to you," he replied and then looked at Mack. "Do you know anything about trailers like the one that was taken on the A9?"

"Not really," replied Mack shaking his head, "it was just the trucks I was interested in, but I can do some research." Avalon gave him the briefest smile, and said,

"Good, get on it and find out why they might specifically want *that* trailer." Mack nodded and left, but Frazer stayed, when Mack was out of hearing distance, she asked,

"So what's happenin'? I mean about what you asked me." Avalon thought for a second and then replied.

"I don't know yet, I have to find time to check something out."

"Well I can't carry on tryin' tae do my job not knowing if I'm gonna get suspended or not."

"I can see what you mean, but the only option *is* to suspend you, and that will go down on your record. I'm trying to find out the facts, until then, you'll have to bear with me, or take a voluntary suspension." Frazer folded her arms and glared at the floor, Avalon could see the anger welling up in her but he couldn't see any other option.

"So how long is et gonna take you to decide?" she asked impatiently. Now Avalon was getting angry, he leaned back and glared at her.

"I can decide right now if you wish, but I promise once I do, there's no going back," he demanded. He held her stare for what seemed like minutes, but in the end, she relented then turned and left. Avalon knew she was now lost to him until the matter was cleared up and he wasn't going to find opportunity anytime soon.

By the late afternoon, Avalon was helping Mackinnon with some research on the background of the Priory case but neither of them could find anything to single it out as a perfect place to leave a body. He had to admit that it was probably just a coincidence and as he pointed out to the young DC, that's the line he was following.

"So it's a just a random site?" asked Mackinnon.

"I don't know if it's totally random but the more I think about it, the more I think the body was put there to ensure it was found quickly, and publicly," he explained.

"But that doesn't make any sense, it goes against the MO of every murder case I have ever read about."

"So don't think of it as a murder case, think of it more as a..." Avalon tried to think of the best words to use, "a hit, a contract killing, whatever you want to call it but think of it in *that* way and you get a different perspective of it." Rory considered this and after a few seconds he blinked and said,

"I see what you mean but it's a bit more involved than being 'double tapped'." Avalon smirked a little at the lad's use of professional killer's language.

"It is more involved but the manner in which it was done and the way the body was arranged, probably means something to someone out there. He also knows our methods, so some things have been done to put us off the scent."

"I get that," nodded Rory, "but to my way of thinking the person who orchestrated this *doesn't* know police methods that well," he said rather hesitantly.

"What do you mean?" asked Avalon.

"There are certain details that we have kept back from the press and public knowledge, such as the parchment and the wound in the neck," Avalon nodded

236

to confirm he was correct, "so if he knew police methods that well, he would have known we would do something like that and so he would have left his clues where they would be more obvious, making sure that we couldn't hold that information back." Avalon raised his eyebrows for a moment.

"You know," he began with surprise, "I hadn't thought of that," he paused, "no I hadn't thought that through at all," and he went quiet for a moment. Mackinnon began to feel slightly uneasy, the boss was now side tracked and it was *his* doing.

"I mean, it's just a theory," he added as if to apologise.

"No, it's a valid point," began Avalon coming out of his thoughts, "and you may have just given me an idea," smiled Avalon, he stood and patted Rory on his shoulder. He went to the booth and Mackinnon could see him looking on his computer as if checking something. He wondered what the DI was thinking and looked around the room but there was just Ross near the windows talking quietly on his phone. Frazer and Mack were out preparing some equipment for surveillance and Wilson was out, giving Pottinger a 'whistle-stop' tour of the station and getting him settled in. Rory looked back to Avalon, just in time to see him beckon Rory to the booth.

"Sir?" said Mackinnon with a questioning tone.

"Something occurred to me, I am still looking at this out of context." Rory was quiet, Avalon was making no sense. "Okay," continued Avalon, "we have assumed that the planning of this was meticulous and that is making us think they are one step ahead of us," Rory nodded, "but what if, as you say they don't know our methods and it was never considered *how* we would pursue the case?" asked Avalon as he looked at Rory.

"Then..." he hesitated, "they probably made mistakes," he hesitated again before continuing, "but if they did, we haven't found any." Avalon allowed a slight smile.

"What if the mistake was meteoric? What if the mistake was the body down by the loch?"

"The wrong person you mean?" questioned Mackinnon.

"Not the wrong person but the wrong place."

"Sorry sir I don't follow," replied Rory. Avalon knocked on the glass and Ross looked up to see Avalon beckon him over.

"What? I'm busy arranging my ballet lessons," announced Ross with a frown as he entered.

"What if the body down at the loch *is* connected to the body at the Priory?" asked Avalon.

"Then there is potentially a connection, if there is a connection, we may find some common ground and if..." Ross stopped and then continued with, "hang on, you can get this sort of information from 'become a detective dot com'."

"Now, here is another question," announced Avalon, pointing at Ross, "*if* they are connected, which as I must point out, we don't know at this stage, but *if* they are," he paused for effect, "how come the Priory body was so public and yet the body at the loch has been there for at least ten days and possibly a month?" Ross frowned, raised his eyebrows and frowned again, finally he pointed to the ceiling with his index finger and said,

"I haven't the foggiest."

"Work the timings back, you want to scare someone by providing a body that had been tortured, so you put it in a public place, but-" Ross interrupted.

"They put the body by the loch in what they thought was an ideal place to be found by passing tourists, but no one found it," he concluded.

"Exactly, after a few days and the body still hadn't been reported, they probably started to think it wouldn't *be* found," explained Avalon, "and if that was the case, their point would be lost, they may even have gone to check to see if it was still there and found an unidentifiable mess."

"So they killed someone else for a more public display?"

"There's a theory to the madness, what the hell made you think of it?" asked Ross.

"I didn't, Rory came up with it."

"Well that's not exactly true," said Mackinnon, with a slight reddening of his cheeks, "I just didn't think that they understood police practice, as was previously considered. The DI put the icing on the cake."

"Good work though Flicks," added Ross.

"If this is correct and they did kill someone else just because the other body wasn't found, it makes these people very sick, to say the least," frowned Rory.

"And very dangerous," concluded Avalon just as the phone rang. He quickly said,

"Excuse me," and lifted the phone, "Avalon."

"*Hello Detective Avalon, it's Sarah Underwood.*"

"Ah, Miss Underwood, what can I do for you?" and he raised a single eyebrow slightly. Ross rolled his eyes and left the booth with Rory following on.

"*I have some news for you, it was quite a surprise when I found it in one of the evidence bags from the autopsy,*" she paused for a second, "*there was a parchment on the body, or rather in it.*"

"What to you mean, *in it*?" he asked.

239

"The coroner, it seems, saw a slight shadow on the x-ray taken of the teeth for the odontologist and he assumed it was just leaf litter, or something inside the mouth cavity. On further examination during the autopsy, he found something wedged in the throat and found the parchment."

"I'm surprised the Professor didn't find it," said Avalon.

"It's likely with the body being in such a poor state he wouldn't have seen it until the autopsy and it wasn't visible on the night, we both looked over the body."

"I suppose so, but why didn't the coroner think to let me know I wonder?"

"He wouldn't think it was that important, he wasn't aware of the first parchment as we removed it and took it away on the preliminary examination," she explained. Avalon could see her point, and so he asked,

"Is there anything else that was found at the scene?"

"Nothing I'm afraid, we have had just about every sort of weather pattern since it has been there, so any trace evidence would have been long gone."

"So, what about the parchment, can you prepare it as you did before, we were able to read the last one, if not decipher it?"

"It's not in as good condition as the previous one, but I'm sure we can clean it up a little." Avalon thanked her and went to tell the others.

"The body at the loch had a parchment with it," he announced.

"Really?" said Ross with a surprised look, "where was it found?"

"In the throat, it must have been pushed in there

240

after death so that it didn't get blown away," suggested Avalon.

"We're lucky it was found then, the neck area of the body was just about gone, it could easily have been lost."

"True, but it sounds in poor condition, we'll have to wait and see," nodded Avalon, "and of course this finally puts the idea of ritual completely out of the running and gives more strength to the theory that this body *was* expected to be found." Mackinnon nodded at this, and said,

"It's looking more and more like some sort of gangland killing then."

"I'm beginning to think you're right," sighed Avalon, "but with a truck haulage theme running within it, how the hell can it be gang related?"

~~~~~~

Avalon was home reasonably early in the evening, in his opinion anything before eight o' clock was early, and it was only just prior to that time but it gave him chance to relax a little.

He had suggested that he and Ross make a show of the 'call-out' rota by doing the first week themselves. With that in mind, they had tried to get away from work a little earlier so they could have time to rest, just in case.

He considered going for a ride on his bike but he felt tired and so decided to stay in, and maybe watch a movie if he could find anything that may be of interest. After a hot shower, he considered food, but the 'pantry' was almost bare with only the single tin of spaghetti hoops and a jar of strawberry jam. That tipped the balance, he got dressed and got in the car, placing the spaghetti into the glove compartment as he wanted to give it back to its rightful owner at some stage. He then drove off to do a little shopping at one of the late opening stores but by the time he had returned, the process had eaten away at the time to such a degree, that relaxing had become a nonsense, he couldn't get the case out of his head anyway, particularly as they were starting to piece it together. He had gone off the idea of food too, so he looked at the bottle of Whisky on the shelf, but even that didn't appeal. It was probably his luck to be called out on their first official rota night, so he stayed well clear of it. He decided to go to bed but as he lay there, unable to sleep, he just kept going through the case in his mind. There was a noise, a weird, echoing noise that was like a whirring sound that became the noise of a telephone, *his* phone. He felt groggy as he turned on the bedside lamp and its glare felt like a two-kilowatt light shining in his eyes. As he pressed the button to answer, he realised he must have been asleep and looked at the clock, it was two in the morning.

"Avalon," he croaked.

"*DCI Avalon, et's PC Conelly from the nick, we have something here you may be interested in.*"

"It better be good PC, I was just making love to Sandra Bullock," he growled.

"*Well,*" replied the PC with a little hesitation, "*we may have caught the Priory murderers.*"

He was up and dressed in an instant, and except for calling down the phone for the PC to get DS Ross out of bed, he was straight into his car, heading towards the station. He was half way there when the reality dawned on him that it was very unlikely that some lowly PC on his Tuesday night rounds had accidentally found the gang responsible for what was now considered a double

242

murder. Nevertheless he needed to be there, and how ironic that on the first night of the rota, almost as he had predicted to himself, here he was on a call-out. The station seemed incredibly busy, he had no idea there were so many officers on night shifts, but then again *they* could have been called out too. The PC on the desk told him the duty Sergeant was down in the cells sorting out the arrests, so that's where he headed. He saw the duty Sergeant, but he seemed to have his hands full, so he headed towards two PCs who seemed to be taking details of a man dressed, or rather half dressed, in tight fitting red trousers and nothing on his top half. Two other men were dressed oddly too, one had a black cloak with a hood and the other seemed to be wearing something that would have been more at home in a stage opera. On a bench were all manner of items that had obviously been taken from the assembled crowd, one item looked like a hat, shaped and fashioned to look like an animals head. All in all, it was a scene of pandemonium, the cells were being overfilled, there were complaints and a little bit of shouting here and there.

"So what's the score here?" he asked. One of the uniformed officers was Dowd. "Hello PC Dowd, have they got you working nights now?" Dowd smiled.

"Aye, et looks like you and me both DI Avalon."

"So what's the story then?"

"Pretty straight forward on the surface," began Dowd, "several people were seen entering the Priory at Beauly around midnight, and et was reported to us. A car was sent and found people inside the grounds acting in a suspicious manner. They asked for backup and entered. The people refused to leave, and so, when the backup arrived, they were arrested."

"Any explanation for why they were there?" asked Avalon, as a voice in one of the cells was complaining loudly.

"The one that seems to be the ringleader, says they were carrying out a sacrifice to their lord." Avalon stared at Dowd, who seemed unmoved by his own statement, and turned to try and deal with the noise.

"Just one moment sir," he said and he left to help one of the other officers put a man back in a cell. He returned and said,

"Where was I? Oh yes," he continued, "several knives were found in their possession, they have been logged and put in evidence bags." Avalon noticed Dowd give a slight smile to someone behind him, so he turned, and saw Ross approaching.

"Jesus, is the circus in town?" asked Ross, looking at some of the more interestingly dressed individuals.

"Good morning DS Ross," said Dowd.

"Have you organised this specially for us Dowd, just because we are on call-out?" frowned Ross.

"No sir," smiled Dowd, "I did think it might be of interest though," and he explained what he had told Avalon who was watching some of those in the corridor. Two of them seemed to have blood on them.

"Is that blood?" he asked to the other uniformed officer at his side.

"We don't think so sir, Sergeant Silver," he pointed to the Sergeant who was, with the help of another officer, trying to calm one of the men down and get him into the cell, "says it's either paint or theatrical blood." Two of the people were female, the one sitting in the corridor close to Avalon, had a woollen blanket around her shoulders and draped over her body. Avalon turned to Dowd as the Sergeant was still having problems down the corridor.

"PC Dowd, this girl has no clothes, I assume she arrived in this condition?"

"Yes sir," nodded Dowd, "we can't find her clothes and the arresting officers said they left nothing at the site."

"Ross," called Avalon, get this girl out of here, take her to one of the interview rooms, and PC Dowd, see if there is a female PC on site, if not, send for one." Dowd nodded, and walked smartly away, Avalon made his way to the other female and led her out of the corridor. One of the men tried to stop him, but the Sergeant and another officer grabbed him and threw him back into the cell. He took the woman to the other uniformed officer, and told him to take her to the same interview room as the other woman and wait with Ross until a woman police officer arrived. He then left the commotion to the Sergeant and his men. After half an hour or so, it quietened down, and Ross arrived, saying that two female officers were looking after the two women arrested at the Priory.

"So what do you make of this?" smiled Ross.

"Well, they certainly aren't our killers, if that's what you are asking."

"I spoke to one of the arresting officers, he says they were practising some sort of Black Arts at the Priory, there was a pentacle drawn on the floor in red chalk."

"This is all we need, more fuel to the fire for DCI Croker," sighed Avalon.

"Well, we're C Section on call, I suppose we better make a start," said Ross. They explained to the Sergeant that they were going to interview all of the eight people straight away, the Sergeant placed two officers at their disposal, one being Dowd. One by one, the miscreants were taken to an interview room where Avalon and Ross did their best to get any information they could, but it was clear that some of them had been using drugs previous to the arrest. As they returned the second one back to the cells, Avalon asked Dowd to send for the doctor.

"He's not going tae be well pleased about coming out at this time," grinned Dowd.

"Let him earn some of that money for once, anyway, I don't want one of these people dying on us, that would really cause us some issues."

The next person to be interviewed was a tall, thin man with long, dark hair. He didn't seem to be under the influence of drugs or alcohol and he had a mean look in his eye. Avalon had been told that this one was probably the ringleader.

"What's your name?" asked Ross as soon as he was seated.

"Zepar," he hissed.

"How do you spell that?" asked Ross. The man gave a slight smile and said,

"However you wish." Ross wrote it down, then looked up and then asked,

"Well you've given us your clown name, can we have your proper name?" The man stared at him. "I'll put declined..." and he spoke as he wrote, "to give... proper... name." He then looked up to the man. "What were you doing in the grounds of the Priory?"

"I would have thought even a tiny mind like yours would be able to work that out."

"Some sort of fancy dress party?" asked Ross. Avalon was wondering if he should intervene, as it was

246

obvious Ross was simply trying the man's patience.

"That's right, Fancy dress party," smirked the man. Ross sighed and stated that,

"It's an offence to carry knives into a public place so I'm going to caution you under sections 139 and 139A of the Criminal Justice Act 1988-"

"I know that act, I also know there is a section relating to *'religious purposes',*" glowered the man.

"You know your Criminal Justice act Mr..." Ross made a show of looking on his notes, "Zepar, but in *your* case, several of your *'congregation'* have admitted that you were there specifically to carry out a sacrifice, and to my certain knowledge, neither the Criminal Justice act, nor the Prevention of Crime act 1953 gives any allowance for human sacrifice." With this, Ross closed the pad and called out, "PC Dowd." The police officer entered to take the man away.

"It's just a mock ceremony, no one gets hurt," admitted the man as he was lead away.

"The charge *isn't* mock however, Mr Zappa," called back Ross.

"I think you're enjoying this," said Avalon, after the man had gone.

"Not really, I keep thinking about the paperwork this is going to generate."

"Do you want the next one?" asked Dowd, as he re-entered the room.

"I need a drink," demanded Ross, stretching his spine. Avalon opened the pad Ross had been writing on.

"Not taking this seriously then?" he asked looking down at the name Zepar circled and nothing else.

"They're just cranks, we won't get anything from them, it's pretty pointless."

"Some take their religion seriously," insisted Dowd.

"What? devil worship?" asked Ross with surprise. Dowd stuck his bottom lip out and nodded.

"Yeah, of course, Satanism es a very old religion and has been going much longer than the Jedi Knights, yet even that's now officially a religion." Ross shook his head and said,

"I'm off for a drink and a pee, in no particular order," and he left. Avalon sat.

"This bunch seem a bit odd though don't you think?" asked Avalon.

"I don't know, a lot of these groups perform mock ceremonies, et doesn't mean they are any worse, or better, than other religious organisations."

"The one who seems in charge, the last one interviewed, seems pretty manipulative though and he doesn't seem to be under the influence of narcotics like some of the others," insisted Avalon.

"Maybe," nodded Dowd, "but ef you're looking at religion, that es always the case, take my religion," he smiled.

"I didn't see you as the religious type," replied Avalon.

"But that's et, like these people, et's not mainstream, et's a freakish religion based on expectation, disappointment and then elation. Et has its manipulative members too and et costs a great deal to get into ets church." Avalon could see a hint of playfulness in Dowd's eyes.

"And that religion is?" he asked.

"Caley Jags, otherwise known as, the Inverness Caledonian Thistle."

"The football team?" announced Avalon with a

smile, "it's not my thing, but I think I know what you're getting at."

"I think most people who go to watch sport with a passion turn et into a religion, we wear uniforms, we chant songs and we swear that our church es the only true church, es et so different?" insisted Dowd.

"In the way that you don't go with the intention of human sacrifice, yes," replied Avalon.

"But people can be killed, property es sometimes damaged and wars can break out, just like other religions," explained Dowd. Avalon nodded and gave him a slight smile.

"PC Dowd, you should become a detective, your view on the world would serve you well."

"No chance," he grinned, "I worked with you long enough to know that you don't get time to crap," he gave a wink, "and I wouldn't get time to go to church would I?" Dowd had come a long way since he had worked in Avalon's team several months ago, he was bright and astute, Avalon liked his appraisal of the world. He would make a good detective, but he also understood his reasons for not going down that route.

As soon as Ross returned, they continued with the interviews and the last one was the girl who had been found naked. Someone had found her some over-alls and some footwear.

"Shona," she said to Ross's question, "Shona McLeod." The girl had obviously been under the influence of drugs, but that was wearing off, and she looked terrible.

"How old are you Shona?" he asked.

"Twenty, no, twenty one," she replied.

"What were you doing at the Priory?" he asked.

"I was the one, et's my destiny, et has to be

249

completed to give him the way through," she said, as if reading a shopping list. Avalon could see this girl had bee indoctrinated thoroughly, she believed what she was saying.

"Can you clarify what you mean?" asked Ross.

"He leads us to the straight path without a book, he es the one true god and I am ready to take my place at his side." Ross looked round to Avalon and gave a dumbfounded expression.

"What happened to your clothes?" asked Avalon.

"There are no uses for such things on the other side, all earthy things are left behind."

"What would you have to do to get to the other side?" asked Ross, thinking he knew the answer.

"Zepar, the high priest will release my soul and et will fly to be with the great lord," she announced staring into space.

"How will he do that?" asked Ross quietly. She paused for a moment and then said,

"He releases my blood onto the spot where previously *he* had been."

"Previously?" asked Ross.

"That earthly shell you found, his soul es with the master, it happened there, et es the portal between his world and ours. He will come soon," and she began to shiver. The shaking quickly became severe, and so Avalon looked at Ross, and shook his head. They left the girl in the care of the doctor, who, as Dowd had predicted, was less than happy to be there, but he said he would check them all out before he left.

"I don't think this was a mock ritual," said Ross shaking his head.

"This bunch do seem rather committed," admitted Avalon. Ross looked at his watch and then asked,

"What do you want to do, carry on, or leave it until the morning?" Avalon thought for a moment, he did feel like he could sleep.

"Let's get a few hours sleep, can I crash at your flat?" he asked, "I don't want to disturb Angie."

Chapter Nine

He hadn't slept very well even though he was exhausted, and yet Avalon had been reasonably comfortable considering he was on a sofa. He put it down to the case, they seemed to be making some headway and he needed to keep up the momentum. The snoring coming from the bedroom hinted that Ross was still asleep even though it was full daylight outside. Avalon looked at his watch and decided it was time to make a move. He soon found the coffee and although it was instant, he could feel his body craving the odd smelling powder, so the kettle was filled just as there was a rather loud snore from Ross's room. Avalon considered that he must have woken himself as the snoring stopped and was replaced by some other groaning noises. He poured the hot water on the instant coffee and cringed at the sickeningly cheap aroma it gave off. The door to the bedroom opened and there stood Ross in his underpants, his eyes, red and bulging through the puckering skin that surrounded them.

"Good god man," called Avalon, "if I had the time I would arrest you for being in possession of an offensive body."

"Are you always this noisy in the morning?"

asked Ross looking at the cup.

"I suppose you want coffee?" suggested Avalon as Ross nodded and attempted to free his mouth from the gummy state it seemed to be in.

"I don't remember going to the pub but I feel like we had a couple of dozen pints of strong lager last night," he eventually said, collapsing into the easy chair.

"There's no wonder you live on your own," insisted Avalon, "what with the noise you were making and this apparition you transform into, it's enough to put females off for life." Avalon passed him a cup of coffee. "Oh and it's not coffee, I don't know what it is but it isn't coffee." Ross sniffed the hot liquid and then tasted it.

"Course it's coffee, what did you think you'd find in a coffee jar?"

"Well if it doesn't smell like coffee and it doesn't taste like coffee, it can't *be* coffee can it?"

"So why are you drinking it then?"

"Because there doesn't seem to be anything else, *like* coffee," he sniffed the contents of his cup once more and frowned, "and how long have you had this stuff," asked Avalon picking up the jar, "it says forty eight pence on the lid?"

"I bought it from the corner shop last week," insisted Ross.

"For forty-eight pence?"

"Well, I admit it's not the best coffee in the world-" began Ross but Avalon cut in.

"How you can have the cheek to come to the office and drink that great coffee I supply and then in secret, consume a blend of sawdust and kitty litter I just can't imagine."

"Secret?" called out Ross, "why would anyone keep what coffee they drink a secret?"

"Right," called back Avalon, "right, that's it, this isn't going to work, the marriage is off and I'm going home." As soon as he had announced the joke he regretted it, Ross was probably still stinging from his own marriage failing but he seemed to take it in his stride.

"Well," shrugged Ross, "at least there won't be a costly court case over the custody of the coffee."

"There were a lot of 'Cs' in that sentence," said Avalon as he drained his cup and placed it in the sink," right I'm off, I'll see you in about an hour. I'm going for a shower and a change of clothes first."

"I'd offer to make breakfast but I need to go shopping," frowned Ross.

"Oh, that reminds me," announced Avalon and he left the house quickly but returned some seconds later. "I forgot I had this in the car," and he tossed something to Ross who was still seated in the easy chair. "Bon appetite," he announced and then left. Ross looked over the object in his hands, it was a tin of spaghetti hoops in tomato sauce. He smiled.

When Avalon entered the Cave there was quite a bit of activity but he ignored it and went into his booth. He sat and read his emails as usual and then deleted most of them, as usual, just as he noticed Wilson coming towards him. He knocked on the wall as a courtesy and entered.

"I'm surprised tae see y' here at all today," smiled DS Wilson.

"No trouble, I feel like shit of course but that probably comes from sleeping on Ross's two-seater park bench," he quipped, "so what have you got for me?" he added, seeing Wilson was carrying a folder.

"Oh et's the forensics report," he announced

254

tossing it onto the table as he sat.

"Anything in it?"

"Not really," replied Wilson shaking his head, the parchment hasn't been processed yet."

"Sarah Underwood warned me there'd be little of value but maybe the autopsy will bring something to light," shrugged Avalon, and as he looked over to DS Wilson, the DS seemed to remember something.

"Oh, Sarah phoned earlier and asked if you could ring her when you get time,"

"Did she say what it was to do with?"

"No and I did'nae ask." Avalon noticed there was a doubtful look in Wilson's face, a kind of 'distance' and he realised he had something on his mind.

"What is it Gordon?" he asked.

"Oh, nothing really," he shrugged.

"Isn't that the exact same quote that the chief engineer told the captain of the Titanic?" asked Avalon raising a single eyebrow.

"Well, et's Frazer, I know she can be a bit of an arse sometimes but she's positively dysfunctional today."

"What do you mean?" asked Avalon fearing the worst.

"She won't talk, she doesn't seem tae want to do anythen and she's just not working within the team."

"I'll have a word with her," nodded Avalon.

"I tried that, she just glared at me," replied Wilson looking down at the floor, "I don't know what's up but it seems serious this time." Avalon knew of course, but he wasn't saying, he just tried to assure Wilson he would try to get to the bottom of it and Wilson stood.

"Oh and the other new face has arrived, y' did'nae say it was a lassie," added the DS.

"Did I not?" smiled Avalon, "where is she?" he asked looking through the glass.

"Mack's showing her around tae get her settled in, they shouldn't be long," and Wilson checked his watch with the clock on the wall and stood as if to get back to his work then he returned to his desk.

Ross entered soon after and went straight to the booth.

"Anything I need to know?" he asked.

"Not really, your new partner has arrived," replied Avalon, but seeing Ross look into the cave, added, "Mack is showing her round, when she gets back I'll have a quick word and then you can take her downstairs and clear up the details from the episode..." he was about to say last night but he amended it, "this morning." Ross nodded and went to his seat. Avalon picked up the phone and dialled Sarah Underwood's number.

"Miss Underwood, it's DI Avalon, you asked me to ring."

"*Oh yes,*" there was a crumpling sound as if she was looking for something, "*we have the results from the original parchment, the other will probably match but the ink is from a printer.*"

"What do you mean?" asked Avalon not quite sure how she meant it.

"*It's same as the stuff that comes from an ordinary desk top printer.*"

"Oh," said Avalon trying to sort out the implications of the information. "Does that mean it was applied by a printer or isn't that known?"

"*There is a good chance it was, the microscopic patterning is consistent with a laser printer, the team say that, given time, they could even tell you which make it is.*"

"Right, well that's interesting. Thanks for the information, I'll let you know if we find something." Avalon replaced the phone and thought about what she had said but he couldn't quite see how it could have been that simple. He began to read quickly through the forensics report from the crime scene up at the loch, just in case there was anything there. There were so few sheets of paper in the report he didn't hold out much hope that there was anything of interest. It took no time at all to read and he dropped it at the side of his desk as being of little importance. He began to consider the printed parchment once more, just as the door opened, and in came Mack with the new detective. Mack brought her through and said,

"DC Boyd es here sir."

"Thanks Mack," he replied and stood to shake her hand. She was fairly tall being the same height as Mack, Avalon was guessing about five feet nine and she was dressed plain but neatly. She offered a broad smile as she shook his hand and Avalon asked her to sit.

"Mack, I want you to check on something," Mack nodded, "see if there is a printer font that closely matches the text on the parchment."

"Printer font, you think et might be that simple?" asked Mack with a surprised look.

"Forensics say it is," replied Avalon and Mack returned to the Cave to start work on it.

"Welcome to C Section," smiled Avalon, turning to the new DC.

"Thank you sir, I'm glad to be here," she replied, her accent wasn't strong but it didn't sound local, not that Avalon was any kind of expert. She had very intelligent, blue eyes that sat in a pleasant face, a face that still didn't show the tiredness and the stress that would surely come later. Her brown hair was bobbed at shoulder length and her build was medium, making her look the antithesis of Frazer.

"I'm sure Mack has introduced you to the team, the only one you haven't met is DS Ross," said Avalon pointing through the glass to Ross who was having some sort of joke with Wilson. "You'll be with him to start with and he's a bit of a joker, so keep your eyes peeled." Avalon considered that, with the exception of Frazer, the description covered them all. "You make the third new detective in this section in as many weeks so we are still treading water when it comes to teaming up," she nodded at this and looked back over to Ross, "but given a week or so we should be able to make a better assessment of our needs." He tried not to make it seem that he hadn't got time for her, so he explained the situation very briefly. "We are in the middle of a major case, so unfortunately, you will have to pick up the pieces as we go."

"Don't worry about me sir, I'm a quick learner.

"Good," smiled Avalon as he stood. She stood too, assuming the interview was over, "you're from Perth I believe?" he said as he held his arm out to steer her into the Cave.

"Yes," she nodded, "do you know it?"

"Not in the slightest," replied Avalon and he looked up to Ross, "DS Ross," he called. He then continued to her. "You even get a window seat, we had to squeeze a desk in at the end," he pointed to the empty desk in front of Ross's position. Ross took over.

"So it's Alison?" asked Ross, she nodded. "It's nothing to be embarrassed about, we'll soon think of something else," smiled Ross as he escorted her to the desk. Avalon sighed as he returned to the booth, he was

258

already tired of dealing with new personnel, he was thinking of letting Wilson sort out the next one, if there were to be anymore.

~~~~~~

"Where're we goin'?" asked Frazer as she climbed into Avalon's new car.

"We need to talk," was all he said and they drove out of the car park. They continued across town and out towards the waterfront but neither of them spoke until they came to the A862 and Frazer eventually said,

"Do you know where you're going?"

"I know exactly where I'm going," he replied. It wasn't long before he indicated to turn off the road and he pulled into a small car park.

"A motorbike shop?" she asked.

"Why not, I like motorbikes," he answered and got out of the car, "and I like water and there's plenty of that," he added as she too got out and looked over the firth. She followed Avalon towards the shop where he looked at the occasional bike now and then.

"Ef you're gonna give me a bollockin' thes seems a very public place tae do et," she said.

"We're here so I *can't* lose my temper."

"So get on with et," she insisted, folding her arms. Avalon pointed down to a part of a bike.

"Look at that, that is gonna get knocked off the first time out." She didn't know what he was pointing at or why it was so delicate, she just wanted to be away from there. "I was going to just carry on until I have more information, but you're not pulling your weight in the office," he explained as he threw his leg over a bike and tried it for fit.

"I told you, I can'nae work thinking I may not have a job," she said impatiently.

"And I gave you the option, as I recall, of taking a voluntary suspension, you didn't, so I assumed you would be patient enough to wait until I have time to sort it out," he insisted, climbing off the bike, "and you are not playing ball with the rest of the team."

"So what do y' expect me tae do?" she said showing some anger, "I can't focus an' I can't think straight, maybe I should just pack et all up," she spat. Avalon noticed a biker in white leathers look at them oddly. Avalon looked into her eyes and said,

"Maybe you should," and he looked back to a bike, "but that would be a shame because you have so much potential but acting like this isn't getting you any friends."

"Ef you think I'm after friends you are sadly mistaken," she began but she noticed Avalon point at a bike and he made his way towards it. She sighed and shook her head, here she was, having to deal with the sort of pressure she could do without and this madman was looking at unfeasibly bright coloured motorcycles as if her predicament didn't matter.

"In this job Megan," replied Avalon, grinning at the bike as he closed in on it, "friends keep you sane and alive, without them, you're just another sad copper," and he allowed his hand to follow the lines of the petrol tank. "For instance," he eventually continued, "those people back at the office watch out for each other, that includes you," he said looking at her for a moment, "and they do it even though they know that the people above know the system is designed to make them slaves to the job."

"I don't need a pep talk on the vagaries of detective work," she insisted folding her arms again.

"Probably not," said Avalon pulling in the clutch of the bike. Another biker was looking at a big Suzuki close by, "but you need to think of the position you are in, I don't have time for this after all," and for a moment he looked away from the bike and straight at her, there was a flash of anger in his eyes. "I don't have time for it but here I am. I've got pressure from above, I'm trying to juggle three new personnel into the team, I have a double murder case that seems harder to crack than the Dyslexia Monthly crossword puzzle, I'm about sixty eight hours down on sleep and yet I'm here trying to sort *your* problems out, problems *you* created," his voice rose in severity a little and then he glared at her and allowed himself to calm. "Just look at this bike," he smiled touching it once more, "Kawasaki ZX10R, it can out accelerate a Ferrari and you could ride from here to Glasgow without the front wheel ever touching the floor," he smiled as the other biker squeezed past.

"Too right mate," grinned the man, surprisingly with a south London accent, "you press the big red go button on that baby and your arms an' head will be in Newcastle and yer' arse will still be in Inverness." Avalon allowed himself an agreeing comment and as the man continued on, Avalon looked back at Frazer, but she spoke before he could continue.

"I'm sorry if I don't seem interested in this conversation," there was a hint of sarcasm in her voice, "but I have no interest en bikes, what can motorbikes have to do with this situation?" Avalon shrugged.

"I was trying to make a point I suppose," he hesitated for a second, "this bike has a lot in common with you, it can be gentle enough to take your granny for a ride to the bingo or it can outpace the fastest super car," he looked into her eyes, "use it without care and planning and you end up as a red stain on the A9," he turned around, left the shop and made his way back to the car. Once there, he leaned on the bonnet looking out across the water of the firth with his arms folded. Frazer slowly joined him and sighed deeply.

"I'll take suspension, I suppose et's the right thing tae do anyway."

"I don't agree, but if you can't hack it..." he trailed off.

"Hack et?" she said raising her voice and then calmed a little, "I know I'm my own worst enemy but I just want tae do my job."

"I know, and you do it well but you have to change your approach, the people in that office are not the enemy," insisted Avalon. She stood upright.

"Let's go, I want tae go back," she insisted, "I've made my mind up an' that's et."

When Avalon arrived back at the Cave, it was noticeable he was alone, he said nothing and went into the booth. Ten minutes later, he called Mack into the booth and told him to sit.

"Can you run the surveillance at the betting shop?"

"Yes boss, no trouble." If he was wondering what had happened to Frazer, he didn't ask.

"Set it up with Pottinger, keep your eye on him though."

"Yes boss," nodded Mack with a smile, "do we get expenses for a wee flutter, et won't look right ef we don't." Avalon gave a quick smile.

"Yes, okay but keep it on the small side."

"Oh and I nearly forgot," he added as an afterthought, "the research on the trailers brought up one

262

thing about this particular trailer."

"Go on," said Avalon.

"Most refrigerated trailers are called 'reefer' trailers and they have connections for the ship's power lines when they are en cargo holds, the one that was stolen was a one-off design from a particular year," he paused for breath, "the refrigeration unit es large and sits inside the trailer."

"How might that be significant?" asked Avalon with a frown.

"I don't know boss but that was all I could find."

"Anything on the text font?" Mack shook his head.

"Nothin' yet, there are hundreds of websites with fonts but it looks promising, there are some very similar ones about." Avalon nodded to Mack as the young DC left to brief Pottinger. Avalon thought about the trailer and the only possible conclusion he could come to, was that the trailers might be useful for smuggling. It was possible that drugs could be secreted into the refrigeration system, but then again, wouldn't customs know to look in these types of trailer?

"Avalon," came his usual greeting to the phone.

"*DI Avalon, et's Sergeant Gregory down stairs, er, we've got the press asking for more info on the murder cases you're running,*" said the voice of the desk sergeant.

"We've released the usual press crap Bob, why are they asking you anyway?"

"*Well they're here at the desk,*" said the sergeant.

"Really?" sighed Avalon, then he continued, "just tell them we'll release any relevant updates when we know something." He heard the sergeant put the phone to his body and then some muffled speaking.

"*I've told them DI, but they say they want to talk to you,*" he had an apologetic tone in his voice.

"No chance, too busy," replied Avalon, and he was going to drop the phone on the hook but a light seemed to come on in his brain, "did they specifically say murder *cases*, as in plural?" asked Avalon with concern.

"*Aye, I'm sure of et DI,*" replied the sergeant.

"But we haven't released anything to say..." he hesitated, "get them to interview room two, I'm on my way."

"I'm Roger Dewart and this is-" the man was holding out his hand, but Avalon ignored it and interrupted quickly as he closed the door behind him.

"Mr Dewart, I'm sure you have received the press releases, I'm very busy at the moment as you can probably understand," insisted Avalon, he noticed the seated figure was female. The man was slightly older than Avalon, probably in his mid fifties and to Avalon's eye, seemed a little too old to still be a reporter. He also seemed hesitant, not like the usual calibre of reporter he had grown used to.

"Well, we er," the man stuttered, "came to see if there was any further information about the murders you are working on."

"If there was, you would have received it as I have just said," frowned Avalon, "and there is just a single murder, not *murders*."

"So you are saying that the body found at the loch was not a victim of crime?" asked the man.

"As I said, we are only investigating one murder Mr Dewart, as stated in the press release, the body at the loch was badly decomposed and we have no idea of the cause of death as yet." his manner became slightly sharp as he folded his arms and leaned on the door, "and I would be interested to know why you considered that it was linked to the death at the Priory." The woman chose this point to speak.

"We have had a tip off," she said but it was clear from his expression that the man didn't want her to reveal the source of the information. She was probably in her late twenties and dressed very casually, she was no doubt new to the job. She spoke in what Avalon called a 'university accent', a mix of middle English and petulant adolescent. He looked down at her.

"Oh really?" and he allowed a slight smile. She saw it for what it was and she glared back at him.

"It's not so much a tip off, as a suggestion by an interested party," interrupted the man. Avalon turned back to him and said,

"Well, whoever 'suggested' it has a tremendous talent, in truth I'd say they must have a connection to the spirit world," he let the meaning sink in slightly before continuing, "as no one in the living world, *including* the coroner, has drawn any conclusions whatsoever," and he unfolded his arms, "and now if you don't mind, I must get back to work."

"We are also getting lots of letters from readers saying that the body down at the loch was torn to shreds like the one at the Priory." Avalon gave a smile and shook his head.

"I came down here to see you because I thought you knew something we didn't, it's clear you are listening to your readers rather than the other way around, good day, the sergeant will show you out," he turned and opened the door. It wasn't that he disliked the press per se, he had often used them in the past to his advantage and he had found them willing to help but these two seemed to be jumping to conclusions and creating mystery where there was none. If there *was* someone feeding them information, it was unlikely they had much or they wouldn't have come down to the station looking for titbits. Avalon walked into the foyer and nodded to the sergeant.

"You can escort them out now Bob." The sergeant called to the young PC close by and he jumped into action to escort the visitors outside. As the man and woman made their way to the door, he heard her speak, it was quiet but he didn't mistake it.

"I've got it boss," said Mack as Avalon entered the Cave. He made his way to MacDonald who had Wilson looking over his shoulder.

"What is it?" Avalon asked joining them.

"The parchment found in the hand of the body, I've found a match, et's a font called 'don't be elfish' an' et's an almost perfect copy."

"Great name," added Wilson. Avalon looked at the font on the screen and down to the photocopied version of the parchment, they certainly looked similar.

"So have you worked out what it says?" asked Avalon.

"Not really, it spells out 'turnatorul'," shrugged Mack.

"Do a search on the internet," suggested Wilson and Mack typed it in.

"No idea what it says," admitted Mack, "but the few sites that it brings up are Romanian."

"Romanian?" asked Avalon standing up straight, "we haven't seen any other Romanian connections have

266

we?" Mack was feverishly typing.

"I think I've got it, translate turnatorul to Romanian and we get 'Snitch'," smiled Mack folding his arms.

"Oh this gets interesting," said Wilson raising his eyebrows.

"Double check it Mack, translate 'snitch' to Romanian," said Avalon.

"Yes boss, same result."

"Well, well," said Avalon taking a deep breath, "we need to look for a Romanian connection with the two victims, we also need to send someone up to the house at Scorguie and bring in any foreign tenants at the house Scobie told us about. I'm guessing they might be Romanian." He looked down at MacDonald. "Good work Mack," and then he phoned Sarah Underwood to thank her and explain that the information was already bringing results. Ross came back soon after, and DC Boyd wasn't in tears so that was a bonus.

"The thing last night," began Ross, "was a little more serious than we gave it credit for. I think they were actually going to hurt that girl, so we have taken statements from those that were able to communicate on a reasonable level and we'll hand it over to the Procurator Fiscal to see if there are any grounds for prosecution." Avalon nodded.

"Okay, we can cope with that," he said and then added, "you and Alison contact the clairvoyant, medium or whatever they're called these days, the one who was in that local newspaper, I want her questioning, she seems to be feeding the papers more crap."

"The glass pusher?" sighed Ross, it was clear he wasn't enthralled with the idea.

"Yes, she stated that there was another body even

267

before we heard about it and I think she's telling the newspapers the two deaths are linked, so drag her in and question her about it."

"She won't be in anyway," he said in a matter of fact way.

"How can you know that?" asked Avalon.

"She'll see us coming in her crystal ball," grinned Ross and he moved off, adding, "Come along DC Boyd and whatever you do, think nice thoughts so she won't detect us," and they left. He seemed to be getting on with DC Boyd but then again Ross would always play the fool in the company of women, even women detectives. Avalon was beginning to feel left out of the picture, he seemed to be sat at his desk sorting out problems and nothing else. He wanted to be out there working the case with Ross, not sat in this cramped office trying to sort out people's problems. But then again, a few days ago he was wishing it *was* cramped. He noticed Wilson coming to the booth.

"So did y' speak tae Frazer?" he asked. Avalon had considered what he would tell anyone that asked and he knew it would be Wilson who would ask first.

"Yes, I think we've sorted it out but I've sent her on an errand so she'll be out for a while." Wilson nodded, he knew better than to ask the boss any more than was necessary.

The coroner's report arrived late in the afternoon and Avalon set about it straight away. There was the usual preamble but the main points of the report were sketchy, as he had expected. The cause of death wasn't confirmed, but it was considered that a wound to the neck was most likely, as that part of the body was where the worst decomposition was found, that meant there was damage

268

and blood loss. That led to the coroner surmising that a knife wound or similar would most likely be the cause of death. The man had not eaten for at least twenty-four hours prior to his death and there were signs of smaller wounds to parts of the body pre-mortem. The body was naked and was unlikely to have been killed at the spot where it was found. The identification was confirmed as William Thomas Ewart by dental records and DNA, he had probably been deceased for between twenty and thirty days, but most likely in the latter end of that period. Other than that, there was little in the report that Avalon didn't already know. He walked back to the whiteboard and filled in a few more pieces of the puzzle. Wilson had been out with Pottinger to check the house at Scorguie and returned with some interesting news.

"So there is no one living there or are they just out?" asked Avalon.

"That, I can't say," replied Wilson, "the neighbours say he left last Thursday and has'nae been back since."

"The day of the truck robbery," nodded Avalon.

"Aye, an' I asked what nationality they thought he was, two said they thought he might be Polish but one woman who goes to Spain a lot for her holidays, says he spoke an odd kind of Catalan."

"That's probably Romanian then," interrupted Mack, "when I was translating that word there were a lot of Spanish similarities."

"So we may have found our truck driver, he's probably still in Holland though," shrugged Avalon.

"Time to bring in his landlord?" asked Wilson. Avalon nodded and then looked at his watch.

"Leave it until the morning though, it's getting late and we will need some time on this one." The door to the Cave opened and in walked Ross and Boyd.

"Find anything?" asked Avalon, though he didn't expect much. Ross had already started shaking his head.

"She's not a medium, I'd say more of a large," he frowned, "but she says that the spirits told her blah blah blah..." and Ross wound his hands around in an erratic way before slumping in a chair. Boyd made a more detailed explanation.

"She says she saw in a dream that the cases were connected, I think she's just guessing sir."

"I suppose I expected that, and well done DC Boyd for explaining the ramblings of Ross. We've needed an interpreter for some considerable time." He then looked around at the team and explained, as he and Ross were still on the call out rota, they would be leaving early.

~~~~~~

Avalon looked at the television screen, it was turned off but he really didn't know where else to look. He wondered if he ought to read, but what? He didn't have any books apart from the well-worn Scottish law books and a single book on Scottish history, and he had read that from cover to cover. He had his poetry books, but he had to be in the mood for poetry to thread his way through their pages. The only other books in the house were romantic novels that Angie kept about the place and several women's magazines. It had always been an issue for Avalon, living alone with time to spare was mentally crippling and he hated it, he was loath to go back to the television but he could feel its draw. He looked at his watch again, it was twenty-five to eleven, he could go for a shower and then, justifiably, go straight

270

to bed for eleven o'clock. Who was he kidding? He never went to bed early, he would just lie there, start thinking, and would have to get up soon after. He needed a hobby, but when would he get time for it? Maybe a hobby he could participate in now and then? He went into his room and opened up the laptop and had a think. At weekends he could go for a ride on the bike but what would be ideal for these odd hours he had spare now and then? Then he looked into the corner of the room to where the old guitar stood. From as far back as he could remember, he had wanted to be a musician, well he actually wanted to be a rock star but his brother had pointed out you had to be a musician first, Avalon had hinted that it hadn't stopped Dire Straights. Either way, he tried various instruments and failed miserably at every one but he had fond memories of the guitar, it had even tempted him back to it when he saw the one he now owned in a pawnshop in Wolverhampton a few years ago. He was the first to admit that he wasn't a born musician but he had managed to strangle the odd tune on the guitar. He wondered if he should throw caution to the wind and pick up the old thing again, he probably couldn't even remember how to tune it. He considered it didn't matter that much as his playing was so poor, being out of tune was the least of the guitar's problems. As he had no idea how to read music, he would be restricted to songs converted to 'tablature'. He looked on the Internet for tablature 'music' and it didn't take him long to find something. It was an acoustic song by Nik Kershaw, something he had once tried before. He picked up the instrument and tried to make a few chords but it was clear he would have to work on his action and his fingers would have to work towards gaining calluses once more, he had forgotten how painful it was on the hands.

Feeling he had achieved something, he put the guitar down to rest his fingers and looked around the house for something else to do.

Twenty minutes later he found himself watching the television but not having a clue what the programme was about. When he finally got to bed, he realised he was still lying there with his eyes wide open thinking about work, the case and his talk with Frazer were prominent in his thoughts and he eventually dozed off without making any decisions for the following morning.

Thankfully, there were no further call-outs and his sleep was reasonable, he was still feeling terrible from the loss of sleep the previous night but he made the first coffee of the day doubtful that everything would go the way he would like it to.

In the Cave, the first job he had to do was the morning meeting and to go through the day's work with the team. There was so much to do and he kept things flowing so that the absence of Frazer wouldn't seem so obvious, it was foolish though, it was clear she wasn't there due to the empty seat and the clear and tidy desk standing out like a beacon in the middle of the room. There was something else he had to do too and that could be the most unpleasant job of the day. He decided to try and get it out of the way as soon as he could and so he picked up the phone.

"Bob, it's Avalon."

"*Oh, morning,*" replied Lasiter, "*what's up, you run out o' coffee?*"

"Can we talk?" he asked.

"*Aye, when?*" replied Lasiter, "*I can come round now ef y' like?*"

"No, I'll come to your office if you don't mind,

272

we need privacy."

"*Okay, I'll order the pizza,*" replied Lasiter. It was ironic that the DI was joking, the timing wasn't great, as Avalon considered there could be some friction over the conversation that they were about to have.

The door to Lasiter's office was open and so Avalon walked in, closing the door behind him, and sat.

"What can I do for y' laddie?" smiled Lasiter. Avalon sighed a little and prepared for trouble.

"I just want to clear something up, it's been on my mind but I have to know what the truth of the matter is," he explained.

"Et sounds serious," replied Lasiter.

"It is," agreed Avalon. He swallowed hard and began. "We brought Bobby Cotter in for questioning the other day." Lasiter didn't react. "He told me about the incident with the handcuffs." Lasiter still made no reaction but Avalon could sense a slight change in the temperature of the room. "So you have nothing to say?" he asked. Lasiter raised an eyebrow and then leaned back in his chair.

"Et was an unfortunate incident," he finally said, "Megan Frazer was a fool, she let the job get on top of her," and he set his gaze on Avalon.

"You covered it up didn't you?" asked Avalon but Lasiter was noncommittal. "Why are you so tight lipped about this, is there something here I don't know?"

"I don't know *what* you know so I can't tell you." Avalon shook his head slowly.

"You have obviously tried to protect her since then too," he continued, "that much is clear and all the time I have been up here, you have been watching over her, trying to protect her career and though I have done some digging around, I haven't found any connection, until now." He took another deep breath before he continued. "Frazer attacked Bobby Cotter in the interview room, her police career should have ended there and she could have gone to jail for it, but someone brokered a deal with Cotter and all the evidence points to you." Lasiter made a shrugging expression and said,

"It could have been DI Davies or even Anderson, et doesn't mean et was me."

"Don't give me that crap," growled Avalon, "I'm not Bobby Cotter and don't treat me like a first year cadet, *I* know, and *you* know, it was you." Lasiter looked surprised at the outburst but was still unfazed. He kept his gaze fixed on Avalon.

"So what do y' want from me?" he simply asked.

"What do *I* want, hey it's you and Frazer who have their arses on the line, because if I go to Croker with this, you can kiss goodbye to your pension." Lasiter had never seen Avalon this angry, he had heard he could get excited but never witnessed it. He nodded though, Avalon was right, his career was a good as ended if it got out and it would be a cruel twist of fate.

"I don't think there es anything I can do for you, though you're right o' course, we both go ef you let this out." Avalon was silenced by Lasiter's attitude, he couldn't believe that he would just allow this problem to fester without any kind of explanation or even a reason for his actions. Lasiter just kept his blank gaze fixed on Avalon and so he gave a slight nod and stood. He looked down at Lasiter once more and turned to leave, he didn't want to report the incident, but he was going to have to, with neither Frazer nor Lasiter prepared to go into detail about it, he had to formally deal with it. One thing he didn't want in *his* career were any skeletons in the cupboard, it wasn't his way and as far as he knew Lasiter had covered up an important misdemeanour of a fellow officer. Avalon opened the door and stopped to take one more look at Lasiter.

"I will be going to DCI Croker in exactly one hour, that should give you time to put your things in order," he said with sadness in his voice.

"You have tae do what y' feel es best, we all do, that's what this job es about," Avalon was becoming angry again, he felt Lasiter was making it more difficult for him. "I know et's in your nature tae do things by the book," continued Lasiter then he hesitated slightly, "when et suits like."

"What's that supposed to mean?" growled Avalon. He was certainly angry now.

"I was thinking about the security van case, when you crawled over Davies's team tae get a result, you seem tae stick by the book when et suits DI Avalon." Avalon closed the door again, walked over to Lasiter, and leaned over, placing his palms on the edge of the desk.

"Moving on evidence that concerns a case to solve it, is what we are supposed to do."

"Not exactly going by the book tae trample on another officer's cases though es et?" hissed Lasiter.

"This is different," demanded Avalon, "you covered up an assault on a suspect committed by a fellow officer."

"That's not how I see et, an' get yer hands off my desk, until you squeal tae Croker I'm still a DI and y' not gonna trample *me*." Avalon could see the fury in Lasiter's eyes and he decided to back off.

"So be it," sighed Avalon, "I thought you would be a little more helpful, I can see I was wrong."

"Does Frazer know?" asked Lasiter. Avalon

looked into his eyes, for the first time during the conversation he saw some humanity in those canny orbs.

"She knows that I found out about the incident," explained Avalon, "I told her to take a couple of days off, mainly because she nearly had a go at someone we were questioning, all he did was ask her if she was Megan Frazer. She changed somewhat after that, to the point that the team were asking questions about her." Lasiter nodded calmly at this.

"So you've known about this for some time?" asked Lasiter.

"No, just a couple of days," the atmosphere in the room seemed to calm a little, "it was a bit of a shock and I didn't know how to approach it, Frazer won't tell me anything beyond the facts of the attack." Lasiter leaned forward and sighed deeply.

"Frazer can't tell you, she does'nae know anythen'," he said and then asked, "what did she tell you?" Avalon hesitated, was Lasiter playing him, or was he about to come clean? Avalon sat and explained.

"She says she expected to get suspended but when she came to you, you told her someone had smoothed things over and done some sort of deal with Cotter, she thinks it was Davies." Lasiter laughed a little then said,

"Davies din'nae know that much about et, he would'nae have sanctioned et anyway. Davies es like you, everythin' by the book."

"There is a reason that we do things by the book, it stops incidents like this coming back to haunt us," demanded Avalon raising his voice once more, "I wouldn't be having to deal with this if you and Frazer had done the right thing at the time."

"Frazer had nothen' tae do weth et!" spat Lasiter,

276

and then as quickly as the outburst began, he calmed and leaned back tilting his head back and looking at the ceiling. Avalon was tired of the game, he didn't want to have to make a demand on Lasiter, but he was left no choice.

"Okay, I'm sick of your secrets, if Frazer doesn't know, then you do and if it's too big to let me in then I have no choice, I have to tell Croker to suspend Frazer and I'll have to report you as a possible accessory," and he stood once more.

"Sit down laddie, I'll tell y', I've had enough o' the damn job anyway," he leaned forward and held his head in his hands. Avalon sat and saw a great deal of worry in Lasiter's face, it may not have been worry for himself, but it was there nonetheless. He slowly lifted his head pressing his fingers into his face as he did, and then, with a deep intake of breath, he leaned back into his chair once more and seemed to calm himself from the inside out. Avalon watched as changes came over him, in his face and his body language, it was as if the Detective Inspector was flowing out of him and the *man* was flowing in to fill the space it had previously occupied. Avalon noticed him take a quick glance down at the photograph of his wife and family that was always on his desk, it seemed like he was the condemned man taking a last look at his past before the switch was thrown. Calmly, he began to explain to Avalon.

"Some many years ago I had a mate, Charlie Logan, a close friend that I grew up with. He became a copper too and we even worked together until we went off tae do our different things. I bumped into him some years after and tae our surprise, we had both joined the CID, I was here at Inverness, and he was down en Aberdeen. We kept in touch now and then and we both made DI about the same time," Lasiter gave a brief smile at this, "we seemed to be livin' the same life." Avalon saw Lasiter's eyes flit about as if he was remembering good times. "Then he called me one night at home, tae sort of ask a favour," Lasiter's face became more serious, "he wanted my advice on somethen', it was tricky then and et's tricky now," and Lasiter looked deep into Avalon's face for a second. "He told me that a fellow officer was in trouble and he told me some o' the story, not the details o' course, but I could'nae help him, because I did'nae know enough o' the case. After a few weeks I heard nothin' an' so I called him but he was en a bit of a state, et was then he told me the *whole* story." Lasiter looked at Avalon as if he was assessing him, trying to figure out if he should be telling *him* the story. He glanced back to the photograph and then continued. "He had sent two officers to a surveillance job, a long term job that was running for a week or so, watching premises that were considered tae be important tae a big case tied en to the oil industry. Both officers were fairly young but competent and he trusted them, they were good at their job and had come up with the goods on several previous occasions." He stopped and looked out of the window, he continued to stare into the distance as he returned to his story. "One night, one o' the two went for a pee, but what they did'nae know was that they had been spotted and somebody was closing en on them. The officer relieving himself was coshed and beaten up and the one left en the car was quick enough to realise she had been spotted, so locked the doors and tried tae get into the driver's seat."

"Frazer?" asked Avalon, Lasiter looked away from the window and straight into Avalon's eyes as if he had been pulled from a dream. He nodded and looked down to the desk.

"One o' the assailants broke the window and pulled her from the car, they beat her and dragged her tae some waste ground," and at this point he looked up at Avalon with a calm but troubled expression on his face. Avalon thought he knew what was coming next, he was half right. "Four of them raped her, then they beat her to a pulp an' left her for dead," added Lasiter with a slight tremor in his voice. Avalon just stared at Lasiter, he was stuck for words yet in his head there were plenty of words, plenty of questions flying around in there. Lasiter looked out of the window again and then continued. "She was en hospital for several weeks and gradually she began tae recover, at least physically, the other officer was also en a bad way too and he fully recovered but left the police force soon after. My mate Charlie was destroyed by et, he never recovered from sending these two, likable young officers, tae such a fate." He looked back to Avalon. "Frazer was made of sterner stuff and she wanted to go back tae work, but Charlie did'nae think she could cope, he knew she had changed and advised her against et but she told him that ef she did'nae, it would be letting those bastards win. He asked ef I could get her a transfer tae Inverness, we managed to pull strings here and there and she came tae work for us." He looked out of the window once more. "She was a husk, I did'nae think we could keep her on but she had decided tae take up self defence lessons, so she would be able to handle herself better, that was when she first met her boyfriend. He was twenty years older than her but was ex-special forces so he knew his stuff. They got on and eventually she moved en with him. It seemed tae be good for her and she came out of her shell a bit." At this point, Lasiter stood and walked to the window, he leaned and put his hands either side of the frame, and looked out into the fields in the distance. "Then we brought Cotter en on a case, no one else knew her history and so, during the interview, she was left alone with him, just for a moment and Cotter decided tae make some kind of move on her. She clobbered him good and proper but et meant she was still unstable, et meant she would lose the job she had fought so hard tae keep," and he turned to Avalon and shrugged, "and that would have been that," he said as he returned to his seat, "I phoned Charlie to tell him what had happened and et was then that they told me he was dead." Lasiter looked once more to the photograph, he held his gaze on it for some time as he continued. "Life es so fragile, DI Charlie Logan had suffered a heart attack at work and had fallen down the stairs. They said he was dead before he hit the first step, I reckon this thing with Frazer did for him." He looked to Avalon and bit his bottom lip. "An, that's about et, I covered up the incident with Cotter, en return I let him go and until you brought him en, that was an end to et."

"There's never an end to it," insisted Avalon in a quiet voice.

"No, you're probably right," sighed DI Lasiter, he suddenly frowned, and added, "Megan does'nae know that I know about this you understand, an' I don't want her knowin', es that clear?"

"She thinks you hate her guts," said Avalon.

"Aye, I'm fine with that, I just don't want her knowing I was watchin' out for her, that's all." Avalon wasn't sure he could promise that, he didn't even know how he was going to react to what he now knew, but he nodded anyway.

"If I *can* keep it quiet, I will," he said, "what happened to the bastards that did this to her?"

"They went down, mainly for the scams they were running en the oil industry, they also got time for assault o' two police officers, but Frazer knew ef she had brought charges for rape she could kiss goodbye tae her career."

"Why? That doesn't make sense," asked Avalon, slightly puzzled.

"What with psychological assessments and all the issues o' sensitive cases they would'nae let her work on anything with assault or rapes in et would they? That's why Charlie covered most of et up and moved her on. Et saved her career."

"And he did this because he felt guilty?" asked Avalon.

"Aye," nodded Lasiter, "but ultimately, none of et was worth et," Lasiter looked directly at Avalon, "but who would know a DI with blazing red eyes would dig deep enough tae find all this out?" Avalon didn't understand exactly what he meant by 'blazing red eyes' but he had to clear up one aspect of the story.

"It wasn't digging that found it, I was unsure why you had so much interest in her, true, but it was Cotter's reaction to her name that puzzled me."

"Aye, Cotter, another lowlife that shouldn't be free tae walk the same streets as decent people," hissed Lasiter, "so now you know et all laddie," he looked back out of the window. Avalon couldn't believe he was in this position, he thought that Frazer was a good detective, he *knew* Lasiter was, but what the hell could he do? Cover it up so that some fresh-faced DC would find something out and the whole cycle would start again? Or maybe go straight to the DCI and tell him what he knew, leave it in *his* dubious hands.

"I need to think on this one," he eventually said.

281

"There's nothin' tae think on laddie, you have nae choice. Ef you don't report et you could get in some serious trouble."

"I don't think you are in a position to offer advice on this subject," insisted Avalon.

"I think I am," replied Lasiter leaning forward with his arms on the desk, "et's clear Frazer has lost et from what y' told me, et's sad an' all that but she es probably a liability now." He glanced down at his arm and to his wristwatch. "I'll tell you what, I'll make et easy for you, I'll go tae Croker myself."

"So after all this time of protecting her you're going to throw it all up in the air?" asked Avalon with surprise. Lasiter sat up and shrugged.

"Ef she has lost et there's nothin' can be done, can you ever see yourself lettin' her loose on a case now?" Avalon thought for a moment, he knew he had already made *that* decision. He rubbed his forehead in frustration, it just seemed like he was backed into a corner. "Ef et's any consolation," began Lasiter, "I happen to know that she has enjoyed working under you."

"How the hell would you know that, she thinks you hate her guts?" Lasiter smiled a little.

"You're good Avalon but not that good," he said, "when I went to Croker to ask for Frazer to be moved to B Section, he denied me."

"You told me that before," frowned Avalon.

"But I didn't tell you *why* he wouldn't't," and Lasiter leaned back, a little more relaxed, "Croker told me that she had put a request in for a transfer some months previous but retracted it. Her reason for the retraction was that she saw more potential here at Inverness." Avalon was staring blankly, so Lasiter

282

continued. "That's 'police speak' for 'things have changed and I'm happy here now'," and he raised his eyebrows a little. Avalon let it sink in, Frazer had almost hinted the same to him, she had come out of her shell, but why the hell had she let the incident at Cheeseman's house effect her? Well, he saw it was obvious now, knowing her past, but it also made it clear she could never work as a detective. If some slight comment could bring her past rushing back, she was never going to be able to work in the police force again. Avalon swore and banged his fist down on the desk so hard that Lasiter's family photograph jumped into the air and fell on its back.

Chapter Ten

Avalon didn't notice the activity when he returned to the Cave, he was too caught up in the agony of what he had to do surrounding the conversation he had just participated in with DI Lasiter. Ross was the first to enter the booth.

"We have made some headway on the..." Ross didn't finish, he could see something was weighing on Avalon's mind. "What's wrong?" he eventually asked.

"Me?" replied Avalon trying to look more upbeat about his situation, "oh nothing, what were you saying?" Ross wasn't convinced, but he continued.

"I was just saying that we've made some headway on the Romanian connection and it looks like we have hit on something."

"Go on," said Avalon.

"Back in 2012 we were involved with an international operation to track and break up several Albanian crime gangs, and though you may not know it, up here we've a few problems with Romanian criminal gangs too, over the past few years several thefts were put down to a gang working out of Glasgow. They hit the Highlands thinking there were some easy targets here. People trafficking is another big problem associated with

Romanian gangs," explained Ross.

"Just because we have a Romanian connection doesn't mean this is linked to a forced slave trade though," shrugged Avalon.

"No it doesn't," agreed Ross, "but think about it, trucks are used for drugs on occasions, why not people?"

"We don't have anything to suggest that though," insisted Avalon.

"No, but it does seem possible, even probable. What does clinch it though is something that DC Pottinger put us onto, he told us about someone his old team were after, connected with smuggling drugs into the country. They broke a drugs ring being supplied by a man named Victor McCabe, sometimes goes by the name of Callum McFee and he's also known to be connected with human trafficking for the sex trade."

"Sounds a nice piece of work, do we know where he is?" asked Avalon.

"Yes, but unfortunately his last known address was Romania."

"Oh," sighed Avalon, "we won't be bringing him in for some time then."

"No, but the pieces are fitting together."

"It's all circumstantial, and he may not be connected with this, we need something stronger than, 'he looks like a villain, let's nab him', don't you think?" sighed Avalon.

"Well we're still working on it but Wilson is downstairs interviewing the owner of the house at Scorguie, maybe something could come of it," shrugged Ross.

"Maybe nothing, we'll see," replied Avalon. Ross stared at him for a moment until Avalon noticed, and looked back. Ross held up his hands in a surrendering manner and returned to the Cave. Avalon sat staring through the glass at the team. He looked particularly at the obviously empty desk of Frazer and wondered what he ought to do. It was *his* decision, and *he* alone had to make it, there was no point in being a DI if he couldn't make this kind of call, the kind of call that could make, or break, his team. He pulled in a deep lungful of air and stood, he then looked at Ross and gave him a beckoning nod and waited for him outside the room in the empty corridor.

"What's up?" asked a concerned Ross.

"I've got to go and see Croker, hold the fort until I get back."

"Do you need to talk?" asked Ross, but Avalon gave him a slight smile and shook his head.

"Come in," called out Croker's voice. "DI Avalon, what is it?"

"Have you got a few minutes sir?"

"I'm sure I can spare a couple of minutes Detective Inspector," replied Croker hardly looking up at him. "Sit down if you wish." Avalon had never been this unsure about talking to a senior officer before, it felt like he was letting his team down, letting himself down. "What can I do for you?" asked Croker as Avalon sat.

"I have a bit of an issue, with one of my team," he announced hesitantly.

"Surely that is your domain DI Avalon, that's what you are paid to do, run your section," replied Croker. Avalon was anxious, if this had been Anderson in front of him, it would have been so easy. He steeled himself, he had no choice, but the way this was worded could be important.

"Normally it is sir, but there are certain

conditions that require me to bring it to your attention." This *got* his attention too, Croker looked up from his computer and frowned slightly.

"I see," said Croker, studying Avalon's face, "then you better tell me about it."

"Without naming anyone of course," added Avalon.

"If you wish," nodded Croker, Avalon was surprised by this, but he didn't want to walk into a trap, so he was careful how he said the next part.

"Something that happened some time ago, before I arrived at Inverness, has been brought to my attention," Avalon was happy with the wording so far, so he continued, "and this incident requires action that I'm not sure I have the authority to do, and I certainly don't wish to do it." Croker was listening intently, he even seemed to be interested.

"I'm not sure I understand DI Avalon but continue," and Croker removed his spectacles.

With Avalon out of the office and to Ross's eye, a little preoccupied, Ross kept up the momentum on the case. Wilson was pressurising George Barber about the foreign tenant he had, Mack and Pottinger had gone back to surveillance on the betting shop, Rory was checking through any records relating to Victor McCabe and Ross and Boyd were pulling out the stops, trying to trace links between the two victims, Alan Clacher and William Ewart. Wilson returned and walked over to Ross.

"Barber is adamant that he does'nae know anything about the man who rented the house, he does confirm he was probably eastern European, his name es Eduard Demetru and he had been renting the house for just two weeks." Ross nodded.

"It's a start," nodded Ross, "Alison," he said looking at DC Boyd, "contact the Dutch Politie and find out if they lifted any forensics or DNA from the truck they impounded. If the answer is yes, we need a readout of it, just in case." She nodded and set to work.

"Where's DC Frazer?" asked Mackinnon suddenly.

"I don't know," replied Ross trying not to show the question caught him off guard, "have you got anything on McCabe yet?" he asked, to quickly get Rory off the subject.

"Quite a bit, it seems he has been running loads of rackets from Romania, most of them directed at Scotland, though it seems he has done a runner in recent weeks."

"Keep at it, we need everything we can get on him," nodded Ross.

When Avalon returned, he looked into the Cave, and then to the whiteboard, it looked like they had been busy, so busy, hardly anyone noticed him return. Avalon walked behind Mackinnon and looked at his screen.

"He's got you chasing McCabe then has he?" Ross looked over and stood.

"I think it's a good direction to pursue," he said in his defence.

"Yeah, I can see that, so what became of the tip off from Alistair Parkes, the man in the betting shop?" he asked. Rory answered that question.

"Mack and DC Pottinger have been keeping an eye on it, they found the guy they think was the contact and brought in some video footage for forensics to look at to see if they can put any names to the faces they have," he sighed, "but there is nothing so far, so Mack and Pottinger have decided to continue close surveillance."

"I don't think Mack has done anything like that before," insisted Avalon.

"Pottinger has," Ross called over, "they used to do close surveillance in his last unit." Avalon nodded and shrugged at the same time, then went over to Ross to see what he and Boyd were up to. He looked over their notes but Ross couldn't be fooled so easily and knew Avalon had something on his mind. He looked up at his DI and Avalon saw the meaning in his expression. He nodded towards the booth.

"You got a minute?" he asked and moved off, Ross followed and, once in the booth, they both sat.

"Have you finally decided to tell me what's going on?" asked Ross with a deep frown as if he wasn't going to take no for an answer. Avalon cast a glance towards him.

"Nothing I'm about to tell you must go any further," Ross just looked at him, if Avalon didn't trust him by now, Ross had seriously miscalculated Avalon's perception. Avalon shuffled slightly, as if embarrassed by what he was about to say. "It's about Frazer of course," and he looked away from Ross as if he was still unsure about telling him. "You heard Cotter talking about an incident during his interview?" he paused, but Ross just nodded, "well, some time ago Frazer attacked him during an interview and the incident was covered up. Cotter was released with a promise to keep quiet about it but his promise is worth nothing of course."

"I can see that causes issues for both Frazer and whoever helped her cover it up," agreed Ross.

"She wasn't responsible for the cover up and she didn't even know who had done it," explained Avalon.

"So who was it?" asked Ross.

"DI Lasiter."

"Lasiter, why would he do that?"

"That part of the story is vague, and I can't tell you what I know, so don't ask, but suffice to say, both he and Frazer get it in the neck if this goes public." Ross nodded slowly.

"Awkward to say the least," frowned Ross, he then continued, "but we have nothing on Cotter, so why should he suddenly start squealing?" Avalon raised his eyebrows and Ross slowly began to understand. "You mean we *do* have something on Cotter?" Avalon opened a drawer, took out a small bunch of keys and unlocked and opened the other drawer. He pulled out a small file and dropped it on the desk. It was the forensics report on the truck abandoned on the B9177, the one that had been stolen. Ross opened the file and read through it, there wasn't much, so it took no time to read, but it stated two small spots of blood were found in the cab, one was identified as belonging to the driver from Crisp Brothers Haulage, the other was a match for Robert Cotter.

"Shit," exclaimed Ross, "this is going to be awkward indeed." Avalon watched Ross as he seemed to read the whole report over again as if he may have read it wrongly. "Normally I would have rejoiced at this, but..." he was weighing up the repercussions if Cotter decided to let the 'cat out of the bag'. He looked up to Avalon and said, "and I'm guessing you're not likely to offer Cotter any deals this time?" Avalon shook his head. "How long have you had this report?" asked Ross placing it back on the desk.

"It came in Monday morning," replied Avalon, "the day after we interviewed Cotter, when I first saw it I thought, great, we've got him, but then realised there was a problem."

"Too right," agreed Ross, "so what's the plan?"

"There isn't one," said Avalon with a blank expression.

"I know you, you always have a plan."

"Not this time," said Avalon placing the file back in the drawer, "we have Cotter in the truck cab at the time the driver was assaulted, he obviously had blood on him from the driver when he was beaten, and he probably injured himself in the attack, so there is no doubt he was responsible for the theft and attack, or at least involved." Ross nodded, it was strong evidence, the sort of 'smoking gun' that was important in any case.

"So we're gonna cut Frazer and Lasiter loose?" Avalon noticed Ross changed the context, he had said 'we're', he was showing his support for Avalon and that meant a great deal.

"Not if I can help it, I went to see Croker about it."

"Croker?" spluttered Ross, "what the hell for, he's not going to give a flying-" but Avalon interrupted him mid flow.

"That's where you're wrong, it took me by surprise too I admit," explained Avalon, "the DCI listened and seemed to be keen to help. I thought he was trying to trap me, but it turns out, underneath he isn't the total sociopath we had him down for." Ross blinked several times, he considered Croker being reasonable was more of a shock that finding two officers he had known for some time were involved in a cover up.

"So what did he say?" asked Ross.

"He said, as long as *he* didn't know who the officers were, he would go along with whatever I thought was right but if he learned their identities he would be forced to act."

"Understandable I suppose," nodded Ross. There were a few seconds of silence and then Ross continued. "You realise that he now has something on you, leverage for the future." Avalon nodded with an air of inevitability.

"I know, but I have to make a decision and I would rather him have something on me than anyone else." Ross looked into his eyes for a moment and then nodded and said,

"So when you said there was no plan, did you mean there was no plan, or did you mean there wasn't a good plan?" Avalon stared back and allowed the corners of his mouth to curve, it wasn't a smile, more a *hint* of a smile.

"Let's say, it's an idea, not quite a plan yet," he said.

"I'm listening," said Ross almost as a question.

"Cotter has us over a barrel because he has something on Frazer and Lasiter, what if we take that leverage away from him?"

"Get Frazer and Lasiter to own up you mean?"

"Sort of," replied Avalon.

"Set Cotter up is what you're saying?" smiled Ross.

"Sort of."

Avalon had rung Megan Frazer up to explain he needed to see her, when he arrived at the address, he saw that the road up to the house was a dirt track and with pot holes and mud up to the axles, he decided to leave the car on the road and walk up the to the house.

"Come en," announced Frazer, as she showed Avalon into the small farmhouse.

"It's quiet out here," he said taking a seat in the

cosy room.

"That's why I live here," she replied, sitting opposite. Avalon looked at her, she looked frustrated and bored and he could imagine someone with her quick mind would find an amount of tedium out in the countryside, quiet or not.

"I'll not beat about the bush Megan, I've spent too much of my time on this already, but I have to ask you how much you want your job?"

"That's a stupid question," she frowned.

"Look, I'm trying to help, I can walk away and my life stays the same, but yours changes dramatically, I can possibly help but you have to do some work." His tone said it all, he was tired with her attitude, he knew more about her than she knew, inside he understood what was driving her, the nightmares she probably still had, the doubt, the shame, the horror of it all but he also had his job to do. Sympathy was one thing but if she wouldn't help him to help herself, then he would turn away and get on with his job.

"I don't see what you *can* do," she replied.

"I'm not sure I can do anything but I'm willing to have a go, but *you* need to do something," he insisted, "you also need to change your attitude," he added. She glared at him for a moment. He understood the glare, it said 'you don't know the hurt I feel', but he did and that was why he was trying to help. Her look subsided and she asked,

"What would I have tae do?" He sighed a little and after a short pause, he began.

"You have to meet Bobby Cotter in an interview room, you will have other officers with you and you will be safe, but you have to do it," she looked worried but after a moment she said,

"What else?"

"First you have to know something," Avalon paused, he didn't know how she would react to the next part, "it was DI Lasiter that covered the incident up."

"Lasiter!" she called, "et was'nae him, et wasn't." Behind him, Avalon was aware of someone entering the room.

"You alright?" asked an English voice. Avalon looked up to see a medium built man, probably in his fifties but lithe and in good shape, wiping his hands with a cloth.

"Yeah," said Frazer, "get back tae what y' were doin' an' leave us be." The man looked down at Avalon. There was no expression, but Avalon felt he was in some danger, he couldn't explain it, but he hoped he never had to try and bring that man in. He assumed he was Frazer's partner, the ex-special forces chap. The man eventually turned and left. Avalon looked back at Frazer who seemed to be considering a million options all at one moment. "Why would Lasiter do that?" she asked but Avalon knew he couldn't tell her, he left everything unsaid.

"I don't know," he eventually said, "but he did, and you have to accept that. You also have to forget that he did, because if you admit to him that I told you, I will drop you like a stone," he insisted, "you also have to tell Cotter you have come clean to the DCI and a few things that you won't be happy with, it's tough but that's the way it is."

"But ef I do that I'm sunk anyway," she pointed out.

"You are just gonna have to trust me on that one," he said, just as he heard a sort of muffled 'crump' sound. He looked around just in case the man had returned, he

294

felt uneasy. He turned back to Frazer, she seemed to be considering the situation.

"An' what do y' mean about attitude?" she eventually asked.

"Well," he sighed, "you haven't always been the easiest person in the office to work with, you have to integrate into the team, you have to stop seeing them as the enemy."

"I don't have anything in common with them, why should I?"

"Because in this line of work, all you have are the people you work with," he insisted, there was something else he had to tell her, and he knew damn well she wouldn't like it. He took a deep breath and said,

"And if you come back, you will be full time office based," and he looked up so see her expression change to pure disappointment but they were interrupted.

"Hey fella," said the man as he re-entered the room, "did you have a black Saab?"

"Yes," answered Avalon, "and why ask in the past tense?"

Avalon stood looking at his car, the delivery van looked like it had tried to go straight through it and the driver said he just didn't see it, as he wiped blood from a small cut on his head. He looked at the wreck of the car again and pulled out his phone. What else could go wrong in his life he wondered?

~~~~~~~

Robert Cotter sat in interview room one with Ross seated opposite.

"Have you sent for my lawyer as I asked?"

"Course we have Bobby, we'll make a start as

soon as he arrives," smiled Ross. The door opened and in walked Avalon, Cotter looked up at him but made no comment. Avalon stood by the side of Ross and looked down at the man opposite.

"Before we bring in your solicitor, there is someone who wants to speak with you," he said. Ross hadn't been particularly happy with this part of the plan, but he realised it was necessary. Avalon opened the door and Frazer walked in. Cotter immediately reacted by pushing his chair back.

"What's she doin' here?" he spat.

"It's quite safe Mr Cotter," announced Avalon. Frazer was dressed in jeans and a tee shirt and her hair was down, a look that neither Ross nor Avalon had ever seen before. The scraped back look was considered the only position Frazer's hair would ever accept. Avalon stepped to the side of the table between Frazer and Cotter.

"Go ahead Miss Frazer, you have one minute." She looked down at Cotter who was visibly unnerved.

"Robert Cotter, I'm not here to apologise to you though I *am* sorry for what happened. I just want to thank you for ruining not just my career, but that of a fellow officer," she glowered down at him, "and ef I ever see you out after this, I will make you pay, you worthless-"

"Now then Miss Frazer, I warned you," interrupted Avalon, "DC Ross, escort Miss Frazer out." Ross nodded and took hold of Frazer's arm.

"I know the way Ross," she spat and left the room escorted by the DS. Avalon sat and opened a case file.

"What was that about?" asked Cotter.

"If I had my way Mr Cotter, I would let her and

the other officer have twenty minutes in here with you, but as it is, I'm here for something totally different," Avalon had kept a calm voice and had not even looked at Cotter as he spoke. The man looked astonished, he was obviously confused and unsure of what was to come, he fidgeted uneasily in his seat.

"Has she gone then?" he finally asked. Avalon looked up to him with a blank face, said nothing, then continued to read the notes in the file. The door opened again and Ross returned with Cotter's solicitor. Avalon began recording the session, announcing the details of the interview, the time, the date, and those present he then began the questions.

"Can you confirm that you are Robert Timothy Cotter, currently living on the boat, 'Sally Anne', at a moorings at Muirtown Basin?" When Avalon had heard the confirmation that he was indeed whom they had in the interview room, he began by stating that Cotter had been questioned informally on a previous occasion and had denied any involvement in the theft of the truck. He was then questioned again and still denied it. When they told him they had forensic evidence to prove he was at the crime scene, the solicitor told his client not to answer any further questions and the interview was terminated. At this point, it was a formality, there would be meetings, paperwork, more meetings and more paperwork and along the way it was possible that Cotter may try to broker a deal to get a lighter sentence. That would be beneficial to the case of course as it may implicate the rest of the team and save some time and some police resources. Time would tell though if Cotter would see through their deception, if he did, both Ross and Avalon could be in trouble, although nothing really illegal had been done, just immoral and against proper practice.

As Avalon and Ross climbed the stairs, Ross sniffed and then asked,

"So what have they said about your car?"

"Oh, it's a write off of course."

"Shame, it wasn't a bad looking car."

"I thought you said it was an old man's car?" asked Avalon looking over to him.

"Well it was, but it wasn't bad looking for an old man's car." They entered the Cave, Avalon poured two cups of coffee and they went into the booth.

"So what are you going to do for wheels, I think the Beemer I told you about is still for sale," said Ross as he sat. Avalon shook his head.

"There's a car lot in town, they had an old Ford, I may go and have a look at it," and then he added, "it's cheap enough," but then he noticed on the calendar, that had been a fortnight ago. The time was slipping away and though the truck theft case was coming together, the double murder was still not showing any sign of being solved.

"Back to a crappy old Mondeo then?" said Ross bringing Avalon out of his thoughts.

"Hey? Oh no, not quite," he blinked, "did you find anything connecting the two victims?"

"Nothing concrete, I'll go and have a word with Alison," he replied and he went into the Cave. Avalon followed, taking his coffee with him.

"I got the records from the Dutch police, they have his DNA on record and confirmed the name Eduard Demetru, though he isn't wanted for anything here," announced DC Boyd.

"What about connections with the two murder victims?"

"Well," began Boyd, "I'm not sure if this is relevant, but I've done some digging this morning, knowing that there could be a Romanian connection, and with a bit of assistance from DC Mackinnon, I found an odd connection between our two victims, they were both called as witnesses in a case involving human trafficking last year." She looked up at the two men with a slightly unsure expression.

"Was that the same case or two different cases?" asked Avalon.

"The same one, their names appear on a list of witnesses and the addresses check out too," she insisted, "it's all I can find though."

"Are you married DC Boyd?" asked Ross knowing the answer.

"Yes, why?"

"Because if you weren't, I would marry you today," he smiled, "this is probably the connection we have been scouring the earth for."

"Don't get your hopes up yet, it may be nothing to do with our case," insisted Avalon.

"Pull up the information Alison," instructed Ross, "let's have a closer look at the case they were involved in." Avalon left them to it, he had a mountain of paperwork to attend to, so he returned to the booth and finished his coffee before starting.

MacDonald and Pottinger arrived back in the office soon after and they went to Avalon with some information.

"We have a confirmed name for the contact that was going tae pay for an HGV driver, he has been positively identified from the video footage that Ewan..." he hesitated, "er, DC Pottinger took en the betting shop," smiled Mack.

"Anyone we know?" asked Avalon.

"Yep, Toby Cheeseman," he beamed.

"Good work Mack," smiled Avalon, "and we have his partner, Bobby Cotter downstairs." Avalon then went into the Cave to tell everyone, but Ross still had doubts.

"So what's the Romanian connection," he asked.

"I'm not sure, maybe the customer was in Europe and the driver had been brought over to ferry the trailer back," offered Avalon. He then considered something he had gone over previously, something he had thought about when he was at home. "Hang on," he suddenly said, "Mack, have you still got the info on that trailer?"

"Yes boss," nodded Mack and he brought it up on his screen, "what do you want to know?"

"Well, to be honest I'm not sure but that trailer was, I think you said, fairly unique."

"Well not exactly unique but there aren't that many of this type of refrigeration trailers around these days," explained Mack.

"So the trailer type is significant, we need to know what it is about that particular trailer that these people wanted," insisted Avalon.

"But we've gone through that a couple of times and come up with nothing," said Ross.

"Then we are missing something," insisted Avalon, "so let's find out what it is we're missing." Avalon looked towards Ross and nodded to the booth. Ross got up and followed him.

"I've got to go and let DI Lasiter know what we have done regarding Cotter, hold the fort until I get back," and he turned to leave but hesitated and turned back to Ross.

"There was something Lasiter said to me that I

300

can't get out of my head."

"What's that?" asked Ross folding his arms.

"When we were having a heated discussion about the cover up he said he didn't expect an 'English detective with glowing red eyes' to find out about it," explained Avalon, "or it could have been 'flaming red', what do you think he meant by that?" Ross shrugged and then said,

"Maybe it's that photo of you at Wilson's birthday party."

"What photo?"

"You mean you are the only person at this nick without a copy of it on your phone?" smiled Ross. Avalon stared blankly. "Course," continued Ross, "your phone is probably so old it doesn't have the facility for photo's." Ross unfolded his arms and went into the Cave and called out,

"Hands up anyone who doesn't have that photo of the DI at Wilson's party." Three hands went up slowly, Mackinnon, Boyd and Pottinger. "There you go, the only ones that don't have it are the recent arrivals," said Ross holding his arm out to the room in general.

"I want to see it," insisted Avalon not having any recollection of seeing the image. Ross fetched his personal phone from his jacket and began to scan through the photographs. Now and then he smiled and even sniggered once at an image he saw on his search.

"Here we are," he finally said, handing the phone to Avalon. The image was a strange shot of Avalon near the bar with his mouth wide open and a red reflection in his eyes. It looked slightly demonic and Avalon found it quite embarrassing.

"Well it's obviously the reflection from the camera flash..." he trailed of for a second.

"Obviously," grinned Ross looking round at some of the others in the room.

"And the open mouth is because... I was in the middle of saying something... like..." he began to mouth the same shape as in the picture, "overkill, or Ovaltine, or something like that."

"Gordon," called Ross towards Wilson, "to your knowledge, how many times did the DI say Ovaltine at your party?"

"None as I remember," smiled Wilson, "but he may have said 'overtime' on a couple of occasions."

"So everyone has this image?" asked Avalon still staring at it.

"I don't think the DCI has a copy, but there can't be many, oh and I emailed a copy to Sarah Underwood," he paused, "for scientific purposes you understand." Avalon shook his head and handed the phone back to Ross, then said,

"Get back to work the lot of you, it looks like being a late night for you all," then he turned and left the room, still shaking his head and directed himself towards Lasiter's office.

Avalon had decided that his team needed some time off, and so he set a rota for the weekend as there was little they could do to further the case until Monday morning. Wilson, Mack and Rory would be off Saturday and Avalon, Ross and the two new faces of Pottinger and Boyd, would have Sunday at home. It was going to be an odd day for Avalon as it seemed quite some time since he had seen a whole day for his own use. They spent Saturday clearing up a few loose ends and catching up with paperwork. It had been a tedious day, to break the monotony they had talked about what they would do

302

with that precious day of relaxation. Pottinger would go fishing, Boyd would drive down to see her mother and Ross was planning an afternoon at the rugby club, followed by too much to drink in front of the television. Avalon had made his plans clear, he would take the bike out, weather permitting and then he would spend the evening relaxing, he may even spend some time to practice on his guitar, but he didn't admit to that.

When Sunday morning finally arrived, Avalon wondered what catastrophe would befall him to send his plans into freefall, but nothing happened. He felt almost guilty when the phone didn't ring as he drank his second cup of coffee. Angie also had the day off, so they had a couple of hours to catch up before Avalon pulled the bike out of the shed and dressed for the occasion. He sat on the bike first to feel it under him, it seemed so long since he had been on it, then he pulled his helmet on, 'tickled the carb', switched on the ignition and gave it a good kick. Nothing, but that was usual, he gave one more kick, then 'tickled' the carburettor again until the unmistakable petrol fumes danced in the air and then gave another kick and the machine jumped into life with Angie stepping back from the noise that it made. She waved him off and he was on his way, heading out towards Glen Affric after stopping to top up with fuel.

It wasn't such a bad day, if a little windy, but it looked like there would be the odd sunny spell so he was enjoying the ride like it was the first time he had ever ridden. The freedom that he felt was so soothing, he had almost forgotten what it was like to be out on a bike. As he rode, he considered that he might buy a more modern bike as a runabout, to save the old triumph for the sunny days, not that there had been any in recent weeks.

He decided not to go down the glen as the wind was

303

increasing a little, so instead, he took some of the minor roads around the hills to see the scenery and he wasn't disappointed, stopping several times to admire the view. The sun came out now and then and all was well with the world, the trees flashing past, the burble of the engine and the wind forcing its way through his clothing. As he returned towards Loch Ness, he decided to stop off at Drumnadrochit, he knew the place quite well and he remembered that there was at least one cafe somewhere on the main street. He pulled into the car park in the centre of the village and put the bike on its side stand. The village was protected from the wind by the sides of the glen, so off came the gloves and the helmet and he leaned on the toilet building and looked back at the bike. The heat from its engine was making a distinctive ticking sound as he opened his jacket and dropped the gloves in his helmet and went to search for the cafe.

As he crossed the road, he decided to have a look around the place first and he covered most of the village. There were shops but he had no means of carrying anything, so he decided to leave that until later, he could always go out in the borrowed pool car he was now using. As he walked back over the bridge away from the Loch Ness centre, he was quite taken in by the place, not just the village but the way it sat, nestled in the glen, tucked back from the great loch. He headed towards the centre once more and as he drew level with the pull-in where the coaches stopped, he noticed a woman cross the road from the opposite side about fifty feet ahead of him. She was wearing a flowing dress and had a very confident walk. Her hair was fairly short and neat, cut to collar length at the back and turned under. The colour was a mix of blonde and brunette, a colour that Avalon heard his ex-wife once call 'caramel'. It looked like a very expensive cut but suited her to a tee. She was wearing sunglasses with large lenses though the brightness of the day was giving way to the usual cloud, so he couldn't make out her face. All in all, he was very taken in by her, it made him realise that unless he got out more, he was going to spend the rest of his life a very lonely man. But that was the dilemma, he couldn't see himself in a relationship, it wouldn't work. It didn't work with Carol and she was an angel, so how could any ordinary woman be expected to cope with his mood swings and his marriage to the job? He followed behind the woman for a few yards until she stopped to look in a window and as he walked past, she looked towards him, he deliberately moved his eyes away from her for a second and she looked back at the window and then suddenly looked back to him as if she had recognised him. She couldn't have of course, but it made his stomach release several small butterflies which seemed to flutter about inside until they flew up his windpipe and threatened to choke him. The woman continued to stare at him as he drew closer and he was beginning to feel embarrassed. She removed the sunglasses and still stared at him, then a slight grin appeared on her face. For a moment he thought he recognised her and then he realised.

"Detective Avalon, I didn't recognise you in the motorbike clothing," she smiled. It was Sarah Underwood.

"Miss Underwood," he returned the smile, "I didn't recognise you either with your rather fetching new hair style."

"Please, it's Sarah, I think we can dispense with the 'Miss Underwood' by now, and thank you, it is just two hours old," Avalon smiled again assuming she was referring to the hairstyle.

"As I said, it really suits you, and it's Jim..." he hesitated, "or James if you prefer."

"So I assume you have a motorcycle, or do you drive the car dressed like this at the weekend?"

"Yes, it's parked over there," he pointed in a rough direction but she didn't look, that probably meant motorbikes weren't her thing. "So what are you doing in Drumnadrochit?" he asked.

"My sister lives just outside the village, so when I come over, I sometimes drop off to do a little shopping, there happens to be a cafe just out of the village that does vegan cake so I sometimes indulge," she smiled.

"Then I'd love to treat you," he said but then hesitated, "though that's probably out of order, you must have things to do." She looked at him for a moment, then looked at her watch and said,

"Why not? I'll pass on the cake as that cafe is a little more than a stroll from here, but I'd love a coffee," she smiled again and placed her sunglasses in her bag. They sat inside as the wind was swirling a little more. Avalon couldn't get over how much the new hair colour and style suited her, she was pleasing to look at before but Avalon found something soothing about her manner as well as her look. When they met in a professional way he just accepted she was one of the best forensics technicians in the country but here, she was a woman.

"So why are you in Drum?" she asked sipping at her coffee.

"I was out on the bike admiring the scenery and noticed the wind was becoming stronger, so I headed back, remembering seeing a cafe here somewhere and decided to stop," replied Avalon.

"The scene of your first great case in Scotland,"

she smiled.

"I wouldn't say great case, it had its moments though."

"I like coming here, it's quaint and friendly."

"I find most places I've seen round here friendly, but I only realised a couple of days ago how outstanding it is up in Glen Affric, I fell in love with the place," he explained.

"Have you been up to Plodda Falls by any chance?" she asked.

"I haven't heard of it, so I doubt it."

"Oh you'd know if you'd been," she said with a thoughtful look.

"It sounds like I'm going to have to seek it out."

"I love it up there, and if you get the time walk down to the bottom, the air is so clean and clear, but of course, there are so many places to visit. I'm sure some of your colleagues can give you ideas." She seemed to suddenly change her tone, as if something had popped into her mind. One minute she was wistfully talking about where to visit and then just as quickly went quiet. Avalon wondered if she wanted to leave.

"I hope I'm not keeping you from something..." he said expecting a reaction of sorts but she just shook her head gently and said,

"No, I don't get many days off but when I do I like to relax, it would be nice to get a sunny day now and then though." Avalon gave a quick smile but it didn't quite say how he felt. He too was missing this sort of afternoon, it was the kind of afternoon he always seemed to see other people participating in as he flew past in a car to yet another crime scene. This was peaceful and relaxing, the rest of his life was hectic and demanding, probably not that far removed from Sarah's lifestyle, did that make them compatible or was he jumping the gun? He was probably running the race before the starting pistol was even loaded if the truth was known. He felt so far out of his depth, his doubts were jostling for room in his mind, what the hell was wrong with him anyway? Why didn't he just ask her out? She sipped at her coffee once more and he decided he didn't think it was wise to get involved with someone he worked with on occasions, at least that's what he told himself, it wasn't what he wanted to hear however. He decided to find out more about her instead.

"So your sister doesn't accompany you then?" he asked picking up his cup.

"Sometimes," she nodded, "but she's busy today, she's the hairdresser that did this," she smiled rolling her eyes up to her forehead. "She ran a successful boutique in Inverness for some years but stopped to have a family," and she looked into Avalon's eyes, "do you have family Det..." she stopped, and changed the name, "sorry, *Jim*?" Avalon swallowed the coffee and shook his head placing the cup back on the table.

"No, I was married though but this job..." and he shrugged, "how about you?"

"No," she replied lowering her eyes to the coffee cup and making a wrinkling effect with her nose, "it's not really me, I like to see other people's children, like my sister's, but that's about it." Avalon nodded and wanted to ask about boyfriends or ex-husbands but he thought it was too forward and instead asked,

"So what do you do with your spare same," he leaned back as much as he could in the flimsy seat, "apart from drinking coffee in Drumnadrochit of course?"

"Not much really, I get so little free time that I

usually keep it simple."

"No hobbies or interests then?"

"Not really, nothing you would care to hear about anyway," she smiled.

"I might surprise you, what would you be doing if you weren't here?" he asked and he saw her glance up and smile a little.

"Gardening," she said, "I don't have much room but I have a tiny vegetable plot at the edge of my lawn and I love to grow at least one crop through the year."

"A very admirable pass-time," smiled Avalon.

"Do you grow anything?" she asked.

"Only older," he grinned and he searched his mind for a line of verse, "*Behold the dark green file of long lank weeds, that all at once, a most fantastic sight, still nod and drip beneath the dripping edge, of the blue, clay stone.*"

"What's that from?" she asked.

"It's from a poem by Coleridge but that is the only part of it I can quote."

"I'm impressed, poetry as well as motorcycling."

"Yes," he grinned, "I'm not sure the two hobbies go together seamlessly."

"What got you interested in poetry, it's not exactly mainstream?" she asked resting her hands on her lap.

"It's odd really, I usually tell a lie when asked that, but today I'll tell you the truth," and he raised his eyebrows. She gave a slight laugh at the comment. "It was my uncle who actually brought poetry to my ears. It was at my father's funeral," he paused to explain, "there was no love lost between us but I went and stood at the graveside like the dutiful son. My uncle decided to read part of a poem, and though I was young, it made an impression on me."

"What was it?" she asked.

"At the time I didn't know what it was, the only part I can remember *now* is the last part of it," he paused and tried to recall it verbatim. "*Ye, who perchance behold this simple urn, pass on, it honours none you wish to mourn,*" he hesitated, trying to remember the last line, "*to mark a friend's remains these stones arise, I never knew but one and here he lies.*" She nodded slowly. "I can see by your expression you don't think it's a great classic, but the thing is, the poem was written by Lord Byron."

"I wouldn't know if he was a good poet or not," she laughed.

"I used to think he was in those days and I thought the poem was a touching tribute until in later years I found it, it's called 'Epitaph to a Dog".

"So your uncle recited a poem about a dog?" she laughed.

"Yes," smiled Avalon, "to this day I don't know if he meant it as a joke." Sarah laughed and then she said,

"What *is* touching is that Lord Byron was moved enough by the death of his dog to write a poem." Avalon nodded.

"From what I have read about the man I wouldn't read too much into it though." She smiled again and glanced at her watch, Avalon decided to give her the excuse to leave and said,

"Well, this has been a much more pleasant afternoon than I could have expected, I suppose we ought to make a move."

"Yes I have enjoyed it," she smiled and they both stood. "Well, I suppose we'll see each other soon," she said and then added, "thanks for the coffee."

"Thanks for a pleasant afternoon." And they parted company, she continuing down the road, he crossing the road and into the car park, to where his bike still stood. He went through the ritual of starting the machine and with his helmet fastened, he exited the car park and made his way back to Inverness as the wind began to rise in strength.

As he rode, he realised he was somewhat taken in by Sarah Underwood, he wasn't sure what the feeling was, it was so long since he had experienced it that he didn't quite know what species of emotion it was, he just knew it was uncomfortable, but thrilling.

He didn't go straight back to the house, he took a detour onto Harbour Road and stopped off at the car lot to have a look around. The gunmetal grey, Ford Focus was still there, at less than a thousand pounds, Avalon considered it would be good make-do transport until the insurance company sorted out his claim. He looked at some of the other cars too but he knew an old Ford was what he needed, his bike said who he was, not his car. The wind was intensifying and threatened to become gale force, so he jumped on the Triumph and rode back to the house. He thought about what to do for the rest of the afternoon and evening and he considered he might pull out some of his poetry books from the box under his bed, but then again, he would probably give the guitar some more pain, after all, it was giving him pain, his fingers were becoming quite sore. For sure his Sunday had been pleasant in many ways and he wanted some more, so one thing he decided not to do, was think about work. It would soon be Monday again and the case could wait until morning.

Chapter Eleven

"I was thinking last night," said Avalon.

"Well there's always room for adventure," replied Ross in a flat tone.

"Something doesn't add up," insisted Avalon as he poured his second coffee.

"Welcome to my world," frowned Ross.

"Can you be serious for just *one* moment?" said Avalon sitting on the edge of the nearest desk, "why would Toby Cheeseman be looking for an HGV driver if they already had one to take the truck back to Romania?"

"I don't get what you mean," replied Ross squinting his eyes.

"Well, if Cheeseman and Cotter were part of the team that stole the truck and the Romanian up at Scorguie was the one brought in to drive the truck back to Romania, why would Cheeseman be looking for another driver?"

"To drive the other unit to the rendezvous," explained Ross.

"But anyone could have done that, it didn't need an HGV driver to take it," insisted Avalon. Ross thought for a moment, he could see what Avalon was getting at.

"Right, why are they still looking for a driver if

they already have one." he said.

"Exactly, are we missing a large part of this or were Cotter and Cheeseman expanding their operation?"

"Could be," shrugged Ross, "I suppose it isn't planned as an isolated attack, they probably intend to continue." Avalon stood and paced the small space left in the Cave.

"Yes," nodded Avalon as he thought it through, "they would certainly need a new driver each time, but wouldn't they bring in more European drivers? Why would they be looking for drivers this side of the water?" he admitted, "Something just doesn't make sense."

"Does it ever?" asked Ross.

"Another issue is," continued Avalon, "who was the other man that told Alistair Parkes where he could find a driver, the one with a foreign accent? He can't have been part of the team so why would he know about the Romanian?" Ross thought about the problem but there was nothing obvious that sprung into his head.

"Maybe it was just coincidence, it could be someone who came over with the driver, there are so many possible options," he shrugged.

"I suppose so, it makes sense that the driver would be in contact with the Romanian community over here," sighed Avalon.

"Do you want me to try and find out if he knew anyone here?" asked Ross.

"Not yet," replied Avalon shaking his head, "we still have a lot to go through."

"Okay," said Ross looking round the room. There was only Mackinnon and Boyd in the Cave, it was still early and no one else had arrived. "So what do you want doing this morning?" he asked.

"I'm not sure yet," replied Avalon, "I want DS

Wilson to continue the interviews with Cotter and Cheeseman once their solicitors get sorted out and I also want him to work on George Barber again, I think he knows more than he's telling."

"What about-" began Ross but the door to the Cave opened and Frazer walked in. She nodded to Avalon and made her way to her desk.

"You were saying?" asked Avalon but Ross had been about to ask about Frazer, the fact that she had entered the room made the question surplus to requirements and he quickly devised another one.

"What about Pottinger, do you want him with Wilson?" Avalon nodded at this.

"Yes, Gordon will need some help," nodded Avalon and he looked over to Mackinnon.

"Rory, bring DC Frazer up to speed and then I may have an errand for you." Mackinnon nodded. "Megan," continued Avalon looking over to Frazer, "I need you here to recap all the information we have and bring the whiteboard up to date, Rory can help until I need him." She also nodded and moved over to Mackinnon's desk taking her chair. Ross was surprised, he had never seen her do anything like that before, if you needed something from Frazer, you usually had to go and get it. Mack walked in with Wilson following close behind.

"Morning all!" came Wilson's usual greeting. Avalon explained what he wanted him and Pottinger to do and then he returned to his booth to finish his coffee and look at his emails, but it would have to wait, the phone was ringing.

"Avalon," he said.

"*James, et's Robbie,*" said Lasiter's unmistakable voice, it sounded as if he was on his mobile phone.

"Hello, what's wrong?"

"*Well, I got a shout before I got tae the station so I came straight here, we've got a body.*"

"Where?" asked Avalon wondering if it was in his patch.

"*Longman Industrial estate,*" replied Lasiter.

"Sorry old chap, that's your area, welcome to the 'I've found a body club'," replied Avalon. There was a slight pause and he heard Lasiter talking to someone then came the reply.

"*Aye, et es but y' see, the body was found en the back of a trailer, the sort that y' pull about on a truck an' I know you are working on somethin' with a truck flavour,*"

"We are, have you an ID for the body?"

"*Not yet, we're still waiting for the FME but Tom Murrey has just arrived and he says et looks like a 'small timer' named Ali Parkes,*"

"I'm on my way," replied Avalon and he immediately called Ross and Boyd over and they set off to the site.

It was easy to find, there were police cars and taped off areas everywhere and as they were waved through they saw the yard where the trailer was parked. The haulage company that owned the yard hadn't come up in the investigation and Avalon doubted there was any connection with their case but if the body was that of Alistair Parkes, could it be just co-incidence that he had been questioned by them previously?

"Mornin'," said Lasiter as they approached. Tom Murrey nodded and then winked at Ross. Avalon looked in the back of the trailer and saw the forensics team processing the inside but Avalon couldn't see the face of the dead man.

"So what's the story?" asked Avalon.

"Not a great deal to et," began Lasiter, "one of the drivers started work at six this mornin', pulls his truck up tae this trailer and couples up. He then went round the back and opened the doors to make sure et was ready tae go and found this en the back." He pointed his thumb in the direction of the body.

"Is there any ID?" Avalon called over. One of the team was checking the pockets of the dead man and found what seemed to be a wallet and he brought it over. Lasiter pulled on some rubber gloves and checked through the wallet, it seemed that indeed it was Alistair Parkes.

"You were right Tom," said Lasiter to DS Murrey.

"Aye, I thought it was him, he always wears that brand of training shoe," explained the soft spoken man, "he was a bit of a rogue but I wouldn't have wanted to see him end like this." Avalon looked around the inside, as much as he could do from ground level and as he saw the blood pooled on the floor of the trailer he turned to Ross and said,

"It could be connected I suppose," and then he turned to Lasiter and added, "we questioned Parkes about a truck theft, he was asked to find a driver by Toby Cheeseman."

"That's a name I hav'nae heard for a while," frowned Lasiter, "he was well into truck hijacking but I would'nae think he was a killer."

"I'm not saying he is, I think whoever did this work in a much bigger league," replied Avalon. Lasiter nodded and glanced back into the trailer, the forensics team had covered most of the trailer and as one of them jumped down Avalon recognised him as one of Sarah Underwood's colleagues. DS Murrey climbed up and

316

carefully stepping over the blood looked at the face of the dead man.

"It looks like a knife wound to the throat killed him," said the forensics technician, "just a single wound as I can see but the pathologist will confirm it I think."

"Any guesses on how long he's been there?" asked Lasiter. The man shook his head slowly.

"I'm not sure but I would say sometime last night as a pure guess." Lasiter nodded.

"Aye, it's him governor," nodded Murrey from the trailer, "the poor bastard has had his throat cut." Lasiter looked at Avalon and said,

"Well this es a bit of a heid scratcher, your case, but my area according to the gospel of DCI Croker."

"This is where his system becomes a real nightmare," nodded Avalon.

"Well the only thing I can suggest es that B Section begin work on et and then hand et over to you ef there es any connection with any o' your cases."

"Sounds good to me," nodded Avalon, normally he would have protested but due to the recent issue with Frazer, he decided to show good faith and let Lasiter continue without any demands.

"Sir," interrupted a uniformed officer.

"Aye, what es et?" asked Lasiter.

"We think we've found where they got in, there's a hole in the fence," explained the PC.

"Okay, I'll get forensics tae have a look," and he shrugged and walked off. Avalon walked back to the car followed by Ross and Boyd and as they reached it he turned.

"You know, when we were at the trailer, something occurred to me." Ross just stared at him with a questioning expression. "What if our first victim was

317

killed in the back of one of these things?" he nodded towards several other trailers. Ross thought for a moment and then stuck out his bottom lip in reflection.

"It could be, I suppose if he was tortured on the move it would ensure no one would hear him screaming," he suggested.

"And it would explain why there was no insect activity until the morning the body was found," suggested Avalon.

"Easy to wash the thing out too," Boyd offered. Ross nodded.

"Yeah, the trailer he was killed in could be anywhere in Europe now too." Avalon was beginning to see that the death of Parkes was likely related to the case but it was going to be difficult to connect it. He though for a moment and then said,

"Let me give Wilson a call, this might be information he can use," and he pulled out his phone.

"You think that Cotter and Cheeseman won't know about this?" asked Ross.

"I don't know but it may come in handy during his interviews," and he dialled. "Gordon, it's Avalon, we are over at this murder site in town but the thing is, we are sure the body is Alistair Parkes."

"*Shite,*" replied Wilson, "*that's gonna complicate things a bit.*"

"I just thought you should know, it may come in useful if you catch my drift?"

"*Aye, et will, thanks for the info boss, how was he killed?*" asked the DS.

"It looks like a knife wound to the throat."

"*Okay,*" replied Wilson, "*I'll get tae work on et,*" and Avalon put his phone back in his pocket.

"I suppose we better make a move and let DI

Lasiter do his job," and then he climbed into the car.

As they drove back Ross was deep in thought, he was considering all the angles and possible permutations of what they knew.

"The first two killing seem like revenge killings, right?" he asked, Avalon glanced over to him and nodded, "so if this last body is connected, it doesn't have the bells and whistles of the first two so we can assume the reason was different."

"Punishment," interrupted Boyd from the rear seat.

"What?" asked Ross turning around to look at her.

"It's a punishment," she repeated.

"I don't follow, I would have thought that being stripped, tortured and then killed qualifies as punishment," he insisted with slight amount of sarcasm in his voice.

"Sorry," she apologised, "I'm not making it clear, what I mean is, the previous killings look like they are orchestrated, designed if you like, to get the most impact out of them yet this one in the trailer is just a murder."

"I know what you mean Alison," said Avalon, "an assassination so to speak."

"Yes," she nodded, "as if they couldn't be bothered with the 'bells and whistles' as DS Ross so quaintly put it," she smiled.

"Okay," began Ross, "that's assuming it is connected and yes, I accept it seems like it could be but there is another option," and he paused to think the argument through. Avalon glanced quickly over to him as he turned to face forwards once more. "What if," he paused again, "what if," he repeated, "Parkes knew about the Priory and loch murder and what if, when the

319

unidentified man with a foreign accent who Scobie witnessed, pointed out their driver as a possible, Parkes would have reported back to tell the head man that someone knew about the Romanian?"

"It's a good idea," agreed Avalon, "and this 'head man' would want to know who the unidentified person was and who was asking."

"But would that get him killed?" asked Boyd.

"It would if Parkes was found to have been interviewed by us, which he was," suggested Ross, "they may even begin to suspect that Kevin was actually a copper."

"Who's Kevin?" asked Boyd.

"Kevin is the unidentified man, he's almost like family now, so he ought to have a name," explained Ross.

"You have to bear with Ross, Alison, his idea of humour doesn't seem to conform to the rules other humans use," interrupted Avalon as he turned into the car park of the police station.

"Heads up everyone," announced Avalon as he entered the Cave with Ross and Boyd. "As you've probably heard we have been out to another body in the town, B Section are dealing with it for now but it looks like it's Alistair Parkes, the man we interviewed," he explained noticing Wilson and Pottinger were still out. "At this stage we don't know if it is connected to any of our cases but if it is, we may still have to work on it." He looked over to the whiteboard and saw that Frazer had been busy there. He walked over and wrote the new victim's name in the corner with a question mark at the side. "So," he continued, "Though I doubt there is a connection, I want everyone to look into any links between our two victims and Alistair Parkes. DS Ross and DC Boyd, I want you to continue looking into the court case that Alan Clacher and William Ewart were involved in, pull all the records if you have to, carry on" and then he nodded and returned to the booth to telephone Scobie.

"Scobie, it's Avalon."

"*Oh, hello Mr Avalon, to what do I owe the pleasure of this call?*" he replied. Avalon didn't really believe Scobie had gone 'straight', even if ex-cons wanted to, the pressures of their peers and the difficulty of making an honest living brought problems that far outweighed the perceived risk involved in crime. For the time being however, he was prepared to give him the benefit of the doubt.

"Do you think you could identify the man in the pub, the one with the accent who gave the directions to the house at Scorguie?"

"*Maybe Mr Avalon, have y' got somebody?*"

"No but if we got you together with a police artist, do you think you could help him out?" asked Avalon.

"*I could give et a try, but you'll have tae arrange et somewhere other than the station, I can'nae afford tae be seen callin' en there every verse end, ef y' know what I mean?*"

"Okay," agreed Avalon, "I'll see if I can find an alternative venue," replied Avalon and then he asked, "the other thing is I want you to have a look at some photographs, mug shots, to see if you can pick out the man you know as Parky?"

"*Oh I see,*" replied Scobie with a little doubt in his voice.

"Can you identify him?" asked Avalon again,

omitting to mention that the man was now dead.

"*Aye, why not, I could give et a go anyways,*" replied Scobie.

"I'll call you as soon I have something sorted out," concluded Avalon.

Wilson returned with Pottinger and he came straight to the booth and knocked on the side wall.

"Got a minute boss?" he said.

"Yes, take a seat Gordon," he replied completing the sentence he was typing on his computer, "have you got something?" He noticed Pottinger stand close by as there wasn't any other seating in the booth.

"Aye I think so, that info you sent me earlier on proved tae be very useful."

"Go on," said Avalon giving the DS his full attention.

"Unfortunately, Toby Cheeseman isn't playing ball with us at all but Cotter es a different matter. His brief has told him that due tae the DNA evidence found in the cab and en the light of 'new evidence'," Wilson held up two fingers of each hand to indicate quotation marks, "that Mr Cotter's best interests would be en helping the police with any information he has."

"Good, so has he said anything?" asked Avalon.

"He wants some assurances first, he says he won't talk about anyone else involved en the truck robbery and insists that he didn't know any of them anyway," Wilson raised his eyebrows a little, "but he says he 'might' be able tae help with identification of a man concerning the death of Alistair Parkes."

"That's big of him," sighed Avalon, "but he has to do time, he's not getting off the hook again," insisted Avalon, and then realised that the 'again' part of the

322

sentence could give something away to Wilson.

"I hinted that a lighter sentence may be arranged," shrugged Wilson.

"Maybe, but don't make any promises we can't keep," added Avalon and Wilson nodded. "Make it clear to him that the effort we put into lessening his sentence is directly relative to the amount, and importance of any information he imparts."

"Aye I understand," nodded Wilson. Avalon knew he didn't have to explain all this to Wilson, he was an 'old lag' when it came to interviews, it was more for the benefit of Pottinger.

"Okay," said Avalon, "keep me informed, I may come down and look in if I get time." Wilson nodded and stood, then he and Pottinger left the Cave just as the phone rang.

"Avalon," he growled.

"*DI Avalon, et's PC Kirk, there's a guy here says he's delivered your car.*"

"Oh crap, yes, I forgot about that, tell him I'm on my way down," and he hung up and went to see Ross. "I'm out for ten minutes," he said but Ross and Boyd were busy staring into Boyd's computer screen. Ross nodded without looking up and said,

"Okay," then to Boyd, "it's not there so bring up the records from the Procurator Fiscal's files."

"My car has been delivered so I'm going down to sign for it," explained Avalon expecting some comment but there was nothing, they seemed so busy, he left, surprised that Ross had passed over a chance to make some idiotic comment about cars.

Avalon signed the paperwork and took the keys from the young lad who had delivered it and then he checked round the vehicle, got in and drove it to the rear of the building and into the car park. He locked up the car and looked at it. It was old, it was ordinary but it was cheap and he could always find a better car once the insurance money came through. As he passed through the foyer he thanked Kirk who asked him what the car was.

"Oh, just an old Ford, I don't seem to be lucky with cars." She smiled and he headed back up the stairs to the Cave. As he made his way to the booth he looked over to Frazer, he seemed to find the need to check what she was doing all the time and that made him uncomfortable, she seemed fine and was typing but she looked unhappy. But then again, Frazer rarely looked anything other than unhappy. He understood that her life hadn't gone to plan and she had done extremely well to pick up the pieces and continue but he didn't think the future looked bright for the DC. He sat casting another glance towards her before continuing with his work.

Ross entered the booth and sat down, Avalon looked up and said,

"Why don't you take a seat?"

"No thanks I've got one," replied Ross and he leaned forward, "we think we have found the link between Alan Clacher and William Ewart from the court case they attended."

"Go on," nodded Avalon.

"The reason it's taken so long to find it is that the trial was postponed due to a witness going missing," explained Ross as he raised his eyebrows, "and the eventual trial date was much later, but we found the details."

"You said previously that this was to do with human trafficking,"

"Yes, it was," explained Ross, "but we also found

324

some other bits of information that Alison is still sifting, namely that Mr Clacher might not have been squeaky clean himself." They were interrupted as Boyd knocked and came into the booth.

"It's all here," she said handing Ross a sheet of paper. Ross quickly glanced through it and began to smile a little.

"Yes, it certainly is," and he offered the sheet to Avalon who refused.

"It's your find, tell me a story, and Alison, find a chair and bring it in." Ross began to tell Avalon what they had found.

"A Romanian gang working from Glasgow were bringing both drugs and young girls into the country, they would sell the drugs on the streets and set the girls up with regulated pimps and set them to work as prostitutes," he looked to Boyd as she returned with a chair and sat close by. "The gang were so successful that there was a great deal of money changing hands, possibly half a million a year, and the trade was outstripping demand and so they took chances to get more slaves into the country," he paused and looked down at the sheet. "Police Scotland with the Romanian police co-ordinated raids with Europol and broke up the main ring. It was celebrated on the news that it had been a great success."

"I think I remember that," nodded Avalon.

"The problem was they weren't even close to breaking it up. That seems clear as there is another operation being planned at this very moment."

"But what has all this to do with two bodies in public sites, and is it Romanian or not?" Ross could see Avalon was impatient so he shortened the story.

"It is, and it isn't. One of the key facilitators of

part of the racket is a Scotsman, a Scotsman living in Romania."

"Victor McCabe," offered Avalon.

"Yes," nodded Ross, "he was making so much money that any disruption to his trade route could seriously effect his lifestyle and as it's so much cheaper to live the high life in Romania, it became a lifestyle he couldn't hope to continue back here."

"So where does Alan Clacher come in to all this?" asked Avalon.

"We found that over the past twenty-eight months, two of Mr Clacher's drivers have been arrested for concealed drugs on their trucks, they denied knowing about it but the record of Clacher's haulage company is poor."

"It doesn't mean he was involved though," insisted Avalon.

"No," agreed Ross, "but we have to assume it's possible he either turned a blind eye or was active in the scam."

"What about the chap that runs it now?" asked Avalon but Ross was already shaking his head.

"Hunter? Not very likely he was involved, he took over the duties after the court case," explained Ross.

"Well you need to bring in this Hunter *and* the wife, they must have known about the court case," said Avalon.

"Yeah, we have already arranged to see them but Hunter has insisted he knows little about Clacher's business practices before he agreed to take over."

"Maybe, maybe not, we'll see," said Avalon, and then continued, "so, they were called as witnesses you said?" Ross nodded.

"Yes, I have ordered the transcripts of the trial but it seems that six men were called from the haulage industry, our two victims, a man from Fort William who has since gone missing and two others we haven't managed to track down yet. The only one still living at his original address is a self employed driver from Bonar Bridge."

"If your theory is correct, it's likely this chap from Bonar Bridge may need police protection," frowned Avalon.

"We thought about that sir," began Boyd, "I've asked if a car can be sent to check on the address."

"That could take some time," said Avalon looking at his watch, "come on, I'll take us there, we could do with asking him some questions anyway."

"Did you say you had a new car earlier?" asked Ross with a puzzled look.

"Yeah, just another old Ford."

As they walked across the car park Avalon turned to Ross and asked,

"Do you think that the type of trailer that was stolen could be converted for more than drugs?" Ross thought for a moment as they reached a car.

"Maybe, I suppose if the refrigeration unit was removed and a false back was installed it would have a bit of room in there, but the trailer wouldn't be cold inside and would make the deception obvious."

"But we know they sometimes move loads that aren't perishable in those trailers," suggested Avalon as he clicked the key fob.

"It's worth a look, but it would be a small space," frowned Ross as Avalon clicked the fob again and again, nothing was happening and the Ford Mondeo was still locked. "So is this your car?" asked Ross. Avalon stopped clicking the fob and looked at the car, he stepped back as if the thing had suddenly appeared when previously there was no car there.

"No," he insisted, "for Christ sake, I've gone back to Mondeo mode," he frowned tapping the side of his head with his index finger.

"Well, if it's of any interest to you the dark grey Ford Focus over there keeps flashing its lights as if it knows you," smiled Ross. Boyd tried to keep a straight face, it wasn't working so she turned away.

"I reckon this job is driving me bloody nuts, and who the hell buys a Mondeo these days?" he hissed as he headed towards the Focus. As he reached it he stopped in horror.

"I don't believe it!" he said and Ross couldn't help seeing the similarity between Avalon and the Victor Meldrew character from the 'One Foot in the Grave' comedy show, "some callous toe-rag has knocked the driver's side mirror off."

"Well, it happens," shrugged Ross.

"In the police car park for Christ's sake?" growled Avalon, "I mean if you can't expect a bit of honesty from fellow officers who the hell can you trust?"

"Well," sighed Ross wondering if the boss would be in the mood for humour, "it's made it look more 'Avalon Authentic'."

"What the hell's that supposed to mean?" spat Avalon, clearly humour *was* off limits for the time being. Avalon looked up at the building searching around.

"What are you looking for?" asked Ross not giving a damn, humour was his lifeblood, "Scottish pigeons are hard as nails but I've never seen one pull a wing mirror off a car," he noticed Boyd trying to stifle a laugh.

"There, that's what I'm looking for," he said pointing to the security camera, "I'll be checking our monitoring system when I return," and he finally got into the car.

~~~~~~

"Now where do you want tae start?" asked Wilson looking directly at Bobby Cotter. He and Pottinger were seated one side of the desk and Cotter and his solicitor the other.

"That depends on what y' want to know," replied Cotter looking at the recording device at his side. DS Wilson had announced all the details on the device before starting and now Cotter looked worried that the machine would be listening in, he knew he had to be careful and Wilson saw this.

"Anything you can tell us about an incident that happened this morning, namely a body found in a trailer on the Longman Trading Estate," announced Wilson. Cotter rubbed his hands together nervously and then looked into Wilson's eyes.

"I had nothin' to do with any killing I want that made clear," he paused a little, "an' I can't tell you anything for sure as I haven't been near the place but I can tell you what I have heard." Wilson nodded and said,

"Go on." Cotter glanced quickly at his solicitor for reassurance but the man simply gave a single nod.

"I was asked to help with the hijack of a truck, I was to go with the driver and meet with another truck and help swap the trailer from one to the other," he swallowed, "when we got the trailer swapped someone," he glared at Wilson suddenly as he continued, "and I don't know his name," he calmed again, "asked me if I knew 'Parky' Parkes." He stopped to take a drink from the water provided. "I said I knew who he was but I didn't know him as such. This guy then said 'well his time is up'."

"What did he mean by that?" asked Wilson.

"I suppose he meant they were after him, I don't know," shrugged Cotter.

"Did they say why?"

"Aye, sort of, this guy said that he had been asked if he knew any truckers, drivers I mean, but he had been too obvious and had been questioned by you lot."

"The police?" asked Wilson, Cotter nodded. "Mr Cotter nodded his head," added Wilson for the benefit of the recorder. "Who are these people who you were working for?" continued the DS.

"I'm not all that sure, I was asked to work on the hijack, nothing else," insisted Cotter.

"But someone must have been the paymaster?" said Wilson.

"Aye, there was but I didn't know him from Adam, a big bastard with an attitude. The idea was that the hijack gang would get the haul but the trailer would be moved on," explained Cotter looking down at his hands. He was looking at a small nick on the side of his wrist, that very same wound that had left his DNA at the scene of the crime.

"Do you know where the trailer was going?" asked Wilson. Cotter shook his head.

"No, they told us what we needed to know, nothing else, the driver was foreign though and the second truck had foreign plates."

"Is this him?" asked Wilson as Pottinger handed him a photograph.

"Aye, that looks like him, he looked shit scared all the time, I don't think he was very happy about what he was doing."

"Did you recognise anyone else?" asked Wilson.

"No," replied Cotter shaking his head.

"Was Toby Cheeseman there?"

"Who?" asked Cotter for the recording machine but he gave a blank stare to Wilson.

"One more question Mr Cotter," began Wilson, "why did you decide to tell us about this?" Cotter looked to his solicitor again, this was the part of the recording that mattered to Cotter, he had to make it sound like he was washing his hands of the whole thing because it didn't sit well with him. The solicitor nodded again.

"I was there to hijack a truck, yeah we had to get a bit rough with the driver but we only slapped him about a bit. These other nutters are way out of my comfort zone, they'll kill you as soon as look at you. That just isn't what I'm about." The solicitor looked over to Wilson and made a sign to intimate the interview was over. Wilson wound it up and then switched off the recording device.

"So off the record Bobby, who's the top man on this one?" The solicitor stood and said,

"The interview is over Detective Sergeant Wilson," and he nodded up towards the camera still showing it was recording. The two men started to leave the room but Cotter stopped at the side of Wilson and said quietly,

"I'll tell you what detective, if it's who I think it is, there'll be more bodies before this is over."

"We know *who* et es, Bobby, we just need tae know *where* he es," frowned Wilson.

~~~~~~~

"Thank you for seeing us at such short notice Mr Pentland," said Avalon seated in the small office that Tyler Pentland used as his base of operations. It was a shed by any other name but it had all the expectations of being an office for a business such as Pentland Haulage. It was so small that Boyd stayed outside and arranged for someone to watch Pentland's house for protection.

"Not at all Detective, what can I do for you?" Avalon looked over to Ross who began the questions.

"We understand you testified for the prosecution on a case last year concerning human trafficking."

"That's right, it was a shambles, we turned up day after day and then it was put off and then-"

"We know the bare bones of the case Mr Pentland, we just wondered if you could tell us exactly what you knew about the case," interrupted Ross. The man was off balance from the question.

"Well, it was in the papers," he began but Ross gave him a direct look that told the man he wanted him to explain, "there isn't that much to it. Several drivers were saying that they were being approached in Europe to smuggle things into the UK, if they refused they were getting items hidden on the trucks without their knowledge, then as soon as they came back here they were arrested for smuggling."

"So it was blackmail, work for us or we'll get you into trouble?" asked Ross.

"Yeah," nodded Pentland, "that's about it. I was approached several times by the same faces but I checked the whole truck every time to be sure. I never found anything but I wasn't taking the chance," he replied.

"So when the human trafficking trial was begun you were called as witnesses?"

"Yes," nodded the man, "mainly because some of the bigger haulage companies were trying to get them closed down, it was costing us all money, it takes time to check a whole truck so when a few drivers went to prison the bigger companies banded together."

"Like Alan Clacher?" asked Ross.

"Yes, he was one of the men who stood up and said 'no more'," nodded Pentland.

"Did you know he was dead Mr Pentland?" asked Ross but the man went sheet white.

"God, no I didn't, what..." but then the realisation struck him, three detectives and questions about the case. He blinked and then asked,

"Was he murdered?" Ross nodded and then said,

"He was and William Ewart was also found murdered."

"Jesus," exclaimed Pentland looking down to the floor, "Bill Ewart used to drive for the same firm as me, a nice bloke."

"I have to inform you Mr Pentland that you are the only one of the haulage witnesses we can find, the others have gone missing or moved away," explained Ross.

"We think you could be in some danger," added Avalon.

"I don't watch the news or have a paper, I wouldn't know, I'm in the truck most of the time," he said shaking his head.

"We are arranging to give you a police presence around the clock Mr Pentland, for your safety," explained Ross. The man snapped his gaze from the floor and looked at Ross.

"But I just can't sit here, I'll, I'll go out of business," he stammered.

"You'll go out of business if these people come after you Mr Pentland," added Avalon.

"But the people responsible went to prison, the ring leader was a Romanian," insisted the man with a worried look.

"He was just one of many," replied Avalon, "there are others and one of them is not happy you helped close his business down."

"Jesus," exclaimed Pentland again.

"What was the main evidence used against them Mr Pentland?" asked Ross. The worried man thought for a moment.

"There wasn't that much really, just the evidence from the Dutch police and the bogus company, oh and our testimony of course," croaked the man.

"Bogus company?" asked Avalon.

"Yes, it was used as a cover for the smuggling, it was called Shee-an Haulage as I remember, it's a Gaelic word," he explained.

"How is that spelled?" asked Ross ready with his notebook.

"I'm not sure," said the man shaking his head and then he remembered something, "oh, wait," and he opened a filing cabinet. "Here it is, I saved some of the letterhead paper for the trial," and he handed it to Ross. Ross read it and with raised brows handed it to Avalon. There on the top of the page was a letterhead that looked like the same font that was used on the parchment found on the bodies. Below it in English typestyle were the words, 'Sithean Haulage'.

"We need to take this as evidence Mr Pentland," insisted Avalon.

"Yes of course," nodded the man.

"You were saying," added Ross, "about the case?"

"Oh yes," continued the man obviously quite nervous, "there wasn't all that much, I gave my accounts how I had been approached on several occasion to bring drugs into the country but one of the drivers said he had found a crate in the back of his truck that shouldn't have been there. The Dutch authorities were called and the crate was opened to reveal three young girls," he stopped to shake his head, "they were drugged and packed like sardines." Ross looked over to Avalon who looked back impassively.

Once it was confirmed that there was to be a police presence at the address, they left to return to the office and Ross said,

"So we were wrong all along."

"Not totally wrong," frowned Avalon, "we knew the killings were a warning and we knew we were being thrown a red herring or two," he paused, "we just didn't realise this was *just* revenge killings."

~~~~~~

Avalon entered the Cave followed by Ross and Boyd and he went straight over to Wilson to see if there was any news. Wilson explained what had happened at the interview with Cotter but Avalon seemed troubled.

"It's not much is it?" he frowned.

"Cotter was holding out I admit but I doubt we'll get anything more out of him, he's not going tae grass on his team," said Wilson in frustration.

"I think he'd open up if we pressured him," added Pottinger.

335

"I doubt et, Cotter isn't a hard man but he's wily," replied Wilson shaking his head. Avalon was looking out of the window, he had obviously been hoping that Cotter would see his position as hopeless. With his DNA at the scene, no alibi because his girlfriend didn't know about his other life and wouldn't protect him and people around him were turning up dead, it was a surprise that he wasn't telling them everything he knew. Avalon shook his head to clear his thoughts, he would just have to look elsewhere. He turned and looked at Mackinnon, he wanted the young DC to co-ordinate the session with Scobie and the police artist, but other things had got in the way.

"Rory, wind up what you're doing, I have a job for you." Mackinnon nodded waited for further instructions.

"What do you want *us* to do?" asked Ross. Avalon thought for a moment, it seemed that the leads were running dry again and he was wondering where to turn for the best.

"I suspect there's little else to be found from the court case concerning the Romanians but it may be worth going through the transcripts. Other than that use the time to catch up on paperwork," he said but his tone gave away his thoughts. "Rory, get your coat, we have a short journey to make," and he made for the door, the eager Mackinnon close at his heels.

When he had gone Ross sighed and sat at his desk, Boyd did the same and looked over to Ross.

"What first?" she asked. Ross shrugged.

"Not sure, we can go through the transcripts as the DI asked but if there was anything there we would have picked it up from Mr Pentland." She nodded her agreement.

"I'll make a start, we've got nothing better to do," she said and began work on the pages of transcripts of the case. Ross looked out of the window and thought for a moment, then he looked back to Boyd and stared at her until she noticed.

"What?" she said slightly embarrassed.

"If I were to ask you who the main man in this case was," he began, "who would you say it was?"

"Victor McCabe, I think we all know that," she shrugged. Ross looked out of the window again and asked,

"And we can't move on that information because of what?"

"Well," replied Boyd, "lack of evidence for starters, neither do we know where he is and the DI doesn't like chasing rainbows."

"Chasing rainbows?" smiled Ross looking back from the window, "I like that," then he tapped his fingers on the desk and continued. "So forget for one minute what the DI has to say about this, we need McCabe's location and something to connect him to the crimes."

"No," insisted Boyd, "I said evidence, we *have* a connection."

"You're starting to sound like Avalon."

"If I am it's because I agree with his opinion," she grinned.

"Jesus, I've never met an Avalon groupie before," he mocked.

"Call it what you like but it's evidence we're looking for not connections, so what's your point *sir*?" she emphasised the title. Ross smiled again and shook his head.

"Well," he continued, "*evidence*, is going to be hard to come by but as to where he is, we have a good idea."

"Do we, it's news to me?" she frowned.

"We'll, he's in Inverness that much is clear, maybe he doesn't soil his hands dealing with his minor officers but these killings would probably require his attention, so *I* think he's here."

"That may be the case but Inverness is a big place," she insisted.

"It is but as dangerous as this McCabe is, the local, resident villains are not going to be all that keen on him being here are they?"

"True, but how are you going to track someone down who would be willing to help?" she asked with a hint of doubt in her voice.

"Easy," smiled Ross, "find-a-villain-dot-com," and he stood and reached for his coat, "come on we have to see a dog about a man." Boyd raised her eyebrows and sighed. She was considering asking the DI if she could be partnered up with a normal person.

Once in the car and on their way, Ross began to explain a few things to DC Boyd.

"The man we are going to see is someone that I have to admit is utterly crazy, he's dangerous and I wouldn't be going to see him if I had any choice."

"Oh," said Boyd doubtfully, "thanks for telling me before I got into the car."

"He comes over, educated and gentlemanly but don't let that fool you," added Ross.

"So how do you know him?" she asked.

"I'm never going to tell you the truth, do you want to hear a lie instead?" replied Ross.

"Maybe not," said Boyd.

"Let's just say he can be good for information

338

when it suits him, but I don't tell anyone about this contact so I expect you do respect that."

"Of course," nodded Boyd, "so he must be one of the bad guys, what's he done?"

"Oh, he's a bad guy alright," smiled Ross, "he spent twenty five years in the nick, he's not nice, not nice at all."

"Are you going to tell me what he did then?" she asked again.

"Rape and dismemberment of women," said Ross as if he was telling her directions to the nearest shop.

"Oh," she said with a tone that said she wished she hadn't asked, "in any particular order?" she added.

"I like you, I like your sense of humour," laughed Ross glancing over to her, "okay I admit, I lied about the rape." And he went quiet as he continued to drive. She swallowed, but then again, it was difficult to tell when Ross was lying and when he was not, it seemed he explored every sentence for humorous potential. She noticed he was even the same with DI Avalon.

"So what's the story with you and the DI?" she asked trying to change the subject a little.

"What do you mean?" asked Ross glancing over to her again.

"Well you seem to get away with a lot, much more than I would expect."

"Do I?" he asked not quite sure he saw he point of view.

"Yes you do," she replied, "and although he calls the rest of the team by their first names he always calls you Ross."

"Yeah, I noticed that a long time ago," he nodded.

"And you never call him sir or boss."

"I don't, what do I call him then?" asked Ross

slightly puzzled.

"You don't, I don't think I have heard you call him anything except 'the DI' and then it's in the third person." He remained quiet. "So you don't want to talk about it?" she asked.

"There's nothing to talk about, I've only known him for about four months, beyond that I can't say much else."

"So you don't think it odd how..." she paused, he needed the correct words, Ross was her superior and she didn't want to get his back up, "you get on?" she finally concluded.

"The truth is I hadn't really seen it as anything more than the camaraderie that goes on between most officers but I have to say you have made me stop and think," admitted Ross. It was the truth, yes he realised they had the same sort of humour and Ross was beginning to see how Avalon played along on occasions but he didn't think they had a great deal in common.

"That episode in the car park, you were winding him up and any other DI would have chewed your arse off for the way you were with him," she added. Ross thought back to the incident. She was right, Ross would never had done that with Lasiter. Was it disrespectful? He wasn't sure, it hadn't occurred to him previously, after all it was Avalon, Avalon the detective inspector with the same sense of humour as him, Avalon his... Ross considered it, yes, that was it. Avalon wasn't just his Boss. He had listened to Ross as his marriage crumbled, he had helped him through the first few weeks when Ross's world was upside-down and yet Ross hadn't seen it before. Avalon was his friend, his mate. He looked quickly over to the DC.

"Thanks for that Alison," he said as they pulled

up at the side of a small house.

"For what?" she asked, genuinely perplexed.

"For opening my eyes," and he looked forward out of the window, "you'd think that someone who earns his living making sure he misses nothing would see the most obvious things." She looked at him for a moment until he blinked and turned back to her. "Anyway, let's go and see if the axe murderer has anything to tell us?"

"I thought he was a 'woman butcherer'?" she asked.

"Did I not mention the axe attacks?" he smiled as he climbed out of the car.

Chapter Twelve

It was late in the afternoon when Avalon sat down again and, noticing Ross and Boyd were out, he decided to do it with a cup of coffee. He had left Rory Mackinnon with Scobie and the police artist at the forensics lab, the only place he could think of at short notice. He was just about to take his first sip when a quiet knock was heard and the door to the Cave opened. It was Kirk and she was carrying a sheet of paper.

"This one's just come en," she announced handing him the sheet.

"Thanks, I thought it was too quiet to be true," he replied taking the sheet, "oh, and I returned the Spaghetti to its rightful owner." Kirk looked bemused for a moment and then she realised.

"Oh, right," she frowned, "what wes that about, he just said 'see ef you can get thes into the DI's cupboard?"

"Just another one of Ross's pranks," smiled Avalon. Kirk thought about it for a moment and then shrugged.

"I guess you had tae be there," she said and then left. Avalon looked down and read the sheet, he then looked into the room, after another sip of the coffee, stood, and walked towards Wilson.

"What are you doing Gordon?" he asked.

"Ah, just finishing the reports on the interviews with Cotter and Cheeseman, why, got a problem?"

"Get DC Pottinger to finish that, take Mack, this needs looking at," he said handing the sheet to Wilson.

"What es et?" he asked as he glanced through it.

"Hit and run down at Fort Agustus, the victim is in hospital but we need to have a look at the site as soon as we can," explained Avalon. Wilson rose from his seat and reached for his jacket. "I know it's late in the day but there may be something to find before they open the road up," added Avalon. As Wilson and MacDonald left, Avalon returned to his coffee and began to wonder where Ross was, maybe he had found something in the transcripts he was looking through. With just Frazer and Pottinger in the Cave, it was quiet, very quiet. Frazer had never been talkative but now she was almost silent and Pottinger hardly ever spoke anyway, though Wilson said he had no issues with his work. He sighed a little and then began to think through the case once more. It was clear that Victor McCabe was heavily involved but there was no evidence to connect him and as far as Avalon could see, nothing whatsoever to bring a case against him, even if they could find where he was. They had a long way to go yet. He reviewed what they knew and wondered if the large man that Cotter had described could be McCabe's henchman, could it be that they travelled together? He began to work the dates back, it was a long-shot and it would take some considerable time but the airport records may contain something, if they were lucky, the records of the passenger lists may contain the arrival of two Scottish nationals.

"Maybe not," said Avalon quietly to himself, it

was doubtful they would travel under their own names as both of them were probably wanted, what's more, they may not have come into the country by the local airport. They needed something concrete to link McCabe to the killings. He researched the name on the letterhead paper, 'sìthean' but all he could find was a translation in Gaelic to mean 'fairy' or 'fairy hill'. It sort of explained the 'runes' on the title but made no connection with anything else. Avalon noticed movement in the Cave, it was Frazer, and she was heading to the booth with a sheet of paper.

"Megan, have a seat," he said and looked into her troubled eyes.

"I've been thinking," she began, "I can't just continue tae be a shiny arse, et's not what I'm about."

"What do you mean?" asked Avalon.

"I'm giving et up, this es no good for me or C Section," she replied. Avalon stared at her for a moment and then leaned back in his chair.

"I think you're making a mistake but it's your life," he sighed.

"That's just the point, this isn't my life, my life is out there doing my job," she insisted, pointing to the window.

"But what would you do, just transfer to uniform?" he asked.

"No, I'll find something else tae do, I think my time in the force is finished." Avalon looked at her and shook his head, he wanted to give her options, but he simply couldn't think of any.

"Why don't you just take some time off and think about it, you have plenty of time in lieu," he eventually said.

"I *have* thought about et, I'll work the rest of the

344

week and tidy up any loose ends and then I'll use my holidays for the rest of my notice," and she placed the sheet of paper on his desk. He didn't look at it, he knew what it was and he felt completely helpless, he could think of nothing to say and there was no advice he could give her. He wanted to tell her that he knew all about her past, he wanted to say that he understood why she felt the way she did, but he couldn't, he had made a promise and he wasn't about to break that confidence. All he could do was watch her shrug, stand, and walk back to her desk and all the time he wanted to rant and rave and throw things at the wall. But he stayed quiet and seethed inside instead, thinking about the injustice that could come from working within the law enforcement system. He stood, and walked to the windows, trying his best not to catch any eye contact with Frazer. He stared long and hard across the fields and still nothing came to him. When the door to the Cave opened, Avalon had no idea how long he had been staring. It was Ross and Boyd, Avalon turned to face them and raised his eyebrows in a questioning manner.

"Well, it wasn't a totally wasted journey," said Ross as he removed his jacket, placing it on the back of his chair.

"Care to elaborate?" asked Avalon.

"I have this contact, well more of a face from the past, but he knows quite a bit that goes on in this area," explained Ross as he sat.

"He's an ex copper, a private detective now," added Boyd. Ross turned to her and said,

"I thought you said you would keep it quiet?"

"I did but the DI made me the official 'Ross interpreter' remember?" said Boyd shrugging slightly, then added, "he told me the guy had spent twenty five years in the nick," she pointed to him with her thumb.

"He did," Ross paused slightly then added, "it's just that he was *this* side of the counter."

"Paterson?" said Frazer suddenly, but just as suddenly looked slightly apologetic and continued with her work.

"Yes, Paterson," sighed Ross rolling his eyes.

"Who's Paterson?" asked Avalon, sitting on the edge of the nearest desk.

"Andy Paterson used to be in the CID, he took early retirement some years ago to start up his own business but he's got loads of shady contacts and he can get information by means that we can't," explained Ross.

"He's also a rapist, murderer and diamond thief who once turned over half a mill' in one year according to Ross," added Boyd.

"Oh really?" questioned Avalon, "so can we leave the fantasy aside for a moment and get back to police work?"

"Paterson told us that he had heard McCabe was back in town, but that was all," explained Ross, "what he did tell us however, was the name of McCabe's lieutenant, a big ugly guy that goes by the name of Steven Calloway."

"Do we have anything on him?" asked Avalon.

"New to me, I'll check records though," replied Ross. Frazer looked over again.

"Have you heard of him?" asked Avalon.

"No," replied Frazer, "but Paterson has a poor record when et comes tae information."

"True," agreed Ross, "but he has his moments and what do we have to lose?" He tapped several keys on his computer and waited for it to sift the database. "Here we go," he eventually said, "Steven Calloway, not

346

from our area by the look of his record, armed robbery, attack with offensive weapon and blackmail, all in Glasgow or Paisley," he paused, "and he's on the run."

"So he'll be on a false passport," sighed Avalon.

"Probably," agreed Ross just as the door opened and in walked Mackinnon.

"All sorted?" asked Avalon, Mackinnon nodded and said,

"Yes, Scobie positively identified Parkes from the photo and the artist says he'll have the image sorted by the morning," and he returned to his desk. Avalon turned back to Ross who was still looking at his computer screen.

"Get a printout of this file and a picture of Calloway," said Avalon, "we need to circulate his image and get the uniform branch on this one, and while you're at it," Avalon glanced out of the window as he continued, "do the same for McCabe, even if we can't pin anything directly to him yet, we could do with knowing where these two are."

"Er boss?" interrupted Mackinnon. Avalon looked at the young DC and nodded slightly, "if you're talking about McCabe and the big man I had already asked for passenger lists from the airport to cover the time before the first victim went missing."

"Flicks will soon be a 'Vertigo' if he carries on like this," smiled Ross.

"Sorry?" said Mackinnon with a questioning look.

"It's old slang for higher ranking officers, they rise so quickly and so high they get vertigo," explained Avalon with a slight smile.

"I haven't found anything yet though, so I can't see them making me Chief Superintendent yet." admitted

Mackinnon with a smile.

"They may have come through the ferry terminals, Paterson seemed to think that Calloway has drug connections in Amsterdam or Rotterdam," added Ross.

"I could try that," suggested Mackinnon.

"It's worth a try, Megan, you and Rory give that a go, widen the search to three weeks before the first disappearance of the victims," suggested Avalon and he returned to the booth. The rest of the day was spent on endless searches and a towering mountain of paperwork.

~~~~~~

For the first time since he had been in Scotland, Avalon felt low, he was tired, but it was more than that. The incident with Frazer was depressing him and the struggle to solve the murders wasn't helping. Even the weather was against him, it seemed like everyday it rained at sometime and most people admitted it had been one of the dreariest summers they could remember. Above him the canopy was more like a ceiling than a sky and it seemed like the sun was never going to shine again. As he got out of the car, he looked over at the missing mirror, even that had ceased to annoy him. He felt like tearing the other one off to match it. As he climbed the stairs to the Cave, he wondered if someone had added a few more extra steps as it seemed to grow in length and height each day. He stood silently outside the door of the Cave, pulled himself together, and at least tried to 'fake' the idea that he was upbeat about the day. Morale had to be kept up, as the next few days would be difficult for everyone. He opened the door and walked in. Mackinnon, Pottinger, and Boyd were already there and

Ross followed by the time Avalon was seated. Ross looked over and raised his eyebrows as he walked into the main room. He knew Wilson and Mack would probably be late, so he went to pour a coffee and then stood, looking out of the window.

"Another shite day," insisted Ross readying himself for the day's work.

"At least it isn't raining," replied Avalon, in a quiet voice.

"Yeah but it's pretty bad this year even for Scotland," groaned Ross.

"I have to admit, it's getting on my nerves a bit," agreed Avalon.

"What really gets my goat," began Ross, "is that down in Cardiff, they go on about the Millennium Stadium and how it has a state of the art roof, we've had one up here for sixty years, it's called 'permacloud'." Avalon allowed himself a slight smile at this as Frazer entered the room and nodded to anyone who looked, she then went to her desk. Ross joined Avalon at the window, he too had a cup of coffee in his hand. "We've issued a BOLO on McCabe and Calloway but as it stands I can't see there is anything else we can do to find them," said Ross. Avalon nodded silently. He turned away from the window and looked into the room across to the whiteboard. He couldn't quite read all the details but as he looked at the general picture, something occurred to him.

"The one thing we *do* have on him, is that he intends to start his human trafficking route again," he suggested.

"We don't know that for sure," said Ross.

"No, but we have a good idea that the refrigeration trailers are needed specifically for that purpose and it does look like he was involved with the theft." Ross nodded.

"But it could be just be for drugs," he suggested.

"Well humour me then," insisted Avalon, looking over to Ross, "if he is planning to start that up again, he's going to need resources and a team to do the finding and stealing of these trailers."

"Yeah, so what?"

"Well I would think that we have some of his truck stealing team on remand at the moment," and Avalon looked at Ross again.

"There are plenty of villains out there ready to do his bidding for hard cash, I don't think that will slow him down," insisted Ross.

"With respect sir," cut in Boyd, "I can't see McCabe continuing with that caper knowing we have some of his hijack team and the trailer they pinched in an impound yard in Amsterdam."

"I don't suppose I can either Alison, but is there something we can use knowing that?" Avalon asked. There was silence and blank faces. Rory looked up from his computer and Avalon saw thought processes bouncing around his features. "What is it Rory?" asked Avalon.

"Oh nothing boss," replied Mackinnon.

"It didn't look like nothing when you were thinking it," insisted Avalon with a stare.

"I was just thinking about Cotter and Cheeseman," he shrugged.

"They sound like an estate agent when you say it like that," added Ross.

"Go on Rory, spill the beans," insisted Avalon ignoring Ross.

"They just seem in a crappy position, particularly

Cotter, and yet they're doing nothing to make their situations better."

"I suspect they don't fancy being opened up in the back of a trailer like Mr Parkes," suggested Ross with some irony in his voice.

"Well, if that was the case, what does Cheeseman have to gain?" asked Rory, "as I see it, we don't have anything conclusive on him, just a statement from a dead man saying some chap in a betting shop was asking for an HGV driver."

"We'll have to let him go soon, I admit," nodded Avalon, "I was hoping Cotter would play ball, but..." he tailed off.

"But that's the point boss," insisted Rory, "he's going to walk free and that doesn't seem to bother him, we brought Parkes in and now he's dead, Cheeseman must be thinking the same fate could await him once he's released."

"Definitely vertigo material," nodded Ross.

"Unless he knows something," added Avalon ignoring Ross again, "or has a reason that makes him immune," he added.

"Or his wife," cut in Frazer. She had been so quiet that her statement took everyone by surprise. She just stared at her computer screen as if it hadn't been her that had spoken, but the comment wasn't lost on Avalon.

"Cheeseman still lives with his wife and they still have a connection," he nodded, "and I think what Megan is getting at, is that Cheeseman may want out, so that he can get to his wife and then run."

"Et's a thought," she said without looking round.

"So," suggested Rory, "can we use this against him?"

"Better than that," smiled Avalon, we can use it

against them both." He looked to Ross.

"You and Alison go down and inform Cheeseman he's free to go, but point out all the obvious things as you process him," explained Avalon, Ross nodded an understanding of what was required. "Rory, you come with me, let's see if we can prise some more information out of Cotter."

"Shall I send for his solicitor?" asked Mackinnon.

"No, not yet, let's try him out first," he replied, with an impish grin.

~~~~~~

"Bobby," announced Avalon as he and Mackinnon entered the cell, "I've come to let you know how things are going."

"Oh aye," replied Cotter, looking up from the betting section of the newspaper he was reading, "I'd offer you tea but it's the maid's day off." Avalon gave a fake smile as he threw Cotter's feet off the bench he was laying on, Cotter put the paper down and sat up.

"I'm glad you can still joke about it, you're not going to do much more though when you hear what I have to tell you."

"What do you want from me, I've told you all I know?" he scowled.

"Maybe, maybe not," said Avalon linking his fingers and leaning forward on the bench. Mackinnon folded his arms and leaned on the doorframe. "We've got most of what we need," continued Avalon, "evidence that links Victor McCabe and his lieutenant, Steven Calloway to the murders, the thing is, we just can't find them."

"That doesn't surprise me," replied Cotter, Avalon thought he was about to say more but he didn't.

"It doesn't bode well for Toby Cheeseman though, we're letting him go at this very moment, and I'm guessing he's going to end up in a pool of blood in the back of a trailer." There was a spark of something on Cotter's face.

"I didn't know you had him here," sighed Cotter.

"Oh yeah, he didn't say anything, but to be honest we had what we wanted from you," said Avalon in a relaxed way.

"It won't wash with me," began Cotter with a smile, "go on, tell me how you told him I spilled my guts, tell me how things look bad for me. It's all bullshit and you know it, I've had harder coppers than you try to get me to talk," and he sniffed.

"Like Megan Frazer?" said Avalon. Cotter remained silent at that comment, he folded his arms, and stared at the wall. "Anyway," sighed Avalon as he stood, "that's not why I came, I just came to tell you that the information you gave us isn't going to be used, so we can't offer you a deal," and he nodded to Mackinnon who opened the door.

"But you promised you'd come up with something," called Cotter.

"We promised nothing, we said if the information was good, *and* we could act on it, we would try for a more lenient sentence," replied Avalon looking back at Cotter.

"I should have known you bastards would lie," he hissed.

"We didn't lie, the investigation moved on, we found out more through police work than your pitiful information gave us," Avalon's voice rose in volume, Mackinnon wondered if this was one of those moments Mack had told him about. Avalon paced the room slowly

353

looking down at Cotter, still seated on the bench. "You identified the driver, true but we already knew who he was, you told us about the big man but we already knew his name was Calloway," spat Avalon, Rory was intrigued how Avalon was working the facts to suit the situation, was it lying? yes it was, but it was having an effect, "so, then you hinted to DS Wilson that you knew who the top man was, but as DS Wilson told you, we already knew who he was, it was Victor McCabe." Avalon had raised his voice to a shout now, he stood directly in the front of the man and bent towards him saying, "so what have you told us that we didn't already know Mr Cotter?" Avalon straightened up slowly and made to tighten his necktie, Cotter was speechless but both Avalon and Mackinnon could see doubt in Cotter's face. "Anyway," continued Avalon, "I'm a busy man, must crack on," he concluded, as if they had just been talking about the cricket results then he turned and headed out of the door.

"What if I give you something?" called out Cotter. Avalon stopped in his tracks, he stood perfectly still for a moment, then blinked and returned to the cell.

"Like what?" he asked. Cotter swallowed and said,

"I don't have an address I swear, but one of the team I was working with knew a bit about McCabe, and he mentioned a place."

"Where?"

"Do I get a deal, and I mean a real one or do I not? I'm saying nothing until I have assurances this time," insisted Cotter.

"If you give me something we can work with, I will do my best to get you a lighter sentence," nodded Avalon. Cotter swallowed again and gave a very deep sigh, he hesitated and then said,

"Okay, I may have something."

~~~~~~

Avalon returned to the booth with Mackinnon, he noticed that Ross and Boyd were back and Ross was approaching.

"Anything?" asked Avalon. Rory was about to get up to let Ross sit, but Ross stopped him and leaned on the wall instead.

"No," he frowned shaking his head, "I thought he was going to roll over at one stage, but he resisted and we let him go, I considered putting surveillance on him, what do you think?"

"Worth a try but I think he'll just run now," shrugged Avalon.

"How did you get on," asked Ross.

"Not bad, Cotter is wily but he's also a coward and we got some information out of him, though I'm not sure how good it is."

"What is it?" asked Ross folding his arms.

"Have you heard of a place called Inverarnie?" asked Avalon, Ross nodded.

"I couldn't place it on the map, but I've heard of it."

"Well, Cotter says he heard 'second hand' that Steven Calloway was staying in a caravan on some waste ground in that area, it could be, if he's there, he'll lead us to McCabe," explained Avalon.

"Or McCabe could be with him," offered Ross, Avalon nodded. "Shall we go and have a look around the area?" Avalon thought about the story that Lasiter had told him regarding Frazer, he didn't want the same sort of thing to happen to *his* team.

"No," he shook his head, "this lot are highly dangerous, I think we need a dedicated surveillance team and probably armed response officers close by before we move closer to them."

"What if the info is a load of crap, it's going to look grim if we send in the ARVs to a group of travellers," frowned Ross.

"So be it, I'm not risking people's lives on this," demanded Avalon. Ross nodded, he was going to suggest Frazer be involved, but he wasn't at all sure what was going on with Frazer. Avalon looked over to Mackinnon.

"Rory, get on the satellite maps and see if you can track down some waste ground in that area." Rory nodded and set to work on his computer.

"It's near the Cairngorms, it's all waste ground," smiled Ross.

"I'm sure the Cairngorms National Park Authority and millions of tourists would disagree with you there," insisted Avalon as Rory walked back to his desk with a smile on his face.

"Are you worried about this then?" asked Ross as he sat.

"A bit, yes," admitted Avalon, "but if we plan well, and keep to procedures, we should be fine," and he gave Ross a sudden puzzled look. "That reminds me," he began, "I have a question for you, something that has been buzzing around in my head for a couple of weeks," and he leaned forward with his arms on the desk, "I overheard something from a reporter that came to see me and I have now heard it again down in the cells." Ross shrugged as if to say 'then ask'. "I want the truth," he insisted and lowered his voice, "do I have a nick-name at this station?" Ross stared at Avalon for a few seconds, at first there was a slight smile on his face and then Avalon wasn't sure, Ross could have been suffering from indigestion, it certainly looked like it. Then Ross drew a deep breath and said,

"Yes, but it didn't start in this section."

"Oh," said Avalon, not sure if he now wanted to know what it was.

"I wouldn't pay much attention to it, I never did to the one they used to call me," he smiled explaining in a whisper.

"So what is it?" he eventually asked. Ross squeezed his lips together in a restricted grimace and then looked back into the office.

"Don't shout when I tell you, or everyone will know that *you* know," he said as he looked back.

"What's that got to do with anything?" asked Avalon with a deep frown.

"It will break the spell, it's the same as you knowing that Croker is called Toad behind his back, it changes the way you see people." Avalon didn't see it that way, and wasn't sure what Ross meant.

"So what is it?" he asked again.

"Auld Clootie," said Ross quickly, and stared with wide-open eyes. Avalon stared back but he had a puzzled look.

"Well that explains a great deal, but how the hell did I get that name?"

"Do you remember the old chap we brought in last month for flashing at young girls?"

"Yeah," nodded Avalon, "what of it?"

"You gave him a hard time in the interview room as I recall," sniffed Ross.

"Yeah, we thought he was a pervert and a sex offender, okay he turned out not to be quite as malignant as we expected, but he was still breaking the law."

"When we went to interview him later, Mack said we were there to ask him a few more questions and the old chap said that was fine as long as he didn't get 'Auld Clootie' again. Unfortunately, there were several uniforms present so it sort of got out." Avalon sighed.

"So I got the name through the bent brain of an old flasher?"

"Kind of, yes, but to be honest, the photograph at Wilson's birthday party probably sealed it." Avalon nodded again and then looked up.

"Tell me you didn't really send that photograph to Sarah Underwood," pleaded Avalon.

"No, course not, I was just pulling your leg," smiled Ross as he got his phone out and began scrolling through images. "This is the one I sent to her," and he passed the phone to Avalon. The image was pretty dreadful, Avalon looked to be asleep, his head was tilted back, and his mouth was wide open.

"When did you get this?" he asked with a high pitch to his voice.

"When you stayed over, I came back into the main room to bring you an extra pillow but you were already asleep, I thought it was only right to take a picture."

"You are quite evil, you know that," insisted Avalon handing back the phone after deleting the image.

"It's on my computer at home too," smiled Ross seeing the image had gone.

As Ross walked back to his desk, he considered that Avalon finding out what his nick-name was hadn't been as bad as he expected, he hadn't told him *all* of the reasons for the name but he didn't think the DI would thank him for that information.

The following day was cold, even for Scotland it was cold for August, and the rain came down most of the day. Avalon sat in the booth preparing what he could for the Procurator Fiscals Office in the hope that something would come in to tie McCabe with the murders. The case against Toby Cheeseman wasn't looking very good, though Avalon *had* asked for surveillance on him. He had also asked for a team to be sent to the Inverarnie area to search out the caravan that McCabe and Calloway were thought to be hiding in. It would be unpleasant in the poor weather, but it may also ensure that the two suspects stayed there. One good thing was, that Cheeseman had indeed decided to go into hiding, the surveillance was being carried out by two specialist officers but there were not enough of them to keep a twenty-four hour watch, and so Avalon had agreed to put his team at their disposal when they could and take over to allow around-the-clock cover. They had reported that Cheeseman had collected his wife, bundled some basic items into their car and driven off towards Aberdeen. The most recent communication said they were heading along the coast to Nairn and had stopped at an isolated farmhouse near Auldearn. That was going to cause problems for them. As Avalon looked on the map, he saw that it was twenty miles away, even with Ross's driving it would take thirty minutes, clearly, if they were to move further away, Avalon would either have to get another team involved or just forget about Cheeseman. Wilson and Mack were now committed to the hit and run case that had recently come in, Ross and Boyd were out interviewing George Barber again. He looked at his watch, and then checked it by the clock on the wall, he then looked back into the Cave. He couldn't send

Pottinger out yet, he didn't trust him, even though Wilson had said he was good enough, particularly as he would have to go with Rory. Avalon thought back to Frazer's fate down in Aberdeen and he didn't want to send anyone inexperienced on surveillance, he would have to go himself, but who with? He realised that Ross and Boyd were not going to return before it was time to leave and so he tapped on the glass, three faces gradually looked up, but Avalon beckoned Frazer. She entered the booth and leaned casually on the glass looking at him but saying nothing. He had thought of telling Frazer to hold the fort until Wilson or Ross arrived but at the last second he changed his mind.

"Fancy a run out?" Frazer looked at him with squinted eyes.

"Yeah but doesn't somebody have tae relieve the surveillance team?" she asked.

"Yes," nodded Avalon, "I was thinking of me and you," he replied.

"I thought you would have to be here, y' know seein' as you're the boss an' all that."

"Normally yes, but I'm not willing to send Rory out with Pottinger," he paused, "not yet," and he glanced through the glass to them, "only if you fancy it of course," he suddenly added looking back at her remembering she had told him she wanted out of the force. He had been on surveillance with her before, she was good and showed no sign of worry that might have come from her previous experience.

"Okay," she nodded and she returned to her desk to tidy up there.

In the car, as they headed towards the rendezvous, she asked if anything had happened. Avalon glanced over to her as she tried to find somewhere in the small car to stow away the flask of coffee they had brought.

"They're at a farmhouse somewhere I've never heard of, the other side of Nairn," he replied, as she nodded. "It's a half hour or so run."

"I would have thought he would have gone further tae be honest, ef they really are at risk, twenty or thirty miles is'nae gonna be far enough."

"I think they'll continue, they must know someone there and I'm guessing they're making plans, once they move, we won't have the resources to follow them."

"But ef we know where McCabe es, why are we following them?" she asked.

"Well, we're not sure McCabe will be there and we don't have the rest of the truck theft gang. I've also got an odd feeling we might need Mr Cheeseman when this all comes to trial." Frazer sniffed as if she didn't agree, Avalon didn't care, he just didn't want to leave anything to chance, not now they were so close.

The surveillance team watching the farmhouse had an excellent spot overlooking the house, it was a small pull-in and there was a low bank just ahead, but with the rain still coming down they had retreated to their car. They handed over the operation explaining that nothing had been seen for several hours, no one had come or gone but they had confirmed through their binoculars that there were still several people in the house. Then that was it, they were left alone with the windows cracked open to stop them steaming up. Avalon took the first watch of the house with Frazer watching other areas. After an hour, they changed places and Avalon poured them coffee which, once again, steamed the windows. Avalon was soon bored and his mind drifted off several times, but he could see why Frazer had been good at this work. Her focus stayed, and she never took her eye off the subject, on occasions he noticed her jot down details of the site and even then she hardly took her eyes away from the subject.

"How do you do that?" asked Avalon, "I mean, write without looking at the sheet?"

"I got used to et en dark cars, sometimes the slightest light can give you away, so you learn tae write en the dark," and she lifted the binoculars to her face once more. "Another tip es take the fuse out of the interior lights, or paint them out, she added, dropping the binoculars to her lap. Avalon wondered if that had given them away when she was attacked, Lasiter said the other officer got out to relieve himself. He looked across to her again.

"Are you still going ahead with it then?" he asked.

"With what?" she asked, still concentrating on the job at hand.

"Packing it up," he elaborated. For the first time she stopped her observation and turned to him, studying his features before turning back to look out of the window.

"Yeah, there isn't any option, I know I have a problem with authority and I know I have a violent reaction tae most things," she admitted, "even if I get over this episode there'll be somethin' else." She picked up the binoculars and scanned around the farmhouse again.

"Ironic," sighed Avalon, "those attributes would have been a positive trait in the eighties and nineties, these days it has no place in the force," he sighed again, "you may be right, I just think you would make a good

DS if you could control it," and he tried to get comfortable in the seat.

"Me, a DS?" she chuckled, "that seems so much of a pipe dream now."

"Not impossible though," insisted Avalon resting his head on the window. There was quiet in the car again for a few minutes until Frazer said quietly,

"A car has just come down the road from Nairn, et's stopped just the other side of the farmhouse."

"Keep your eye on it," said Avalon, "it could be someone to pick them up." There was silence again until Frazer said,

"This looks dodgy, two guys have got out o' the car and they have gone behind the hedgerow."

"Where?" asked Avalon as he sat up to look, she handed him the binoculars and pointed.

"The other side of the hedge, near that big tree, I think they're moving." Avalon looked, but could see nothing.

"I can't see them, but if they are heading to the farmhouse, they'll be hidden all the way up," he explained and passed the glasses back to Frazer. "Can you see them?" he asked, she looked and said simply,

"No, I can't." Avalon jumped out of the car, reaching for a flashlight as he did.

"Get on the radio and ask for some back up," he said.

"From base or local?"

"Local and get an ARV on the scene just in case." Avalon knew the Armed Response Vehicle would take time to get there but he was worried that the two men were looking for Cheeseman, he couldn't see any other reason they would be moving towards the house in cover. If someone had come to pick them up, they would have simply driven their car up the drive, not parked out of sight. "I'm going to cross the fields and try and get behind the farmhouse where those barns are," he added and set off on foot in the cold drizzle of the afternoon. His feet were soon drenched but the adrenaline that was coming from his apprehension overrode the cold and the discomfort. He tried to keep to the grassy edges of the fields to prevent a build up of mud on his shoes and he gradually made his way to the rear of one of the barns making a dash once he was in cover. He waited for a moment and listened. He gripped the flashlight in his pocket, he had brought it just in case he needed to see in the barns but now he was thinking of it more as a weapon. A taser would have been comforting at this moment but he wasn't firearms trained, so didn't carry one. He would have to improvise. He could handle himself that was true, when he was a bike cop he had to deal with tricky situations because he was usually the first to an incident so he was reasonably confident, but, if these were McCabe's gang... He swallowed and entered the barn and made his way through using the flashlight to guide his route and stood near a doorway looking through a crack in the door to a courtyard outside. He could see and hear nothing. He then thought about the flashlight, it wasn't much of a defensive weapon so he looked for something in the barn and found a shaft of wood. He slid it into his soaking jacket sleeve. It was better than nothing and after all, the gang had never used guns, but then again, it didn't mean they weren't carrying firearms. He tried to force those kinds of thought from his mind and opened the door carefully and scampered across the yard to the side of the house. He waited and listened once more. To his right, the way he had just come was a noise, he looked and saw Frazer

364

coming out of the barn so he put his finger to his lips to tell her to keep quiet. She nodded and slowly made her way towards him.

"Anything?" she whispered. Avalon shook his head, he was wondering if they had been wrong.

"Did you make the call?" he asked quietly.

"Yes, local force in ten, ARV later," she frowned. Avalon was going to look a complete fool if he had got this wrong but then a large man appeared from the other side of the courtyard and behind a shed. Avalon knew he would see then both so he stood away from the wall.

"So who are you?" he called.

"Who wants tae know?" replied the big man coming forward with a grin. Avalon recognised him as Calloway from his file notes and he also noticed Frazer move slowly out wide and the big man seemed to ignore her for a moment, Avalon was the obvious target and he allowed his arm to drop and the shaft of wood to sit in his palm, still hidden by his sleeve.

"We're the police Mr Calloway, we have this building under surveillance and we require you to accompany us to the station to answer some questions," insisted Avalon. The man made little reaction to hearing his name and continued to advance as he pulled a large knife from his pocket.

"I repeat, we are the police, drop the knife, you are under arrest."

"Both o' you's have got one chance tae run," called the man and he slowed slightly being just twenty feet from Avalon. Frazer was circling and it put the man off his guard for a moment so Avalon let the shaft of timber fall into his hand and brandished it repeating that the man was now under arrest. The big man ignored him and advanced. Avalon cringed as he saw Frazer move forward and the man react to it but he knew he wasn't quite close enough to help, he tried anyway. It didn't matter all that much, quicker than his eyes could register it, Frazer had dived under the man's attack, used her left arm against the lunge of the knife and struck the big man in the throat with her right hand. The man just collapsed on the floor choking, Avalon finished the job by walloping the man across the elbow of his right arm causing the knife to fall on the floor. The flexi cuffs were on even though the man was still retching and trying to grasp at his throat. Avalon stood and quickly moved back to the wall just in case the second assailant arrived. He held the wooden shaft again and felt Frazer move in behind him.

"You okay?" he whispered. She nodded and raised her eyebrows, he actually thought she looked as if she was enjoying herself. They slowly moved forward towards where the kitchen door to the house was and Avalon explained he would take a peep around the side of the house but he noticed there was blood on Frazer's jacket. He pointed it out.

"I can't feel et, et must be a slight nick," and she felt under her clothing. Her hand was covered in blood as she withdrew it and Avalon felt worried, he couldn't take his eye off the job at hand but Frazer obviously needed attention.

"Sit here," he said pointing to bench just behind them but Frazer didn't fancy sitting on the wet bench and so leaned on the wall. Then the second man came round the corner and Avalon gripped the shaft tightly. The man advanced and he too had a knife but he didn't seem quite as anxious to engage as the big man. Then with no warning, the door to the house opened and as the man turned to see what it was a shovel swung down onto his

366

head and laid him out cold. The shovel was raised again and was about to come down onto the man's face when Avalon called out.

"Toby, no!" The shovel stopped and Cheeseman turned to Avalon raising it above his head once more.

"What are you two doing here?" he spat.

"Saving your arse by the look of it," growled Avalon. Cheeseman hesitated as he looked at the big man still breathing erratically and then over to Frazer with blood dripping down her arm. Someone then stepped behind Cheeseman, it was his wife.

"That's enough Toby, ef these bastards can find us here we hav'nae got nowhere tae run, et's over." Cheeseman dropped the shovel and Avalon called,

"Mrs, Cheeseman, my officer is hurt, do you have a first aid kit?"

"Aye, et's my sisters house, bring her en, we'll see what we can do." Avalon nodded to Cheeseman and then went to check on the assailant who had been hit by the shovel. He seemed in better shape than the big man who was having trouble breathing but Avalon could hear the sirens of the police cars on their way.

"*It's Avalon,*" came the voice down Ross's phone.

"Where are you?" he asked.

"*In an ambulance heading for Raigmore hospital, now listen,*" demanded Avalon. Ross could tell the DI meant business so he listened without any interruptions. Avalon asked him what was happening at the waste ground at Auldearn and Ross had told him exactly what he knew from the surveillance team, that it had been confirmed that people had been spotted at the site.

"It isn't a caravan though, there're several trailers parked there and the sergeant in charge says he thinks they are living and working from the back of one of them," explained Ross.

"*Well this is what you need to do,*" began Avalon and he explained that the sergeant should be instructed to work with armed officers and make arrests at the site, particularly if McCabe could be confirmed to be there. The gang were most definitely dangerous however and must wait for the ARV to arrive. Ross was to drive there too with Boyd and oversee the operation once the arrests were complete.

"But we don't have anything to link McCabe to the murders," insisted Ross.

"*We do now, you're looking for a knife that McCabe always keeps with him, it's made from an old first-world war bayonet, shortened and fitted with a bone handle, the blade has been honed to a fine point but it's triangular in section. You must find it,*" Ross knew Avalon was deadly serious about the instructions so he questioned them no further but he did ask about the current situation.

"Why are you in an ambulance?"

"*I have to go with Frazer, she's not seriously hurt but we have to get her there.*"

"Oh," said Ross with concern, "what about you?"

"*I'm fine but get Rory to drive to the hospital to pick me up, we'll follow on as soon as he gets here.*" As soon as Ross put the phone down he shot into action.

~~~~~~~

"Hells bells, you look like shit," exclaimed Ross as Avalon came walking towards him.

"Did you get the knife?" asked the DI.

"Yeah, sealed in an evidence bag, so what

368

happened to you two?" Avalon and Frazer looked like they had been dragged across a ploughed field by an angry gorilla, their clothes were in a mess and at some point they had obviously been soaked to the skin. To add to the horror of the shambles, Frazer seemed to be covered in dried blood down her arm and left side and her hair was loose and curly, which no one had ever witnessed before. It didn't look very fetching however as she had spots of dried mud on her face.

"Oh we took a tumble," was Avalon's understatement, "did you have any problems?" he then asked.

"No the ARV chaps waved automatic rifles about and the gang gave up almost immediately, but do we have enough to charge them?" he asked. Avalon gave a quick nod as he looked around the waste ground where the truck trailers were parked. It had finally stopped raining and Avalon was beginning to feel cold and tired.

"Yes, Cheeseman came good at the end, he told us that rumours had been circulating that McCabe had a special dagger with a triangular blade that he had reputedly killed people with in Romania, it all came together," he paused for breath, "and he also suggested that Calloway was one of the people who took the body to the Priory, that also figures as he is a big chap and if that is correct, we should find his DNA matches that found on the Priory wall."

"Unfortunately, Calloway isn't here," pointed out Ross.

"No, he's in Raigmore Hospital in a oxygen tent, under guard along with a Romanian," replied Avalon.

"How come?" asked Ross with a puzzled look.

"Well Megan tried to push the back end of a police issue flashlight through his neck, she got a nick under the arm for her trouble but she'll live," and he turned and smiled at her, she just shrugged. "Toby Cheeseman took a shovel to the Romanian," he continued, "so all in all it was a good arrest."

"Doesn't that come under 'unreasonable force' or something," smiled Ross.

"Et does'nae matter tae me," said Frazer, "I'm-" but Avalon cut in before she could finish. He didn't want her to admit to anything she may regret later and neither did he want the team to know of her plans just yet.

"If anyone used unreasonable force it was me, I broke Calloway's arm trying to get a knife out of his hands," sniffed Avalon as he brushed down his ruined suit. It made no difference to how he looked whatsoever.

"So how much was Cheeseman involved then?" asked Ross.

"No more than we thought, he was hired by George Barber to put a team together for the truck hijack but he became more involved when Calloway met him and asked if the team could repeat it. They needed four more trailers."

"For drug running?" asked Boyd.

"That and human trafficking, McCabe was starting up the whole thing again using converted refrigeration units drastically altered as we suspected, when they couldn't find girls they would bring in drugs."

"And what about the victims, were we right about that?" asked Ross.

"Sort of," began Avalon, "Parkes was really killed because McCabe didn't like him he thought he was a 'grass', he probably sent out Calloway to get rid of Cheeseman as soon as we let him go too. Alan Clacher and William Ewart were revenge killings for the evidence they gave at the trial and Cheeseman says that he heard someone else was silenced too, but he doesn't know much about that."

"Well, at least we were pretty close then," smiled Boyd. Avalon nodded.

"So how long do we think forensics will be here then?" he asked looking at the white suited team picking through items at the site.

"I don't think they'll be long now but Sarah is over by that trailer, you could always go and ask her," suggested Ross suppressing a slight smile. Avalon looked down at his suit and then round at Frazer.

"I think we'll just leave them to it, I need to get a shower and a change of clothes I think," he grinned back, "it's late anyway," and he turned and nodded to Rory who was standing with Boyd but scurried off to fetch the car. "Let's go team, and well done, I think this will be one I'll remember for some time," he announced as he turned and walked back to where Mackinnon was starting the car.

"It's been an odd one I admit," replied Ross.

"One thing I don't quite understand," asked Boyd as they walked, "why was is done so publicly?"

"To tell the others he was coming," replied Avalon, "it's something that tends to happen in the drug world, it's a warning, a message that they are coming and they don't care who knows."

"And McCabe es an arrogant bastard," hissed Frazer, "that's why. He's been running circles round the Romanian police for so long he's forgotten what et's like over here."

"And he didn't reckon on Auld Clootie and his minions," grinned Ross to Frazer raising his eyebrows. Avalon glanced back for a second then said,

"I hope you're not alluding to your superior

371

officer DS Ross."

"Perish the thought," replied Ross shoving his hands into his trouser pockets as he walked. Avalon continued with Ross, Frazer and Boyd close on his heels, or was it his cloven hooves?

The Avalon Series, by Peter Gray.

The Drums of Drumnadrochit
By Peter Gray.

Introducing Detective James Avalon, a man in turmoil. Both his
private and professional life is at an all time low and to make things
worse he is seen as a liability to his senior officers. He has to make a
change in both aspects of his life, but how? Though he is still on
good terms with his ex wife she is beginning to despair with his lack
of compromise in his life until a chance meeting with another
officer shows promise of opening new doors to his future.

Auld Clootie
By Peter Gray.

James Avalon faces a new menace in the second book in the Avalon
series. Change and upheaval within the police forces sees him
struggle with the problems of a reorganisation of the team. Trouble
visits once again in the shape of a major crime that seems to have no
clues or motives and Avalon has to work with limited resources to
solve a crime linked to religion, ritual and legend.

The Brollachan

By Peter Gray.

After just twelve months based in Inverness, Detective Inspector James Avalon now feels more at home than any other time in his career. With his personal life still a shambles, Avalon takes solace in the landscape and his work, but when a woman disappears from her car in plain sight, he wonders about the accuracy of the report. When a body is found, the case becomes more serious. Is the woman's disappearance linked to the body or does Avalon need to reassess his methods?

The Black Clan

By Peter Gray.

When Avalon becomes embroiled in secret societies and Masonic rituals he soon finds out how far up the food chain the rot has climbed. Once again the Inverness detective is on the streets and this time he's angry.

Out 2018

Caledonian Flame

By Peter Gray.

Out 2019

See website for details.

www.avalon-series.co.uk

Also by Peter Gray

A Certain Summer

Sam's Kingdom

With Feeling

Please visit:

www.petergrayauthor.co.uk
www.acertainsummer.co.uk
www.avalon-series.co.uk

www.trickyimppublishing.co.uk